The Holy Terror

BY THE SAME AUTHOR
ALL PUBLISHED BY HOUSE OF STRATUS

FICTION

ANN VERONICA
APROPOS OF DOLORES
THE AUTOCRACY OF MR PARHAM
BABES IN THE DARKLING WOOD
BEALBY
THE BROTHERS *AND*
   THE CROQUET PLAYER
BRYNHILD
THE BULPINGTON OF BLUP
THE DREAM
THE FIRST MEN IN THE MOON
THE FOOD OF THE GODS
THE HISTORY OF MR POLLY
IN THE DAYS OF THE COMET
THE INVISIBLE MAN
THE ISLAND OF DR MOREAU
KIPPS: THE STORY OF A SIMPLE
   SOUL
LOVE AND MR LEWISHAM
MARRIAGE
MEANWHILE
MEN LIKE GODS
A MODERN UTOPIA
MR BRITLING SEES IT THROUGH
THE NEW MACHIAVELLI
THE PASSIONATE FRIENDS
THE SEA LADY
THE SHAPE OF THINGS TO COME
THE TIME MACHINE
TONO-BUNGAY

THE UNDYING FIRE
THE WAR IN THE AIR
THE WAR OF THE WORLDS
THE WHEELS OF CHANCE
WHEN THE SLEEPER WAKES
THE WIFE OF SIR ISAAC HARMAN
THE WONDERFUL VISIT
THE WORLD OF WILLIAM CLISSOLD
   VOLUMES 1,2,3

NON-FICTION

THE CONQUEST OF TIME *AND*
   THE HAPPY TURNING
EXPERIMENT IN AUTOBIOGRAPHY
   VOLUMES 1,2
H G WELLS IN LOVE
THE OPEN CONSPIRACY AND OTHER
   WRITINGS

.

The Holy Terror

H G WELLS

HOUSE OF
STRATUS

CONTENTS

PRELIMINARY NOTE

Every person, place and thing in this story – even the countries in which it happens – are fictitious, and any resemblance, though it runs to the pitch of identical names and circumstances, is at most a realistic device and free of any libellous intention whatever. It is an imagination about everyone and nobody, about everyland and nowhere, justified by the *Lives* of Suetonius and our present discontents. Maybe it is lifelike, that is the incurable ambition of the novelist, he will not disavow it; but if so it is because its characters have come alive. Their motives run about in our world also, and it is our problems with which they wrestle in their distinct and perhaps simpler but similar world. The England, the America, the London in this book are not the England, America and London of geography and journalism, but England, America and London transposed into imaginative narrative. The tampering of J W Dunne with popular ideas of space and time is having its influence upon fiction. So far as the writer may judge his own story, it seems to begin on earth somewhen in the nineteen twenties, but it goes on and on unrestrainedly, into the years to come. The writer has let that happen, he calls your attention to it to prepare your mind for it, but he offers no explanation or apology.

BOOK ONE

INCUBATION

CHAPTER ONE

Tender Years

"It's a Holy Terror," said Betsy Barnacle, the monthly nurse. "I never heard such a baby. Scream and scream it does. *And* its little fists!"

"There ain't nothing *wrong* with it?" asked cook.

"Only it's a little Turk," said Betsy. "Goes stiff it does and if you tried to stop it, there'd be convulsions. Hark at it now! You'd think it would rupture itself."

The two women listened judicially. Their eyes met in a common wonder.

"I shouldn't have thought its father had it in him," said cook.

2

The baby grew into an incessantly active, bilious little boy with a large white face, a slight scowl and the devil of a temper. He was a natural born kicker; he went straight for the shins. He was also a wrist-twister, but he bit very little. On the other hand he was a great smasher of the cherished possessions of those who annoyed him, and particularly the possessions of his brothers

Samuel and Alf. He seemed to have been born with the idea of "serving people out." He wept very little, but when he wept he howled aloud, and jabbered wild abuse, threats and recriminations through the wet torrent of his howling. The neighbours heard him. Old gentlemen stopped and turned round to look at him in the street.

By the time he was seven or eight quite a number of people had asked: "What can you *do* with a boy like that?" Nobody had found a satisfactory solution to the problem. Many suggestions were made, from "Knock his little block off," to "Give him more love."

Nowadays many people deny that the unpleasantness of unpleasant children comes naturally. They say they are love-starved. His Aunt Julia, for example, did. "You think so," said his mother, and did not argue about it, because at times she was very doubtful indeed whether she did love him. She was for a mother unusually clear-headed. She was affectionate but she was critical. And what to *do* with him she did not know.

His name was Rudolf, not perhaps the wisest name to give a child, which shortened naturally into Rudie, but which after he had heard of the existence and worldwide fame of Mr Kipling he insisted upon shortening further and improperly – since it altered the vowel sound – into "Rud." He was also called Young Whitlow, Whitlow Tertius, Wittles and Drink, Wittles and Stink, Grub and simply The Stink. He objected strenuously to the last and always attempted the murder of anyone not too obviously an outsize who used it. It referred to some early accident in his career which he desired to have forgotten.

His relations with his brothers were strained. Samuel was inclined to mock and tease him – a perilous joy. He threw a dinner knife across the table at Samuel and nicked a bit off the top of his ear. Samuel had either taken an overdose of mustard or, as Rud declared, twisted his nose in such a way as to imply "Stink." The subsequent enquiry never settled this. The ear bled copiously into Mrs Whitlow's handkerchief and nobody could imagine what would have happened if the knife had gone four inches straighter. "Might have blinded me," accused Samuel, from under Mother's arm. "Might have cut my eye clean out." It was a tremendous scene and Mr Whitlow, who disliked the job extremely, took little Rudie upstairs and spanked him, calling him "You little *Devil!*" between each smack, and left him in the bedroom.

Thither presently came Mother.

"Why did you *do* it, Rudie?" she asked.

"He's always teasing me. He drives me wild," said Rudie.

"But to throw a *knife!*"

"He won't do it again," said Rudie, smearing his wet, dirty, woeful face and nose with the back of his dirty little hand.

"Your own brother!"

Later he threw a large, wooden toy horse at Alf and missed him and smashed the parlour window. "Your father will beat you again!" cried mother in distress. "Say you were playing catch with him, Alfie!"

"I didn't catch the horse," brother Alf prevaricated stoutly to Father, and the beating was averted.

But little Rudie never thanked Alfred for that. He never thought very much of Alfred.

He stole his brothers' things, he played with their things and broke them and they had no remedy – for you cannot sneak on a younger brother and they were forbidden to take the law into their own hands. All three of the boys drew and painted. Alf's work was the more delicate and he copied meticulously, but Rudie's had a sort of splashing originality. When Alf took a bright and careful bit of illumination to school the drawing master praised it in front of the whole classroom, and he had never once had a word of praise for Rudie's frequent and hasty performances. So Rudie got hold of and tore up Alf's masterpiece and, when the master wanted to exhibit it again, the story came out and Rudie was reproached by the master before everybody. He went home with a bursting heart and scribbled all over a number of pages in Alf's favourite book.

"What can you *do* with a boy like that?" asked Mr Whitlow in the bar parlour of the *Bell*.

"He's got spirit," said Mr Cramble, the grocer.

"An evil spirit," said Mr Whitlow.

"He'll change as he grows up," said Lozanda, the vet. "Adolescence. They often do."

"If he doesn't," said Mr Whitlow, "he'll face a jury one of these days. I tell him that. But does he mind me? Not him."

"Spare the rod," hinted Mr Cramble.

"His mother don't like his being touched," said Mr Whitlow, "and *I* don't much like it eether. I suppose I'm a bit modern."

"You see," said Mr Whitlow after reflection, "he's not over-strong. He has these headaches and bilious fits. And he seems to be able to make himself look pale when he wants to. I used to think his brothers would keep him in order a bit. But he kicks them, he does, and they can't very well kick back, him being delicate. Their mother'd never forgive them if they left a bruise on him. All they seem able to do with him is to get him upstairs in their bedroom and suffocate him with pillows. He certainly

6

don't like that. But he's got artful about it. He used to kick and try to yell and so they knew he was all right. *Now* he goes limp right away as soon as they've got hold of him. And naturally they take off the pillows to look at him and see they've done him no harm and he sort of comes to very slowly. Last time they did it, he got away down the passage and then went back and buzzed an old croquet ball at young Alf and raised a lump – so big."

"Sort of Problem Child," said Skindles, the watchmaker.

"What's going to become of him?" said Whitlow and straightway abandoned further enquiry.

3

Mrs Whitlow was a woman of some intelligence and she had had a good modern education, which had confused her mind considerably. Nevertheless she kept up her reading. She thought that women were the race and men merely incidents, and that every great man in the world owed nearly everything to his mother. She thought that if Adam had had a mother things might have been very different, and that the story of Ruth and Naomi was the most beautiful story in the world. And she thought that after Sam and Alf she ought to have had a daughter, and when Rudolf came squalling into her life she repined gently.

Once or twice she said to him, wistfully but unwisely, "If only you had been a dear little girl," and so sowed the seeds of an enduring misogyny. The sex war was all alight in him from the age of six onward.

The first girl he hit was his cousin Rachel, who had recited:

7

> "Sugar and spice and all things nice
> That's what little girls are made of
> Slugs and snails and little dog's tails
> And that's what little boys are made of,"

to him. He hit her, and all she did was to slap back – just a stinging slap – and then he got her by her long hair. Whereupon she pinched – so painfully it made him yell with surprise – and then got hold of his wrists in a strong sort of grip that immobilised him and then she put out her tongue at him. "Yaaaa!" she said. He couldn't get free of her. Not for the moment. Of course he would have won all right, in spite of the fact that she was nearly a year older, but just at this point the mothers came in.

Her mother completely misunderstood the situation. "Rachel!" she cried, "what are you doing to that poor little boy?"

(Jimini! What *wasn't* he just going to do to *her!*)

He brooded on this affair afterwards. If left an uneasiness and an aversion. There was something queer about these girls; they were like insects; you didn't know what they might do to you next. And their shins were difficult to get at. They weren't as soft as they ought to be, not nearly. What properly ought he to have done? Jerked his wrists free of course, and then?

"He's not a gently child," said his mother to Rachel's mother. "He's *not* gentle."

"Love him all the more," said Aunt Julia who was also present.

But after one or two attempts to take him to her bosom and sit him on her lap and reason with him gently or talk to him beautifully about the child Jesus, about whose entirely undocumented youth she invented the most unwarrantable stories, she realised her sister-in-law's difficulties better. Rudie fought her love like a wild cat.

They tried to soften his nature by giving him pets. But they had to take the white mice away from him again because he wanted to teach them to swim and submerge themselves in the bath at the word of command and was inclined to be punitive when they failed to realise what was expected of them. Dogs he regarded with suspicion and had a way of picking up stones when he saw them. The suspicion was mutual. His white rabbits died either of eccentric and irregular dietary or by being dropped suddenly as a punishment for squirming about and kicking in sudden disconcerting jerks. For a time he seemed really to like a gay little kitten that pursued a rabbit's foot on a piece of string with the most ridiculous nimbleness and waggery. Then something happened. A great running and banging-about upstairs was heard. The kitten came headlong down the staircase incredibly scared. Rudie followed in pursuit – armed with his little cricket bat.

"She won't play with me any longer," he bellowed. "She's *got* to. Where's she gone?"

What can you do with a boy like that?

4

Aunt Julia's earliest attempts at changing Rudie's heart by love had not been very successful, but she was a persistent woman and full of ideas of the most diverse sort about the bringing up of children and the lamentable foolishness with which people in general set about that business. People marry for passion, a most improper motive, and their children take them by surprise. They don't deserve them. Maybe in a more scientific world only spinsters will have children. She knew she was on the right track – or tracks – in disapproving of whatever had been done, was being done or was ever likely to be done with Rudie. Children are right, and parents and pedagogues never understand them. That is the privilege and compensation of the observant spinster. Very likely she had been a little precipitate with Rudie, but she felt she would try again.

She had a nice long talk one evening with Mrs Whiltow. "You ought to have him psychoanalysed," she said. "It lies too deep for us untrained observers. Very likely that Oedipus complex. But what we have to remember always is that, like every child, he is intrinsically *good*."

"At times," said Mrs Whitlow, "that is very hard to believe."

"I copied some bits of wisdom out of a book by Mr Neill," said Aunt Julia. "Listen, dear: *'I cannot say the truth is, but I can declare my strong conviction that the boy is never in the wrong.'* What do you think of that? And *'the self that God made'* – isn't that beautifully put? – *'the self that God made is in conflict with all our silly teaching and interference.'* And this! – what a comfort it is in these times of war and trouble! – *'Human beings are good, they want to do good; they want to love and be loved.'* When one thinks of all those poor lovestarved young aviators bombing – what was the name of that place in India – yesterday? Just unsatisfied love-hunger. And then this again: *'Criminality,'* he says, my dear, *'springs from lack of love.'* "

"On the part of the criminal – "

"Oh, no, dear! No. *No!* NO! On the part of the people who make the laws. And so you see what we have to do, is just to find out the complex that is tying poor little Rudie down to all his naughtiness. When he broke the leg of his rabbit when he was playing with it the other day, that was really a *protest* – a symbol."

"It wasn't a nice symbol for the rabbit."

"We have to discover his complex – that is the next thing."

"He keeps so quiet about that."

"Naturally. We have to discover it. Now tell me – do you and George, do you ever quarrel in front of Rudie?"

"My *dear!*"

"Does he ever see you caressing or making love?"

"Julia, *darling!*"

"Does he – is he disposed to *avoid* his father?"

"He keeps out of his way – especially when he is up to mischief."

"A pure Oedipus," said Julia, nodding her head several times. "Probably a chemically pure Oedipus. Now tell me: When you and he are together and his father comes in, does he seem to want to get close to you – edge between you, so to speak? As if to protect you?"

"It's generally the other way about. He wants to be protected. Not that his father ever ill-treats him. But the boy has that sort of conscience. He always feels his father may have found out something."

"Exactly. And now tell me – tell me – do you think – has he any particular feeling – any sort of aversion," – Julia became very red in the face but her eyes were bright and resolute – "*Steeples?*"

Mrs Whitlow thought. "He certainly hates going to church for the children's service," she said. "If you mean that."

"Exactly. Transfers it to the church – where dear Mr Woolley presides. And no doubt to Mr Woolley. The Oedipus in perfection. The radiating father-hate. But don't trust my untrained judgment, dear. Go to a proper psychoanalyst and have all this cleared up. Then you will know..."

Thus Aunt Julia.

But Mrs Whitlow did not go to a psychoanalyst. She had seen only or two in her life and she had not liked the look of them. But the idea of getting some advice took hold of her and she decided to go to old Doctor Carstall, who was so big and deliberate that you felt you could put the utmost confidence in him. And by making an excuse of Rudie's bilious attacks, old Doctor Carstall looked him over.

"He's the most ordinary boy I ever met," said old Doctor Carstall, "except that he has a certain excess of – *go* in him, and a lack of self-restraint. He's fairly intelligent of course – in his way."

"He's not an *ordinary* boy," said Mrs Whitlow, defending every mother's dearest illusion, "not by any means."

"As you will," said old Doctor Carstall. "But keep him out of the hands of these faddists and send him to the most conventional school you can find. He'll probably do as well as most ordinary little boys – get scholarships, play games and all that. He has – well – *tenacity*. He doesn't feel scruples if he wants anything. Don't imagine he's anything out of the way for naughtiness. It's just that that curious *go* of his brings it out..."

"Nasty little kid," soliloquised old Doctor Carstall, when Mrs Whiltow had departed. "There's millions like him – more or less.

"Millions," he repeated... "Most people forget what nasty children they were themselves. They forget it.

"Just because children are small and pink – or small and sickly like this little beast – they imagine them angelic. If you magnified them, everyone would see plainer what they are."

He reflected. "Tenacity? That's no virtue... Though of course it may by an advantage..."

The great lines of Wordsworth floated protestingly through his memory and were ill received.

"But trailing clouds of glory do we come from God who is our Home," he said and then added irreligiously, vulgarly and outrageously: "I *don't* think. His clouds of glory would smell of sulphur all the time."

Aunt Julia was never able to put her finger exactly on Rudie's complex – if so be he had one. Whatever it was, presumably it remained unresolved and festering in his soul, and this story can tell no more about it.

5

Under the influence of old Doctor Carstall, Rudie went to Hooplady House instead of having his subconsciousness explored, cleaned up and made over in a suitable establishment on soundly psychoanalytical lines. Probably the results would have been very similar. Hooplady House, as an educational institution, never gave a thought to character and the fine shades of conduct – except on Speech Days. Then the headmaster said the boys were a household of young English gentlemen, and the parents and prefects heard him with quiet self-approval.

By way of teaching, the school devoted itself to satisfying the requirements of various respectable examining bodies, and unless your behaviour militated against the attainment of that objective, the school, as an organisation, did not concern itself about what was happening to you inside or outside or between the hours devoted to that purpose. Beyond the lines laid down by these examining bodies it did not adventure. Why should it? If they did not know what arrangement of obligatory and optional subjects constituted a proper education, who did? Most of the boys were day-boys, and by ordinary standards the tone was good. Filth was furtive, and such vice as occurred was inquisitive, elementary, infrequent and obscure. The head boy was a son of Doctor Carstall's, a taciturn, fair, good-looking boy who seemed to do everything he did well and with a minimum of effort. He won a sort of qualified hero-worship from Rud, quite at the beginning of their acquaintance.

Rud was engaged in an all-in scrap with a boy who had called him "The Stink." He had been jabbing at his adversary with a penholder with a broken nib. But the fellow had got him by the wrist now, only his left fist was free and he was getting the worst of the punching.

Carstall appeared, tall and calm, standing over them. "Don't fight with things like that, Whitlow. We don't *do* it here."

"He's bigger than *me*."

"Kick his shins if you must, junior's privilege, but don't use a filthy thing like that. Might poison his blood. Or jab his eye. What's the trouble?"

Explanation.

"Well, *I* say he's not to be called that. Nicknames ought to be tolerable. And Russell, you; tease someone your own size. Get our of it, both of you."

There was a splendour, Rud thought, about such authority. "Get out of it, both of you," he whispered to himself presently and wondered how long it would be before he was head of the school. He'd make 'em get out of it all right. But it seemed hard to him that he wasn't to use pen-nibs or scissors in warfare. Very hard. He was the sort of scrapper who would have invented knuckledusters, if they hadn't already been invented.

On the whole he was less aggressive during his junior days at school than at home. He was not much of a success at games and he was held to all sorts of rules and customs he had been accustomed to disregard at home with his brothers. He learnt quite early the inadvisability of mowing down the wicket with his little bat when he got out at cricket, or of quitting the game ostentatiously and vindictively directly after he had had his innings, and he grasped the necessity of having the football somewhere near at least, when he desired to hack another player. He ceased to bawl and threaten loudly when annoyed, but on the other hand he acquired a complete set of the recognised English bad words, and he muttered them ferociously whenever exasperated. Brother Sam he saw little of in the school; he was in the upper division; and brother Alf just drifted about him quietly, pursuing ends of his own. There was a lot of smouldering goodness in Alf and a touch of religion. "You didn't ought to say words like that, Rud," he protested.

Rud replied with practically the complete vocabulary.

Alf put his hands to his ears and said: "You might be struck dead for that, Rud."

"He'd have to strike pretty near the whole school then," said Rud, who had a keen sense of justice when he himself was concerned.

He speedily displayed an active, insensitive intelligence beyond his years. His memory was exceptionally good, his reception uncritical. He bolted the feast of knowledge and threw it up again with ease, completely undigested. He was indeed a born examinee, and his progress up the school was exceptionally rapid. He competed for marks vehemently. He was best at English, Geography, History, French and Latin. He found mathematics tricky and problems irritating. He could not ponder. Formulae he could tackle but not problems. He got hot and cross in the face of difficulty. He was all for cutting the Gordian Knot instead of fiddling about with it, and he saw nothing idiotic in the classical story of Columbus and the egg. Downright action was in his nature.

He read voraciously. His imagination was fired particularly by the history of wars, conquests and campaigns. Then forthwith he became Caesar, Alexander, Napoleon or Genghis Khan, whichever Rud it happened to be. He conquered America with all Washington Irving's Conquistadors, and subjugated Ireland with the sword of Cromwell. He was Clive; he was Gustavus Adolphus. Fiction, generally speaking, he did not like, there were too many of those incalculable girls in it. He had no use for Fenimore Cooper and the noble Indian, and books about big-game hunting merely strengthened his innate distrust and dislike of animals. If ever he had to hunt tigers, he decided, he would do it with explosive bullets from a *machan,* a good high, strong *machan.* When he saw the elephants and gorillas in the zoological gardens he thrilled with hostility, and dreamt afterwards about fighting them with machine-guns and catching them in the most horribly spiky pitfalls. And when in his dream they just came closer and closer to him, bleeding, half-blinded, but persistently undying and intent upon him, screamed and woke up in a frenzy of fear and hate.

Savages, barbarians, "natives," he "mowed down," he had no other use for them. Omdurman was his ideal battle.

Since he was a day-boy and not very fond of games, and since he could do his school work very quickly, he was free to take long, solitary walks in which he could let his imagination run riot in anticipatory reverie. To the passing observer he seemed to be a small, rather slovenly boy, with a large, pale, egg-shaped face, big end up, and usually a sniff, but in imagination he rode a magnificent charger, or occupied a powerful car, and his staff and orderlies and messengers buzzed about him, and his embattled hosts stormed the farmhouses and villages of the landscape and swept over the hills, while his pitiless guns searched their recesses. The advance was always victorious, and with thee homecoming came the triumph. Usually Hooplady House was involved in that. The prisoners stood before him. That drawing-master, a proven traitor, was shot out of hand. Several of the upper boys shared his fate. The rest of the staff were shot or reproached and insulted according to the mood of the day. Sometimes his father and mother appeared on the scene and were put under protective detention. Cousin Rachel, the pincher, now in a greatly chastened mood, submitted to her fate. Sam and Alf were rarely given rôles.

But one figure was very frequent in these dreams. He was sometimes the second in command, sometimes the opposite general surrendering with all the honours of war, sometimes an ambiguous political associate in the revolution, or the counter-revolution, or the war of liberation, or the great conquest, which-ever it happened to be. His admiration for the generalissimo was extreme, his loyalty amounted to devotion. This was Carstall. "My trusty Carstall." Rudie never seemed able to keep Carstall out of the phantasy. He never wanted to do so.

17

He whistled to himself as he took his imagination on these excursions. He never learnt to whistle normally. It was a sort of acid piping through his teeth and it lacked any consistent tune.

And always he got home by twilight. For in the dark the kings and captains departed, the fighting and the conquests died away, and the small boy was left exposed to those bears and tigers and gorillas, which escape so frequently from menageries even in the most settled districts, and to criminals and homicidal maniacs and hedge-bogles and all the shapeless terrors of the night.

As his mind grew and his reading expanded his reveries became more realist and coherent, and darkness less menacing. He began to study maps, particularly maps in which each country and its foreign possessions were done in the same colour; he began to collect picture and comparative diagrams of armies and navies and air forces. He was particularly keen on air warfare. Dropping high explosive bombs together with printed warnings and proclamations, appealed to him as just the perfect way of making war. He read the newspapers with an avidity uncommon at his tender age. He knew the salutes and symbols of all the dictators in the world and the inner singificance of every coloured shirt. And as he grew up towards them, these heroes, these masters of men who marched like lurid torches through the blue haze and reek of contemporary history, seemed continually to come down nearer the level of his understanding and sympathy.

So it was our Holy Terror nourished his imagination and anticipated his career.

His extensive reading fed a natural disposition to accumulate vocabulary. The staff realised that he could write the best examination paper in the school, and told him so. He used long words. Some of the assistants, and particularly the games master, were disposed to discourage this, but the English master applauded. "Nevertheless, take warning from our Hindu brethren," said the English master, and lent him a facetious book about Babu English. "If the new word sticks out among familiar usage like an unset gem – excise it delete it. A new word is like a wild animal you have caught. You must learn its ways and break it in before you can use it freely."

Rud took that to heart. He learnt to write a good, nervous prose. He developed a certain gift for effective phrases.

6

His early religious experience did not amount to very much and they played only a small part in his subsequent career. Still, one may say a word or two about them before dismissing them.

He was never God-fearing.

Nowhere in the world in his days was there any atmosphere in which the presence of God was felt. The general behaviour of people everywhere made it plain that whatever they professed when they were questioned, they did not feel any such *Power* within or about them. For most of them it would have been an entirely paralysing thought to have been living in the presence, in the sight and knowledge of an unseen and silent Deity. With indefinite powers of intervention. The tension would have become unendurable; they would have screamed. They dismissed the thought, therefore, and they dismissed Him, not explicitly, of course, but tacitly and practically. On most of their occasions, even the professional religious people, from popes and archbishops down to confirmation candidates, behaved exactly like atheists – as well but no better.

Young Rudolf indeed heard very little about the supreme immanence. Mrs Whitlow had a delicacy about mentioning Him except in connection with the Lord's Prayer and the Ten Commandments and similar formalities, and Mr Whitlow only mentioned Him on occasions of dismay – as for example when he heard that Aunt Julia had come in to see them. Then usually he would exclaim: "Oh, *God!*"

From the outset young Rudolf put up a considerable God-resistance. He read such portions of the scripture as were chosen for his learning reluctantly and with incredulity and aversion. Father was bad enough without this vaster Father behind him. From all the world around him Rud caught the trick of putting divinity out of his mind in the ordinary affairs of life. But only by degrees. He had some bad, times, usually about judgment-day and hellfire. They were worse to dream about than falling into tigers' dens. He had called Alf a fool several times. That, he learnt, was a hellfire business. And there was very little on the other side of the account. He had tried praying – as, for example, at cricket for a score of twenty and then he had got out first ball.

"All *right*, God," said little Rudie. "You see."

Then he heard tell that old Doctor Carstall was an atheist. The schoolfellow who told him that spoke in hushed tones.

"What's a Natheist?" asked Rudie.

"It's – he don't believe there's any God at all. Ain't it *orful?*"

"He'll have to go to hell," said Rudie.

"He'll *have* to go to hell. And him so respected! It's a frightful pity."

At his next opportunity Rudie had a good look at Doctor Carstall.

He seemed to be carrying it off all right.

Then Rudie had an impulse to ask young Carstall about it, but he did not dare.

There was something about this sinister idea of Atheism that attracted him. It was frightful. Oh! Unspeakable, but it had a magnificence. Suppose really there *was* nobody watching…

The things you might do!…

He did not talk very much about high matters. They came too close up to him for frankness or the risk of self-exposure. And even had he wanted to do so most of the other kids would have been too scared. But he listened to his elders. When he heard one of the senior boys arguing that "somebody *must* have made the world," it seemed a perfectly valid argument, though for any practical purpose it led nowhere.

Gradually his thoughts took the shape of feeling that the God one heard about in school did exist, that they didn't mean it whatever it was about the Trinity, but that nevertheless there was a God – another God, that Maker – who went away – so that you could do any little things you wanted to do – who was indeed away generally, but who might at any time stage a tremendous comeback. Then he would ask everybody what they had done with the things of his making, and Rudie's impression was that most people would look pretty silly long before it came down to him. There was no reason Rudie could see why he in particular should be pitched upon. He was quite prepared to turn God's-evidence against one or two people he knew.

So far as Aunt Julia's edifying inventions about that examplary Christ Child were concerned, he believed in them only to the extent of disliking him almost as heartily as he did his mother's hypothetical dear little girl. And as for gratitude to anyone, who needn't have done it, mind you, getting himself crucified (knowing quite well he would rise again the third day) to save Rudie from that hellfire from which nevertheless he still somehow went in great danger, that was something too spiritual altogether for his hard little intelligence. Long before he was adolescent he had put religion outside of himself and thought about it less and less.

His mother puzzled about him and tried to feel loving and proud about him. If she had been quite frank with herself she would have confessed to herself that this dome-browed son she had borne was a little cad in grain, to whom unfeeling ruthlessness and greediness and implacable wilfulness were as natural as night-prowling to a hyena or an evil odour to flowering privet.

The chances of the genes had given her that, but her spirit struggled against her luck. It was too much to admit. She knew better than anyone how easily and meanly he could lie. She had found him pilfering, and his instincts seemed furtively dirty, but she could not think of her own flesh and blood in such harsh terms. "His soul is unawakened," she told herself, "one must be patient."

And after all, he *was* very clever at school, continually top of his class and passing examinations with facility. His essays were always "excellent"; he had an "instinct for phrasing." (If only he would not boast to her so much about these things!) And if he was horrid, he was interesting. That at any rate could be said for him. With a certain compunction his mother realised that she thought much more sbout him than she did about Sam or Alf.

They were no trouble. They were ordinary like their father. You loved them, of course, but calmly. You did not distress yourself about them.

For a term or so there was an earnest young assistant master in the early stages of evangelical mania at Hooplady House. He perceived the moral obscurity in which Rudolf lived and tried to throw a ray of light into it. He got the boy to have a long walk with him and, beginning artfully by botanising, led the talk to ideals and one's Object in Life.

It was mostly his own Object in Life he talked about. Rud was as hard to draw as a frightened badger. The earnest young assistant master confided that he himself might not live very long. He believed he was tuberculous. Once or twice he had coughed blood.

"I spew up all my dinner sometimes," said Rud, faintly interested, "and last Easter my nose bled something frightful. Until mother got a cold key."

"That isn't like tuberculosis, which just eats your lungs away."

"Don't worms?" said Rud. "I saw a picture the other day of liver fluke in a chap's liver. Something horrid. You get it from eating watercress."

The earnest young assistant master shifted his ground abruptly. "I'd hate to die before I had done something really good and fine in the world," he said. "Sometimes I think I'd like to take orders. After I've got my BA London it wouldn't be so difficult. And then I could do God's work in some dreadful slum. Or go to a leper colony. Or be the chaplain of a hospital or prison. It would be fine to go to a war – as a chaplain, just upholding the fellows. Helping them. Toc-H and all that. Don't you ever want to do things like that?"

"I'd like to be a machine-gunner," said Rud.

"Oh, but that's *killing!*"

"Well, what will *you* do if this next war they keep taking about now really comes?"

"I should certainly *not* be a solder. Among other things, I doubt if I am physically fit. I should either get into a Red Cross Unit or go as a padre. Under fire, of course – into the front line. But without a weapon in my hand – ever."

"Everyone isn't like that."

"There would be no more war if they were. What a death it would be, stand out boldly between the lines and cry aloud, 'Peace,' holding out bare hands to both sides."

"You'd get peppered to rights," said Rud, regarding the young man's exalted face with extreme disapproval.

The assistant master was lost in a vision. He stood still with shiny eyes and face uplifted and his thin, white, knuckly hands were tightly clenched. He made his companion feel uncomfortable and absolutely resolved never to come for a walk with him again.

"There's a shorter way back over this next stile and across the fields," said Rud after a lengthy pause.

And that is as much as need be told of the spiritual circumstances of Rudolf Whitlow in his youth.

There is no record that his soul ever awakened. There is no record that it stirred even in its sleep. There is no evidence indeed that he ever had a soul.

CHAPTER TWO

Début

The country was already in a very disturbed state when Rudolf Whitlow's schooldays drew to an end. He had believed that his facility in passing examinations would lead up through a ladder of scholarships to university distinction, security and authority. In the stabler past he might have made such an ascent and rounded off his career as a formidably malicious, secretly vicious, conservative don, the sort of don who is feared and propitiated during his lifetime and forgotten gladly almost before he is dead.

Father Whitlow wasn't doing at all well in business just then, and he had heard that a son at the university was an expensive responsibility. Neither of Rud's brothers was doing well. Sam didn't like his job. He complained that it gave him no hope whatever of promotion, but he was afraid to quit it because jobs were now so difficult to find, and Alf, after one or two futile starts, became conscientious to a painful pitch and deeply religious. He hung about at home being inconveniently helpful, and on one occasion his mother, going quietly upstairs, was horrified to find him praying on his knees. After a time he got tentative employment in Doctor Carstall's dispensary and brightened up a little. Carstall found him slow but very careful and exact, and spoke well of him in a faintly contemptuous way. And also he increased his pay and said encouraging things to him.

But Rud's white face during his last two terms at school became more and more resentful and lowering.

He resolved to have things out with his once-dreaded father.

"I'm going in for these scholarships whether you like it or not. And you'll have to pay the fees."

"I tell you it's no *good*," said Father Whitlow.

"What else can I do?"

"Edjicated proletariat – and what good's that?"

"If I get top – "

"You won't get top."

Rud, regarding his father, looked still capable of knife-throwing.

"Couldn't you do something to help?" intervened his mother. "Write for the papers? Do tutoring?"

"And eat up all my blasted time and energy!"

"Better than nothing," said Father Whitlow.

"Look at my brothers! Look at old Sam stuck in the mud from the very start – for good and all. Look at Alf! Undereducated. Underqualified. Making pills in slow time. Meek and holy. While young Carstall soars away to be a great physiologist. What have you done for us? Give me my chance. See? Give me my chance, while there is a chance."

"Look here, Rudie, you've got to be reasonable. How was *I* to know that business was going from bad to worse? I always meant to give you a chance."

"*Meant!* What's *meant* to me?"

"This depression; it's *got* us. It's got everybody."

"And did you ever do anything to prevent it? Or dodge it? Some of them have dodged it. Got you – of course it's got you. Did any of your generation ever think of escaping it? And so – here I am. One of the victims. I won't stand it, Father, I tell you. I'll fight. You let me go for those scholarships. See? You let me go in. Time enough to tell me I can't do it when I've failed."

"I can't face the expense of it."

"As though you had a choice now. Not a bit of it! You owe it to me. D'you hear? You *owe* it to me. What did you bring me into the world for? What did you bring me into the world for? To let me down *now!*"

Tears of indignation shone in his eyes.

Mrs Whitlow has been watching the disputants. "Rudie dear," she said.

"Did I *ask* to be born?" said Rudie.

"Rudie!" she said, and put her hand on his.

He snatched his fist away. "Ow! – Rudie! Rudie – *rot!* It makes me *sick*."

"Listen, Rudie."

He glared at her.

"Maybe we could manage it. Maybe – "

"What?"

"There's my insurance – "

"Well?"

"It was always meant for you."

"*And* the others," corrected Father.

"Never mind *him*," said Rudie. "Tell me."

Mother made a halting explanation. The policy had a surrender value. It might make things possible.

"But the other boys – !" protested Father.

"You give me my chance" said Rudie, "and I'll carry the damned lot of you – I'll be an omnibus camel for the whole blessed family. Trust me. But if I can't take up these scholarships, I'm done. I'll blow my brains out. I'll throw myself into the canal. And I'll leave a letter to scald the skin off you."

"I'm sure you'll do yourself justice, Rudie," said his mother gently, "if you have half a chance."

And so he was able to do himself justice, and the large, white, bilious face with the permanent, resentful scowl, frequented the streets of Camford beneath the exiguous tassel of a second-hand mortar-board cap, for four hardy and strenuous years.

2

While Rud Whitlow pursued his studies at Camford, such as they were, the disintegration of the civilisation into which he had been born went on steadily. Human society had in fact been progressing too fast; it had slipped up on mechanism and dislocated its class disciplines and traditions. It was in a bad way; it was possibly in need of a major operation. History was passing into a new and very perplexing phase. The scale and pace of life had altered and mental habits had failed to keep pace with the alteration. The social cog-wheels were failing to mesh with one another and they ground and jammed more and more violently. At first he did not apprehend this at all clearly, but the perception of it seeped into his mind.

Mankind put to the test was indeed displaying the most extraordinary inadaptability, politically, economically, educationally. The sole ideas for relieving tension that anyone seemed able to entertain, were the suicidal alternatives of blind social insurrection to shift the stresses to other nations on the other. No one seemed to think of relieving the stresses. One resounding crack followed another in the mighty edifice of confidence and traditional usage which was the essential framework of civilised society. Abyss after abyss yawned open wider and wider. Insecurity appeared at the most unexpected points. And amidst it, like an ant in an earthquake, our hero ran about and grew up.

It did not take him long to realise the advancing malaise of his world. Hints of disillusionment, impalpable but cumulative, gathered in his consciousness. Doubt accumulated in his mind and would not be dispelled. The ladder of academic competition and of promotion to assurance and dazzling opportunity, that he had started to climb, which by all precedents should have made him more or less a member of a definite governing class and opened the door to legal distinction or political opportunity – or at very least to the higher civil service and security – acquired a quality of unreality, became less and less credible until at times it seemed more like some inaccessible spiral staircase seen in the central incandescence of a burning house than a permanent method of ascent.

It was hard for him to believe that he of all people had misjudged his world, that even now that he had got to Camford, it was going to be a much more difficult world than he had supposed. He thought about it at nights and he betrayed an intense exasperation when people made banal remarks about it to him. Apparently the whole system of things had conspired to anticipate his ambitions and corner and defeat him.

But indeed the whole system of things was not thinking of Rud at all. It was thinking and thinking very incoherently about itself. More and more of the two thousand million or so who constituted humanity were falling into very much the same line of thought and feeling as that along which he was drifting. It was like the way particles change their orientation in a magnetised bar. It was like bits of crumbling ore falling one after another into a flux. This sense of insecurity was spreading about the entire planet, and though people went on doing the things they usually did, they had none of the assurance, the happy-go-lucky "all-right" feeling, that had hitherto sustained normal men. They went on doing their customary things because they could not think of anything else to do. They tried to believe, and many did succeed in believing, that there would presently be a turn for the better. They did nothing to bring about that turn for the better; they just hoped it would occur. All the same, they were worried. Rud was very seriously worried. He had no disposition to believe in the natural benevolence of the universe.

"They ought not to have let things come to this," he said, but he was never very clear even to himself who or why "They" were nor what "This" was. Some person or persons unknown was to blame. He hated these unknowns in general. But he was unable to focus his hatred into hating some responsible person or persons in particular. If only he could find who it was had neglected to do something, or had done something wrong or messed about with things, they would catch it. He'd get even with them somehow.

There had been a time when Camford was the very heart of conservatism. It was a bilateral conservatism in those days – and one half of it was called the Liberal Party. It dominated the country without effort as a matter of course. It changed and remained the same. It radiated out over an unresentful empire in a state of unindicted exploitation – on which a sun of unimpeachable loyalty never set. Odd specimens of the more coloured subject-races came up to Camford and objected to something or other, but in such funny Babu-English that their complaints dissolved in laughter. In these happy days the tradition of the careless, wealthy, young gentlemen ruled the whole university from the richest Fellow Commoner to the poorest scholar. The only use for subversive ideas was the opportunities they afforded for privileged rags. People with revolutionary minds and "advanced" notions were invited to address meetings and conduct debates, and were then kidnapped, ducked, personated and so forth, all in the most perfect good humour and with the unostentatious approval of the authorities.

But when Rudie went up, those golden days were already ancient history. He had read about them in books, but behold! they were over. The Great War had strained Camford, and Camford, after a phase of hectic optimism while it was reconstructing what was left of the old undergraduates who had gone to the front, remained strained and began even to realise how strained it was. A subtle change in the quality of the multiplying students and the younger dons, due to the belated but extensive expansion of lower middle-class education and the development of what was called the educational ladder, had gone on and continued. A new, uneasy type was swamping the ancient confidence of those venerable colleges, young men who said: "Yes, *but* – " to everything, over whose apprehensive minds the perception of decaying privileges and of imperial enervation, shrinkage and decline, hung more and more heavily.

For a year and more Rud stuck to his lecture and books. The teaching of Hooplady House had been urgent for examination successes rather than first-class in itself, and he had much to revise and supplement. Then he began to take notice of events outside the classroom.

Camford, since the mediaeval cosmogony had broken down and the Catholic scheme of salvation had fallen into disuse, had never made the slightest attempt to give any coherent picture of the universe to the new generation that came to it for instruction. Its Church of England orthodoxy broke down with Catholic emancipation and an influx of Dissenters and Jews. Since then nothing in Comford except a few dreaming spires had pointed anywhere. Inertia had carried the old place on for the better part of a century. It resisted novel ideas and scientific aggression as long as possible by the method of slight and innuendo, and when it could resist no longer it yielded in the true Anglican style with ambiguous and nearly inaudible acquiescences. This lulled the minds of a certain proportion of the young people and diverted their energies to games, rage, amateur theatricals, amateurish poetry and amateurish literary criticism, and the less easily tranquillised ones resorted to the bookshops in the town and to a diversity of intrusive movements that promised in the most various ways to satisfy that impatience for plain direction towards a concrete objective which is one of the natural cravings of ripening adolescence. At first these uneasy ones had been a small and derided minority, but in the post-war days they multiplied rapidly.

In his school days he had devoured books whole. Now he was realising that standard history had little to tell about what was happening in the world. He began to attend political gatherings and discussion circles; he took to reading and comparing a number of newspapers; his large brow and lowering expression were to be seen at the back of stuffy and draughty rooms, disliking and scrutinising the speakers and watching every reaction of the audience. He was puzzled, but he hung on, and his mind became more and more involved in this extra-academic stuff. He joined the Union and snorted and growled and indulged in ironical and imperfectly audible comments through three discussions. Each time he wanted to speak and didn't dare. Then at a debate upon the resolution: "That a drastic change in our economic life in the direction of collectivism is long overdue," he wrenched himself up from his seat, drew a deep breath and began his maiden speech.

He spoke for the motion. Words came. He found he could think on his legs. He could forget himself in his subject. Once started, his speech rambled indeed, but rambled interestingly. His sentences flowed easily. They were going over, he realised. He was less and less scared and more and more fluent. He was keeping his head and quite aware of what he was doing. He found he could hold a sentence, even quite a long sentence, bring out its conclusion with an emphasised clearness and a punch at the air that made it seem significant even when it was not. He worked himself up into a generous indignation. He ended in a whirl of patriotic anger.

"This is what they have made of our country! This is our inheritance!" The "old men" caught it, the privileged incapables, the greedy, short-sighted business organisers, the military caste, finance, the party "gangs." All the recognised cockshies. Indeed they caught it. Even "people in high places."

"Wake up England! – that was said thirty years and more ago. And see where we are! We of the new crop! Where are *we* to go? Go into the cadet corps, go into the flying corps! Yes – yes. Though those others died, they thought, to save us! We're in the soup and we've got to do it over again, my masters. We've got to do 1914 over again. It'll be our turn sure enough. The way they're going. We've got to face up to it. But not under the old fools and rogues, Sir, this time – not with the profiteers at our heels. No, *Sir!* This time we fight with our eyes open, with our eyes wide open."

And so on, growing loud and harsh, but still keeping pretty clear, more and more sure of himself. Betsy Barnacle would hardly have recognised the voice that had squalled upstairs in Mrs Whitlow's room eighteen years before, but it was the same voice growing up now, as protesting and as unquenchable. The speech was the success of the evening. It was what so many of his hearers had been feeling. But they had not been able to let themselves go as he did. More and more applause broke into his flow. They liked him. They really liked this thickset figure with the punching gesture and the big head. His words had the rather attractive bitterness of quinine.

He sat down amidst a buzz of applause.

In one crowded half hour Rud had become a Camford personality. Men discussed him in their rooms that night, and young dons talked about him.

"That was a pretty good speech," said a voice beside him as the gathering broke up. "A bit angry of course."

He looked up and saw Carstall at his elbow. That gave him a thrill. Carstall was already a research Fellow and his work in physiology was being talked about.

34

"How did you vote?" he asked.

"I voted with you, of course," said Carstall. "I'm all for a revolution – maybe more of a revolution than yours. I don't know. Mine is the cold deliberate sort and yours is the hot indignant stuff, but we're revolutionaries all right. It takes all sorts to make the world budge."

"We're revolutionaries all right," from Carstall, gave a peculiar confirmation to Rud's self-approval.

We!

Other hands got hold of his sleeves and caught at his elbow and drew him away from Carstall. Or he would have liked to have lingered for a moment over that. Men who had ignored him and even avoided him were asking him to come along to their rooms for a talk. Others were obviously intent upon questioning him.

He was not prepared to answer questions, he realised. He had made a strong impression and he must not complicate it. A natural turn for tactics came into play. "I'd love to," he said, "I'd love to but I've two hours of work tonight before I got to bed…"

"No. No. It's work that won't wait…"

He hoped they got the faint flavour of mystery in that work that wouldn't wait.

"I didn't mean to speak at all tonight. My ideas ran way with me…"

He felt he was doing it all magnificently. He was elated with himself. He disengaged himself, got away to his own rooms and locked himself in.

It required a considerable effort to do this. There was something intoxicating in this sudden transition from contemptuous negligence to interest. It was the first time he had felt visible in Camford. But he knew that he had to get out of it. He had to adjust himself before he betrayed how little he was adjusted. His speech quite as much as its reception had taken him by surprise. He hadn't thought it was in him. Even the ideas he had expressed struck him as new. They had come up out of him.

He sat before his fire for a long time in a state of confused self-congratulation. If he could go on with this sort of thing! Dreams he had kept at arm's length before he now accepted frankly. "Leadership," he whispered. "The quality of leadership. Maybe I have it. Maybe I really have it.

"Man to man I don't count for much, but man to meeting – ! It's going to be different. I wonder why. And – yes – *I can do it.*"

He began that acid whistle between his teeth that had been the common accompaniment of the walking daydreams of his schoolboy years – at first very softly and then loudly.

"A great speech, Rud, my boy. A magnificent speech!"

To that he had expanded Carstall's "pretty good speech."

"Leadership. Leadership. Leadership." The word sang through his brain.

He found himself in a vast dreamland auditorium compelling great waves in that time-honoured "sea of faces."

He thrust out his fist, held it up to the level of his forehead and glared at his armchair. It was his natural gesture, arrested and held. The room was filled with phantom applause.

3

"Your son, I see, Mr Whitlow," said Mr Skindle, the watchmaker, "has been getting into the papers. Seems he's been making speeches."

"Whe-where? I didn't see it," said Mr Whitlow.

"It's in the *District Weekly*," said Lozanda. "*I* saw it too. 'Local scholarship winner' they called him. Just a paragraph copied out of the *Camford News*."

"Says he's a Rising Red," said Mr Cramble the grocer, with a stern eye over his pipe.

The paper was handed to Mr Whitlow and there was silence while he read the news.

"Now that's serious," he said. "You never know what to do with that boy. Always breaking out in a new place. It won't do him any good at Camford to be figuring about as a red."

"It will *not*," said Mr Cramble.

"Seems he don't like the idea of this new war that's coming," said Lozanda. "*We* had a dose. I don't see why these kids shouldn't be soaked a bit. Make men of them."

"Or crosses," said Mr Skindle. "You don't know what it is to have a cross out there, Lozanda. *I* do. Ain't there no way of escaping it?"

"Not by talking Red Treason," said Mr Cramble. "I don't know what's happening to all these youngsters nowadays. Restless they are – extravagant. No respect for established things. As if they were all waiting about for something they didn't quite like, to come out of the night and happen."

"I *did* think Rudie had settled down to work," said Mr Whitlow with a rising sense of grievance. "We made sacrifices for him."

"Seems the generals are old fools and the admirals old fools and the bankers and businessmen fools and knaves," said Lozanda with the *District Weekly* as evidence in his hands. "He's got a hot tongue, that boy of yours. Hope it won't get him into trouble."

"Always had a hot tongue," said Mr Whitlow. "Fancy his breaking out at them like that... *Silly* young fool! Always talk, he would. Always. Burst out – like. After our sacrifices."

He took his troubles home with him. He walked about the bedroom undressing, and delivering his soul. "I ain't going to stand for it. I sent him to Camford to get a first-class degree and a permanent job. I didn't send him to Camford to get ideers. Who's going to listen to a young fellow like him telling them off? I ask you."

But Mr Whitlow answered nothing, because she had been reading over again Hans Christian Andersen's story of the Ugly Duckling. Ugly, Rudie certainly was. Nasty, too. Cunning and mean to his brothers. He could say the most horrid things... He seemed always angry about something... Why should he be angry?... Maybe if one understood him better...understood him better...

She went to sleep.

4

Rud did not make another speech for a week or so, and even then attempted nothing so elaborate as his first outbreak; his instinct told him that a second oration in the same term would not *do*; he wrote nothing but lecture notes, gave four hours a day grimly but with a watch on his desk, to textbooks, and talked with the utmost discretion. He felt that something very important had happened in his life and he did not quite know what. In such brief leisure as his steadfast pursuit of a good degree permitted him, he would catch himself dreaming over a gazetteer and an atlas, or reading books about Napoleon and Hitler and Mussolini.

Or simply he dreamt and schemed. If he could move people once, he could move them again…

Her did his best to control those extravagant reveries. For they went even beyond the range of his schoolboy battle-dreams.

People made his acquaintance now – almost with an effect of seeking him. This did much to confirm his newborn sense of his own value. If there was something they valued in him, then he would be a fool to give it away. Of course these reveries were reveries, but for all that there might be something in them. He could not help posing a little. He regarded his various visitors with a faintly hostile expression, hands behind his back, replied without committing himself to anything and summed them up one after another in his own mind.

The latest thing in religion presented itself one afternoon as a man too old for an undergraduate and too oily and shiny for a don, a queer fish with a slightly American accent. He had called, he said, and stopped. Whitlow thought he might be a canvasser. But he was much too rich and smug-looking for that.

"I heard your speech," resumed the intruder. "You have, what shall I call it? – mental energy. You have persuasive power – oh – great persuasive power. There was something *contagious* in your indignation. I feel it imperative upon me to implore you not to waste these gifts."

"I have my ideas," said Rudolf. "What do *you* suggest?"

"Where do they take you?"

"Nowhere yet. I asked you what do you suggest?"

"Have you Guidance?"

"Tell me about it."

The visitor wanted to walk about the room. He had played for the hearthrug but Rudie had got that. "*Do* sit down," said Rudie.

"In that chair there, the low one. No; I cannot listen to you if I have to keep on watching you moving around. It distracts me. What is this Guidance?"

"*Guidance*," said the visitor, sinking into his chair. "Just that."

Rudie replied with an uncivil monosyllable.

The missioner was spurred to exposition. "You don't know," he said.

"I'm asking you."

"Let me illustrate."

"I'm attending."

The illustrations rambled a good deal. Rudie listened with a lowering expression, that hampered the teller. He spoke of the fear and uncertainty in so many lives nowadays, the constant struggle against sinful impulses, of suicidal moments and how when at last it broke upon them –

"*What* broke upon them?"

"Guidance!"

"Ugh!"

"Guidance and the fellowship of those who *share*. Then everything grew simple, everything grew plain."

Rudolf remained in a pose of enigmatical attention. He realised that he was embarrassing this spiritual windbag. He liked that. There was power in this still silence; it was giving him an ascendency. It was a sort of hypnotism. He must try it again. "Don't you feel *something* – ?" said the visitor, trying to break this stony irresponsiveness.

"You go on with what you came to say," said his host.

Presently he brought the interview to an end. It was a sudden inspiration came to him. He lost his breath for an instant and then forced himself to speak.

"Tell me," he said. "This Guidance brought you here?"

"I felt impelled – "

"Yes, and now, don't you think it about time that Guidance packed you up and took you away again?..."

When his oak closed on the intruder, Rudie's stern face relaxed into a delighted grin. His mature earnestness fell from him like a mask. He stuck out his tongue at the door and then put his thumb to his nose and spread out his fingers in twiddling triumph. "*That* for you and your Guidance," he said.

By which it is manifest that he was still only very partially grown-up.

5

That was the only approach made by any sort of religious organisation to our emergent young man. Whatever other forms of faith flourished at Camford were apparently under the impression that Rudie might just as well be damned. But various politicians of a markedly "junior" character enquired about him. They waylaid him in stony corridors; they accosted him in the reading room; they came to his room. There were Liberals who just talked party politics of the most arithmetical sort and failed to pass quite elementary examinations on what they meant by Liberal principles; there were rather beefy Conservatives, one of them titled, with an ill-concealed quality of condescension, who seemed to regard the Empire as a sort of alluring Juggernaut to whom one would naturally and gladly prostrate oneself; there were shrill Indians who tried to win his respectful adhesion to their dusky cause, by proving with chapter and verse that the English were cheats, liars, oppressors and only temporarily necessary to India; there were Pacifists, some of whom were total abstainers from life, neo-gnostics in fact, while others seemed to make an exception in favour of serious eroticism. And there were middle-class Fabians, those painless permeators, with schemes for expropriating the rich and powerful so subtly that they would never know it had happened to them, and various leftists, Stalinists, Trotskyites and so forth, including several earnest young peers, who agreed that what was needed was a vehement class war and a proletarian revolution. And also he had a call from two oafish, unprepossessing young men in purple vests who talked against the Jews. Their indictment of the Jews was a little flimsy, but there could be no question of the earnest gusto with which they advocated the ancient sport of Jew-baiting. They wore broad leather belts and their jersey sleeves were rolled up as if on the off-chance of finding a pogrom round the corner. They told him Judaism was a wicked conspiracy to rob, corrupt and enslave Gentile mankind. He did not believe them for a moment. But he was quite polite to them because they were so very hefty. He did not argue with them, but he paid visible attention.

"You aren't called upon for any action," said the largest of them. "Just speak. We want speakers with ginger."

"I couldn't make a speech on the Jewish question to save my life. I haven't got it up."

"We could give you material."

"No," said Rudie, shaking a smiling face with modestly resolute conviction.

"You aren't by any chance a Jew yourself?" said the smaller (but still considerable) purple-shirt, and his eye roved about the room as if in search for convenient breakables.

Rudie had a nasty moment and then decided upon a virile line. "If I was about four stone heavier," he said, "I'd smash your blasted jaw for that."

It got a laugh, and the situation eased.

"Come along, Colin," said the big one. "He's not even a Pacifist. But you ought to read the Protocols of Zion, you really ought, Mister – ? I didn't get your name?"

Rudie felt now that he was safe on the bantam tack. "I haven't got yours," he said.

They pulled up their jerseys in search of pockets and produced cards. They handed them to Rudie with a friendly solemnity, bowed genteely and, forgetting all about a return card, louted off down the staircase with an air of something accomplished, something done.

"Blaggards," said Rudie when their footsteps had died away and the door was safely shut. "If I was a Jew I'd get a revolver. I'd get a razor like niggers do."

And his mind went back to his shin-kicking days, when he had thrown knives and jabbed with scissors and pens...

But it did not go forward to the time when myriads of such "blaggards" would march at his bidding.

6

Of all the movements fermenting through the venerable halls and colonnades and the narrow lanes and winding streets of Camford, the Communists had the most convincing air of meaning something and definitely going somewhere. Their scientific pretension, the aggressive confidence with which they sustained their remarkable, though incomprehensible, Hegelianism, impressed him, and their bias for revolutionary violence was all in their favour. But their doctrinaire inflexibility and intolerance did not attract him.

A large, fat young man at one of their meetings was quite interesting about the Seizure of Power. That sounded like sense. Of course one must seize power.

But Rudolf did not join the "Party." He spoke at a meeting and intimated a certain sympathy, but he kept outside. He did not speak very well on that occasion. There was something uncongenial in the atmosphere for which at first he could not find a name. It was as if he lacked some shibboleth and was out of court from the beginning. And not only that. They set their new adherents, he gathered, to do all sorts of undignified and time-wasting jobs, such as distributing unconvincing leaflets and selling newspapers full of stale provocation. And they were shepherded – shepherded was the word – by a postgraduate, one Jim Mortland, who had been four times to and fro to Moscow and behaved like a Malay who had been to Mecca. He had the languid authority of a rather jaded sergeant-major with a batch of new recruits. He seemed always to be transmitting orders from higher up and far away. Moscow? Why the devil should wisdom centre at Moscow? Why should Spain be the only arena for revolutionary activities? What had all this stuff to do with Rudie's perplexities and English social and economic unrest? And moreover, there was this Stalin-Trotsky, split, a worldwide scolding match, irrelevances, personalities, alien issues, imported stuff. Where was it likely to take this bunch of English trailers? He attended one or two meetings; there were one or two young peers and hardly a single real proletarian – and suddenly he found the missing word – *dilettante!* That settled Camford

Communism for him. It wasn't good enough. So for a time he remained politically indeterminate.

Yet his reveries now were all of political adventure. The success of his speech had lit and given a direction to his ambition, an everyday it burnt more brightly. He felt in his bones now that he had the making of a political figure. Once he started. His very indecision about the line he had to take marked the seriousness of his intentions. He found his inclination towards a sort of scheming reverie more and more of an interference with his work.

A day or so before the end of the term he went for a walk by the Cramb meadows to get tea at Chuck's Hill Farm. He had cleared up all his work and he felt free to indulge to the full in that ancient vice of his.

His thoughts ran over these various movements he had sampled. His ruling thought was what he could do with them and what they could do for him. "One has to take a line of one's own," he said, "and all the same, if one is to get anywhere, one has to have an Organisation – with a capital O. One must go over big or not go over at all. You've got to have a newspaper. Newspapers. Radio talks. Great halls. Stewards. It has to be paid for. You've got to have backers…

"One might *capture* some organisation…"

In his reveries capturing an Organisation involved a good lot of timely shooting.

What was it caught people? What was it caught backers? What got faithful adherents? What was it made them believe in you? So that you got started? Other people got supporters. You had to be obviously successful to hold them and you had to give them something, something that they felt they could not get or do or be themselves...

Brooding in the warm afternoon sunshine over the Chuck's Farm tea things, with unlimited supplies of Mother Braybone's newish bread and admirable butter and home-made strawberry jam, all things became possible. His thoughts were like the printed text of a book that has been over-illustrated by a far too enthusiastic illustrator. The text kept to a certain level of possibility, but the reverie soared fantastically and magnificently. He found himself presently with a group of intimate colleagues, devoted to him. (They really were devoted to him.) And behind them was the party, *his* party.

Would they wear a shirt?

Shirts were overdone. Brown shirts, green shirts, black shirts, purple shirts; the idea was played out. The Whitlow men wouldn't have that. They'd have belts. They'd have trousers with elastic webbing in them and belts with heavy buckles that could be whipped off in a moment for a fight. Good. And by a way of recognition, a badge, a badge worn *inside* the jacket, like the sheriff's badge in an American gangster film. A good idea that!

What to call them? The Whitlow men? The Rud men? They'd have to have a slogan. Something to shout, something to stick on their banners.

And an idea? He had long thought that the separation of the United States and the British Empire was a terrible waste of strength, that a drive for reunion could be made very popular, and that gave him, "The man who speaks English is my brother." Because nowadays, now that we were drawing so near to America by air and radio and common dangers why should not our political movements straddle the Atlantic?

So far it had never happened. Even their Communists and our Communists were different. But that needn't be so now. And that altered everything. This was a great thought for Ruide.

The reverie produced a vision of the mighty canyons of the New York City streets as he had seen them in photographs and pictures and films, and people were scattering torn-up paper from the windows upon the milling swarms below, and great banners hung across from one side to the other bearing his slogan. "The man who speaks English is my brother." There was an immense excited crowd, all displaying badges, all Rud men. It was a tremendous occasion. Rud had arrived in America. The Big Union had been achieved.

Why not? Various things stood in the way, of course; the monarchy, ancient prejudices, irritations, suspicions on both sides of the Atlantic. Rud's imagination swept them aside.

The reverie suddenly produced a touching meeting between a British monarch, a very hypothetical British monarch, and Rud. "Our family," said the monarch, opening his coat suddenly and displaying the hidden badge, "have been Rud men and Rud women for some time. If it is necessary to Anglo-American coalescence for us to efface ourselves, we are prepared."

An almost religious reverence came into Rud's eyes as he contemplated this beautiful present from his imagination, over an unusually large, an almost fervent bite of jam-spread bread and butter.

He found he had to assist that excessive mouthful with the back of his disengaged hand.

Then he blushed at his own puerility, finished his slice in a more businesslike way, emptied his cup of tea and produced and lit a cigarette.

"The problem," he whispered, "is to find those nuclear associates. Then we could start something...

"But we have to give them something *new*...

"All these things that are going on now – communism, fascism and all that – they are nearly played out – they are three-parts dead. By the time *I* get going it would be like crying stinking fish to go for any of them. A new appeal. It has to have a freshness, whatever it is..."

And then suddenly it seemed to him that he saw an idea, a programme, a scheme of operations, a way to success plain before him. For a moment he had the impression of something full and completed, the exact thing needful. His mind just stopped at that and stared at it – as one might stare, if suddenly a door opened in a hitherto impenetrable and unclimbable wall and revealed – the dark and indistinguishable landscape of some unknown land on which no sun had ever yet risen. And then it was as if the door slammed again.

"If they're all *out*," he whispered. "And if there is a right way –

"*They* haven't got it. Any of them...

"But if one *did* get it!"

He seemed to see the confusion suddenly crystallising under the spell of a magic word – some missing elusive word – surely he had had it quite plain only a moment before! – and in his reverie, he it was who had shouted that word. And now it had gone. Gone altogether.

What was it? That missing Sesame?...

What was it? What was it?

There was an extraordinary blankness upon the sunlit meadows and the steel-blue, winding Cramb...

He sat stockstill for some time realising his hallucination only very gradually. His cigarette went out between his fingers. Then, still with a dazed expression, he roused himself and began rattling his spoon against his cup to get his bill.

Returning to college he was still trying to recall something that had never really been in his mind.

7

Old Doctor Carstall, whom Mrs Whitlow considered so big and deliberate, had often wanted to talk things over with his son, things in general, fundamental things, what everything was for and what one thought one was up to, and things of that sort, and like all intelligent fathers he was afraid of his son and shy of him. These young people, he felt, know so much more than we do and so much less than we do; one ought to make some sort of show-down to them and get some idea of what they thought they were doing. There ought to be that much continuity between the generations. His son's visit to his home *en route* for the Alps, that trite and wholesome and not too expensive playground for the earnest young don, seemed to give just the occasion needed. They sat at dinner, an excellent dinner, for the doctor was an easy and stimulating master to his cook.

"The world seems in a queer state nowadays," the old man began. "what do you make of it all, Dick?"

"An old world dying, a new one unable to get born – who was it said something like that?"

"Only worlds don't die and get born again," said the doctor. "If a world dies, it dies, and there's an end to it. There's no more on its line... You *might* perhaps – Of course, if you're thinking of

49

obstetrics, the image might just pass... Died in childbirth... Phoenix... Something of that sort... *Is* your world dying, Dick? And what are you doing about it?"

Young Carstall had been sitting at his ease and he had answered his father after the manner of casual conversation. Now he sat up a little. He felt the slovenliness of his previous response. "No one of my age, sir, thinks his world is dying," he said. "It isn't natural. But we're certainly in for troubled times. Dangerous times."

"Those fellows who lecture to us about the world and who talk on the radio and write in the magazines and papers and all that have got hold of a phrase lately; what is it? Ah! – *imperfect adaptation.*"

"Not bad as an elementary statement. Don't you agree, Father? Imperfect adaptation to all the new powers and implements in the world. Following them up clumsily, using them vulgarly and not keeping pace with the new possibilities and dangers. Particularly the dangers. Air-war and disorganisation generally. It seems fairly obvious."

"A few years ago we used to talk about morality failing to keep its ascendency over – what was it? – material progress?"

"Said by bishops usually, Father. I don't attach much value to all that *scolding* of aeroplanes and the cinema and the radio and motor cars and so on. No. It's the moral side which has to adapt. It always *has* had to adapt. There's no such thing as fixed and final morality. Though the bishops like to think so. The immutable laws of Heaven! They're like obstinate men with a dying patent – or a vanishing trade. Their stuff doesn't *go* any more and they won't give it up. No, they won't give it up. Until the church files its petition in bankruptcy and there are no more stipends forthcoming. But their game is pretty nearly over, all the same. We have to get new values and ideas to fit these inflexible new facts we've got ourselves up against. Or come a cropper."

"You mean?"

"Political ideas. Religion. History. Ownership. All the ideas we have about such things are threadbare and rotten and splitting. I suppose they've all got to be changed. The material facts won't change."

"Such facts as?"

"Three hundred miles an hour travel. News almost instantaneous. Limitless power. Overproduction – whenever you try in the least, that is. Health control. Population control. No animal has ever faced such changes in what it can do and what it can bring down on itself, and survived."

"I know that song, Dick. Yes. I can sing it almost in unison with you. I guess we agree pretty completely about all that. Man is now a new animal, a new and different animal; he can jump a hundred miles, see through brick walls, bombard atoms, analyse the stars, set about his business with the strength of a million horses. And so forth and so on. Yes. Yes. But all the same he goes on behaving like the weak little needy ape he used to be. He grabs, snarls, quarrels, fears, stampedes and plays in his immense powder magazine until he seems likely to blow up the whole damned show. Eh?"

"That's on the face of things, Father."

"That's where we stand. That's our situation."

"That's our situation. Yes. You read your *Nature*, I see. You keep up with the times."

"I shan't do that much longer, Dick."

51

"You're good for another twenty years. I don't need to be a doctor to tell you that."

"Not very good for action now. Retiring from active practice. Quite soon. Yes. I see the distant land of the future like Moses, but you – you have to carry on... The problem comes to you. Sixty years of life may be in front of you. Sixty tremendous years. What are you going to do about it, Dick? Is it all going to happen to you or are you going to do something about it? It's for your generation now, you know, to do something about it. No good blaming us. That won't help you."

"Inform ourselves, I suppose. Readjust our imaginations. Think out a new behaviour."

For an internal the elder man answered nothing.

"I suppose," he resumed presently, "that some sort of mental renascence *is* possible. A sufficient renascence. I hope so. But I see very few signs of it. That adaptation you talk about... There's a lot of unteachable stuff in humanity. Down here I've been watching a little section of mankind, bringing new individuals into the world, seeing the old ones drop out of it, seeing the insides and the undersides and the backsides of the creatures. Queer stuff and weak stuff, they are. Mean. A lot of malice in them. And also a sort of obduracy. Do you know that almost always they lie to me about themselves. Their doctor, I am, and they lie to me. Out of self-protective vanity – mostly. They come for advice and then they fake their facts and dodge their medicine. Only just a few work with me. Silly, they are. Intricately silly."

"All of them?"

"Most. There's differences. Considerable differences. They vary. Their imaginations vary. And their *go*. Very widely. So widely that at times I seem to be dealing with different species of creature. But on the whole I don't *see* that renascence of will and understanding which is needed to head off catastrophe. No..."

He paused, but his son remained silently attentive.

"Maybe it isn't altogether hopeless. Maybe there are different species in mankind – all mixed up. That idea seems to be getting about, Dick. You must have heard of it. Maybe the real differences in men lie in the kinks of their brains. Scattered about among the silly multitudes there *may* be men of a different quality – with a different power of vision."

"A sort of anonymous unsuspected aristocrats?"

"Exactly."

"So you don't believe in democracy any longer?"

"I never did. Look at 'em! Do you?"

"I'd like to."

"But you don't."

"But during your forty years of practice," said the younger man, "hasn't there been a certain amount of general, all over, mental progress? More education, more books, more information? Not enough, I admit, but some. If only we were able to increase the tempo of that sort of thing?..."

The old man shook his head with a smile of unbelief.

"You'll never get the whole lot intelligent. You'll only widen the gap. A born fool is a fool to the end. Maybe there will be more and more of the right sort proportionally. As they get opportunities to emerge. But the crowd will remain a crowd and behave like a mob... That's where I stand, Dick."

"I don't like to feel that is right. Somehow – at my age – and with a sort of implicit reservation about our noble selves, you know, Daddy..."

He made a grimace.

"You don't like that, and neither do I. At my age, too, Dick. It makes me feel – uncomfortable, to admit even to myself that there are these differences. But if the truth is that all men are not equal, then is it *fair* to treat an inferior as an equal? Even at golf you give a handicap. And I don't ask my patients to vote on their treatment and then blame them for the result."

Then with a chance of manner that his son found very characteristic, he said: "This is getting academic, Dick..."

Dick didn't seem to mind. He was plainly interested in this evidently long-meditated discourse. He waited for his father to resume.

"Well, anyhow, the practical outcome of all these crude democratic ideas, is that men of our quality – yes, damn it! we *have* a quality – excuse themselves from the hard and thankless service they owe – not to the crowd, Dick, but to the race. (Much good it will do us to shirk like that in the long run.) We will not presume, we say, no. We shrug our shoulders and leave the geese, the hungry sheep, the born followers, call them what you will, to the leaders who haven't our scruples. The poor muts swallow those dead old religions no longer fit for human consumption, and we say 'let 'em.' They devour their silly newspapers. They let themselves be distracted from public affairs by games, by gambling, by shows and coronations and every sort of mass stupidity, while the stars in their courses plot against them. *We* say nothing. Nothing audible. We mustn't destroy the simple faith that is marching them to disaster. We mustn't question their decisions. That wouldn't be democratic. And then we sit here and say privately that the poor riff-raff are *failing* to adapt themselves to those terrible new conditions – as if they had had half a chance of knowing how things stand with them. They are shoved about by patriotisms, by obsolete religious prejudices, by racial delusions, by incomprehensible economic forces. Amidst a growth of frightful machinery..."

He stopped short and stared at his son and his son smiled back at him faintly and nodded for him to go on.

"You haven't been watching a community for four full decades, Dick. I have. My practice here is a fair sample of mankind... I have seen a sort of self-confidence fading out of this world. Like a twilight. When I bought this practice everyone who came to me, every man Jack of them, felt he had a place in the world, that there were things he ought to do, and things he mustn't do. Maybe people were a little lower then, nearer the earth, but that was how things were. A normal man got along in a system he thought he understood. *Now* −

"Dick, people aren't nearly as straight in business as they were. They've ceased to feel that honesty is the best policy. They've found themselves put out of business by competition they think unfair. They try to get even by counter-cheating. And they aren't clever enough. They find the incomes they had counted on, their pay or whatnot, raided by taxation, shattered by currency manipulation and slumps, knocked to pieces, by all this messing about with money, this inflation, deflation, and all the rest of it. Even the wages-earners never know now what their money can buy. And more and more of them are pottering about with poor little parcels of stocks and shares, hunting after Capital Appreciation. That's the great phrase now. I've heard it three times from three separate people this past fortnight. There's ten men speculating in a small miserable way for one who knew his way to a broker forty years ago. Ten, do I say? −

fifty! They lie awake at nights. They get chronic indigestion. They get neurasthenia and neuritis. Some are frankly betting. These football pools are a sort of disease of vain hopes, social dropsy. The *women* bet. It was unheard of in the old days. There's hardly a man in my area now, Dick, under fifty, who finds any satisfaction in a job well done, or believes that it will secure him any sort of reward. Think of what that means in social stability...

"And the women I have to deal with, Dick, the younger women; they're *all* demoralised as we understood demoralisation. They don't understand themselves. There was a certain amount of sly adultery and still slyer fornication going on then, but it didn't disturb the even surface of things. It was just healthy incontinence... Chastity now is out of fashion. Children are an encumbrance. The women want, or feel they ought to want, a sort of gadding-about amusement and a man has to pay for it. They sell themselves almost frankly, wholesale or retail. They aren't steady because the men aren't steady. The men are insecure and rattled and the women follow suit. You'd be amazed, Dick, at the people who come along nowadays hinting at abortion..."

He hesitated and plunged. "What are *you* making of women, Dick? What are you going to do about all that?"

"I like them," said Dick after a long, downcast pause for reflection. "I like them a lot."

"And they like you?" said his father.

"Things have changed, Father."

"Mutual comfort, eh? That's all got relaxed. It's all different from the repressions of my time. Perhaps it's not worse, perhaps it's better, but it's all shockingly different... And that sort of thing is not going to eat you up?'

"I don't think so. No. So far it hasn't done any harm to my work, and I don't think it will."

"Sex," his father reflected, "used to have certain biological significance. And social aspects. And a kind of idea of mating, Is all *that* changed?"

"It's changed in a way, yes."

"And what becomes of your young women in the end? Rather jaded little bitches, eh? Some, anyhow. Some don't seem to suffer much damage, but most who go loose stay loose. And a loose woman who is getting old is a damn nasty thing... And yourself, Dick, as *you* grow older?"

"I think I shall marry. Long before I grow nasty. *You* ought to have some grandchildren, you know. It won't be a grand passion... Maybe it's a defect, Father, but the truth is I don't like romance in love. I like humour..."

"I'm not so sure of that *mating* business either. Women's minds don't seem to move with ours. They don't keep step with us. I've seen that. I guess I shall have time to think about it some more before I fix myself. When Adam delved and Eve span, there was a sort of partnership. But now – do men and women hunt in couples? *Can* they? Under the new conditions. My work... I'd hate to have a wife who knew too much about my work. When I was going slack, when I was casting about in my mind, preoccupied, in that sort of exasperating, dissatisfied worry one *must* go through, when one is feeling about for something missing. Think of the horror of a nice intelligent question at the breakfast table! 'Tell me all about it, darling'... But all the same I'd hate to have a wife who knew nothing about it."

"There's a middle way," said his father. "Maybe you'll not marry, Dick, maybe you'll never *find* a wife at all, but all the same some woman will come along, who will think you over and decide to marry you. And do it. I'm inclined to think that's the way things are going. Anyway it's the way things *ought* to go. It's *their* business really. Damn it! What else are they for? You aren't likely to be too rich or too conspicuous, to attract the exploiting sort. But you're not unattractive, Dick."

"I take after you, Father, a bit."

"*You'll* be picked all right. But it will be more her business than yours, and if things go an as they are going, she'll probably ask you. I've watched people. Picking out women by men is silly. They don't give their minds to it. Far better have it the other way about. Though I doubt whether they ought to pick much before two or three and twenty. That's the way. Be sure she has our sense of humour, Dick, and then marry her and thank God for her – even if she gives you moments of doubt. A woman with unsatisfied desires or a craving vanity is the worst thing in life, but a woman with living and responsive things to protect and take care of, is the best. Believe me…"

And then the doctor made what he firmly believed was an entirely original, outstanding and remarkable statement – the statement that a countless multitude of widowers in his position have been moved to make.

"There never was a woman in the whole world," he said, "so good and uncomplicated, so generous and self-forgetful, as your mother. I wonder if you remember her. I never knew anyone with so swift and sure a judgement of character. You couldn't harbour a mean thought when she was about. And yet she regarded politics as a kind of male silliness – like a hunt or race-meeting – she thought science was wool-gathering and she hadn't the slightest idea of the – the blundering uncertainties of medical practice. She thought I cured whenever a cure was possible. Fifteen years ago, she died, and I talk to her in my dreams still. I think of things I should like to tell her. Sometimes when I am in trouble and sometimes just because I want to share something with her. But one can't do things like that, Dick. So that's that... I'm wandering, Dick, from what we were talking about..."

He mused for a moment and returned to his original drift.

"You think your scientific work is good enough to hold your imagination and carry you on? It opens out, eh? That second paper of yours certainly had a periscope. It ranged... Sometimes I think we biologists may find ourselves coming into politics from our own angle. If things go on as they are going – We may have to treat the whole world as a mental hospital. The entire species is going mad; for what is madness but a complete want of mental adaptation to one's circumstances? Sooner or later, young man, your generation will have to face up to that."

He stopped and looked at his son's face.

"Those – what was it we said – anonymous unsuspected aristocrats," said the younger man, and thought.

He leant forward on the table and picked his way among his ideas as he spoke. "I have an idea, Father, a half-formed idea, that before we can go on to a sane new order, there has to be a far more extensive clearing up of old institutions... The world needs some sort of scavenging, a burning up of the old infected clothes, before it can get on to a new phase. At present it is enormously encumbered... This is just a shadowy idea in my mind... Something like breaking down condemned, old houses. We can't begin to get things in order until there has been this scavenging phase. And, you see, what one might call civilised men can't do that sort of rough work.'

"I suppose it *has* to be rough work?"

"What do you think? Conservatism insists on it. The old order of things, the patriots, the priests and the old laws won't *deal* with reasonable men. They won't hear of it. They're cunning, they're subtle in their way. Subtly stupid. They've got an unintelligent suicidal instinct for what they think is self-preservation. They *won't* stand criticism; they *won't* adapt. They'll listen and seem to agree and they'll play tricks. They're afraid of any light, any clearness. They fog education. They obstruct. What! Deal with *us!!* They're much more disposed to deal with the roughs and turn them against us. You've got to capture the rough from them, you've got to use the rough against them, educate him, civilise him – as far as he will stand it."

"A bit roundabout and underhand," said the old man. "Modern Jesuitry. Rather on old Marx's lines, eh? Call these roughs 'proletarian' and there you are! Flatter them until you've organised their discipline. Maybe I misunderstand you?"

"I'm telling you my ideas, Father, as well as I can. You've asked for it. But I see no way out of the present break-up, but 'Let the best rough win.' Then so soon as you've got a top rough in the world, he'll have to organise efficiently to save himself from the next possible rough, and he'll have to be quick about it. The bigger he grows – and you know the next rough may be worldwide – less of the administration, and less of the planning he and his gang will be able to control, and the more he'll have to use and trust the able, resolute, relatively unambitious type..."

"Meaning our sort? Our virtuous sort? Eh?"

"Well – yes."

"After the democracies, the demagogues who become dictators and after them a World Civil Service? Fabian permeation and all that. And I'm not so sure of that Civil Service. It may develop a high standard of comfort and a taste for dependants."

The young man reconsidered it. "All sorts of complications and interludes," he said, "but, like it or not, that I take it is the general shape of the story ahead. A World Civil Service if you like – but based, that's the restraining force – on a World Public Opinion."

"Something of that sort," said the doctor, with a grape in his mouth, "existed in Egypt. In Ancient Egypt. Which was practically a world in itself. BC two thousand. Charming cultivated people."

For a time they gave their attention to desert.

"Civilisation has always been something of a patch-up," reflected the doctor. "You seem pretty convinced that it had to be worse before it is better... I agree... This particular earthquake looks likely to be the biggest so far. How do you see it in terms of yourself, Dick? You may not be able to keep out of the way of these – what do you call them? – scavengers. Concentration camp or prison examination. You cannot smash and remake a social system without breaking men – incidentally and accidentally – and the chances may pick on you to be broken. It may degrade you, Dick. You won't be able to help yourself if your skull gets burst open or your brain or your mind gets exhausted or poisoned. After all, it won't be the end of the world, but it may be the end of *your* world. That's as may be, you say... I agree... It will mean you will begin your decay before you are dead. A slight but nowadays not an uncommon inversion of the normal order. But an end comes to all of us. Until then and while you are yourself, you mean to keep a stiff backbone. Eh? No cringing, no compromise."

"I want that," said his son. "A stiff backbone, I mean. As long as possible I will keep out of money-making and politics and the scrambles and stampedes, and go on with my special work. You've made it possible. But if a straight challenge comes, if I'm absolutely prevented from working or if I see a plain occasion before me and my sort..."

"Working, waiting and watching for something that may call you and compel you... Waiting for the time when dictators dwindle and roughs relax... You might do worse... For the life of me, I don't see what else there is to do now. If you fight them now you'll only fight for the old system."

With a palpable effort not to seem self-indulgent and to throw a sacramental flavour about the gesture, Doctor Carstall poured himself some of his own very excellent brandy. "Good luck to you, my son. I'm glad we've had this talk."

CHAPTER THREE

Exploration

Rudie went down home for the Long Vacation because there seemed to be nowhere else to go. But in his state of adventurous unrest he found home altogether unendurable before a week was out. His father with a manifest disposition to administer discouraging advice, his mother with her general air of asking him not to (whatever it was) for her sake, and his brothers with their ill-controlled jealousy of his Camford advantages, were all so tiresome, and the district when he tried a lonely walk or so, so full of stale memories, that he felt himself driving towards one of those smashing and screaming and abusive outbreaks that had disfigured his childhood. But among the disciplines he was imposing upon himself for ambition's sake, was the practice of self-control. He had buried, even if he had not killed, little Rud the knife-thrower. But he had not buried him very deep. Once or twice his father exasperated him almost to the verge of a resurrection.

"You've got to work hard at Camford, my boy, and mind what they tell you," said his father, "for it's your only chance. And you mustn't make enemies, my boy. You mustn't make enemies."

"Ow! *Who's* making enemies?" snarled Rudie.

"I didn't say you *were* making enemies, my boy. I didn't say that. You catch me up too quick. I said you *mustn't* make them."

"Ugh!"

"What I say is for your good, my boy. you've got a quick tongue and you may give offence before you know where you are. I know. I've lived. I've given way to wit in my time or I might have been a better-off man than I am today. When I was young, before I learnt better, I was a good deal like you, my boy. Very like you. *Quick*. And something of your gift of the gab. No sooner did I think of a thing than I was out with it. It made me enemies. And all this saying things about politics and socialism and people. Seems clever at the time…"

"Oh, *Criky!*" said Rudie *sotto voce*…

He decided that somehow he would wangle five pounds out of his mother and go off for a walking tour. Anywhere. He was wasting his time here. He couldn't even study; he had no room to work in and no seclusion. He felt perhaps if he went through the country looking in on meetings, listening to speakers at street corners, talking to people, he might get ideas. He'd wear old clothes, take his stuff in a rucksack, be a university gentleman, incognito, so to speak. A lot of fellows nowadays were doing that. Old lodgings and doss houses. And weren't there hikers' camps and roadhouses? He'd manage all right.

He would head for Birmingham or Sheffield and then turn north. He might find a strike going on and anyhow he'd get a glimpse of industrial conditions. There'd be unemployed men to talk to. He'd find out what kinds of organisation were possible among them. If the weather was fine he might cultivate a sunburn by a few days on the Lancashire moors or in the Peak country. What he would have liked to do was to have gone to New York and prowled with his eyes and ears open. He was now very keen to learn about America, and in the vacation away from the Union he could not even see *Time* or the *New Yorker*. He hadn't the money to buy them. And as for crossing the Atlantic, he had neither fare nor time now. America must wait. He might get in touch with those Mass Observers one was beginning to hear about, but they might keep him too busy for his private concerns. He had no desire to do jobs for other people. If he had thought of it before he might have joined one or other of the conferences that were always afoot now in some hostel or other, but that might have involved a subscription he could ill have afforded. But anything was better than stagnation and more father.

Mother had been watching him. She was ready for his appeal and helped him out with it. She got the five pounds somehow. She got together six pounds ten shillings.

"Of *course*, dear, you want more of a change than you get here…"

2

He found little to excite him in the first two days of his pilgrimage and he was beginning to feel more than a little solitary when he came upon Chiffan. It was in the late afternoon and he was consuming as big a tea as he could manage with eggs and cake and jam at a pleasant generous little wayside cottage. He was going on a two-meal system, hearty breakfast and late high-tea and that was all. He found it the most economical way of feeding. And perforce he had become a strict teetotaller.

Chiffan, it seemed, was on the road in much the same spirit. He was an older man than Rudie, he might have been twenty-six or seven, and he had a pale, intelligent face with a decided nose, a faint, wry smile, bright, rather distraught, grey-blue eyes and untidy, dark brown hair. His trousers were relaxed grey slacks and he wore a knitted blue pullover in placed of a jacket. His gear beside him was in an ancient Japanese-cane valise which he carried by a strap, and he had a stout cabbage-stick laid across the table. He studied Rudie for a time and Rudie, looking up from a copy of the *Daily Worker*, found he was being accosted.

"Doing a lonesome hike?" asked Chiffan.

"Looking about at things," said Rudie.

"Sociology? Mass observation? Something of that sort? I see you're reading the *Daily Worker*. Communist, maybe?"

"No-o," said Rudie, finding himself hard to explain and making a mystery of it. "No. just interested. What are *you* doing?"

"*I* make no secret of it. I'm a disgruntled communist wandering about like a lost dog. The Left's gone to pieces... Stalin and Trotsky...

"Spain...

"United Front rot. When there is no sort of unity..."

Rudie was in the completest agreement.

"Anti-Fascist. Anti-Purple shirts. What a lot they are! What good is it being just Anti-? It lets the other side choose the battlefield and you have to run after them and attack. *They* say it first and you say 'No.' Look at this rag."

He smacked the *Daily Worker*, so to speak, in the face.

"Now *that's* an idea!" said Chiffan alertly, taking in what Rud had said. "That's a real good idea. Yes. Anti-. If you're just

66

Anti-. That lets the other chap choose his battlefield. Good! Oh, *good!*"

Rudie felt he could like this stranger. "Well, that's how I see it," he said modestly. "We want something positive. Surely we do. I've been feeling that lately. I tell you – "

Chiffan stuck out a long forefinger. "The old game is up," he said. "You've got it. We want a new formula. That's what we want – a new formula! *As* you say. Exactly what I have been saying! And until we get it, I'm going back to my brother's at Booksham to help him get out the *Booksham Messenger* and do general printing. I'm disgruntled, I tell you – deadly disgruntled, and that's all about it. I'm just going to drop in to the New World Summer School at Wexley on the way, but I don't expect anything much from *that*."

"And what might the New World Summer School be?" asked Rudie.

Particulars were forthcoming. They discovered themselves similar and sympathetic from the outset. There seemed no reason why they should not visit this school together.

They set out for a four-day tramp to the New World Summer School and as they tramped they talked, and while they ate they talked, and they talked while they sat in woods and under shady trees beside pleasant rivulets or hung over the parapets of little bridges during the heat of the afternoon, and when they shared a bedroom they talked most of the night, and when they slept in a Youth Hostel they talked and argued until the consensus of opinion that they ought to "Shut Up" could be disregarded no longer. Chiffan declared loudly and frequently that he had rarely met anyone with the freshness and lucidity of Rud, and Rud knew that in Chiffan he had found just that experience, response and appreciation that would bring out all the best that was in him. As he talked he discovered brilliant opinions in his mind that he had never even suspected were there.

Chiffan was in a phase of disillusionment, and his disbelief in people and especially in the leaders of the left world was acute and acid. But he had a gift for admiration. It is a winning gift. He was prepared to admire Rudie, but at first only on condition that he joined in a general denigration of the distressful world about them. He wanted a world revolution and everything completely upside down more passionately but much less hopefully than Rudie. He had the advantage of eight or nine years of experience. He knew more people and he had watched the careers of many more people. He had done a considerable amount of journalistic work. He had always been against the Government. He had picketed. He had rioted. He had been locked up. He had been married in some imperfect way that had come undone, but he laid no stress on that. He could talk more abundantly than Rudie, though he lacked his facility of phrase. And he found something very sustaining in Rudie's manifest belief that there were still possibilities of revolutionary activity in the world. With reconstructed formulae. (Great phrase!)

Three main topics interlaced during their four-day tramp to the New World conference. One was Rudie's notion that the revolutionary movement in Great Britain should cut away from continental associations altogether and get into the closest co-operation with American revolutionists.

"You can't work with people who not only speak a different language," said Rudie, "but who're in a different phase. None of these Communists ever seem to think of that. We are laying out a revolution in a democratic country. That's *our* phase. Isn't it?

But Russia is in a phase of" – he scarcely hesitated before the words rolled out – "precocious Communist senescence."

"Precocious Communist senescence! Oh *grand*, man! Oh, simply grand! And you're *right*."

"Spain, on the other hand, isn't even up to Marx. This anarchist syndicalism of theirs! It's pure Rousseau. Read Sender. It's hundred and fifty years behind us."

"You're so *right* about this."

"But America and here are not ten years apart. Some things they're ahead and some things we are. *That's* our fight. Hands across the sea. One tongue. One culture. Take a hint from the Anschluss…"

That was Rudie's chief contribution.

Chiffan brought in the second theme and that was the monetary question. "It took me a time to see it, and most of them don't see it themselves, but those currency cranks have *got* something. Mark my words, Rud! They've really *got* something. They've *got* something fundamental. Money, you see, is the key to the whole property problem. Socialism is just William Morris and *News from Nowhere* until it has a theory of money. Socialism has been poking about in the factory when it ought to have been going through the books in the counting-house. Setting the worker against the employer has been barking up the wrong tree. It's the banker, Rudyard, it's the private banker. The Bank is the key position in the social war. Go for that. Control banking, control the issue of credit – and money, you know, is only a credit counter – and private enterprise is yours to do just exactly what you like with."

This took some explaining and wrangling. It was newish stuff for Rud. But Chiffan was tremendously equipped for that argument. They went about the whole question and came back to this bit of it or that. Rud would get new ideas and objections in the most unexpected circumstances and hurry to find Chiffan and expound them. Before they got to the summer school Rud was no longer talking of "Capitalists," he was talking of "Money Barons."

(And here in parenthesis we may note that henceforth we must call our Rudie, Rud and nothing else. Because Chiffan had assumed from the outset that Rud stood for Rudyard. When he had used "Rudyard" for the third time, Rud reflected upon the matter and decided not to correct him. He had always had a faint dislike to the foreign romantic flavour about Rudolf, and he felt now that for a potential demagogue in the great English-speaking community, it would be a serious handicap. He began to think of himself as Ruyard. A time was to come when he would not even recognise himself as Rudolf Whitlow.)

The third and more absorbing topic between these two young men was the possible creation of a New Revolutionary Party. It was all very well to be a great revolutionary leader in reverie, but at first it seemed almost indecent to Rud to expose that secret thought in conversation in the sunlight. Still it had to be brought forward.

"These other fellows," he said, "after all, compared to us, they aren't so *wonderful*. How did they get there?"

How did they get there? Or to be nearer the intention of the question; how can we get there?

Here Chiffan's eight years of observation and detraction was of the utmost value. Rud became his lively and intelligent pupil.

They canvassed this leader and group and that. Chiffan explained the faults and failures of the endless imperfect coagulations and dissolutions and recoagulations of leftism with the utmost lucidity. He had an astonishing memory. The two of them began to shape out more and more definitely the movement and organisation that was needed to correct that tangle of faults. It was to be Anglo-American (*and* Dominion. *Certainly* Dominion) from the start. It was to adopt an attitude of self-respecting co-operation towards the good industrialists. It was to promise abundant money and abundant cheap goods in a world relieved of rent and financial overheads. It was to pursue the banker and the Stock Exchange and all "speculation" pitilessly. There were to be no rent, no debentures and no sort of mortgages in the new world, and the State was to take care of the people's savings and lend their money for them to initiate profitable enterprises – guaranteeing an adequate return. "The land," they would say, "is the State's and the fullness thereof."

"Not a bad slogan," said Chiffan. "I like that biblical twang! Fullness thereof!"

"The land for mankind and the fullness thereof," tried Rud, always a little fastidious about phrasing.

A tremendous benevolence welled up in them, especially on the finer afternoons, as they sketched their economic programme. They seemed to feel already the grateful response and the eager support of mankind. They settled the little matters of shirts in favour of Rud's badges and they tried over a lot of other slogans and argued out the main conditions of launching a movement.

A point Chiffan made that seemed fresh to Rud was the necessity for invading and "capturing" already existing groups and parties.

"We've got to capture people," said Chiffan. "You can't be like Cadmus and the dragon's teeth; you can't call a party out of nothing. Nearly everybody who is politically minded enough to join a party has joined a party already. Our party would have to raid..."

"Now *that's* an idea," said Rud.

"And where?"

"You know better than I do."

"I've cast about in my mind," said Chiffan, "since I chucked communism in London. But not very hopefully until I hit upon you. Now things look different somehow and I'm casting about in my mind more than ever. There's these Guidance people... No. No. Not to be sniffed at like that. They gather a lot of raw stuff. They're worth raiding. Then there's that fool Lord Horatio Bohun and his purple shirts – mauve shirts really they are, for he never had the wit to get his shirts fast colour. There's a deuce of a lot of money behind him a lot of meaty young men and precious little in the way of ideas. Sort of vaguely anti-communist and that's about all. Fancy dress and ragging. Aristocratic – nothing to do with the blasted bourgeoisie. They might be ready to take on a good set of ideas – and there you are!"

"They *do* want speakers," said Rud. "In fact... I was approached... You know they're anti-Jewish?"

"Because that fool can think of nothing else. He's quarter Jew himself. It obsesses him. He's always running away from that nose of his and it annoys him by keeping just in front of him. However I merely mentioned him by the way. For the sake of illustration."

"New York," said Rud, "is the greatest Jewish city in the world."

"You think ahead," exclaimed Chiffan in warm approval. "You certainly think ahead. Mind you, Jews are not always easy to work with. They're as *clever* as anyone could wish, but they've always one foot in the Ghetto."

"I don't know anything about Jews," said Rud compactly.

"You will," said Chiffan...

And so discoursing, elaborating in common a magnificent reverie of revolt and power, our two young men, with their heads pleasantly swelled by these imaginative exercises, and their confidence erect, arrived at the New World Summer School at Wexley and found that with a little squeezing there was room for their admission.

3

They got on very well at Wexley. They had much to say, and Wexley found it fresh and lively stuff. Things there had been going rather slackly. The school had been feeling the need for new blood. And here it was. Chiffan saw fit to play the rôle of impresario, an admirable impresario, for Rud. Chiffan too was made of imaginative stuff. He was elaborating his own reverie about Rud. Rud's peculiar type of ugliness attracted him. He conceived himself as a sort of deferential elder-brother tutor to this new acquisition. He knew just when it was time for Rud to speak, he advised him quite sagely about the temper of the place, suggested lines of action, talked about him loyally behind his back and set the school remarking Rud's exceptional quality.

The New World Summer School was a fair sample of the continually increasing chaff of mentally unsettled people that was being winnowed out of the social order by the advancing disorganisation of the period. It was a sort of lodgement of wind-driven minds in a cranny of the Yorkshire hills. They had one thing in common, an enthusiasm for progress. The New World Society was pledged to progress in any direction, to anywhere, and to any idea about a New World its members chose to entertain. It was of all ages above fourteen and it included everything from barely cryptic nudists to extremely woolly vegetarians, and from single-taxers to Douglasites; there were Swedenborgians, Spenglerites, modern spiritualists, aberrant Fabians, seers and great thinkers, teachers of all grades, sex-reformers, thoughtful people who listened intently and never said anything, professional and genuine refugees from Nazi tyranny, Indian nationalists and one Chinaman of incomprehensible speech and consequently unknown attribution, who bowed very politely. The school led a hardy, healthy and extremely inexpensive life, sleeping crowdedly in austerely simplified dormitories at night, and eating in tumultuous refectories on trestle-tables covered with marbled white American cloth by day. There was much walking and swimming, table-tennis, medicine-ball and Badminton, and a series of conferences that it was bad form to cut altogether. There were a number of young women, brightly rather than over-dressed, who supplied little more than applause to the discussions, but manifestly appealed and set themselves to appeal to the pairing instinct of mankind. One or two of them decided to betray an interest in Rud, but he was wary and unresponsive. Chiffan after a slight resistance lit up and responded almost too much.

Rud never discovered who was running the assembly. There was a secretary, an anxious-looking spectacled lady of the hard mistress type whose name he never learnt, who stood up and made proclamations and stuck up notices, and there was an omnipresent white-bearded old gentleman in a state of earnest inactivity, who may have been her husband. And there was something that met somewhere called the Committee. The essential interest for Rud were a score of nuclear individuals, who did seem to be trying to shape out some sort of ideas about the current world drama and the roles they might have to play in it. Chiffan made rapid and quite plausible estimates of their quality and Rud concentrated upon them to learn and impress.

It was not that he was indifferent to the sexual stir that was going on around him. Indeed he was acutely aware of it, but his habits and instinct in these matters were becoming increasingly solitary and secretive. He did not like to give himself away to a fellow creature even amorously. He made no advances and no responses. He wouldn't go near the bathing-pool or look a girl in the face if he could help it. He was acutely jealous and at the same time contemptuous of Chiffan's gallantries and of all the other scarcely masked love affairs in progress.

Nevertheless he showed off as brilliantly as he could in the meetings.

Mainly the newcomers summarised and decanted what they had discussed during their four days of interchanges. There was an earnest ex-ophthalmic little man with a black beard and an uncontrollable feather at the back of his head who had swallowed the Douglas gospel whole and apparently digested some of it. His mind ran on certain definite rails, and if an argument knocked him off them he just picked himself up and put himself on his rails again. He had already been making Social Credit unattractive by dragging it in as an irrelevant topic and so disorganising other issues, but Rud, talking across the table at supper, seemed to take a fresh sort of hold upon the question, and the little man, when it came to his turn to give a conference, was pleased to find an unexpectedly full room awaiting him. He did not realise at first that he was to be the victim at the feast. He read a paper that most of the School had already heard in fragments several times.

Chiffan sat and listened with a growing admiration while Rud, who had had only the most rudimentary and casual ideas about the whole business three days ago, now not only repeated but expanded and filled in and rounded off what he had picked up in their conversations. Chiffan watched the bulging forehead and the pugnacious profile with an almost parental interest and kept up a *sotto voce* endorsement to the sentences that came clear and emphatic from Rud's determined mouth.

"You can't deal with money questions in this way," said Rud in the magisterial tones of one who had studied the subject for years. "You can't do it like that. Before you can begin to talk about money you must settle in your mind what you mean by property – for money is only a ticket for property – and before you can talk about property you must have made up your mind about the social system you want. How much private property is there to be? What can be bought? What can be sold?"

"Hear, hear!" became audible from Chiffan.

"In a theoretically complete socialism, it goes without saying, the only property you will be able to buy will be consumable goods, and the only way you will ever get hold of money will be as anticipatory or current or deferred wages. It won't matter whether it is cash down or cash held over because there will be no interest."

"Dole?" said someone.

"Dole is jut vacation wages," said Rud. "It's the duty of the community to find a man work."

"Hear, hear!"

For a time the assurance of his manner carried the meeting. Then objections arose.

A young man from Belfast, Figgis, raised the issue of foreign trade and started an excursus about the Workers' International. That and one or two unfamiliar phrases promised trouble for Rud, but Chiffan, to whom no current political phrase seemed unfamiliar, came to his help and pulled the debate back within his reach.

That Was Rud's début. After supper nine or ten of them sat and talked round him for a good three hours, they talked of "Socialism in our Time," and the talk went wide and far. "Socialism," said Chiffan, "has got to rejuvenate itself. Prewar socialism was sentimental and insufficient. He and I have been talking about that for days. Socialism's got to dot its *i*'s and cross its *t*'s. Marx ran away with it and lost bits as he ran. It never understood money."

"What I told you," said the ex-ophthalmic young man with the black beard. "Exactly what I told you."

Next day a well-trained Marxist from the Black Country, named Bennet, took on Rud with considerable vigour.

"All this sneering at Marx," he opened, "I don't know who started it…"

It was a live discussion and once or twice Rud felt himself cornered, and broke through with some effective rhetoric.

"Talk every time you can," said Chiffan late that night and with the manner of a trainer. "It's all you can do here."

"As long as they listen," said Rud.

"They'll listen to *you*," said Chiffan.

Rud displayed no gratitude for Chiffan's aid and support. He took Chiffan as a matter of course. He was always to take Chiffan as a matter of course. He trusted him, he relied upon him; he expected everything from him and gave nothing in return. He took credit to himself for everything Chiffan taught him or told him to do. That was Rud's way with life and it worked very well for him...

When Rud was disposed to guy the Swedenborgian's account of the Master as Socialist, Chiffan kicked him on the ankle.

Afterwards Rud discussed that kick with some heat. "Never ridicule a man except for a definite party purpose," said Chiffan, "And then *kill* him. Guy him so that he will never rise again. But don't make an enemy of him for fun. Oh, yes, I know I do. But I'm different."

Two tepid discussions on "Agriculture in a Socialised world" and "the Nationalisation of Mineral Products" were instructive rather than provocative for Rud, and Chiffan did most of the talking. Rud began to realise that the level of information in the School was higher than he had assumed. Several of these non-university men were much better read than he was.

Things livened up to flaming reality with a discussion of pacificism and non-resistance.

"Are we to Use Force and if so How Much?" was the question mooted, and before the two days' debate had lasted for an hour Rud realised that hitherto he had consistently shirked this particular and very fundamental issue in political affairs. In his reveries of a stupendous political ascent there had been great marches and demonstrations, flag-waving and cheering, there had been battles (heard off) and tremendous displays of armament, thousands of planes in the air and the like, but so far the rougher stuff had always been fairly remote from his person. Once or twice he had been under fire in dreamland, undismayed and unscathed. When he had imagined himself arrested and put on trial, it had always been an open trial, numerous reporters present, the whole world wondering, the judge cowed or secretly sympathetic, and himself practically in control of proceedings. Prisons, concentration camps, domiciliary visits, disappearances and secret examinations had been far beyond the actual margin of his picture.

But now in, clumsy and distressful speeches, in broken sentences and broken English, came harsh reality, at first hand. One of the refugees had been crippled and broken. He limped. He clung to the chair in front of him as he talked. "Even here," he said, "among friends, one hesitates to tell."

He spoke admirable, bookish English, slowly, carefully and with a German flavour rather than a positive accent.

He told them of the foul indignities that men, when they encourage instead of discouraging each other in cruelty, can put upon their victims. "And your martyrdom," he said in a faded voice, "is in vain. Your courage is wasted. You suffer and you are hidden away and lied about. Your persecutors are more horrible than apes, because they are subtler. Beasts and diseases and accidents can cause men pain and misery, but such things do not torment you with hope and snatch it away, they do not caricature and disgrace you as well as destroy. They do not leave your friends in doubt whether you have betrayed them. They do not make those you love vanish without a trace or put them to pain and indignity before your eyes. I did not know it was in my fellow creatures to do such things as I have seen – such things as I have been through. Let me tell you – I will tell you – a part of it. What happened to me. If I *can* tell you…"

It was a hideous and circumstantial tale he had to tell...

The speeches of the inexperienced which followed seemed helplessly feeble and pale. It was difficult to listen to them with that man's story fresh and vivid in the mind. Then came a woman recounting at second-hand, but no further off than second-hand, the frightfulnesses that had happened to her family.

Rud wished he could go out of the room; he felt inadequate. His self-satisfaction evaporated.

He wanted to get up and say: "Stop all this! What do you imagine *we* can do."

A little old Jew from Vienna suddenly jumped up with a great discovery. "I will tell you something. I will tell you something. A Magna Carta for the whole vorlt. No force except in the hants of disciplined men. Vell paid, vell fed, vell cared for, *disciplined* men, with officers who know exactly – vat dey may do. And go no more beyond. Exactly. Yess. No wappens. No munitions. Nothing. Except for them. And *no secret police*. No force used out of sight ever. No dossier – or if there *must* be dossiers, I do not know, but if there must be dossiers, then every man the right to know exactly what you hold against him. Right to inspect and protest. And no secret examinations. No. Wherever there is an examination, then gif me a sort of people to be able to walk through the room, at any time, able to say, What's did? What you doing? A sort of people able to go through all these things. Valk in. Doctors, mind or body – all controlled – in their examinations. Visitors. Guardians of men. See? A Magna Carta. Until you haf that. Always there will be darkness and abominations. *Always* – to the end of the vorlt. Better law and order, I tell you, even if it is bad law – then lawlessness and evil in the night. For by night, louts, hooligans touch hell – you haf heard – and rejoice in it. I know. I know. Always, always gif me *law*."

His face was flushed. His bright eyes glittered with tears of excitement.

"Gif me my Magna Carta. Then – you need not bother. Everything will be all right. No force, you understand me, no force to be used on anyone except in the hants of *disciplined* men –"

He went right through what he had said already almost word for word.

He repeated his speech with variations three times and was resuming, *da capo,* when the chairman overwhelmed him with clock and bell. Whereupon he sat down, sat very subdued for a minute or so and then twisted himself round and began to explain it all in harsh whispers to the people immediately behind him. "My Magna Carta for all the vorlt. No force, you understand me…"

Rud sat in his place during the outbreak of this little old Jew from Vienna, digesting the ugly realities those other two refugees had retailed. They stunned him so that for a time he could not find anything to say. The thought of violence filled him with angry fear and the urge to savage reprisals. He felt just as he had felt when he read of gorillas and wolves in his childhood. The shadow of it lay plainly across the path of his imaginations. What the little old Jew was saying meant nothing to him. What stirred his imagination was the thought of himself being treated brutally and filthily, mutilated, subjected to subhuman indignities.

"Get your blow in first," he thought. "Nothing else for it. Always carry a gun. Carry poison."

When at last he spoke, he raged against Nazis and Fascists, he spoke of the little ways of the British police with mobs and repeated rumours that came out of prisons. He was all for vehement reprisals.

"Never forgive a bully. Mark your man down," he said, "and wait for him. Even if you have to wait for years...

"You've got to attack. Your only safety lies in attack. Choose your moment for attack. Strike first at the devils, strike first."

His voice became a scream.

"*Easy,*" whispered Chiffan.

The meeting was divided. There was still a rather shaken minority for non-resistance, but most of the men and nearly all the girls were with Rud, for fighting and fighting bitterly. But the refugees said little and the little old Jew shook his head and whispered. "If you had my Magna Carta," he whispered.

That night the summer school talked long and late and loud. "And well we may," said Chiffan, "for, after all, violence is the fundamental thing in life. As old as hunger and earlier than lust...

"Before there was even a beast; before a single animal came on land, there was this attacking and defending, devouring and fighting for life. If you think you can escape by being lambs, ask the wolf."

"There's such a thing as Mutual Aid," said the ex-ophthalmic man. "Kropotkin said that ages ago."

"Mutual aid," said Chiffan, "but only to fight better."

"Force you *must* have somewhere," said the little old Jew. "There's only peace under the power of the law. No peace for man but that. In *my* Magna Carta..."

"How about bed?" said a voice.

82

4

Rud and Chiffan sat on a stile on the hillside above the summer school on their way to the junction. "Time we went," Chiffan had said, "before they start packing. Then they'll have time to miss us and talk you over."

He had announced this decision quite suddenly and they had paid up and slipped away without farewells.

They proposed to go by train to Balting, where there was trouble brewing in the minor gadget factories. Chiffan wanted to see it for himself and he also wanted Rud to see it. The stile tempted Chiffan after the long path uphill and maybe there was something else, pulling at him.

"You can't expect anyone to say goodbye," he remarked, "who doesn't know you're going... *You're* not impulsive, Rud."

Rud had nothing to say to that.

"It was a good time anyhow," said Chiffan.

"I've never talked so much in my life," said Rud.

"Or to as good effect...of course –. It's a *gentle* crowd. They're – how shall I put it? – they're flimsy people. They're not the stuff revolutions are made of. But they polish up revolutionary ideas. If it came to a real showdown with violence, they'd vanish like a heap of dust in a cyclone. All the same it's a good school for talking. I'm glad we came. But we had to quit before we caught their disease."

"Ugh?"

"*What?* Enervation of the intelligence.

"Too many ideas and no conclusions to them – like a plague of Manx cats on the brain."

He dismissed that thought and came to something else, that had evidently been brewing in his mind for some time.

"You know, Rud, you could be vetted into a pretty tidy leader. Into a very useful leader indeed for a live new movement. You've got real passion. You speak uncommonly well."

Rud had felt that something of the sort was coming. He had felt that for some days. He had already thought out his reply thoroughly and cunningly.

"It isn't impossible," he said, "I believe I might make something of a figurehead and something of a foghorn, but I shouldn't be any good, Chiffan, unless there were *men* in the ship behind me. And one man in particular…"

It needed no ceremony to bind that tacit treaty.

"I think," said Chiffan presently, "we ought to keep in touch with Figgis and Redwood. There was something *in* those chaps."

He was already organising, imaginatively.

5

They pursued their way and their several lines of thought.

"I doubt if I got hold of the women," Rud reflected.

Chiffan roused himself from profound calculation and gave his mind to Rud's question.

"The women?"

"I doubt if I got hold of them."

"You did exactly right about them. I wish I had your self-respect."

"I don't think I touched them."

"You didn't. And two I *mauled*. That's where we differ. I got my face slapped. I'm sorry but I did. It – it accelerated my departure. But you just impressed them. That's the difference between us – and why I shall never be a leader. I can't keep my hands off a pretty girl. It's a second-rate quality – for all my wit and wisdom. I have to admit it. *You* kept absolutely aloof from them. Exactly what a real leader has to do. You were concentrated on bigger things. 'All the world loves a lover' they say. Don't you believe it. Not in politics. Supposing you had started to philander. It wouldn't have been so difficult. That yellow-haired girl – "

Rud had noted the interest of the yellow-haired girl, had felt it even when he was standing and speaking with his back to her, had dreamt about her; but he gave no sign.

"You'd have started a lot of jealousy and irritation among the girls. Even if they didn't want you for themselves, they'd not have liked another girl monopolising you. And you'd have just come down to competition with the other men. Every man is more or less jealous of any man who gets a girl. Even if she isn't *his* girl... That's one of Lord Horatio Bohun's advantages. He can't keep his profile and his aristocracy and his touch of sex appeal out of the picture. Maybe they won't let him... Women disciples are dangerous animals... If I hadn't felt you were a natural leader for ten other reasons, I'd have known it from your handling of those women. Cool. Sure. I was a bit silly out of school, I admit – but all the time I was watching you. One or two of them said things about you."

Rud could not resist asking what they said.

" 'He's aloof,' they said. 'There's a sort of mystery about him.' "

And then Chiffan produced one of those maxims for statesmen that Rud was beginning to find characteristic of him.

"A political leader," said Chiffan, "to be successful, must either be an ice-cold bachelor entirely devoid of sex appeal, a manifest cuckold or the faithful husband of some ugly, unpleasant or ridiculous woman. Run your mind through history. All history stands for it. Napoleon, for example; Caesar, – *all* Cleopatra's bunch; Marcus Aurelius; Justinian; Oliver Cromwell…"

Rud looked anything but elated.

"It's part of the price of greatness," said Chiffan. "And, after all, it isn't as though you *wanted* them Rud."

"No," said Rud, relaxing into his primitive self, "If I wanted them – "

"Everything would be different," said Chiffan firmly. "But you don't – either for show or use. Not even out of rivalry."

He regarded Rud, with his head cocked on one side for a moment, and then confirmed his impression. "No."

He went on for a time preoccupied with some train of thought of his own. "Philandering," broke out at last. "Philandering. That's the matter with most of us intellectuals. We philander with women. We philander with ideas. We philander with violence… Rud, the real world is a *bloody* world, a world of beatings and bruises and cuts and fights and dead men. And men not quite killed who're sick. As that Austrian said. Those dying men who were sick in that room. You heard him? Gods! I can see it still! That's the raw meat of life. What are ideas alone? Ideas – ideas are shapes but not substance…

"That discussion on non-resistance, Rud! Did you ever have a better show of Ideal versus Real? Elegant sentiments and then suddenly those actual things that cut like a knife…

"Idealists! Nothing serious in this world was ever settled by nice little rabbits putting their little votey-poteys into boxy-poxes and going home again. The next thing you have to get, Rud, on your way to leadership, is – "

"Yes?"

"Well, I don't want you to get too much of it."

"What do you mean?"

"A broken knuckle, say – a tooth knocked out and a black eye."

A glow of amused animation appeared upon Chiffan's countenance, a brightening of the eye, a shining effect on the face. It was his nearest approach to laughter.

"Bloody knuckles, black eyes and continence, Rud. The way of the leader is hard…"

"I suppose I've got to face up to it," said Rud after a slight pause. "It's all in the day's work I suppose…"

But that night there was not the faintest intimation of a yellow-haired visitant for him. Instead he had a disagreeable nightmare about those two hefty young men in purple shirts who had come to his room at Camford. But their methods of controversy on this occasion were emphatic and not verbal. They never made a sound. They set about doing frightful things to him. He shot them both dead but they came to life again and he had to keep on shooting them. They were soon covered with blood, but still they got up again. He got his back to the wall and woke up screaming faintly when he had fired his last cartridge and they still came on nearer and nearer.

He lay awake and was still aquiver. What would have happened, he thought, if he hadn't awakened? What would they have done? Then as he got more awake he knew clearly it was only a dream.

He lay staring at a dim ceiling and listening to Chiffan's faint snore.

87

"No good running away," he whispered. "They'll dig out all the rabbits…"

6

On their way to Balting they took a day off for a rest, because Chiffan knew of a little lake where there was someone who would lend them an old punt. And they would borrow a rod and line and fish.

"Fish for what?" asked Rud.

"Just fishing," said Chiffan. "Think of all we've got to turn over in our minds."

It was a very pleasant day indeed, much sunshine and a glowing stillness upon the lake and upon its great trees. Chiffan's friend was a gamekeeper by profession and a socialist by resentment and conviction. He cooked them a mighty meal of rabbit and onions. They had small beer (departing from their normal austerity) and cheese, and he relieved himself or much long suppressed radical opinion and gave them a shakedown in a little outhouse with a fire. And while he was busy about his work Chiffan did his fishing.

Rud did not even attempt to fish. Chiffan caught nothing, and for the most part they paddled about the lake, pulled yellow and white water lilies out of sheer acquisitiveness, or sprawled in the punt and meditated under a great yellowing horse-chestnut that overhung the water, and occasionally plopped a conker through its glassy surface. Chiffan wasn't inclined for talk, and Rud, too, had a feeling that the bulk of their talking was done. They understood one another. And in his relaxed state Chiffan reflected upon women.

88

"That girl – " he said.

"What about her?" asked Rud. "That Lancashire girl, you mean?"

"I could have had her," said Chiffan.

"Well?"

"I didn't. I didn't want her enough."

"Well?"

"And now I do…

"She was a bore. And yet there was something about her… I think it was her neck attracted me. There was something attractive about her neck. Damn! I wish I either wanted a woman or didn't. I can't get her out of my head. Maybe it's the sunshine or that rabbit. And I made a fool of myself with the other because she piqued me… You're lucky not to be bothered by these things."

Rud, who was lying on his back in the punt, said nothing, but he made Chiffan feel his disapproval by wagging his foot as an impatient cat waves its tail.

7

The next day the purposeful life was resumed, and they went on to study the industrial troubles of Balting. And hardly had they come into the dingy, winding streets of that town before they found a shopfront bright with the announcements of a brand-new political party, the League of Free Democrats; Leader, Jim Flab. Most of the window was adorned with copies of a handbill asking and answering the very natural question, "Who IS Jim Flab?" above the portrait of a cadaverous man of thirty-five or forty with a skew chin, a forced glare in his eyes and a crooked mouth featuring an extremity of resolution to the very best of its ability.

"He is the Leader of the League of Free Democrats," said the handbill, "Consecrated to the Salvation of this Our England, PTO."

The handbill was printed on both sides, and each side was exposed alternately in the window. The reverse contained much further information, which Chiffan devoured, with that exalted pallor on his face which stood him in the stead of laughter. "Come and read it, Rud," he said.

Rud joined him. He found something unpleasantly like a burlesque of his own dreams in Mr Jim Flab's proposals, but Chiffan did not seem to observe that. Mr Flab, it seemed had had an eventful, noble and indignant career, he had "travelled extensively," seen the Pope and the President and Hitler and Stalin, been jailed for political reasons in Russia, Spain, America and Scotland, and was still in the early thirties, mounting towards his self-chosen task of national leadership. There was plainly an instinct for rhetoric in the man, and a large willingness to avail himself of all the current prejudices, antagonisms and suspicions of the time. He boasted of Town Councillors, military men, including "a VC with head injuries," several majors, businessmen and solicitors among his embattled following, and they had met, he alleged, by moonlight at Stonehenge, that "original temple of the British spirit," and there lifting their hands before their faces "according to the ancient rite," taken the Vow of the Free Democrats.

"We've never thought of a vow," said Chiffan.

The League of Free Democrats was still very new. The date of that profoundly solemn occasion was "the Vernal Equinox" of the current year. He was attacking the "Reds" in particular "all along the line," wherever the line might be, and his programme, mostly in capitals, included Fearless Exposure of Red Plots, Smashing of the Rings of International Financiers, Britain to be Strong and Fearless, Kicking out Party Hacks and Old Gangs, the Revival of Simple Christianity, National Plan to Abolish Unemployment and so on and so forth.

Chiffan read these projects over in an appreciative whisper. "Pretty comprehensive," he remarked, and then: "Oh! look at this. *'Lack of finance and lack of speakers are our chief difficulties.'* Chance for you, Rud! *'We want one thousand pounds to found anti-red combat groups all over industrial England.'* Combat groups, eh? Lovely. Vows! Combat groups!"

"It's wild," said Rud.

"It's not a bit wild."

"But who's going to – "

"Lots maybe. You mustn't suppose, Rud, this chap doesn't know what he's up to. This is the stuff to give them, he thinks, if you want to be a Leader. Consider him as a reporter. He's got something to tell us, Rud. He's a very useful reporter on the state of the country. He talks to crowds that answer back, while you, so far, have just talked in your Union. And back there at the summer school. This stuff has been tested by cheers. He's been heckled. He's gone home and thought out answers. And that stuff is what goes... Would-be leaders of his kidney... All over the country they're breaking out like spots on a boy's face. Competition. We aren't going to have it all our own way, Rud. And the Colonel Blimps are rolling up behind him..."

Chiffan considered for a moment and then moved towards the door of the shop. "Come along," he said.

"What are you going to do?"

"I am going in."

"The man's a blatant bosher."

"He's not. He knows exactly what he is up to. Master Jim Flab is no fool, whatever else he is. I want to feel his bumps. I want to find out who pays for all *this*."

"But what are we to say?"

"*You* – nothing. You just listen for once."

In the shop there was a counter with some piles of handbills, walls draped with primitive flags of black and red (the League Flag), a large photograph of Stonehenge framed in wilted laurel, enlargements of the inspiring likeness of Jim Flab, and in charge of it all a lumpish young man drowsing over a crossword puzzle. He stood up with a start and made a hasty and uncompleted movement as if to take up something hidden behind the counter. Possibly a weapon. He decided that was unnecessary. "Whad you *want*?" he said.

"Enquiring souls. Camford men both of us," said Chiffan, annexing a university for himself. "Long Vacation. Seeing England. We're sick of the Reds and all that, and we want to hear what your leader has to tell us. He seems good stuff."

"He *is*," said the lumpish young man. "But he isn't here. You can see the Major."

"What Major?"

"Major Fitz Blessington. Sit down there, will you…"

After the delay of ten minutes which the importance of the major necessitated, they went upstairs to a large shabby room over the shop, in which there were letter files and card indices, odd tables and windsor chairs, a bookcase of reference books, a telephone, packages of stationery, a small safe, a rack of what

Chiffan suggested later were hosepipe bludgeons, a row of clothes pegs bearing a number of berets and two waterproofs, the portrait of the Leader over the empty cast iron fireplace, and a large map of England marked with blue and red wafers. In the centre was a writing desk of painted and grained wood, littered with papers and with the apparatus and litter of a slovenly pipe smoker, and at this desk sat a small but sturdy little man with a hooked, red nose and a tumult of chins in full retreat, dissimilar blue eyes, a moustache as wild as an excited Persian kitten and a pipe in the corner of his mouth. He was dressed in a shabby old khaki uniform from which all badges and indication of rank had been removed, and diagonally across his chest was a black and red scarf after the fashion of a French mayor's. He pretended to be busy with important documents.

"Sit down, my lads," he said, pointing with a pen. "I'll be through with this stuff in a moment."

Chiffan made to examine the map of England.

"Siddown," said the major.

Rud and Chiffan disposed themselves in free and undisciplined attitudes on two of the windsor chairs. "Mm. Mm. Mm," said the major, and slapped a folder on his desk. "And now let's have a look at you, my boys."

He came round the desk towards them, leant against it and contemplated them. There was a smell about him as though his uniform had recently been cleaned with benzine and his breath enriched by whisky. It came to them through the rank smell of his pipe, and there was also a flavour of leather and something else that was probably idiosyncrasy – altogether a thoroughly manly smell. People with leftish prejudices might conceivably have said the major stank.

"So you want to join the Free Democratic party," he said. "Good for you."

"I don't know whether we do," said Chiffan. "We want to hear about it first."

"You'll soon hear about it, my boys. All England is going to hear about it before very long, by God. *You'll* hear about it. You're sick of the Bolsheviks and the white-livered peace skunks and the Jews and all the rest of 'um. You want to do something about it, and you've found your way to the right place. We're out to clean up England. Jim there is the man for us. He's the man for us and the man for you. He's *white*. True-born English, a pukka democrat, if you understand me, and straight as a die. You ought to hear him. It's grand. It's grand."

"Yes," said Chiffan in a digestive tone. "And you started all this – these new ideas – this spring?"

"At Stonehenge, with a bit of a ceremony. *And*, my boys – and don't you forget it – a prayer to God. Whom you've all been pretending to forget. Jim Flab hasn't forgotten the Old Book."

"Why didn't you start before?" asked Chiffan.

The major replaced his pipe, with which he had been making generous circular movements indicative of the greatness leading and sustaining the party, in his mouth, and he spoke about its stem with a snarl that set his moustache flying high and wild, and revealed a wealth of irregular yellow teeth. "Because we've given those other slackers and humbugs rope to show their quality. That's why."

"Meaning old Bohun and his purple shirts?"

"Meaning, sir, whomsoever it may concern. To hell with postures and posers, say we! We start free and clean."

"I suppose people are just pouring in on you?"

"By the hundred. The people of this country know a good thing when it's offered them. They've waited long enough. God knows. We can't keep up with them – taking their names. We put out our programme. Here it is – if you haven't seen it. 'Join us and fight for us' we say, and that's enough for them."

"I see that," said Chiffan. "There were five or six hanging about outside when we came in."

"*No!*" cried the major. "Where?" and went to the window, so evidently astonished, that Chiffan was able to convey a solemn look of derision to Rud.

"I don't see 'um," said the major, turning back.

"Shyness, I expect," said Chiffan.

A faint suspicion passed momentarily across the major's countenance. There was a pause. "So you wish to join us?"

"There's trouble in the Balting shops, I'm told," said Chiffan.

"*Fomented,*" said the major.

"It always is. And you're doing something about it?"

"Balting men must deal with Balting men."

"You mean?"

"We're running Bolsheviks and paid agitators out of the town. We give 'um notice to quit. That's our particular task here, *if* you want a job with us. We saw Mr Harry Bellows off the premises the day before yesterday."

"Stand all right with the police?"

"Mr Supe is heart and soul with us."

"Supe?" said Rud.

"Superintendent of Police, my boy."

"And the Town Council?"

"Fifty-fifty. There's some rotten radicals and pink parlour Labour men. But we've got good friends on the bench. Good sound men and good sound patriots."

"And half the strikers are girls? More than half, Major? Not much chance for *them*. If you cut off help from outside."

"What's that got to do with it? Eh?" The major was suddenly on the defensive again.

"Trying to get things clear in my mind," said Chiffan.

The major removed his pipe from his mouth, walked across the room and spat with an air of extreme deliberation into the empty fireplace. "Look here, my lads, what do you think you are doing here? Joining up – or smelling round?"

Chiffan stood up and Rud followed suit.

"It doesn't smell so fresh," said Chiffan.

"Get out, you scabs – you Bolshevik spies," said the major with concentrated intensity. "I've wasted my time on you."

"We were only enquiring."

"*Get* out," said the major. "D'you hear me? Get OUT." He made truncated gestures of assault. He was transparently disposed to kick. Rud felt himself going white.

The major caught Rud's eye. An eye like that might mean a knife or a pistol. The major abandoned his impulse for immediate violence. "Get out – before I blow my whistle."

The departure was wary and stiff. Chiffan led the retreat. Rud kept a watchful and dangerous eye on the major and went downstairs sideways. There was tension but no actual violence.

The major continued audible above in abusive soliloquy. Apparently he had risen from the ranks, a promoted drill sergeant of the old school...

The young man in the shop had clutched a truncheon, but apparently only for self-defence.

"That," said Chiffan, when they were in the street again, "was as plain and diagrammatic as you could have. You didn't say much, Rud, but I guess you didn't miss much. This town, you see, is a nest of small factories making bits of things; half the workers are girls and kids, and helpless as mutton. The law protects them, but who cares for the law here? The employers are cowardly sweaters, and they think that industrial discipline is cheap at the price of Jim Flab and that major and the few casual roughs they have enrolled. It isn't; but they think it is. And so Jim works himself up, half rogue, half dreamer – such dreams as *we* dream. While the major sells the stuff."

"Such silly stuff," said Rud.

"Silly stuff, you think? P'raps no more silly than ours. P'raps less. Wait till war gets nearer and the bombing and shooting starts, wait till the people above begin to have that back-to-the-wall feeling... Same as these sweating magistrate manufacturers here have... Then you'll get it all – magnified. The big people will come in. They will put guns in the hands of chaps like that, put bombs in their hands, teach them the authority of a uniform, set them to suppress strikes... Put them at last in control of things... After which they will get out of hand. It was stinkers like that little major who ran about in Ireland during those ugly years, Black and Tans versus rebels. You don't remember. I just do. Gods, the foolishness of the Tories to touch such muck! So they lost Ireland. So in the end they are going to lose everything they ever clutched under God's sky. There's hundreds of that dirty little beast – ex-temporaries – looking for gangster jobs now. The last war bred them like maggots in a dead dog. The next war will breed thousands more.

"I'm glad we went in. That's the sort of thing ahead of you, Rud, like a dangerous back street at night, and there's miles of it that you'll have to go through before you can even begin to get that successful feeling…before you can dare to dictate peace and plenty in good earnest…before you can feel independent enough even to start our great programme – and put out that Strong Right Arm of yours…"

8

"It all gets into the boiling when you come to a revolution," said Chiffan. "You can't even make a garden without slinging mud. The raw material of politics. What is it? Mud, blood and fools. There's nothing else… What have you been dreaming about, Rud, if you haven't faced up to that? That's the stuff of life for our generation – leaders or led, bleeders or bled. Our feet are set on the path of revolution. The stars in their courses insist. There's no turning back. But I'll tell you, Rud, who I would rather be than any dictator that ever lived."

Rud asked "Who?" as he was plainly expected to do, though he knew nothing rational was coming.

"Omar Khayyàm," said Chiffan. "Yes – old Omar. Bless him! I am a revolutionist by conviction but I am a poet by nature… That loaf of bread, that jar of wine. And the sunshine of the desert…

"As for 'Thou beside me in the wilderness – ' I should want an occasional change. Like the books of a circulating library. But I suppose I should begin with that girl with the neck..."

"There are times, Chiffan," interjected Rud, "when you talk like an ass, like a Priapean ass... I don't like it."

"And I have devoted myself to making a great man of you," said Chiffan with a monstrous sigh. "It's true, Rud. I've found my job in life. And when they try to shoot you – I shall be – behind you. No avoiding it. There won't be any Wilderness to go to in the Wrath to Come, and they'll have burnt the vineyards and slashed the wineskins."

9

Rud returned to Camford at the end of the Long Vacation very nearly if not quite a grown man. In every life cycle there are phases of swift development alternating with intervals of comparative unchangeableness; there comes a time when the child almost suddenly becomes a boy and again at adolescence when puerility falls off in a few amazing days, like a cloak suddenly abandoned. So now in a brief tale of weeks, Rud had passed from the phase of dreaming youthfulness and begun to assemble himself for a purposeful attack on life. He spent the last two days of the holiday at home, and his mother saw with unspoken satisfaction the change wrought by that six pounds ten of hers in his voice and eye and bearing. Where he had been defensive and irritable he was now tranquil and resolute.

"All that fresh air has done him a lot of good," said his father.

But she felt that it was more than fresh air had happened to him. What it was she could not imagine. His development followed laws of its own. She knew exactly how Aunt Julia would account for it, and she knew quite certainly that Aunt Julia would be wrong.

So she said nothing about it to Aunt Julia.

BOOK TWO

THE HATCHING

CHAPTER ONE

The Group Assembles

One brilliantly sunny morning two years later found old Doctor Carstall in his dressing gown, sitting in a capacious wicker chair in his garden, lost in thought. His devastated breakfast tray was on a rustic table beside him, and various letters, circulars and a couple of morning papers occupied a second wicker chair within arm's length. A wastepaper basket had been put conveniently for his envelopes and wrappers.

On his tray lay a letter and an original paper, a reprint from a scientific publication, by his son. The paper was entitled *Certain Relations between Nervous Strain and General Metabolism,* and the letter explained: "This is a sort of premature birth brought on by the Crisis. Some of the most interesting threads lie loose. I meant this research to be an epoch-maker, but what will you? All my work is interrupted – for Heaven knows how long. I've been grabbed by the National Nutrition Emergency Committee, damn it. How the devil research is to get along under this sort of thing I can't imagine. The Committee is fundamentally futile. But there's no escaping it."

Two headlines of the crumpled newspapers were visible. One proclaimed a "Further Slump in Industrials," and this had suddenly brought home to the doctor that his tenure of this pleasant red-brick house and this garden in which he had expected to spend his declining years, was now extremely insecure. If he hadn't sold his practice so soon it would have been better for him. And if he hadn't bought United States Steels. No good fretting about that now. Anyhow, Dick had had his start, and not even the NNEC could rob him of that now.

The second newspaper, at which the doctor had scarcely glanced as yet, was being emphatic about "The Fight for the Purple House."

"Damn the world," said the doctor, and began filling the pipe that for reasons of economy had replaced his former customary cigar. "Nothing is safe any longer. Nothing is steady. I could have bet my life on those Steels."

He smoked slowly, and presently his breakfast tray was carried indoors.

There seemed no end to this slump. No end at all. He found himself going over the steady development of the world peril that had thrown its shadow across the security of his morning sunshine. How had it begun? He recalled the follies of the victors in the Fatuous Twenties, the gathering resentment and bitterness of the losers in the war, and the wave of pacificism that preceded the armament race of the Frightened Thirties. How obdurate France had been, how ambiguous England! How futile the League! He recalled the Great Peace Ballot of 1936 which had passed like the sigh of a sleeper reluctant to awaken.

Then had come, not formal war, all declared and set, but a gradual decline into warlike violence and destruction all over the world; Abyssinia, Spain, China and Japan, Macedonia, Syria, the social disorder in the Cotton States, the Ukraine business,

Brazil, the Argentine, Ireland, and now these ever-spreading troubles in India. Everywhere there appeared the same phenomenon of unemployed and discontented masses of young people milling about in revolutionary movements; everywhere demagogues rose to exploit them, everywhere the gangsters fought more openly, everywhere were shrinking markets, mounting taxation and monetary inflation, conscription for military service, conscription for munition making. The formulae of the gangsters varied from extreme leftism to extreme rightism, but the material facts were everywhere the same. Governments everywhere were afraid to declare war definitely or to restore an effective peace, because so long as the military necessity ruled there was at least an excuse for unqualified repression. It made one's mind fret and ache to open the morning paper.

Civilisation as he knew it, was going to pieces.

He thought of the world before the Great War and it seemed a Golden Age. In those happy days a man lived his own life, and politics were no more than a noise offstage. Government was as remote and benign as the sky. You went about nearly all Europe then without a visa and you talked with absolute freedom wherever you went. Your personal liberties were rational and immense, you could do anything short of violence to frustrate the government, and when you earned money it meant you had that much money – less a slight diminution of pay for the roads and the policeman. You could invest and assure your future and provide freedom for your children after you. And all over the world a pound was a pound. Of course the poor were poor then, but were they any better off now, except that they felt their poverty more acutely? The subject races were subject and equally

105

unawakened. Life had some dignity then in a decent Englishman's home. Art was subservient and not subversive, its mission was to please and evoke a feeling of complacent approval, and literature, as free as it is today, had infinitely better manners. Philanthropy, real charity indeed, prevailed remarkably.

It had been a good secure time for a quite considerably number of gently-living people, and all about him, all his world, had assumed that that really very good life was getting better and better, carrying a higher polish and spreading out steadily to an ever-increasing proportion of the population. Presently the whole world would be gentle. And no one dreamt that this expanding civilisation was being undermined and outgrown, was living on its moral capital and wasting its abundant material resources. That pleasant world of his in which he had been born and which had seemed so permanent and settled, had been indeed hardly more than a passing gleam of sunshine upon the overcast, stormy, incalculable stream of life. It had seemed to be the normal course of life.

How rare indeed are such patches of sunlight in history! Now and again, in China, in Greece, in Egypt, in Japan, in the early Roman Empire maybe, in a few cities in the Middle Ages and rather widely through the eighteenth and nineteenth centuries, there had been phases of well-bred, humane, cultivated living, free talk and liberal behaviour. Gentlemen and their womenfolk had walked the world without weapons and lived in pleasant comfortable houses. Gardens had multiplied and men of his type had sat in them, secure in their dignity. Surely wherever you find a cared-for garden you have a symbol of goodwill and wellbeing in life.

Probably, thought the doctor, few of my sort of people who have lived this life had realised, what I am beginning to realise, that ours is not the normal life of man. Over vast regions always, and for long ages even in the favoured lands, our sort of life had been impossible. True that in a few half-illuminated regions there had been a sort of penumbra to our civilisation, little gleams of comfort, refinement and loveliness, cringing in courts or carried on precariously behind high walls and locked doors. But the rest had been blackness, the blackness of natural violence, the black struggle of the brute to survive and triumph. A general blackness leaves no books or pictures or traces behind it; only the bright phases are remembered. The old proverb is wrong. Unhappy is the breed that has no history. In all those vast unlit intervals, the life of man, just as much as the life of any other animal, has been red in tooth and claw, suffering greatly and signifying nothing.

Am I growing old? Questioned the doctor, or am I beginning to see reality plain?

Never before had it dawned upon him, how flimsy was civilisation, how limited and incidental and flimsy it had always been.

"A few precarious patches of civilised life," whispered the doctor, "a few decades here, a few there, and before and behind and around and beyond that an animal – that craves, that cowers and is beaten. *Homo vapulans.* And back to that we go.

"*Burr!*" he said and knocked out his pipe.

He sat polishing the bowl of his pipe in the palm of his hand. His eye fell on Dick's letter and paper.

He recalled that talk they had had at the beginning of the Long Vacation. Two – three? – no, two years ago. Before that bad bout of neuritis had set his mind towards thoughts of senescence. Fine chap Dick was, but a little strange. So like and so intensely different from himself. They had had a long talk…

The doctor had hoped the boy wouldn't be disturbed in that psychovisceral work of his, but the rising tide had got him. The tide of disaster was coming in faster than they had thought…

They had discussed this breakdown towards war and disorder. Dick had been very strong on – what was it? – the idea of "scavenging". All this present disorder in the world, he had said, was the breakdown and clearing away of outworn creeds, dynasties, classes, nationalism, bad industrial organisation, bad monetary and financial methods. Possibly – Oh! Probably – It was so. But what had Dick to put in the place of all this debris when the scavengers had taken it away? There was no doubt we were going to have the ruffians and scavengers, no doubt at all now, all over the world they were busy, hyenas on the battlefield, wolves following the retreat, but who were these other fellows, where were these other fellows Dick had talked about, who were going to take hold of things and set up the great modern scientific world-state of our dreams and hopes? That was where Dick had become mystical.

What was it he had said? Something about a lot of tacit fellows, with a common clearheadedness. Secret natural aristocrats – something like that. Yes, he had the words now, a World Civil Service, based – that was it – a World Civil Service based on a World Public Opinion.

"But my *dear* Dick," said the doctor, addressing his absent son aloud, "how the devil do you propose to get a World Civil Service based on a World Public Opinion when all the good school-masters and mistresses have been beaten to death, when all the universities have been turned inside out and filled with bullies and subservient professors scared out of their wits? When all free publishing is over. I ought to have said it that night, only we got on to something else…"

He nodded his head.

The fact of it is, he reflected, Dick makes up that story in self-defence. It's just self-protection from the reality of the case. It's the reckless optimism of youth. He wants to get on with his work – and very pretty work it is, too – and not be invaded and wasted by politics. He is shirking the issue because it is too complex and disagreeable to face. That is how it is; that is how it has always been with these scientific men. Dick had invented these phantom natural aristocrats of his, this imaginary new breed of mankind, who would all know each other and exactly what has to be done when the time comes; he has invented them, just to save himself from the distraction of political things. And so until the ultimate smash-up overtakes him, please don't bother him.

"*It's not good enough, Dick.*"

Something occurred to the doctor. He decided to smoke another pipe on it. He had a faint memory that he too had been rather bitten at that time by that idea of a better sort of men appearing on earth.

A nice easy way out of our troubles. Here comes the Super Man, the Super Man, the Super Man! He'll see to it. In the nick of time.

Things weren't going to happen like that…

For the stresses of the new world we wanted a new education. Such a lot of people were saying that and still doing nothing about it. If we had only realised that thirty years, twenty years, ago. *Then* Dick's World Civil Service, which was to be

109

indispensable for successful dictators whether they liked it or not, and his World Public Opinion which would be unavoidable if you are to have the education for an adequate Civil Service, might be something more than dreams. But now?

Wasn't all that too late now? Too late? The world was becoming a warfare in fragments. There might not even be great dictators any more, not widereaching Caesars like the early Caesars, but only a succession of little bloody men who would come and go, little Francos and Francolets, getting baser and less civilised step by step. And if that was so, there would be no intellectual revival now, much less a great educational reconstruction, and no effective World Public Opinion anywhen. That World Civil Service was a dream...

"Pessimism of old age?" asked the doctor.

"But isn't it so?"

Enough of this thinking! Who had enough knowledge for prophecy? No one. We had to take the blows as they came. Maybe it wasn't going to be bad as it looked. Not so bad as all that. Maybe he was missing some hopeful possibility...

"And now for the morning's disasters!" he sighed.

He picked up a newspaper and read: "The Fight for the Purple House. Political Monkey – Lord Horatio or Rud Whitlow."

"Whitlow?" he repeated. "now where have I head that name before? *Rud* Whitlow?"

A small recalcitrant white-faced boy appeared scowling before him. Of course he *had* gone up to Camford! On some scholarship. There had been talk of speeches he had made...

"That infernal little beast!"

2

The two years that followed his encounter with Chiffan had been crowded with experience for Rud. He had come up again to Camford with a greatly enhanced self-confidence. Chiffan had inflated and confirmed and strengthened him enormously. A certain shyness in making personal contacts had diminished. He began to expect things from people, to demand them and get them. His revolutionary conviction increased. He knew the world was in a phase of revolution and that inevitably he had to play a part in it. He talked much as Chiffan had talked to him. He took a first class in his stride though he did not get a fellowship. Then for a while he felt his progress checked.

He came down, he found himself at home for a time without a job and the vaguest of plans. He got some lecturing in a London college and took mean lodgings in a back street in Bloomsbury. His assured income, he found, was less than in his scholarship days, and in London poverty is more obvious and galling than at Camford. He added to his income by writing a book for a publisher fortunately affected by the series mania, and by doing a little reviewing of sociological and historical books. For the better part of a year his political prospects ran along cramped, unpromising lines.

But nevertheless he had supporters now and a sense of reality about his activities. At first he had been disposed to conceal Chiffan from Camford; he did not want Camford to notice how much he owed to Chiffan; then he felt the need of him and got him to come up for a weekend of talk with the new associates. They had formed a discussion circle and Chiffan came as their common guest. He did much to confirm and develop their impression of a certain large flexibility about Rud's imagination, his capacity for political enterprise and the political effectiveness of his storms of passionate speech.

Now after a phase of loneliness, doubt and depression in Bloomsbury, Rud found his friends turning up in London and resuming their Camford conversations with him. One of his most steadfast supporters was a rich young man named Steenhold. Steenhold was half American and he was in his middle twenties. He had come up to Camford explaining himself rather copiously; he did not want a degree, he had said; he did not need a degree, but he wanted to learn; he wanted to see what Camford had for him. He wore strange clothes, he drank excessively and then took to living on carrots and water, he tried poetry of a mystical inaccurate sort; he got as far with art as investing in a painter's outfit, he tried on a purple shirt but stuck at Jew-baiting, he was drawn to "Guidance" for a while, he was a member of the Communist Party for a fortnight, and then he decided that what Camford had for him was Rud. And he settled down to be Rud's disciple with a quite unprecedented steadfastness. He liked in particular the idea of a common revolutionary movement in Britain and America. He displayed a strange prophetic insight. "Rud's real," he said. "Rud's going far."

He established himself in two large flats in Camborne Square just out of the Euston Road. In the upper one he lived, in the lower he set up a sort of headquarters for Rud and such Rudites as were gathering round him. He refreshed them with a sideboard bearing bread, which they cut for themselves, cheese, carrots, plentiful carrots, apples, bananas, cider, water and beer. The cider and beer were in casks, and there were blue chequered earthenware mugs but no plates. The floor of this lower flat was covered with cork carpet, bathroom and kitchenette included, and the walls of its four rooms were adorned with a disorderly collection of election posters, caricatures and very modern pictures with a political bias. There were chairs, forms, a settle or so, two sofas, five or six folding beds, a spinet and several tables bearing piles of old newspapers, and warmth was supplied by electric radiators and light from cornice lights and casually placed reading lamps.

A queer miscellany of people drifted into this place. It had points of resemblance to the crowd at the summer school, but there was a greater reality about it. There was a sprinkling of young scientific workers, there were rising and ambitious artists, there were unusual looking young women who were models, there were incidental, bright and excessively usual looking American girls, some rather encumbered with disconcerting mothers, there were journalists, the secretaries of one or two politicians and various peculiar friends of Steenhold's too diverse and irrelevant to describe. There were fewer school teachers and pairing arrangements played but a minor role in the interests of the company. Here Rud would sit in a corner and talk and improve his talking powers. The political atmosphere was much more various than the unchallenged, uncorrelated progressivism of the summer school, and he learnt to parry and deal with a number of new points of view. He learnt with a sort of angry reluctance – he would rather he knew without this learning – but he learnt continually. He was moody; he was often manifestly sulky; he seemed to feel a smouldering hostility to many of them; and yet the discipleship of Steenhold infected

113

most of the crowd. Occasionally his brain seemed to light up and then there could be no doubting his originality and vigour.

His onsets of political clairvoyance took him by surprise almost as much as they surprised his following. He had little introspection; his disposition was to be consistent and always right, and he passed from phase to phase almost unwittingly. At one moment he would be sullen, rather angry, disinclined to speak, with a cloudy confusion of facts and impressions, things he had heard, partial suggestions he had never tackled, old reveries and present impulses swirling about in his brain, and then suddenly like a crystallisation, everything fell into place, with a conviction, an absolute certainty of rightness and fitness, and with it came words and phrases, coherent, continuous. Life, which had been like a dispersed jigsaw puzzle, appeared then as a stateable and manageable problems, and the only astonishing thing about it for him was that it was not as clear and compelling to everyone as it was to himself. It was as if some different intelligence, a sort of parasitic lucidity, was hidden in his brain, with contacts and a range that went far beyond his personality; it was a genius he had, a genius in the Socratic sense, like that of a musician or a calculating boy or a poet. It seemed not to affect his general character at all.

Gradually he became aware of the alien nature of this mental being within him, and shaped his conduct to exploit it. Generally he would sit in a corner drinking little and smoking less, and waiting. It became a leading interest to "get Rud going." Sometimes when he had a feeling of inadequacy, he would stay away for days at a time, so as not to spoil the impression he perceived he was creating.

He would sit in a corner under a chalk caricature of himself that one of the artistic contingent had made. It was on brown paper and the forehead was exaggerated and done in white. His normal scowl was exalted to intensity, his eyes were alight, and he raised one eloquent fist to the level of his forehead. It was one of those brilliant caricatures that seem to exercise a moulding influence upon their originals.

Since the war scares of 1937 and 1938 the process of world armament had been going on with an ever increasing intensity and an ever increasing stress and dislocation of the ordinary life of mankind. Everyone now was being regimented, enrolled, enlisted, taxed beyond all reason, intimidated. If a new world was being born, it was being born very uncomfortably. A feverish exacerbation of human consciousness was manifest under these conditions. Overt criticism was dangerous and suppressed, but doubt and unbelief gathered intensity through their lack of expression. One dogmatism destroyed another and was in its turn destroyed. Everything was being openly accepted and furtively questioned. No tacit assumption and no established institution was safe from this seeping away of belief. A mean superficial cynicism spread like a miasma over every land.

Compared with any former period in human history the second and third decades of the twentieth century saw a stupendous diffusion and ferment of ideas round and about the earth. The only approach to a parallel is the intellectual, moral and religious confusion of the world that occurred between the break-up of the ancient localised paganisms and mythologies and the onset of the first syncretic, universalist experiments, Christianity, diasporic Judaism and Islam. And that was an infinitely fainter and slower mental turnover. One instance marks

115

the difference in tempo and the change of scale. In the eighties of the nineteenth century, communism was the imagination of an obscure group of exiles in London. Marx wrote his articles in Highgate and made a scanty living, and young Mr Bernard Shaw, after speaking, chiefly for his own amusement, at a little meeting in Hyde Park, was accosted by an unrecognised stranger who proclaimed himself: "I am Friedrich Engels!" It did not seem to be anything very wonderful in the way of an encounter at the time. Engels indeed struck Shaw as a needlessly self-important person. "O-o-oh! – *Engels!*" he said, with the rising inflection of surprised enlightenment. Yet within thirty years there was not a country in the world, from Quito to Lhasa and from Greenland to Papua, where the names and doctrines of Marx and Engels were unknown; and communism and the doctrine of the class war were as widespread as Christianity and far better understood. It was a diffusion ten times as rapid as the former instance – and with a vastly greater range.

One evening Rud found himself eloquent upon this point, rephrasing – and greatly improving – some of Chiffan's remembered wisdom.

"Revolution so far!" said Rud. "Bah!...

"Just class bickering, rows in the street, changes of management! The mere beginnings...

"The real revolution," he went on, "is still going about the world like a mighty spirit seeking a body. For a couple of centuries now the world has been troubled by needs that have never once found a suitable working expression. All the time the stress had been getting worse. Life gets more unbalanced, more dislocated, clumsier and more abundant. Then tension of population increases. More and more people suffer. Pointless, silly, bloody warfare! Pointless, silly, bloodless unemployment! This *real* revolution going about the world – "

"Like an evil spirit," said one of the models.

"No! A great spirit, a monstrous spirit beyond good and evil, resolved to embody itself somehow…"

Steenhold murmured approval. "Beyond Good and Evil," he thought. "Nietzsche! *Good!*"

"I tell you," said Rud, becoming more and more prophetic in his manner, "Social trouble has been growing and growing, ever since civilisation began to use money and roads and ships. All the religions, all the loyalties of the past three thousand years, are just the childish palliatives, the insufficient clothes, the *shapes,* men have tried to impose upon this growing monstrousness to prevent it from disorganising life too frightfully.

"And it's growing now – faster than ever – always more intolerant of these shreds and patches, these *Gulliver strings,* we put about it."

"Gulliver strings?" queried Steenhold, and then with delight: "Oh! *Gulliver Strings,* tying him!"

"Yes, tying him," said Rud. "the real revolution, mind you, will never endure these limitations – not for another ten years. 'Damn you,' it says to us, 'clothe me *properly,* equip me properly! I am the Age of Plenty, I am the new life.' The new world is getting impatient. It is a new life – absolutely – and it wants the shape and it wants the endorsement of a new life. Communism wasn't enough for it. Not nearly enough. A mere feud of existing classes. The new world *has* to burst all these racial and national and class ideas, Fascism Judaism, Nazism, Sovietism, by which people are trying to incarnate it. It is bursting them now. They are being tried and found wanting. All of them. They were all experiments. All experiments. Temporary – to the last degree. It is the turn of our generation, of our sort, now, to try and fit the case better. It has come to us, now. *Now!* Now! We have to solve the problem or go down in our turn. Go down! And every generation that goes down will go down heavier. There is no fury like a revolution frustrated – no disorder like a world in which a new pattern of living has failed to realise itself."

"Now that's *real* stuff, Rud," said Steenhold. "that's real life stuff. That goes on to something. That goes on."

"*But* I don't *quite* see – " began a spectacled Bloomsbury intellectual, sitting on the floor and nursing his knees.

"I tell you, he's *fine*," shouted Steenhold, quenching the intervention. "Let's have more of it, Rud. Tell us some more."

"That's the gist of it," said Rud.

He was trying to remember exactly what he had said. He himself felt he had said something fine, It was like his first outbreak of eloquence at the Union all over again.

3

To these conferences in the Steenhold flat there presently came a bunch of young men from Lord Horatio Bohun's once hopeful Popular Socialist Party. At first they argued with Rud, and then they crystallised about him. "But this is our stuff," they said. "No," said Rud, "it's what your stuff ought to be. If it had more bones and less white meat."

They were ripe for Rud. The spirit of their movement was changing, and they realised the need for a renewal of its vitality. They were growing up mentally, and the idea of being thoroughly disagreeable to Jews and long-haired communists no longer satisfied them as an objective in life. They no longer flaunted it in decorative purple shirts because the wearing of party uniforms was now rather heavily penalised, and that loss of colour also was reflected in their bearing.

The biggest of them was a man named Rogers, some sort of amateur boxing champion, with a streak of almost maternal protectiveness in him and a bias for a good clean vigorous fight. He did not mind very much what the fight was about, and he hated to think it might lead to bad feeling. Bodisham, another of them seemed to be a born director; he would have been an able producer of films or plays and he played chess and was said to play bridge with a swift, uncanny realisation of how the game was going. Later on he was to justify his reputation and become a brilliant controller of meetings and party manoeuvres. And he was to end as one of the greatest of constructive statesmen. Rud perhaps had a quicker grasp of a general situation, but it was instinctive, not reasoned; Bodisham's turn for either massed details or isolated details was not to be equalled. And when it was a question of the scientific handling of a problem, Rud gave way to Bodisham perforce. Bodisham had come out of the London School of Economics; his first ambition had been to supplement the mental deficiencies of Bohun. When he had found that they were not be supplemented, he had turned to Rud. He was the only one of the Group who wore spectacles; it seemed to accentuate his claim to be the intellectual influence in the party. Irwell came in from a stockbroker's office. He was living by sub-editing a financial paper, and when he talked of money the others listened with respect.

Another of this bunch was a man whom Rud had a haunting sense of having met before. His name was Colin Dreed. At first

Rud could not think where they might have met, and then he identified him, though not with absolute certainty, as one of two purple shirts who had visited his rooms in his second year. Dreed perhaps had an equivalent doubt, and at times Rud would catch a slight perplexity in his eyes, an expression of inadequate recognition. But nothing was ever said about it. Dreed was now nearly an adult and no longer that bright potential furniture-smasher of Rud's second year. But he was still essentially a partisan. He did whatever he was told, and he always did it with a faint suggestion of surprise at not having thought of so obvious a thing himself. But he never thought of it himself. One or two other purple shirts and ex-purple shirts came less regularly and talked less freely, but these were the nuclear personalities of what was destined to be Rud's primary organisation.

It was evident to him that all these young men were extremely dissatisfied with Bohun's leadership, and that they did not know clearly what to do about it. They felt misdirected and frustrated, and yet they still retained something of the good intentions that had brought them into his movement. Many years ago Lord Horatio had come into British politics with a considerable flourish, as a young man of wealth, position and influence, destined to play a brilliantly unorthodox role in public affairs. He had also evidently proposed to himself a wide conspicuousness as a splendid individual. He had narrowly escaped the House of Lords; his brother was the Duke of Wybrow, a defective so defective as to be unfitted for anything but procreation, in which indeed he had been eminently successful. So Horatio, cut off from any hope of a dukedom and a senatorial career by a growing zareba of nephews, had decided to be the British Julius Caesar; the Duce, the leader of a renascent patriotic Britain. Plus Byron without the limp. At first everything seemed to favour him. There had been only one insurmountable obstacle to his ambition, but that was hidden from him, a complete lack of originality in his make-up. He was so completely destitute of ideas that he had no idea he had no ideas. He behaved therefore as though he had ideas, and for a time there were admirers to share his illusion.

He had been what is called a "spoilt" child, the favoured younger brother, and he was still essentially "Lord Horry." He had one of those faces whose features seem asymmetrical and confused when seen in front, but which have a certain resemblance to handsomeness in profile; he was pale, freckled and red-haired, with the rebellious forelock so frequent with romantic personalities, and his voice was arrogant and adenoidal. He carried himself with a certain solemn haughtiness, breathing heavily, with a projected chest balanced stiffly against a projected behind. At first he had proposed himself as the rising hope of the Liberal Party; but in those days very little was left of the Liberal Party except rising hopes; many of them were already middle-aged, and they had shown very clearly that an addition to their numbers would be unwelcome. He was an imperious rather than a patient wooer, and so he had transferred his proffer of leadership almost convulsively to the Communist wing of the Labour Party.

Here again his reception was inadequate; the Labour Party did not seem to realise in the least what an accession this splendid and brilliant young aristocrat would be to its all too pedestrian front, and while he was still reluctantly realising this poverty of the leftish imagination, the successes of Mussolini and the Nazis gave a new turn to his ambitions. He became the sedulous student and ape of the Italian and German adventures, not realising that there was a certain incongruity between their methods and formulae and the peculiar large scepticism of the Anglo-Saxon tradition, with its lamentable disposition towards facetiousness on serious occasions. What was more natural than for the rejected romantic leader of the Reds to invert himself in another swift transformation, become an anti-Red, and stretch out his strong right arm to protect the rich old ladies of the land from the Red Horror? They responded to his heroic gesture with copious subscriptions and profuse press support. Lord Thunderclap and all the *Daily Clarion* group of newspapers hailed him with enthusiasm. He was speedily in a position to provide headquarters, highly decorative purple shirts, brown belts and a sense of purpose to a perceptible following of unemployed young men. So far as the police would let him – and at first they let him quite a lot if only on account of his rank – he induced the Jews to advertise him by a campaign of annoyance and menace against these far too responsive, expressive, tactless and unendearing people.

So it was Lord Horatio after his abortive explorations of the alternative avenues to the Left of life, made his definitive entrance upon the political scene from the Right. No further transformation was possible for him for there was nothing more for him to copy. He was now past the first blush and beauty of youth, and he found himself in a bright limelight of expectation. For a time – indeed until the dynastic trouble about the Duke of Windsor in 1937 superseded him – the first question the travelling Englishman was asked was "what is this new man, Lord Bohun, going to do?"

To which the more intelligent Englishman said: "He isn't much of a man and he isn't going to do anything."

"But that's what they said of Hitler."

"But Hitler was a national growth, and Bohun isn't even a growth…"

What the less intelligent Englishman said about him varied, and anyhow, it does not matter now.

There he was upon the British scene in a nimbus of expectation. He took large halls and addressed meetings at which he regurgitated the masticated leading articles of the opposition press – and more particularly those of the *Daily Clarion*. He never made an original remark, he never coined a phrase of his own, not even by accident. He organised processions, which had a diminishingly irritating effect, in Jewish districts. Nothing ever ensued from the meetings and processions except a dribble of police court proceedings that died away. Then he would pass out of the headlines for a space and then again would come another great and entirely vacuous meeting and another temporary obstruction in the streets.

Slowly, incredulously, the world realised that Lord Horatio was doing nothing, and did not know how to do anything. But he kept up his movement with all the dignity of Tristram Shandy's bull.

He was too vain and jealous to associate any original or vigorous intelligence with himself. Helpful people of initiative and ambition joined him, only to drop off disappointed. Instead he gathered about himself parasitic adherents of impeccable dullness, and he organised a wonderful "training school" of Popular Socialist speakers. They were given little books of pros and cons – remarkable pros and cons – and general advice. But it is hard to train men to meet the unexpected interruption. These trained and paid supporters did not so much speak at his meeting as imitate speaking. They learnt the sounds and gestures of demonstration and conviction, but nothing more. They brought down the emphatic fist upon the suffering palm in the vain hope of giving platitude the flavour of inspiration, and a few determined interruptors could make a dreadful mess of them.

Sometimes Lord Horatio was out of the papers for weeks at a time, and then he would be back again, delivering the same old speech and demonstrating nothing by the same old demonstration. He was especially prevalent in spring. May and June seemed to excite him. It looked as though he was destined to become a seasonal feature in English life, like the Royal Academy or the Boat Race. Whenever there was a socialist or pacifist or communist gathering, or indeed any sort of mass meeting, the purple banners of the Popular Socialists with their golden tassels turned up in slowly dwindling force, always under almost excessive police protection, and always making a scuffling rather than triumphant exit from the field of debate.

The nimbler years slipped, by, and even his loyalest adherents were forced were forced to realise the progressive ravages of middle-age upon his former fatuous *élan*. His pogroms, such as they were, lost pep. The *Daily Clarion* ceased to feature him. It did not so much turn against him as fade away from him. It looked as though he and his Popular Socialists were going to sit down and fade out altogether. This sessile disposition on the part of their leader was a source of grave discontent to many of the youngsters who had got into belts and purple shirts and broken their adolescent voices shouting "We *want* Bo-oó-un" in those so much more promising early days. More and more he had to rely on the subsidised element in his following. More and more did the growing tension of the superarmament period emphasise his essential unreality, his amateurism.

At one or two of his recent meeting unidentified and disregarded voices had cried out "Get *on* with it!"

The world situation darkened. The sense of impending catastrophe increased. All over the world it was felt that the now-or-never moment was approaching. There was a sort of paralysis of grim expectation. In 1940 the chief employment of human leisure was anti-aircraft drill; a quarter of a million bombers were in commission, and everywhere men excavated. Political life changed its character. Political thought intensified. The taste for mild rioting was declining under a burthen of apprehensive responsibility. The newspapers bore anxiety on their foreheads.

The publics in the old democratic countries had had the educational spectacle of a decade of blustering dictatorship in Europe. They were capable now of immense scepticisms and increasingly resistant to the vague promises of merely personal leadership. "You are anti-Bolshevik and anti-Jew, you declare the government is corrupt and incompetent and so forth, and that's all very acceptable," said the mind of the common man. "But what are *you* going to make and what are *you* going to do if we put you in power?"

Beneath Bohun's feet, at his headquarter, the germs of a "Ginger Group" stirred and grew. Out of deference to his ruddy forelock it called itself "*Real* Ginger". It desired a programme, a creed. It desired explicitness. It took a definite form in Steenhold's flat one evening when, after a dissertation of Rud's, certain letter of power, namely, "BMG" were pronounced. Which letters being interpreted signified no longer "Balfour must go" as they had originally done – but "Bohun". And the man who said them was Rogers.

He hit his knees with his fist, he said the mystical letters and glared around him.

4

The talks in the Steenhold flat had benefited considerably by the accession of Chiffan. He had returned rejoicing to London, having got a job as printer-editor of a small suburban newspaper, and he brought with him much precise information about the gathering unrest in the North. "They despise and hate the government more and more, but they don't know how to set about changing it. The country is dying for some sort of lead, and so far all it is getting is a crowd of fresh professional leaders. Who never get anywhere. Who do not seem to be aiming anywhere. We are living in a world of *jaded* politics. Poverty increases, prices rise, unemployment spreads, mines, factories stagnate, and nothing is done."

At first Chiffan was wary and a little jealous of Rud's Popular Socialist friends, and also, quite inadvertently, he developed an earnest and sympathetic friendship with a frizzy-haired, amber-eyed young woman who had been regarding Rud very earnestly for some weeks. (They began by talking about Rud, his gifts, his character, his possibilities, and their devotion to him brought them closer and closer together, and at last so close that Rud became a benediction over their liaison. Chiffan made a sort of party sacrament of it, but for all that he was rather ashamed of himself. The relationship excited and occupied him for a week or so, and then it bored him, and when Rogers smote his knees and said "BMG", he lit up and became a fount of shrewd suggestions.)

"BMG. *Great!*" said Chiffan.

"BMG. *Great* idea!" said Steenhold.

"I am not so sure of BMG," said Rud, nursing his knee in his corner. "I agree that the Popular Socialist organisation has to be given a new start and a new programme – it's what I've been saying all along – and as things are, it is probably the only organisation in the country on which you could base a real efficiency campaign outside the party machines. There it is. It is the only quasi-voluntary organisation just now that could take liberties and not be suppressed at once. The left organisations now, if it came to a scrap, could be shut up in a week. It's the Popular Socialists for us or nothing. But why shouldn't one keep Bohun as the nominal head and work through him?"

"You don't know him yet," said Bodisham.

"I've got to see him. We join up tomorrow, Chiffan and I. I told you. When I see him I shall know better about him. What is there impossible about him?"

"Wait till you see him," said Irwell.

"He has personal contacts with the West End and the City."

"Had," said Bodisham.

"The sort of immunity this Party has had – it certainly has had an immunity – may vanish if we chuck out Bohun."

"That depends on the opinion the authorities have of us," said Bodisham.

"There are three reasons why BMG," said Chiffan, "so far as I understand the situation. Firstly he will never let any sort of initiative exist in the party except his own, so long as he remains the leader. And he has no initiative of his own. Secondly, the only way the public can be made to realise that the Popular Socialist Party is now going to mean something else, is by not simply making Bohun *go* – but by chucking him. And thirdly we have to publicise Rud. That is the most important. We have to stage a first-class row, so that Rud's restatement of our ideas will be on the front page. We've got to put him there and keep him there. What do you think Bodisham?"

"Couldn't be sounder," said Bodisham.

"I'd like to hear more suggestions," said Rud. "we've talked tonight. We've talked before. We can't always be talking. Now if this Real Ginger Group of yours is to go beyond talking it has to define itself much more plainly than it has done. We must know what we really mean to do and we must have some ideas of the roles we have to play. It is no good, for example, for Rogers to yield to his burning desire to go right out now and hit somebody, unless the group is prepared for the situation that will arise out of the hitting. If I am any sort of leader – "

"But you *are!*"

"Then the first thing is that nothing must be done until the word go – Nothing. For ten days or so at least we have got to meet here and draw up almost detailed particulars of what we mean to do. We have to sound everybody concerned. Now we happen to be alone here tonight, but generally speaking this room is too public, Steenhold. On Saturdays it's half Bloomsbury and stage here, in the small hours. Anyone may come in at any time."

"Well, make a planning room of my room upstairs," said Steenhold.

"And definitely plan," said Bodisham, and took off and wiped his spectacles with an air of preparing for work.

So they definitely planned and became an organised conspiracy. They elected themselves and were chary of introducing fresh blood. They drew up certain articles of association beginning: "The object of the RGG (Real Ginger Group) is to resuscitate, revise, enlarge and invigorate the Popular Socialist movement and make it a Living Power in the Land." Their imaginative organisation of the group proceeded apace, and everybody weighed everybody's character and capabilities and limitation with the utmost solicitude. Chiffan ticked them off with semi-official titles. Rud was the Master Director or "Chief" for short, Rogers was the Fighting Chief, Bodisham was the Organiser General or the Head Strategist, Irwell was the Financial Reorganiser, Dreed was the Chief of Propaganda and Education.

"Everything has to be stated," said Rud.

"Of course! Of course!" said Dreed. "It's all as plain as daylight."

"Times change," said Rud, "and nowadays they change very rapidly. Propaganda becomes more and more a primary thing. One reason why the majority everywhere is so indecisive is because it is becoming intelligent. It is mobile but sceptical. It won't jump at a name or a nickname now. It wants – *definition*. Compared with ten years ago it is critical. It has to be given things straight and clear. But if you give it things straight and clear – it *can* take them and it *will* take them." ("I do so agree," said Bodisham. "I do so heartily agree.") "The primary need in order to get and keep power is bright plain publicity. And more publicity. And then publicity. There never has been a time when ideas are as fluid as they are now. If only one can get publicity, if only one can get the ear of the crowd, anything could be put before it – anything – and given sufficient explicitness almost

129

anything can be put over it. If you put over nonsense it will fall to pieces later, but there is no limit now to the changes of opinion that can be affected in the modern masses. Choose good slogans. Speak loud, speak wide, speak plain and the thing is done."

(Approval from Bodisham, nodding his head so that his glasses flashed.)

"Just consider the fluctuation of the popular intelligence in Britain during the last few years. You had absolute changes in a year or so. Not changes of shade, mind you, but changes of colour. Black to white. There was that Peace Ballot business. When was it? In '36? You had ten or twelve million adults in Great Britain voting against any sort of war. You would have said that a majority of the British people and certainly all the left side of British life would never fight in *any* war again. And by '37 the whole country was boiling for a showdown with Italy about Abyssinia, and by the middle of '38 you got the feeling that the selfsame mass of people, the same crowd of individuals, was beginning to want a war with Germany! Really *want* a war. Getting *dangerous* to Germany! Spoiling for it. And now the current slogan is 'Settlement.' The government says settlement, but the people *mean* it. What will they mean next year if they are still being bored to hell, drilling and arming and paying taxes?

"In Germany too, how many Nazis were Liberals and Social Democrats ten years ago. Yet in '37 and '38 if you woke up a German in the night he said 'Heil Hitler' automatically, and felt it. Then they slacked on Hitler. How easily they slacked on him! How rapidly they developed resistances to the tension, the incessant tension, he made.

"Look at the way people have swung through Communism, Toryism, Liberalism – in vast blocks. In my father's boyhood

130

you were either a Liberal or a Conservative in England, and there you stuck, and in America you were a sturdy individualist Democrat or Republican from the cradle to the grave. But now the Voice does it – the pervading voice. And just now it's come to a point when a Voice – putting it straight and clear. Straight and clear…"

"There speaks the voice," said Chiffan. "You make pictures in the mind, Rud. I see the mind of the world like chaos – a whirling Chaos, and suddenly comes the Logos – the Word. In fact you, Rud."

"You aren't jeering by any chance?" asked Steenhold, always anxious to know exactly where he stood.

"Perhaps I *am* decorating a little. It's my vice, Steenhold… Let us plan."

"Yes," said Bodisham. "Let us plan. Now just where do we begin operations? Where do we first confront the Boss with the unpleasant fact that the movement no longer considers itself properly led? And proposes to give him a push? And what exactly will it do when he splutters and hectors?"

So the conclave in Steenhold's upper room began its deliberations, began to figure out the definite seizure of the party for Rud. It was necessarily highly imaginative work.

At times it was entirely indeterminate whether they were really making plans for definite action or merely indulging in a collective reverie, that might at any time evaporate back into nothingness – as ten thousand other conspiracies have done.

"We now know," said Bodisham, summing up one night, "practically everything we mean to do. We mean to insist upon a general meeting of the party and then we mean to challenge

Bohun fairly and squarely. What we have to do now is to fix times and dates, determine numbers and places."

"Wait!" said Chiffan.

"What for?"

"The Hour. The Moment. Rud's instinct and the word Go."

"Wait, but be ready," said Rud. "wait for the word. It will be like shooting a gun and killing a man. After that there is no turning back. I've seen the Boss once. H'm! I want to give him one more chance. I want to start with a speech on this mess the government is making about the American Situation. Somehow I must make that speech."

5

When Rud met the Popular Socialist Boss he hated him, he hated him immediately and without qualification. His intention of impressing him deeply, winning his confidence, betraying and supplanting him, was replaced by vehement desire to destroy him, humiliatingly, completely and at once. Rud the political learner, at the mere sight of Lord Horatio, gave way to the more primitive Rud, Rud the vindictive destroyer.

He had expected to encounter a foolish figure, but he had not expected to encounter so exasperatingly vain and foolish a figure. He had thought he was bringing a considerable contribution to the Popular Socialist movement in the shape of his natural eloquence, rapid comprehension and gusty energy. He found Lord Horatio incapable of appreciating any gifts but his own.

Lord Horatio was seated before a great, ornamental, unbusinesslike desk with a large inkstand and impressive paper-weights and accessories. He was posed as an eighteenth century

Whig gentleman. But he was smoking a cigarette and there was an ashtray of stubs and a selection of cigarette packages among the more monumental desk fittings. He was wearing a frogged purple velvet Tuxedo. His white shirt collar was open to reveal his neck picturesquely. To his left was a large table bearing a litter of pamphlets, press cuttings, proofs, memorandum, pads and even books, and looking over this barrier appeared the upper part of the face of a small, spectacled, woman stenographer, who had been taking down his Lordship's correspondence.

She rose to go at Rud's entry.

"No, no," said Lord Horatio, with a restraining gesture of an elegant hand, "we shan't be long."

He had given Rud the benefit of his profile, the ruddy forelock, the Corinthian nose, the rather underhung jaw. Now he half turned to face him. The expression of his rather too closely set eyes was designed to convey hypnotic penetration.

"Well," he said with a certain condescension. "What do *you* want?"

He had made no suggestion that Rud should sit down. Rud had an impulse to seize a chair and plant himself, but there was no chair. His scowl intensified. He came up to the desk and stood over Bohun. He had the infuriating thought that he must look rather like an under-gardener applying for a situation.

"The Popular Socialist programme express very much what I feel," he said. "I'm prepared to throw in my lot with it."

"That means work."

"What else can it mean?"

"What can you do?"

"Speak."

"Have you been trained?"

133

"I've debated in the Union with a certain success."

"But in the real world? I said, have you been trained? Our speakers are trained men."

"If you mean that poor little list of pros and cons of yours…" For once Rud was at a loss for words.

"Do you fancy you have a platform pairsonality?" said Lord Horatio. "I wonder. How tall are you?"

There was a pause. If Lord Horatio had not been so occupied with his own "pairsonality," he might have remarked the extreme malignity of the face before him.

"I'm two inches taller than Napoleon," said Rud.

"Remarkable! But for platform work you require more than a coincidence of that sort. You want a definite, commanding pairsonality. Even *I* have had to study and drill myself. You have to *dominate*. Frankly I think you're too short. But these are really questions for Commander Hoggin. He is in control of all the training work. You ought not to have come to me. Who sent you up? Rogers? Oh! Rogers… I've no doubt Commander Hoggin can see you, but the first and last thing in a party like ours is discipline and obedience."

He turned the wonderful hypnotic gaze of the leader full upon the new adherent, but it did not have much effect on him.

"But do you know who I am?' said Rud. "do you know what I can do?"

"Hoggin must see to all that."

For a moment Rud was at a loss. He turned to go and then thought of something to say. "Why the hell don't you have chairs here for people to sit down?' he asked. "It's damned uncivil."

He went towards the door.

"One moment, my boy," he heard behind him.

"Yes."

"The salute?"

Lord Horatio was standing up and looking very scandalised and stern and commanding. He had apparently not heard that impossible snarl about the chairs.

"How? Salute?"

Lord Horatio lifted his hand and Rud reciprocated. Lord Horatio dropped his hand and so did Rud. Honours were equal.

Then Rud slammed the door and found himself trembling and feeling sick.

Bohun stood for a time staring at the slammed door.

"*We'll* lick him into shape, Mrs Crumb," he said. "We'll lick him into shape. Yes... By the by, did *The Times* print yesterday's letter? Who is it on *The Times* who makes all these needless difficulties about my letters? It gets worse and worse."

But his mind was on Rud.

"Who the devil was that, Mrs Crumb? I've never seen him before."

"I'll get him documented, my lord. He joined up only last week."

"He's quite an untried man?"

"I'll get whatever dossier we have."

6

Rud second encounter with the Boss was if possible more exasperating than the first. Rud spent four days turning their first meeting over in his mind, and by that time he was ready with an ultimatum. He made it without consulting his associates. He had learnt that Lord Horatio was going to Liverpool for the weekend, and that there was to be a Birthday Meeting in the smaller Saltbag Hall there. The American trouble was growing acute, but the Popular Socialists seemed to be doing nothing about it. They were plainly wasting an immense opportunity. Rud found Dreed on duty at the Purple House and he had no difficulty in making his way up through the lower rooms to the sanctum on the second floor. He walked in without ceremony.

Lord Horatio was sitting at his desk. He had two documents before him. One was the final draft of his forthcoming Liverpool speech which Mrs Crumb had just typed. The other was what she had been able to produce by way of a dossier for Rud. He was looking them over protentously and doing nothing about either of them. The dossier was the result of confidential enquires by Captain Smike, whose duty it was to report upon the internal discipline of the party to the Boss. The last entry noted that Rud had not yet discussed the matter of training with Hoggin. In addition, Smike had some hearsay about Steenhold's flats – he had thought it wiser, he said, not to show himself there until he knew that something was really brewing – and his chief fact was that Rud sometimes talked very well and effectively. "No doubt that several of our older associates think well of him. He has ideas, plentiful if not sound. He has a certain force. But so far – just *talk*. The rest of that crowd is mostly pink carnations with a pansy border."

(So Smike. The Popular Socialists were always very loud and scornful about pansies – whatever pansies might be. "Carnation" seems to have been Smike's own original unaided term for a mitigated "Red.")

Lord Horatio had a way of rolling back his lips from his teeth and playing imaginary tunes upon them with his fingernails, when engaged in stimulating thought. "Has ideas?' he said, and was tapping his teeth and regarding that draft speech of his schemingly, when Rud burst in.

"What the davil!" exclaimed his lordship. "what do *you* want? Where's the Salute?"

"That salute!" cried Rud. "Oh! *How* does it go?"

Bohun fell into the trap again.

"Don't you trouble about a chair," said Rud. "Don't you bother about a chair. I can say all I have to say walking about the room. But I must know before you leave London what we are going to do about the American trouble. Mexico? And the shooting in south Carolina. Particular the shooting in South Carolina. It's the grandest opportunity the party had ever had, of taking a line. Before the Communists get hold of it. Slap against the government and with all the natural instincts of the people behind us. What are we going to *do?*"

He stopped short and stared at Mrs Crumb. She had flopped back in her chair quite audibly. Her eyebrows had risen a full two inches above the rims of her spectacles.

Lord Horatio was speechless for some seconds. One large freckled fist rested on Rud's dossier. He looked rather like a public monument of a leonine character being desecrated by trippers. "You ask what the party if going to *do?*" he said at last.

"Well – evidently! Here's exactly where we come in! Where the government couldn't come in, even if it wanted to. We can put Washington, Wall Street and Westminster into the cart now and shake hands right across the Atlantic with the mass opinion in America. The situation is screaming for it."

Lord Horatio held up a hand.

"Have you come here to make speeches Mr – Mr Whittlelow? I don't remember inviting you to do so."

"I don't want to make speeches here, but I want to make speeches for you in London. I can handle this situation. If you have to go to Liverpool, well anyhow let me have the Hyde Park Platform next Sunday. Let me take a line and get a press for the party. I'm ready to discuss it all with you."

"*No!*" said Lord Horatio.

"Gods!" cried Rud, in a frenzy, wringing his hands. "But *look* at it!"

Lord Horatio was looking at Rud. This sort of thing, he thought, was what comes of what they called ideas. This youngster was going to be a nuisance in the party – probably even a menace. His effrontery was astonishing.

With an extremity of quiet scorn Lord Horatio demanded: "Are you the head of the Popular Socialist movement or am I?"

"Should I come to you like this if *I* was?" demanded Rud.

"I wonder if we want a man of your stamp in this movement at all," considered Bohun, still very cold and calm. "Now let me tell you, my boy, that we know exactly what we are doing in this American affair – exactly." He pointed his remarks with an extended finger. "We have our own sources of information and our definite policy. You can hardly expect me to confide in a neophyte like you, what and why and how and when. You've forgotten your place and you've got to learn discipline. You imagine we have no Party discipline. A day may come when you will know better.

Rud was about to speak, but Lord Horatio was standing up. "Now not a word more of this," he said. "I tell you to go to Commander Hoggin for instruction and to keep your mouth shut until he tells you to open it." He reflected for a moment and then laughed scornfully. "To think of it! *You* deal with the situation! *You* take the Hyde Park platform. *You!* If you come here again to annoy me with this sort of thing I'll have you thrown out of the party. It's only because you're a raw beginner that I tolerate you now."

"Oh *foolery!* Oh Stick in the Mud!" burst from Rud, a cry of agony.

Lord Horatio rapped the desk with a ruler he had seized.

"You *rat!* You little *rat!* Salute, sir, and get out. I'll tell them how to deal with you."

"Salute!" said Rud. "*Me* – Salute!", and then, grinning viciously, "*How?*"

It looked as though Bohun might lose his self-control, and he was a full five inches taller than Rud and generally much larger. Moreover that ruler might serve as a missile! If he thought of it.

Rud closed the door behind himself and stood quivering on the landing.

"Damn the idiot!" he said.

Lord Horatio stood very still at his desk, dilating and contracting his nostrils almost as though he was doing breathing exercises. Anger illuminated him – in the eyes of Mrs Crumb.

"I was *afraid*," whispered Mrs Crumb, all limp in her chair. "I was afraid – you might *kill* him."

"He just wants discipline," said Lord Horatio. "I'll break him in yet... I've dealt with tougher stuff than that... Have you ordered the car? *Hotel?* No. I'm staying with Lady Garbees."

Rud went out of the Purple House in a preoccupied manner.

"OK?" asked Dreed as he came downstairs.

"No," said Rud curtly...

He felt he had made a mess of the whole situation. He ought to have consulted the BMGs before this second encounter with Bohun. He did not want to got back to Steenhold's flat to make premature explanations to him or any of them, and still less did he want to return to his dismal little apartment. He felt he could never make a tolerable story about this paralysing quarrel. He would go for a walk. He would just walk. He would spend his anger in walking. It was a mild, clear afternoon and he wandered for miles, first west until the sunset got into his eyes, and then northward and round by Hendon and the Northern Heights. He sat for a long time in a teashop in Hounslow, brooding; he got a sausage-and-mashed in a little pub out towards Barnet. Afterwards he found a friendly wayside seat and sat on it for some time. Then as his feet were getting very tired and his small change low, he established himself in a belated confectioner's shop at Highgate over a glass of soda and milk, and when that establishment closed he went home, refreshed himself with a wash and repaired at last to Camborne Square.

Saturday night in Steenhold's flat was not one of the BMG nights, and none of the Group was there. Instead there was an influx of uncongenial spirits, interested in the worlds of dramatic art and poetry and literary journalism. Many of the people were quite unknown to Rud, and Steenhold was plainly giving politics a rest. "How goes it?" asked Steenhold.

"Rotten," said Rud. "I'll have a drink and sit a bit and then go to bed."

He sat about ineffectively and he disliked the company very much. The talk splashed about his disregarded sulkiness. He disliked them more and more.

They were all so *irrelevant*, so frightfully irrelevant. The mind of youth is an errant mind and will not always conspire. It loathes concentration. It flits from novelty to novelty. It must be fed by events and challenges and held to its objective by conflict. It pits world affairs on a level with any one of the affairs on a level with any one of the minor arts. That night Rud had the completest conviction that things had slipped out of his hands altogether. He did not talk and they betrayed no desire to hear him talk; he felt that they were convinced they had heard all he had to say, and were talking now about other things, about their damned little plays and pictures and novels and biology and genetics, and time-space and any old thing of that sort, beyond his peculiar range. He was effaced. He drank several mugs of beer and smoked more cigarettes than were good for him, he tried to intervene in two discussions he knew nothing about, and finally went home stiff and footsore to bed.

CHAPTER TWO

The Captured Platform

He woke up on Sunday morning in a state of extreme irritation, or rather, he emerged by degrees from a dreaming exasperation to an aching discontent. He woke up and stared at his discoloured ceiling. A realisation of absolute ineffectiveness overwhelmed him.

"Defeat!" he whispered. "Defeat. *Self* defeat. Here's the Popular Socialist demonstration will be petering out as usual in Hyde Park as if nothing had happened; here's a plain situation before us that won't wait, that can't wait, and I'm doing nothing. My guns are spiked.

"What *good* am I?

"I might as well not exist."

The tension accumulated. It reached the breaking point. He exploded.

"Oh *God!*" he screamed.

He leapt out of bed as though some unseen beast in it had bitten him. He threw his bedclothes into the corner; he gashed his chin shaving; he kicked his shoes across the room, he quarrelled with his shabby suit of clothes and broke his only pair of braces. He made hay of his room in his search for a piece of string or a safetypin to repair the damage. Instead of cooking his egg he beat it up raw in his milk and drank it like that with a trembling hand. He was too agitated to light his Primus and make tea.

He betook himself to Camborne Square.

He shouted Steenhold out of bed and stamped and bawled about the room. He was determined to act, and now, at any cost. It was not only Steenhold he bawled into action, but himself. "Now or never," he said. "The time has come to act. Now, when no one expects it, is our moment. I have waited – I told you the other night I was waiting. *Well* – the time is *now*."

Steenhold received his announcement in a state of stunned admiration. He had always felt the latent explosives in Rud's composition, and here at last, thank the gods, they were exploding!

"You mean get the boys together?"

"I mean get them together now."

"Right, Chief."

Steenhold went to the telephone and began dialling. "Funny!" he said. "Bodisham gave me this list of names three days ago. And I didn't see what it was for. *Really!* Didn't see what it was for... That you, Rogers?... Rogers! – The Hour has come."

The group and its associates assembled bit by bit. A miscellany of odd cars parked outside in the Square. Rud was exalted, and they listened with close attention. He walked up and down, he sat and twisted himself about the back of his chair, reiterating his conviction of a crisis.

"They've shot men in South Carolina. They landed marines to co-operate with the state police. British marines shooting

American strikers. Think of it! The affair can't wait. Don't you see how urgent it is and what it means to us?...

"I begged and prayed the Boss to take a line, and he put a flat veto on the whole thing... I must speak. There are things that must be said.

"How and where? I'll tell you exactly... There's that platform in Hyde Park with one or two trained droolers, drooling his old stuff... We go there. We take control."

Bodisham thought for a while, grasped Rud's idea and began to fill in particulars.

"We go there by twos and threes and gather round the platform," said Bodisham. "Then when Rud thinks fit we put him on the platform. There'll be some raw greenhorn in charge. If necessary Rogers and you other stalwarts can hustle him...

"Can we get reporters? I don't mean newshounds, I mean reporters."

"I know a man or two," said Irwell.

"Shorthand?"

"We could have a man for a verbatim report," said Steenhold. "We *ought* to have a man for a verbatim report."

"And after your speech?"

"I don't know," said Rud. "But get what I say reported. Get it reported. And now I'm going upstairs to be still – perfectly still – until it is time to go."

He vanished.

"He'll do it," said Steenhold, not all clear in his own mind what it was Rud would do.

The conspirators ate casually, wandering about the flat with mugs and chunks of bread and cheese. There was a lot of staring out of the window – as though the Future might be visible there already. After one o'clock they began to depart by twos and threes for Hyde Park.

2

The park was vastly crowded that afternoon, but over it hung a peculiar effect of inconsequence. It had less the quality of a popular forum than of an aimless promenade of useless people. It was a fermenting crowd, uneasy, and with no perceptible direction. There was something of the quality of one of those heavily clouded, brooding days on which there falls no single drop of rain. The processions has been swallowed up in a shapeless swarm of listeners and mockers and lookers-on. Over it all hummed a plane from which an officer was directing the movements of an unobtrusive but numerous police force by wireless. This plane and two little fleets of police vans were a recent and provocative innovation by the new Police Commissioner, but this afternoon it hummed above a stormless, quaking marsh of people. No need to move them on. They kept moving on.

The BMGs converged. Rud made his way, silent but determined, among the platforms, towards his particular objective.

The air was full of voice; the nearer ones patchily audible, saying stereotyped things, the further ones a felt of raucous sounds. All the speakers seemed bored. Everybody seemed bored and dissatisfied. It was all politics and no reality. There was a big Labour Party demonstration, to show once again and for all time that no considerations of human welfare could shake for one moment the stern resolve of the established British trade union

146

leaders to have no truck with Liberal politicians, men of science, men of ideas, Communists, Americans or anyone who might attempt to share the honours and emoluments that come at last to the implacably obstructive in political life. There was a dissentient Labour platform concerning itself with defining the fine differences in organisation that justified its dissent. There was a Liberal platform trying to steal Labour votes by its insistence upon the trouble in the Ukraine and the Mysore prison scandal. There was a Free Indian group and a platform of miscellaneous people pinning their faith to the South Welsh prison scandals as a means of raising a useful indignation. General objectives had long since vanished in the intricacies of party strategy. At every Socialist and Liberal platform the common man was being warned and incited against every other Socialist or Liberal group – probably with justice. One gathering charged the government with responsibility for the recent outbreak of measles. The Ministry of Health had done or not done this, that and the other thing, and at another point the Ministry of Agriculture was being challenged very manfully about some intricate manurial technicality. Isolationist platforms clashed with demands for intervention in Spain, China, Siam, the West Indies and Lithuania. Amidst the confusion religion reared its head to reply to infidelity, and anti-vivisection called on all mankind to end the greatest horror in the world. Communists in alliance with Catholics, Communists of the Trotsky heresy, Pro-Mexican Communists, New Communists and True Blue Communists, beat upon the air and warned the common man against deleterious imitations. It was less of a forum than a fair with every platform trying to sell some monopoly of its own.

Overhead bumbled the plane, directing the unobtrusive movements of the police, mindful of nothing said provided that nothing was done. It was a very symbol of the invincible determination of the government and institutions of Britain to yield to nothing less than blasting operations in their obstruction to any conceivable world reconstruction. And not to argue about it: They did not need to divide and rule. They ruled a fissiparous Opposition. That pervasive, soft droning gave the exactest expression to the aimless, gentle firmness of the British constitution at home and to its incalculable persistence in vaguely Imperialist assertion abroad.

The recent happenings in South Carolina played a minor role in that crowd's confusion of thought and feeling. The press had tempered the facts of the American social war to the mentality of the British public, and the general ignorance of American geography in England had prevented any realisation of the steady extension of the conflict from state to state. The loss of confidence in the remedial powers of Congress and the lapse of the whole South and Middle West first towards sporadic lawlessness and then towards an organised insurrectionary movement, had been masked by the fragmentary nature of the news and overshadowed by the *de facto* war in the Ukraine and the Balkans. No one had yet drawn a working analogy between the Transatlantic and the European situations.

The informal powers that worked through the forms of the British constitution, however, were from their own point of view more alert to the realities of the American situation; they had always had close associations, financial and social as well as political, with the reactionary Republicanism of Big Business, and they were in the closest sympathy with the methods of

148

obstruction, non-co-operation and counter-attack that had defeated Franklin Roosevelt's well meant but not always well balanced efforts to adapt the traditions of private capitalism to the economic and social stresses of a new age. They shared the same disregard of the warnings of the times, the same uncompromising conservatism of heart. They both wanted to pull the community back to the happy eighties, and they were quite prepared for just as much repression of the uneasy masses, repression direct or indirect, legal or informal, and as unobtrusively violent, as possible.

Things were rather larger, more obvious and rougher on the American side, but the issues were essentially the same. The general public voted and demonstrated, but its voting seemed to lead to nothing. It felt that things were done behind its back and over its head but it could never understand clearly how. It never seemed able to get sound news out of its newspapers nor good faith out of its politicians. It resisted, it fumbled, it was becoming more and more suspicious and sceptical, but it was profoundly confused and ill-informed.

Rud's quick realisation that something profoundly significant was happening across the Atlantic, or at least something that could be presented as being profoundly significant, was well ahead of the popular intelligence, but not so much ahead of it as to be out of touch with its latent possibilities.

Spectators far outnumbered demonstrators in the park that Sunday, and never had they found the flow of eloquence so trite. They drifted from platform to platform. For anything fresh they heard they might as well have been at Matins or Evensong. The Popular Socialist platform had as usual contrived to get itself within irritation length of the main Communist gathering. That was now its established place. It was within irritation length, but it has long since ceased to irritate. Its normal function in the past had been to provoke violence and be rescued by the police in a scrimmage which justified the arrest of what the authorities, for the obscurest reasons, regarded as undesirable characters. But now that worked no more.

The orthodox Communist bunch was not taking much notice of the little band of purple shirts that afternoon. From 1937 onward an almost genteel discretion had permeated the Communists. They had found long since that indignation and violence were far less effective against Lord Horatio's once-dreaded following than ridicule. They would kill his trained speakers by listening to them in a pseudo-awestricken silence – in which they stumbled and fell – or they would disconcert them by sudden baffling interruptions. But this afternoon, because of the general vague dissatisfaction, even the sport of ragging the Popular Socialists was providing a poor draw.

Three or four dingy young Reds were attempting to get capital out of the absence of Lord Horatio at Liverpool.

"Where's Horry today? Taking a day off with his girl? Hi Jeams! Long Jeams there! Where's his Ludship?..."

Rud contemplated the scene.

"Well?" said Rogers.

"All our men are here?"

"Yes. And *now?*"

"We go on to the platform. Which way up?"

"Those trained speakers of Horry's are no good at all," said Irwell, leading the way round the crowd. "Sheer waste of money. Listen to that fool – a chick of three days old could heckle him down."

"I'll speak," said Rud.

"This way," said Bodisham

A tall young man wearing one of the prohibited purple shirts (But one costume does not make an indictable uniform.) seemed to recognise Rogers. He was acting as the day's usher of the ineffective Popular Socialist eloquence. Rud found himself hoisted to the platform by his henchmen. He elbowed his way toward the front of the platform.

"You're not going to speak?" said the tall man.

"I *am* going to speak."

"I've heard nothing about it from Hoggin."

"Change of plan at the last moment."

The tall young man turned to Rogers and asked in an audible aside: "Who *is* this fellow?"

"*He's* all right," said Rogers. "You hear him."

"But what are you going to say, Mister – ?"

"You listen," said Rogers.

"When?"

"Right now," said Rud. "Don't you bother me." And he pushed his way to the forefront of the platform and stood glaring. The audience had been having a routine time with the trained "Booners" and they hailed a new face as a pleasant variation of the afternoon's proceedings. "Ullo Beethoven!" said a redfaced, frizzy-haired little man, giving a name that was not unhelpful to Rud on later occasion. "Ullo Bottle-imp! The Things old Bohun catches!"

Rud faced the interrupter with an outstretched hand. "Here *Gollywog*," he said, "listen to me."

"Gollywog" fitted. Shouting and pushing subsided. This might be worth listening to.

"Listen to me, brother Gollywog," said Rud intensely. "And thank God for those *very* big ears he's given you... No! Don't start talking till you've heard what I'm going to say to you. For if there's a platform worth listening to, today here, it's this platform I'm on. You don't know what this Popular Socialism means. You never have known. You're going to know now."

"We know right enough," said the Gollywog. "Anti-Red and all that balderdash! We've heard it a hundred times from your trained purple parrots."

"You've heard nothing. You've just bawled as you're bawling now. Listen, I tell you."

"Listen to him," said a bystander, and an expert in anti-Bohun tactics said, "Freeze him out."

But there was no freezing out for Rud. "Good!" he said. "Now don't make mistakes about me, and don't make mistakes about what's on the platform this afternoon. You thing I'm one of Lord Horry's paid men. I'm not. You think I'm some sort of Anti –. I'd rather be dead."

"Horry said – " began the Gollywog.

"I don't care a rap what Horry said. When Horry talks to you, you answer Horry. But when I talk to you, you listen to me."

"But how about – "

Rud raise his voice. "Listen!" he shouted.

"Look around and listen. Here's a score of platforms and scores of speakers and what they talking? *Anti!* They want to stop somebody doing something, but what they want to *do* themselves, Heaven only knows. They don't know. Turn out somebody from government, from direction, from ownership, and put them in, and they'll show you. Open your mouth and shut your eyes. That's the dream of all these gentry who are shouting themselves hoarse on these platforms. They want to set you *against* something. They're *against* something. Up against something. But what they're *for* – ah! Wait and see. They want you to clean up the men in possession, and then *they* will be the men in possession. And a hell of a lot of difference that will make to *you!* Like your blessed old Labour Party which started out for Socialism in Our Time and ended in the House of lords. You've had that game played on you often enough. Do you want it played again?'

"Well, wot's yer difference? You and your Lord 'Orry!"

"Who's talking of Bohun here?" said Rud.

"Well! What *are* you?'

"The common-sense of politics; that's what we are!"

"And what's that?"

"Unity! Not twenty platforms all shouting away through the afternoon to advertise twenty different gangs of political pushers and Welshers, but One Common Platform to ask for the things that every man needs. In spite of that noisy buzzer overhead. Augh! Shut *up* – up there! We want one great popular movement for social justice wherever the English language is spoken. That's what Popular Socialism means. Certain things are as plain as a pikestaff."

"But Lordorry – "

"Oh *damn* Lord Horry!" said Rud.

"Here!" said the tall man. "You can't say that!"

"Shut up," said Rogers with his beefy shoulder against the chest of the tall man. "Let our man speak!"

"But this is his Lordship's platform. Confound it, man!"

"Does it look like that to you? Go on, Rud, never mind *this*."

"But, boys!" said the tall man, appealing to his stalwarts. He made a move towards Rud, but he found Rogers, Steenhold, Bodisham, Figgis and Redwood intervening. Swift and venomous undertones passed. "Let the man speak!" said the crowd. "Leave him alone Jeams. *Damn* Lord Horry! Right you are. Go on, Mister. What next?"

"Well, I get sick of all this raking-up of what Mr Gladstone said fifty years ago, or what Lord Horatio said last spring. Damn this allusive style, anyhow. Do let us talk for once, about what *all* of us want and all of us want said *now*. NOW!"

"You hear?" said Rogers, still leaning slightly against the tall man.

"Don't you know us?" said Irwell. "You've seen *us* times enough. Can't you trust your own men?"

"But this new chap!"

"Let him go on," said Steenhold at the tall man's ear. It seemed the easiest thing to do. The crowd about the platform was taking notice and growing. "Let him speak," they shouted. "The little chap with the big face!"

"He's got to talk our stuff, mind you," said the tall man, yielding. "*I'm* in charge here."

"Obviously," said Rogers, still fending him off. "Go ahead, Rud."

And Rud went ahead.

"We've been christened Popular Socialists, and I suppose every movement must wear a label, but if I'd been in at the christening, boys, I should have said the Party of the Common Man. The Party of the Common Man, here in England, away in America, in Africa, Australia, China and all over the earth."

"But Horry is a nationalist out and out!'

Rud did not even answer that comment. He waved it away as if it was a fly.

"The party of the Common Man – everywhere. The Plain Needs of Common-sense! First he wants peace and security, and what stands in the way of that? All these damned localised governments that divide us up and set us fighting – set us fighting against our own brothers. Think of it – English guns being lent to the Old Gang in America to shoot English-speaking strikers! We want *one* government everywhere, not all these governments, one common-sense government for our common needs."

"But that's Internationalism! That's Communism!"

"Augh! Never mind those words!" said Rud. "Do we want one law in the world or many, you crowd of cannon-fodder, you bombees of tomorrow? Isn't it plain as a pikestaff that one government means peace, and many war? Well, let's *get* that one government. It's these old national governments out of the past that stand in the way and won't let go. Do we want them? Not a bit. But they want themselves! That's one thing we want. *One* government keeping the peace everywhere.

"And next we want Plenty. Everyone who knows says we can have Plenty today for everyone. All the men of science say that. Why don't we *have* it? Because a few people won't let us get at the earth and get at the work. They've appropriated it, they squat in on it just as they squat in on Power, and they have to be expropriated – expropriated by the sheer common-sense of everyone. They string a net of private property about our futile paralysed world, and they trick us with this false money that they keep on changing and increasing and diminishing so that you don't know from day to day what a shilling is worth to you. They pretend they can't help it. Do you believe that? Do you believe they can't help the boat rocking? Do you believe they can't help supplies being locked up? Do you think they don't know what they're doing? They want Power over us. And do you think *you* don't know that? In your bones you do. They'd rather see the world wrecked than give up their Power game. And we are the pawns!

"It doesn't take ten years of study, you don't need to go to the University, to find out that this is a damned good world gone wrong. Gone wrong, because it is being monkeyed with by people too greedy and mean and wrong-hearted altogether to do the right thing by our common world. They've grabbed it and they won't let go. They might lose their importance; they might lose their pull. Everywhere it's the same. Beware of the men you make your masters. Beware of the men you trust.

"We've only got to be clearheaded to sing the same song and play the same game all over the world, we common men, We don't want Power monkeyed with, we don't want Work and Goods monkeyed with, and, above all, we don't want Money monkeyed with. That's the elements of politics everywhere. When these things go wrong, we go wrong. That's how people begin to feel it and see it in America. That's how we feel it here – when we look into our minds. That's what common people feel everywhere. That's what our brother whites – 'poor whites' they call them – in those towns in South Carolina are fighting for now. Fighting our battle. Why aren't we with them? We speak the same language; we share the same blood. Who had been keeping us apart from them for a hundred and fifty-odd years? Ruling classes. Politicians. Dear old flag and all that stuff!

"Our schoolbooks never tell us a word about the American common man; and his schoolbooks never tell him a word about us. They flutter flag between us to keep us apart. Split us up for a century and a half because of some fuss about taxing tea. And what are our wonderful Labour and Socialist and Communist leaders doing to change that? What are they doing to unite us English-speaking common men together and give us our plain desire? Are they doing anything more for us than the land barons and the factory barons and the money barons? Not a bit of it! These labour leaders of today mean to be lords tomorrow. They are just a fresh set of dishonest trustees. Look at these twenty-odd platforms here! Mark their needless contradictions! Their marvellous differences on minor issues. 'Manoeuvres!' 'Intrigue.' 'Personalities.' 'Monkeying.' 'Don't trust him, trust *me*!' All of them at it. Mark how we common men are distracted, how we are set hunting first after one red herring and then after another, for the want of simple, honest interpretation…"

And so on.

The tall young man listened in a state of great perplexity. He was determined to intervene and shut Rud up when it was necessary, but how was he to determine when it was necessary? This was queer stuff, but it was holding a gathering crowd. It was stealing more and more people from the communist accumulation. Perhaps "Simple, honest interpretation" meant Lord Horatio. Perhaps this stranger would come round to that presently. And always if the man went too far, afterwards it would be possible to say a few words, chairman fashion, and put things right again. If these unaccountably menacing fellows on each side of his had the sense to let him, that is.

Rud unfolded the Chiffan-Whitlow scheme of world salvation in broad outline as the two of them had hammered it out in their early discussions; its insistence on a common Anglo-American basis at any cost – at the cost of "every institution, crown, constitution or what-not, however old, however venerable, "that might stand in the way; its bold proposal to reorganise and control the whole financial apparatus of the world; its assurances of the hope in science of a universal plenty; its wide development of Huey Long's almost fanatic educationalism. "This is what we are for!' he bawled. "*Anti*-be damned! We are Pro-Pax-Mundi. We stand *for* mankind today and tell you mankind will stand for us tomorrow."

He became aware of a change in the situations, a lull to the left of him. The communist platform had gone out of business, and a little knot of their supporters were pushing their way towards him. He welcomed this intervention. He threw them phrases and sentences to provoke an argument.

"This is what Communism stands for?" he answered them, "Stealing *your* thunder? Nonsense! Your old Marx prophesied the Revolution, but he never saw an inch beyond it. He knew nothing of modern scientific production. He never distinguished between financial and material property. He knew nothing about money, not a thing. Why don't you put him back in Highgate Cemetery and forget about him?…Well, put a great, lying, flattering monument over him if you must, and *then* forget about him."

The ascendancy of the platform was an immense advantage to Rud. They had made a mistake in coming down from their own platform to get near him. They had to shout from below at him. He caught up what they had to say at the point when it gave him the most effective reply. He delivered every sentence as though he scored a point against them.

The two officials and the little American-born countess they had with them in the observation plane, noted the increasing accumulation of hearers about the Popular Socialist nucleus, but they heard nothing of the immense subversiveness of Rud's restatement of Popular Socialist aims. A gentle infiltration of the growing assemblage by the forces of law and order was set going. The observers overhead heard nothing of the steady attack upon the American policy of the government, linked with a systematic depreciation of Lord Horatio, upon which Rud was launched.

"Leaders are nothing," said Rud, "Parties are nothing. Governments are nothing. Look at the thing with plain common-sense. Nothing matters but the common man."

"But – !" spluttered the tall young man. "Steady on!" and "*Wait* a moment."

"Shut it," said Rogers.

"We Popular Socialists stand for plain common-sense, put in order and kept clear," said Rud. "Just as Science does. We stand for that and nothing else. We want no dogmas and we want no dictators and leaders... No. We here are the party of the common man – common one and all. Our only theory is to keep our eyes open – *your* eyes open. And to hell with all this strategy and party discipline and leadership and the climbers and the stand-patters who obstruct and divide us." (Futile cry of "But how about Horry?") "What I am telling you is simply and plainly what *you* think. It's *your* natural stuff. I'm no leader setting myself up here to know better than anyone, what ought to be done and what had to be done to bring it about. I don't ask you to open your mouths and shut your eyes and see what I will give you. I'm not leader

159

number six hundred and fifty-nine, to start a new divergence.
I'm just a common man who knows how to put it, and nothing
more, I'm your megaphone. That's the Popular Socialist way...

"Yes, that's democracy. That's what you Communists have
forgotten. You tied yourselves up in a rigid organisation. You put
on Stalin and Stalinism like a gag and a straightjacket." (Uproar.)

"Lord Horry? Popular Socialism made him, I tell you, and
Popular Socialism can break him. He's our figurehead today –
but only in the service of common-sense. As long as he cares to
serve common-sense. And work hard for *us*. Our reality is in you
all, all of you. All of *us*. He'll be the first to admit it. Fall in with
us. Simplify! Unite! Common-sense! Now do you get me? Now
do you understand where we are?"

He paused for his applause and he got it. The tall young man
appeared to be saying something, but nobody heard what he had
to say.

Rud had fired his shot. He stood without an idea in the world
about the next step to take. Left to himself he would probably
have got down from the platform and gone home.

"We can march back on this," said Bodisham suddenly at his
elbow.

"March back?"

"To headquarters. While we're on the crest."

"But where – ?"

"To headquarters!" cried Steenhold, gleefully grasping the
idea. "Oh, great!"

"Headquarters!" said Dreed. "Of *course!*"

"Your meeting's a thundering success," said Irwell to the tall
young man. "Now's the time for the triumphant exit... No. they
don't want to hear you."

Rud had got it in an instant. He was already gesticulating to the crowd. He had made Bodisham's inspiration his own. Mastery returned to him. Of course! Now was the moment to strike. He shouted:

"Now that I've explained things to you, perhaps you'll fall in with us. March with us to the Purple House! We don't mind a red banner or two. Facts, not flags, is our motto. Put down your names with us. Never mind your party or your party wire-pullers. Never mind your leaders! Or ours for that matter. Come and gibe a cheer for the common-sense man, the good old common man, who's the real backbone of all of us. (Let's get a move on, Bodisham.)"

The re-formation of the homeward march was a thing of routine. Rud saw two manifest newspaper men making notes. "The shorthand reporter?" he said to Chiffan.

"OK," said Chiffan. "I looked after that."

"Where's the band? Where's the other banners?" said Bodisham, taking complete control of the tall young man.

"There's one banner about the Jews," said Rud in a quick undertone over his shoulder. "Furl that. We don't want that stuff today – anyhow. Furl *all* the banners. We'll alter those rotten inscriptions later."

"Hustle round, boys," said the tall young man to his posse of stalwarts. "Keep together," said Rogers, close behind him...

And how was the official observer in the air above to know that the Popular Socialist procession that was reforming itself and making a departure so much more spirited and substantial than its arrival, was really a captured procession? All that he remarked was that it seemed to be exercising a suctorial influence on the accumulating crowd round about it. It seemed to be taking three-quarters of the communist crowd with it. That was odd. There might be some sort of trouble presently. So the radio got to work and the police drifted towards the purple banners, to see that law and order kept pace with the swelling crowd.

Rud was borne along with his particular adherents in the midst of the column. He carried himself now in a grave and preoccupied manner. At moments he felt like a mighty commander with everything obedient to his hand; at moments he felt like a cork in a stream. But his prevailing feeling was confidence and exaltation. Everything was going easily. There had been no fighting. The crowd was driving along in a state of indeterminate appreciation. Someone had started shouts of "Common-sense Party. Not too soon." And "Common-sense at last." One voice even cried "Good old Horry," and another tried the old slogan: "*We* want Bohun," But no one took that up. The Popular Socialist band, of two kettledrums and half a dozen fifes, sustained the Popular Socialist marching tune:

> "One, two; one, two, three,
>   Horry Bohun is the man for me."

But a number of men and lads and one or two young women were pressing in on the central group to get a nearer view of Rud. "What's *your* name, mate? What's his name, Mister?"

"Rud," said Rogers.

"*Rud what?*"

"Just Rud."

"Rud. Rud – His name's Just Rud."

Presently they were repeating:

"One, two; one, two, three,
 Just Rud is the man for me."

Rud exchanged rapid opinions with Steenhold and Chiffan. "Nothing more doing today," he said, "A few words from the window?"

"And then take possession," said Bodisham.

"If the crowds hang about?"

"It's going to rain," said Chiffan. "And the police will keep them moving. All that about enrolling them will evaporate quietly. You'll see. The pubs open at seven and the cinemas will be opening now."

"One, two; one, two, three,
 Just Rud is the man for me."

3

Rud went to one of the three drawing-room windows, opened it wide, and stood out on the little pseudo-balcony. His sense of fitness required a few words from a balcony; it was his conception of the part. The band had gone round to the garage behind headquarters, and the few policemen were having no trouble in keeping the crowd moving. The idea of enrolling a great crowd of adherents had evaporated insensibly, even as Chiffan had said. There was a cessation of movement at Rud's appearance, the police stood still for a moment and someone cried "Speech!" Rud held up a reassuring hand to the Inspector.

"Nothing more doing tonight Thank you for joining us, and thank you for giving us a hearing. If I may suggest something; Three cheers for Unity. And three cheers for the Common Man everywhere, and may God help him to his own... Thank you. That's all."

He moved back from the window.

"Not a cheer for yourself?" said Irwell. "you can't be modest as a leader. You had your chance then. Shall *I* tell 'em?'

Rud half-turned towards him and said something Chiffan was never to forget.

"I *am* the common man,' said Rud.

4

Rud turned about and surveyed the room before him...

The Purple House, it should be explained, consisted at that time of a couple of big stucco houses with porticos, in that region of large, white, later-Georgian mansions between Kensington and Paddington. Bohun had wanted to paint it an imperial purple, but the police and the ground landlord had opposed this idea, and so it had the normal dingy pallor of its neighbours, relieved only by purple front doors, now greatly faded, and with tarnished gilt knockers, purple painted ironwork and black blinds. Behind these two houses were garages, one mysteriously locked up, and the other devoted to a store of banners and the band's stuff, with a bagatelle table, table-tennis, a cask of beer and other reliefs to the tedium of the adherents "on duty."

One house, number seventeen, was reserved for his lordship, and its door yielded only to his latch-key, but an internal communication had been made with number sixteen, by an opening between the halls. Number sixteen was the common entrance and there was a "guard room" on the ground floor in which three or four bored young louts were usually "on duty" – rather vaguely conceived. The most definite obligation was a smart salute for the Boss or Commander Hoggin or Major Smike.

The first floor was a common assembly room reaching from front to back of the house, capacious and furnished only with plain chairs and a few occasional tables. Along one side of the back portion was a trestle-board bearing a tea-urn, jugs of lemonade and cakes.

Most of the stalwarts had produced virile pipes and lusty great pouches. They were standing about in knots and talking uneasily. Much of the afternoon's happenings had been incomprehensible to them. In a way it had seemed "all right" and in some ways it had seemed "odd." They were puzzled about the apparition of Rud, they wanted to know about him. Was he going to be the new favourite?

The tall young man "on control" was one of Lord Horatio's later discoveries. It was among his Lordship's little weaknesses to turn against his men who began to "know too much" and to introduce inexperience and incapacity as "new blood." So that all his officials were insecure of their positions and there was a long and growing list of men he had turned down, ready to turn up again. Bodisham had been establishing touch with these scattered rejects for some time. He was forming them into what he called his "reserve." And the Purple House itself was smouldering with uncertainties, resentments and suppressions from roof to cellar.

The tall young man was slowly developing a sense of grievance, as the exhilaration of an unusually effective meeting passed off.

"But what's your trouble?" asked Rogers.

"What I complain of is the want of system – of orders. I ought to have OK'd him before he said a single word. And Hoggin ought to have OK'd him."

"Well, didn't he speak well? Didn't he *get* them?"

"But did Lord Horatio send him?"

Bodisham hesitated and then had an inspiration. He glanced at Rud as if to make sure he was not being overheard, and then he leant forward to the tall young man and spoke in a confidential undertone. "*I'm not sure*," he said, "I don't know – exactly – myself – what relationship there is between them.'

The tall young man contemplated Rud. "You mean?"

"I don't know enough to mean anything precisely."

"But you feel – ?'

Bodisham reflected. He said nothing but he nodded repeatedly in a confidential and deeply significant manner.

"But didn't you come with him?"

"Steenhold brought him. And Steenhold's been in the organisation, off and on, for years."

"I see. All the same I think I was let down about that fellow. On that platform I was made to look – well – a bit of a fool. I didn't know – *what*. I was taken by surprise. I might have given him a clip on the jaw and spun him off the platform."

"You *might*," agreed Rogers, "But you have too much sense. The Boss knew that."

"Yes. What I can report to Lord Horatio I don't know. It's hard to phrase it. I don't want to be hard on one of his friends."

"Better to understate than overstate," counselled Bodisham. "You might claim you discovered him."

The tall young man seemed to be recovering his self-confidence. "In some ways anyhow, that chap is an acquisition, you know. He can spout…"

Rud surveyed the groups in the room for a while, as if he consented to their existence, but meant to keep his eye on them. Then, with his hands behind his back in the manner of a pensive Napoleon and saying nothing to anyone, he left Irwell and Chiffan at the window, walked past them all and upstairs to the room of his two interviews with Lord Horatio.

It was, as he expected, empty. He walked round the great ornamental unbusinesslike desk, seated himself in the much too ample chair of his lordship, took up the large paper-knife and tapped thoughtfully with it as he meditated. This time he remembered most of his speech. He thought it was an extremely good speech for the occasion.

"I *am* the common man," he repeated. It had leapt to his mind out of nothingness. It could be made a cardinal slogan.

Another part of his mind was busy upon quite a different line. He was wondering whether he would keep on Mrs Crumb.

If she could see him now! She'd topple over backwards.

He was still smiling quietly at that thought when the door opened and Chiffan and Bodisham came in.

"Well," said Bodisham. "Here you are in the lion's den."

"For a time," said Rud. "Won't you sit down? There's a chair behind that table where his stenographer sits, and if you shove that pile of pamphlets off the table – they're no beastly good anyhow – *The Heart and Soul of a Great Leader* – Lord! Shove' em off and there'll be the table to sit on too. So's he can find them. Don't *lift* them off. Let' em drop in a heap there. The next move's with him."

"I suppose he's booming and gargling that old speech of his about now," said Bodisham. "Or maybe a little later. He'll get his first idea of what has happened here tomorrow when he opens the morning paper."

. "And then the great purple car will turn its mighty lanterns Londonward,' said Chiffan. "We're well started. There's no going back. I suppose that tall fellow, what's his name – ?"

"Frobisher."

"Won't have telephoned?"

"That's all right," said Bodisham. "He wouldn't know what to telephone, but anyhow Rogers and Steenhold are in charge of him. He's amenable. He has a grievance. He's half with us in a perplexed way already. They're all stale here. Things have got into a kind of routine through sheer lack of inventiveness. Here we are and here in effect we have to stick. There's no way on, but onward – as you said last week. We can do practically what we like here – until Horry comes back. Then the fat will be in the fire. Then the real flare-up will begin. Presently when most of the boys have gone home and there's nobody downstairs but Longshanks and the guards on duty, you and I will look the number seventeen over. It had its points of interest. It's queer –

"In fact," said Bodisham, after a short interval, "It's *very* queer…"

And then: "*Very.*"

He seemed to be thinking very hard about Rud. He seemed to have some sort of uncertainty about Rud.

"There are some locked doors," said Bodisham. "I happen – . As a matter of fact I was put in control here for a time last

September and I have duplicate keys. I had them made. I always had my doubts of Horry. About that underhung jaw of his and those eyes too close together. I made some discoveries, and then I waxed the key. I don't think you quite realise yet what he is. You will see. You think he's an Ass. He's an Ass all right, but he's something more than that... In some ways he's a dangerous Ass... We've got to be prepared. We've got to know the animal we hunt or we may have some nasty surprises. I want you to see.'

5

Rud saw.

The arcana of the basement and cellars of number seventeen and the flavour of the locked up garage behind altered the whole complexion of the day for Rud. He had been living triumphantly in a storm of rhetoric all day, living gloriously by the spoken word. "I am the common Man." He had been carried by the torrent of his own speech into the very seat of the boss. In the absence of the boss. Now here was something more fundamental than rhetoric.

Bodisham had closed and relocked the double doors behind them. The second one was covered with green baize for the evident purpose of making it soundproof. The main cellar was a sort of arsenal, with a newly made bolthole and dug-out below it. There were only about a dozen rifles in the arms collection, but there were three or four guns with short barrels, a considerable miscellany of pistols, life-preservers, assorted ammunition, a trunk of knuckledusters, truncheons, and a number of other murderous looking implements whose use was not immediately apparent.

"*Golly*" said Chiffan. "It's a bit out of a gangster film. It's a schoolboy's dream. At least – It would have been a dream twenty-five years ago. But *now* – Of course, *weapons!*

"Weapons. Human beings have always loved weapons. Hardly a man alive who does not love to caress a good rifle…"

He became exceedingly thoughtful for a space.

"This isn't all," said Bodisham. "There's more yet."

He unlocked a door at the back of the cellar and led the way along a paved passage to a group of ill-lit and cramped apartments, three on either side. They had heavy doors with bolts and locks on the outer face, and each, had a small, square peephole in the upper panel.

"They look like prison cells," said Rud.

"They *are* prison cells," said Boldisham.

"But – Illegal?'

"Party discipline. Kidnapping. How should I know?"

"He's never used them?"

"We don't know. One's rather dirty and has – you know – the prison smell.

"It reminds one a little of the sort of thing they had under the châteaux of the Loire,' said Bodisham. "Or in High Germany. Picturesque, romantic old High Germanee."

"The Boss must be crazy."

"Crazy!" said Chiffan. "But *is* he? NO! It's the new style in politics. He's merely been studying continental models. This sort of thing is current political reality in a dozen countries today Dilettantism – no! Grim reality. It's spreading. Why shouldn't it spread here? *He's* just been doing his best to keep up with the times. Why, in Belgium, for example, there must be dozens and dozens of little caches like this now. And in Czechoslovakia. Not to speak of France and Germany."

"I don't believe," said Rud.

"I'm not telling you things," said Bodisham. "I'm *showing* you things.'

"Kidnapping. Secret arrests," said Chiffan. "There's enough here to show you what the Boss had been dreaming about. Dreaming, do I say? Contemplating. Continental methods. He's just a sample. It's all coming back. It never really left off. The little ways of man with man. I suppose they kept stuff like this in the Tower. The Bourbons did it. *Lettres de cachet.* Napoleon kidnapped and murdered people. The Brown House. The Lipari islands. Quiet corners of the Ogpu life. Under the British raj, in some of the prince's palaces. Under any dispensation. Here it is – right under our noses."

"But to find this in England!" said Rud.

"Why not in England?" asked Chiffan.

"Or America," said Bodisham. "Much more probable in America."

"In a great free country like America!" protested Rud.

"Running the world by votes and resolutions and processions and demonstrations is all very well when things are easy and the other side won't fight," said Chiffan. "But there's always been jails and there's always been cellars and drains under the social fabric, and when houses are pulled down or tumble down, the cellars come up to the surface and the drains stink... Esoteric politics, Rud. You've got to face it, my boy."

6

The BMGs decided to hold a council of war in Steenhold's upper flat. The Purple House was arranged for autocracy and not for conferences. There was no accommodation for camping or sleeping in the place, but Rogers, Dreed and Redwood remained to sit up all night and keep an eye on Frobisher. The rest were to go home or sleep at Steenhold's flat. Roll-call was to be at number sixteen in the morning before nine.

At Camborne Square they sat late and discussed the situation from every point of view. Could they consider they had captured or were going to capture the Purple House? What was the constitution of the Popular Socialist Party?

"What is our status there?" said Irwell. "Are we technically burglars? Or trespassers?"

"We are the Popular Socialist Party, I take it – at home," said Rud. "The Purple House isn't a private house. It's Headquarters.'

"But it's Bohun's house.'

"He's a trustee – at most he's a trustee. He must have divested himself in a sort of way."

"I doubt if it will be matter for litigation," said Bodisham.

"We shall have to fight for that house, whatever the legal position may be," said Chiffan. "And we'd better get ready for that. Knives and kicking and that sort of thing. You may bet on that. Pity we haven't Rogers here. He's our Big Fist, our Organiser of Violence."

"I agree with you," said Bodisham. "I haven't the slightest doubt there will have to be some rough work before we get hold of the Purple House. If we do get hold of it. Horry may not

172

make much show in the way of brains, but you can bet he will show fight – and a pretty nasty sort of fight..."

Presently Rud found his mind wandering from the finer points of strategy.

"None of the Party have ever disappeared?" he asked suddenly.

"Not that I ever heard of," said Rogers.

"You've never heard anything, Colin?"

"Never heard a thing," said Dreed. "all this secret prison business is as new to me it is to you."

"Nor you, Irwell?"

"Nothing."

(Intimidation. Rough handling?... Torture? In London. In 1941! What sort of game were we playing?)

They were looking at him.

"It's just a crazy schoolboy's imagination," said Rud. "I'm – curious. Go on with what you were saying. We are going to demand a general meeting of the Party – and force a sort of want of confidence motion. Good."

"I have some ideas about that meeting," said Steenhold. "There was an Enquiry in Washington – but never mind that now. But I have an idea. A *lovely* idea."

7

Rud slept but little that night. He got out of bed. He got back into bed. He got out again. He went to the window and stared at a blank wall opposite. He tried to assemble the situation in his mind. He murmured and then recited fragments of his speech so far as he could recall it. He was trying not to think of something

— a silly impossible idea, but at the same time very ugly and disagreeable. Kidnapping was in it and thumbscrews, and a vast large freckled face with the eyes too close together, that continually approached, full of menace, full of cruel deliberation. He would not think of it. He would not. If he had to keep repeating his speech all night...

His insomnia exasperated him more and more. Never had the contrast between his immense ambitions and his flimsy body, his lurid imagination and his unbalanced nerves, distressed him so acutely. He wanted to sleep and there was no sleep; no sleep, no repose, no position in which he could keep still. And always these foolish imaginations kept creeping nearer to him and nearer. They wouldn't keep away. He was awake and yet he was dreaming.

He cursed. For a moment he got quite out of hand. He made a feeble slog at nothing with his fist. "No, you *don't*," he shouted. "No, you *don't*. Don't come another step nearer me!" His sudden movement upset a row of books on his chest of drawers and the end one fell with a resounding smack on the floor. He was moved to fling all the other books after it. He realised the need for self-control in time.

He addressed himself as though he was a public meeting. "Get to sleep," he said. "You've things to do tomorrow. Tremendous things! Tomorrow is *the* day. You've *got* to sleep. Got to sleep. Hold yourself together, man. You've got to go through with it now. Hold yourself together. Have you *got* it, Rud my boy? Hold yourself together.

Rap. Rap. Rap on the wall.

A drowsy, angry voice was calling to him through the thin partition. "Hold yourself together, man. Yes, and shut up. Go to sleep, yes, or by God! I'll come another step nearer you and no mistake. I'll come and I'll bloody well kill you."

It was astonishing, but there was a sort of relief in hearing this thick, wholesomely angry, human voice.

"Talking in my sleep," called Rud, after a moment's reflection. "Nightmare." (No good ending a political career prematurely in a fight with an unknown fellow-lodger.)

"Rot! Shut *up!*"

"Good night," said Rud, sitting on his bed.

"Goo' ni', you howling monkey, and don't let me hear you again. See?"

Silence.

The unknown fellow-lodger was presently audible as a formidable snore. Rud sat quite still, thinking and gnawing his knuckles.

He forgot the snore for a moment. His hand gripped upon imaginary weapons of defence.

"Don't think of it," he whispered very low. It was nothing. But he had better sit up. If he went to sleep he'd certainly have a real nightmare and shout again. There ought to be some sort of drug to tranquillise a brain too fatigued to quiet down of its own accord. Perhaps if he jotted down a few notes...

"There ought to be a doctor in the Party," thought Rud. "Someone to stand by me. I wish we had some chap... Carstall for example."

CHAPTER THREE

Rud Becomes a Public Character

L ord Horatio too had not slept well that night, although he had occupied Lady Garbees' pet visitors' bedroom. He was in a state of unusual discontent with himself. He was asking himself whether he had not missed his way in life altogether.

Bonina (Lady Garbees) had almost said as much. "I *hated* this evening. Never have I felt before how uncongenial this English atmosphere can be to all we are and all *we* care for. On that platform, standing up before that dismal crowd of C 3 clerks and errand boys, I pitied myself. You may be English through and through, but all the same, you are alien here. You would be alien in any of these dismal democratic countries. You are – *arbitrary,* my dear. You are like one of those great Florentine princes. You are a born grandee. I don't say that to flatter you. I don't flatter you. You know it's the truth as well as I do."

"Ye-e-s," he said, wanting more of it. "For some time I have been feeling – out of touch."

"We American aristocrats feel the same thing." (She was American born.) "It is the mean, puritanical, *English* tradition. Always – politics without a shred of dignity. Over there in spite

177

of everything – it clings to us still. New England has always been just England and a little more so, but we down in the south went back to the sun and to power over fellow-creatures. In England political life always *has* been *squalid*. How Shakespeare felt that! *How* his contempt breaks out against the many-headed monster and its 'stinking greasy caps!' 'Musty superfluity.' That was his name for democracy. I was reading *Coriolanus* yesterday. Shakespeare would have been with you up to the hilt, the dagger's hilt...

"English people are naturally *common* in grain... Lucy and I when we went to Biskra – A sort of splendour about the Arabs. Nature's noblemen. You could meet the hall porter on equal terms. This English temperament! It is like the mild, mild, old and mild climate. Never really hot, never really cold. Sunshine like genteel compliments and rain like sentimental tears. It's all one with the soft, mawkish scenery. Trimmed trees; polite fields; snug little cottages, hawthorns and primroses. Snug's the word. No mountains, no snows, no stupendous gorges, no *guts* in it, Horry, no *guts!*"

Bonina's purpose may have been to console him for the particular flatness of the great Birthday Meeting in the smaller Saltbag Hall, but her words carried further than that. It was breaking in upon his proud, reluctant intelligence that for – how long was it now? – fifteen years he had been wasting his great gifts and all the potentialities of his vitality upon a community incapable of appreciation, a facetious population, a population capable of nothing but an oafish stare or a derisive grin, too stupid even to bow before wrath and scorn. All that could be done had been done to make these dull mechanic souls walk with a prouder step behind a natural leader. He had sold them purple

178

shirts at 40 per cent below cost. He had drilled them, had them lectured to, sought speakers who could be trained to inspire them. He had been to Germany, he had been to Italy, again and again, to study leadership, to mark the methods of evoking the generous youth and strength and imagination of those nobler peoples. You can make ordinary Germans and Italians out of the streets crow like cocks, strut like peacocks and salute like gladiators about to die. "Serried ranks" are where they are most at home. But these English! They love to be out of step. At some expense he had hired clever literary fellows to write him a song book, and clever musical fellows to adapt notoriously successful tunes to the purposes of the movement. Think of the gusto with which a German crowd would have let out that Birthday Hymn:

> "England awake, salute the Happy Morn
> On which our Movement and our Boss were born."

You would have expected that to stir these urban clowns and open their eyes to what they might be. And then again:

> "Onward Bohun's soldiers, marching as to War,
> With the Jews and Bolsheviks scampering before."

It was a trumpet-call! But for all the result it got it might have been a bray.

He had given those boys a gymnasium, he had given them a recreation room, he had sold them balls, badges, rackets, tents, camping outfits, knuckledusters and sheath-knives at half cost or less...

And they could not even keep in tune! You might think they were ashamed of the song.

He had made his speech, his usual speech, to a scanty audience, too thick-headed to realise that now he was no longer making that speech with his former pleading, winning conviction, but in a spirit of contemptuous irony.

The subtle change in his intonation had been completely lost upon them...

After he had left Bonina in the small hours he had slept for a time and then grown wakeful again. His mind passed through a series of alternations between uneasy dreaming and dreamy wakefulness, in which the one continuing idea was his complete failure to grip the popular imagination or realise himself in these political activities upon which he had launched himself so hopefully and so rashly.

It had been going on for fifteen years. Fifteen years of leadership – with practically nobody falling in behind. His friends laughed at him. A lot of young fools in the West End were making a joke of the Popular Socialist salute. They did it to him in fashionable restaurants where politics should have a rest; they did it at race meetings in enclosures and places where he did not want it done, where he was ready to waive it and be just a gentleman among gentlemen. Things had come to that. A joke. And this was his forty-fifth birthday.

He was bored. He had to admit to himself that he was bored by the whole Popular Socialist movement. Bonina had been very near the truth of the business in their long and penetrating talk, very near indeed. That woman had fire in her imagination. She had a way of illuminating reality with strangely coloured lights. She had cruelty in her nature and she was not ashamed. She liked things to hurt. She wanted to hurt and be hurt. She bit. She had left her mark. She was all for lovers biting – hard. She wanted an intensity in life that ordinary everyday living did not give.

How wise she was! Everyone had queer impulses, she insisted, but the common sort, the "Tag," as Coriolanus put it, suppressed them. The essence of aristocracy was the ruthless refusal to suppress oneself. How had she put it? She wanted to *wring* life. That put exactly what he had always wanted to do. Once or twice he had wrung life a bit; when they expelled him from Eton and during his cadet days, when the chaps chased and hazed him for tying up young Darlington. After that he had been almost criminally subservient to the mild appearances of an essentially middle-class society. He had sinned against his own rich nature. Could there be anything better in the whole of being than having one's grip on a weakly, resisting, overpowered, living creature, and doing one's will, exhausting the grossest fantasy, upon that panting life? All the noble carnivores exist for that, and are they not the lords of creation?

He found himself wide awake in a sadistic reverie. He had a pleasing idea of going back to Bonina and strangling her...

One never knew. She might object and make a row and bring in the servants. She was capable of the greatest inconsistency. Her talk was wilder than her spirit. Perhaps she has just been posing at him. After all – she *was* American.

He dozed and then woke into the problem of getting away from Popular Socialism. In any other country in the world it would have given him ample scope for terrorism, physical intimidation, lurid events. As it was, except for one little bit of discipline – And there even he had been weak. He had feared blackmail.

181

"Ruthlessness," he muttered. "Strange lusts... Quivering flesh...The Tiger is an aristocrat... Nietzsche... Strength... Bleating multitude... Bleating *fools*... All of them out of tune."

He sank down again into oblivion.

2

He slept until nine in the morning and then touched the bell for the valet, who brought him tea and the newspapers, whisked away his purple dinner-jacket and black velvet knee-breeches and departed.

The great carnivore stretched and yawned and stretched again.

New days have a way of beginning afresh, with a clean page, so to speak. He had forgotten most of his nocturnal imaginations and he opened the first paper according to habit to see what space had been given to his Birthday Festival. He was struck at once by the headline: "Popular Socialism still a Living Force. Remarkable Speech."

What had he said?

"But – ?" he murmured.

And then in a terrible voice: "My God! What's this?"

The valet answered his furious bell-ringing. He found Lord Horatio sitting up in his black-and-purple-edged pyjamas on the bedside. Even the valet appreciated a sort of frightful handsomeness about him. He was in what valets call "a great state." "Get, every morning paper you can," he said. "Tell my chauffeur to be at the door by half-past nine. Where are my clothes? Have you run my bath? I have to act and act at once."

"Very good, sir," said the valet.

182

A note was scribbled to Bonina. "These accursed politics! How wise you are! But this time I have a chance to hit someone and hit him hard. You were *splendid*. Glorious memories."

The great purple car stormed Londonward. Had people by the roadside cared to look, they might have seen Lord Horatio sitting still and terrible inside, hatless, arms folded, head slightly bent forward, occasionally tapping his teeth in earnest thought, sometimes smiling darkly. But fewer cared to look than Lord Horatio imagined. They were wrapped up in their own mean little affairs.

There had been sufficient in the papers for him to realise the nature of Rud's coup. He despised Rud immeasurably, he feared him about as much, and he hated him desirously. Rud, dressing irritably in his meagre little Bloomsbury bedroom, had completely reciprocal feelings. He despised Lord Hortio without stint, he quivered with fear at the thought of him, and he craved to defeat, overwhelm and humiliate him to the utmost. The two of them were coming together now at an average speed of forty-odd miles per hour.

3

From the moment when Lord Horatio pulled up outside the Purple House he realised that there was a change in the atmosphere of the place. There were guards in the guardroom of number sixteen and two in the doorway, but instead of saluting smartly, they stared at him in a besotted manner and saluted belatedly. He decided to go into number seventeen. As he fumbled with his latch-key, commander Hoggin came swiftly along the pavement and entered the house on his heels. "All sorts of things have happened," said Hoggin. "It's – it's a mutiny."

"Where's Smike?" asked the Boss.

"He's in number sixteen. He'll come if he can."

Lord Horatio led the way to a ground-floor parlour. "Tell me everything. I've seen the papers. How did that fellow get loose?"

"I couldn't prevent it. I – "

"How did it happen? Never mind 'I.' How did that little beast jump our platform? How did he get the press he did?"

"There's a gang. It's an organised mutiny, m'lord. Smike reported on that Camborne Square flat, didn't he? His business to do so. He's the Intelligence Officer, not me. That rich American fellow is in it, Steenhold, and Rogers, that big fellow, who runs Boy Scout boxing clubs in Pimlico and Whitechapel, and there's Bodisham – I never trusted Bodisham – I told you – and a lot of them. Some new men. Some men who've come back. Ci-devants. They're all over number sixteen, waiting for you."

"Have they been in here?"

"How could they? It's kept locked."

"Good. What about Frobisher?"

"Wavering about. I always said that chap was too tall to keep stiff. The way he let them hustle him on his own platform – "

"What did you do?"

"What *could* I do? I control speakers. I don't control the boys. And he was in command. *You* put him in command."

Bohun scowled at the faint note of grievance in Hoggin's tone. "Wait here for a moment," he said. "I shall go right in there and – handle them."

He went up to his bedroom. There he brushed his hair and stood for a time in front of a cheval glass, assembling his personality to the full. His reflection was satisfactory. He felt stimulated. He liked his tall, sinister presence rising to an occasion.

"Yes, my boy, I'll show you how to *handle* things," he said to an imaginary Rud, and with the habitual rectitude of a born commander of men, he went downstairs again, rejoined Hoggin and led the way into number sixteen. He walked through the door of communication and up to his study, past the first-floor room in which, as he was acutely aware, Rud, Bodisham and the others awaited him. "Get me Smike," he said to Hoggin.

He found Mrs Crumb standing over a young man who was picking up copies of *The Heart and Soul of a Great Leader* from a tumbled heap upon the floor and piling them back on the table. He vanished at a gesture.

"Well?" said Bohun. "Has anything happened?"

"I don't know what's happening downstairs, but – "

"Yes?"

"That dreadful little Whittlelow man suddenly came in just now – took no more notice of me than a dog – and" (her voice fell to an awestricken whisper) "*went and sat down in your chair*. Just sat down."

"Did you say anything to him?"

"I said you might not be pleased to see him there. I said it quietly. Like that. I said, 'Lord Horatio – ' "

"And what did he say?"

"He turned and made a most unpleasant face at me. He *is* ugly. But he hadn't a word to say for himself. Nor a word, and presently he got up and walked out of the room. I don't think he likes me every much."

Smike came in with Hoggin as his lordship seated himself.

"Tell me all about it," he said, leaning back, terrible but calm.

"They're just behind," said Smike, with a backward gesture of his head.

Rud appeared in the doorway, his face white and tense, with Rogers and Bodisham at either shoulder. Behind came Steenhold in a state of ecstatic enjoyment, and Chiffan, almost luminously pale with happy excitement. Dreed followed helpfully.

Hoggin and Smike placed themselves like ministers in attendance on Bohun's right.

"To what do I owe this intrusion?" said Lord Horatio, drumming impatiently on his desk.

"We want to discuss the policy of the Party – particularly in relation to America," said Rud.

"Especially in relation to America," echoed Chiffan.

Mrs Crumb looked enquiringly at her employer. "I shall want a full note of all this," he said, and she sat down in her usual place. "And now?" said his lordship.

Rud stood contemplating the desk. Then carefully and deliberately he pushed aside an inkstand, a large memorandum pad, a book or two and two tall candle-lamps, placed himself sideways to the Boss, hoisted and squatted himself firmly on the place he had made for himself. From this position he proceeded to explain. "You see, Boss, we hate to say it, but we think that either your grasp of the world situation is feeble or you aren't acting – forgive my frankness – in perfect good faith."

"Do you mind *not* sitting on my desk?" said Lord Horatio.

"You don't provide chairs, you see," said Rud, looking down at him with quiet hatred and not offering to budge. "Still – "

He considered the difficulty in a generous spirit. "Dreed, there, would you mind going downstairs and making one or two of those youngsters bring up some chairs? Then we can all sit decently and have a proper confabulation. For confabulate, my lord, we *must*. As I was saying, we feel our party has enormous possibilities. And they are not being realised. Are you prepared to discuss that with us?"

His lordship thought swiftly. No good starting a fight here. The odds were six to three. And this was not the place for it. Cold contempt and deliberation were indicated.

"And what is this discussion to be about?" he said.

"The country wants a lead. We are giving the country he lead."

"The country is inert."

"The country is as quiet as unlit gunpowder."

"You have my lead *there*," Lord Horatio gestured to his piled pamphlet. "There you have my *Mein Kampf*."

"*Mein Kampf* was full of ideas – definite ideas. It told the Germans exactly what to do. *That* stuff is just – personal tootling. It tells nobody anything to do. We want a lead as well as a leader. We want a clear statement of ideas. We want a meeting of the Party to clear up our aims."

Rud paused. Bohun under great provocation remained calm and quiet.

"You want dasapline," he said with quiet intensity. "You want to get these Bloomsbury Whitechapel ideas of yours together and then – wash them all out. That, my boy, is what you want."

"At a meeting?"

"At a meeting? Certainly."

"A showdown?"

"A clean-up. We will have a Dasapline meeting. I agree. Certainly I agree. The Party wants gingering up. You are right about that, anyhow. Maybe it needs a purge. A drastic purge. A conference, a confrontation, and no outside interference. Just among ourselves. That little Canton Hall round the corner here is big enough. A nice quiet little place. A ticket meeting – and no gloves on. No gloves on, mind you."

"You'll fix a date?"

"As soon as you like. What do you think of next week, Hoggin?"

"Sooner the better," said Smike.

Dreed and his chairs and helpers arrived belatedly in the doorway.

"We shan't want these chairs now," said Rud, getting off the desk. "We've done our business for the moment. There will have to be a small organising committee, of course."

"Smike," said Bohun. "Hoggin."

"Bodisham," said Rud.

"*You?*"

"Neither you nor me, Boss."

His lordship considered. "Perhaps best not. No... Dasapline," he said, and some pleasant thoughts seemed to cross his mind. "No reporters. Just ourselves. Smike, Hoggin, Bodisham."

Somebody said: "Frobisher."

"Why not?" said Rud.

"Four is enough," said Bohun, and added a touch that was almost in the Coriolanus vein. "And now perhaps you will allow me to – ah – *ventilate* my room. You have made a note of all this, Mrs Crumb? You will let this Mr Whittlelow and Mr Bodisham and the other recalcitrant gentlemen have copies?... Enough."

He made a gesture of masterful dismissal for which Rud had no immediate repartee. He regarded Rud with an expression of serene malignity. He had not doubt now that the situation had been handled. Now he would show them. And as for that white tadpole dressed up as a man...!

Before Rud could devise any effective counter, Steenhold had taken him by the arm. "That's all settled," said Steenhold, and led him from the room.

4

"It's a queer thing," said Mr Montague Abrahams, the manger of Keen and Battle, who did most of the printing for the Popular Socialist Party in those days; "I have had three distinct orders for this Strictly Private Meeting of the Party, all on the Party paper and all signed by names I know. There's that Mr Frobisher, who's conducted their meetings before. I suppose he's all OK. He wants three hundred tickets sent to Headquarters at number sixteen. Prefectly in order. Yes. In addition we get a private order from Lord Horatio himself for a hundred to be sent to him 'Personal' at number seventeen. Good. But then here comes an order from Mr Bodisham who was in charge last year, and he wants a hundred and fifty to go to this address in Camborne Square. Now that hall won't hold much more than four hundred people. I suppose it's all right so for as we are concerned, but – It's funny. I've had an idea of OK-ing all these orders with Headquarters. And yet I've got a sort of feeling that maybe I would be butting in – "

"The money's all right?" said Mrs Abrahams.

"Well, the only point there might be a doubt about is about that Camborne Square part of the order. But *they've* paid that already. Mr Bodisham called. I saw him. *Quiet*-looking young gentleman. Round-shouldered – "

"I wouldn't interfere," said Mrs Abrahams after reflection. "There's wheels within wheels."

"You keep your fingers out of the wheels, Monty," said Mrs Abrahams.

Mr Abrahams went on with his supper. "This political printing is very interesting work," he said.

"Interested is all very well," said Mrs Abrahams, "but don't get excited about it."

Mr Abrahams said no more until his supper was done. Then he said, almost as though he solioquised:

"Maybe I'll just go round and have a look at Canton Hall on the night. Maybe they'll overflow a bit."

5

There was little excitement outside the Canton Hall when the hour of the meeting arrived. It was a private meeting of the Party and there were no police precautions in evidence. Men and youths arrived by twos and three and were swallowed up by the portals. But presently there were shouts within.

Mr Abrahams could not distinguish anything of the shouting. It grew louder and then there was laughter and more laughter – a jeering sort of laughter.

He made a move towards the door and then restrained himself and turned away.

Whistling pensively, Mr Abrahams strolled to the corner of the road which ran towards the corner house. He glanced about him furtively. He was unobserved. Very quickly he produced a red ticket from his breast pocket, a ticket he had overprinted, he looked at it for a moment with his head appreciatively on one side, shifted it conveniently to his outer pocket, slapped it, and then, with an entire change of bearing, marched back to the Hall, presented his illicit credential, and pushed his way into a room already completely packed.

"Quite at the back," he whispered, as if to an absent Mrs Abrahams. "Quite at the back."

He remained an unobtrusive but appreciative spectator of all that followed. He tried to make a rough computation of the number of people present. It astonished him that there was still room to breathe. He reckoned up about four hundred, four hundred-odd. But he had printed – what had he printed? – five hundred and fifty. And one.

"They can't have come. If they were turned away I should have seen them outside."

The four men appointed to organise the secret meeting had behaved very much in the manner of seconds preparing for a duel. Very plainly it was a duel. It was to be held, they had agreed, with an absolute minimum of notification. All the tickets were to be stamped *Private and Confidential*. The outside public was to know nothing about it. Both sides had insisted that there was absolutely no need for police, no need for any sort of publicity at all. "It is just a little matter among ourselves." That had been accepted with what was afterwards recognised as suspicious alacrity by both sides.

After that there had been some cautious diplomacy about the agenda. Neither side was prepared to name a chairman. "We want a sort of non-interventionist," said Bodisham. "We want our principals to have the amplest play."

The organisers pitched at last upon Forbisher.

It was Lord Horatio's desire that Rud should open with his case. And he didn't want to hear Rud open his case. It would certainly bore him, he said, and he might get indignant and interrupt. He wanted to give Rud fair play. Rud could have all the rope he needed to hang himself. Rud could have the meeting to himself for his charges against the leadership, and at the psychological moment Lord Horatio would come in, come forward and state his own position. "Practically, what Rud will say will be on the lines of the Hyde Park speech?" Hoggin assumed.

"Practically," said Bodisham ambiguously.

It was not in the philosophy of either Bohun or Hoggin that Rud – or indeed anyone – could make an entirely different speech – several different speeches. For the Bohunites, one's speech was one's speech like one's height or one's complexion.

"There is a verbatim report?"

"Mrs Crumb has been given a copy."

"You want Rud to fire off his ammunition first and then you want Lord Horatio to come in and jump on him?" said Bodisham, shaking his head.

"We give him the opening," said Hoggin.

"Any right for reply?"

"Do you think that will be needed?"

"I suppose we must agree to that," said Bodisham with an air of reluctance. "I don't like it. He will have to start from cold. No. It's not fair..."

So that what Mr Abrahams came in for first, when he wriggled into the back of the Canton Hall, was Rud's opening address. And if Rud had started from cold, he had taken a remarkably short time to develop a high temperature. He was indulging in a tirade against Lord Horatio, a torrent of abuse and insult that would have made Milton's controversial style seem propitiatory and Terullian a gentleman. "And there wasn't to be a reporter present," whispered Mr Abrahams to himself, appreciatively, counting three men within range who were more or less overtly making notes. "Oh! This is *jam*."

And the things Whitlow kept saying! Abrahams could hardly believe his ears.

He was not only saying them. He was getting away with them. He was provoking angry shouts and abusive cries, but he was getting support and more support.

"Hear what I've got to say," shouted Rud. "Hear what I've got to say."

Uproar.

"This is a private meeting of the Party and if you don't agree with me – say it afterwards. But hear my case."

The majority was for him. No doubt of it. Abrahams' arithmetic was swift and sound.

If that other hundred try to get in, he resolved, I quit. What was he saying?

"I tell you we've had this – this Guy making us ridiculous long enough. I tell you he's not leading. I tell you he's standing in our way. He's selling us to Bankers and rich Americans. He's setting us against the trade unionists and Communists who have a case – a poor case, but they have a case. He's doing nothing for the Socialist cause, while *our* navy, our navy, the navy this country pays for, bombards American workers' homes... He's making mischief for us with the Jews.

"What's the sense of quarrelling with Jews?"

Abrahams applauded internally.

"Do they do any harm here? Do people mind them? But that's the game they played in Germany and so here – where everything is different – where never in the whole of history has there been such a thing as a pogrom – we have to do likewise! Just to split the workers...

"Come to think of it: – he looks half a Jew himself, a ginger-white Jew, the worst sort...

"I've got no quarrel with a Jew as such – Who *has* here? – but these anti-Jews and these pro-Jews are poison. It's a stale old quarrel from the Middle Ages. Who wants that rotten quarrel in *our* new world? To hell with all this Jew consciousness, either way! I tell you it's a *new* world we're living in – and we want to get on with it and get it in order. Who wants to play Jews against Gentiles, Catholics against Protestants, Socialists against Individualists, Sunnites against Shiites now? It's all old stuff. It's dead stuff. It's Yesterday-ism. Politics from Petticoat Lane. What I say about these Jews is, Smash up the Ghetto and let them run. We want New Against old – and this leader who has been pretending to lead us is so old, so stale; he's sort of antiquarian. He's a curio. He's a collector... I could tell you things... But never mind that.

("Is he ready, Bodisham?" – a swift aside.

"He's quite ready.")

"I said he looks half a Jew. I apologise to the Jews. Anyhow, he's selling you old clothes, boys. Do you want to be dressed up in second-hand Dago tights? Do you want to strut about with your chests and your behinds stuck out, doing comic gladiator salutes? You Englishmen? Salute. Hand out. Can I leave the room please? Eh?... We who are about to die salute you,

194

Horatio!... *Bah!* We want the reality of our own sort. Look here! Here's the sort of animal *he* wants to make of you!"

And forthwith a masked figure mounted the steps at the back of the platform and marched forward, with a sort of staccato goose-step, giving the Popular Socialist salute. It halted, still saluting. It turned this way and that. It opened a large mouth and drummed thoughtfully at its pasteboard teeth.

It was a turn that one of the Sunday evening music-hall group at Steenhold's flat had improvised, and which Steenhold had insisted upon making a feature of this debate. The mask was a cleverly simplified caricature of Bohun's visage and the ginger wig and forelock might have been the Boss' natural hair. The apparition took the meeting's breath away and then, after a silence, the crowd broke into a confusion of booing, applause and protests. But the protests were in a minority, and the noise died down to listen as Rud proceeded, after the manner of a showman:

"That's the model Bohun gave us... Yes – you can shout *shame!* but *that's* shame...

"No don't howl now. You'll have your turn to say things."

Somebody in the front of the hall had to be suppressed. But the very crowding of the hall helped to keep the peace. They were too jammed together there for anything but pushing, face-thrusting and elbow fighting. No one could swing for a kick or a punch.

"Look at him, I say. Do you see how tight he is behind, boys? See his rump? *Ain't* it a behind? It beats his chest, don't it? *Look* how it sticks out! *Why?*"

Various suggestions were made amidst raucous laughter.

"I'll tell you," Rud went on. "He's got his tail there, mates. Hidden in his pants. It's a monkey. That's what it is. A nice furry-tailed Capuchin money. It's a performing monkey on old Mussolini's organ, and it only dances to foreign tunes. Popular Socialist he calls himself – patriot and all that – and not a home-grown idea from start to finish! Can't we do better than that? On our own? I ask you...

"Walk up and down the platform, Horry-boy. There you are, the very picture of him. Salute, please. That's the hero of the society Judys. That's the darling of dear old Lady Ragbag. And our spirited, pro-Nazi, Lady Garbees, who spends her whole life trying not to speak with a nasty native American accent. And old Lady Twinkletoes. And all the rest of them. Eh? Give me a good rough Red every time, if it comes to that. Not that I hold with that Moscow stuff for a moment. That's stale, too. But dammit, if they're muddle-headed, they're *real*. This – this isn't politics." (Angry Voice: "No, it isn't politics." Replies and a slight struggle to suppress the angry voice.) "It's private theatricals."

"Yus!" said the angry voice, and something happened to it; it went under for good.

Something was happening at the back of the platform. "What!" said Bodisham. "Already? Right. *Here* – " to the effigy – "you just stand back for a moment."

The masker was pushed into a corner and out of sight behind the group of BMGs.

Rud wound up his speech.

"Well, I've made most of my case! Here's Lord Horatio himself, the great original, ten minutes before his time. But I've said enough, Mr Chairman. I think I've said enough. Now let us hear what Lord Horatio has to say for himself *once more*."

196

"Those other tickets," checked Mr Abrahams. "A hundred more of them. And I'm as flat as a pancake already now!"

He tried to edge towards the door, but unavailingly.

Frobisher was gesticulating with his long limbs for the platform crowd to clear the way from behind. And then Mr Abrahams perceived Hoggin and Smike opening a path for the advance of Lord Horatio.

It was always his way to advance upon a meeting slowly, portentously. In spite of the congestion of the platform he did so now. He arrived amidst an unusually thin applause at the front, raised his arm in a dignified salute and stood silently radiating his personality upon the audience. Beside him, and a little behind him, was Frobisher. By contrast with these two tall figures Rud looked gnome-like, lacking in dignity, inferior. Yet also he looked much more alive and malignant. A lull in the shouting ensured. Expectation stilled the crowd. Then on the right the masquerader reappeared, advanced sublimely and struck an attitude exactly parallel with Lord Horatio's.

There was not much laughter. It was funny in a derisive way. It was not, however, hilariously funny. It produced guffaws rather than merriment, and everyone was alert for the next incident, which was the realisation of this mocking presence by Bohun himself.

He turned and saw his parody.

He should have featured outraged dignity, but he was too astonished. Sublimity vanished. "You mean to make out I'm like *that!*" he cried, and then, advancing with upraised fist, "You silly Ape, you!"

Then he paused for a moment and cried to Hoggin: "Bring our men in *now!*" he cried.

"I *knew* it," whispered Mr Abrahams. "A hundred of 'em!" For a crucial moment his face was jammed against the broad back of the man in front of him. When he got a clear view of the platform again Bohun was grappling with Rogers, who had intervened between him and his pseudo-double; the masker and one or two others of the platform crowd had been pushed right over the edge and on to the front rows of the audience; and the chairman, who had become as long limbed it seemed as a gibbon, had produced a bell which he was not so much ringing as using as an impartial mace upon the heads about him. A wedge of toughs had appeared from the back of the platform in response to Bohun's cry. One extremely ugly face stood out among these newcomers, and Abrahams seemed to recognise it as the face of the Terrible Slew, the all-in wrestler. Then he felt sure it *was* the Terrible Slew. "Gollys!" Rud had been pushed against the wall to the left of the platform and was apparently having difficulty in keeping his footing and not being shoved down into the hall. He was hitting about weakly with one fist and seemed then to be resisting pressure rather than actually fighting.

But it was very hard to grasp the situation as a whole and Mr Abrahams found his powers of observation confused by the danger of being trodden on and crushed, and by a desire to pull back a chair against the wall and stand on it and see more. There were too many heads and too much minor action between him and the drama on the stage. Everyone was standing up and a lot of men were kneeling and standing on the chairs. The chairs were having a bad time, cracking and collapsing with a sort of squelch. The general thrust, happily for little Mr Abrahams, was towards the platform.

So far as he could grasp the situation, the hall had been packed against Lord Horatio, but now a formidable counterattack from the back entrance had been unmasked. "Slew!" said Mr Abrahams. "He'll *hurt* somebody."

A lot of people were shouting: "We *want* Rud Whilow!" But that cry was not sweeping the meeting. It was just as if some cue had gone wrong. "We want Rud!" bawled a youngster close to Abraham's ear. "Why aren't you shouting, sir? What's the matter with *you?*"

"Oh, I'm neutral," said Mr Abrahams.

"Neutral are you? Then what the devil are you doing here?"

"I'm the printer."

"Printer be damned. You lift your voice, sir, and show your colours."

"I *want* Rud!" shouted Abrahams perfunctorily. "What's happening now?"

The attention of the young man who had challenged him was happily diverted.

The milling crowd on the left of the platform reminded Abrahams of swarming bees. He saw a chairleg go spinning across the hall to no definite address. Somebody in the front row began yelping shrilly with pain.

Bohun, the Terrible Slew, Rogers and Steenhold towered over the swaying platform battle and there seemed to be a convergence of conflict towards the back entrance. And then there were cries of "Where is Rud? What are they doing to Rud?"

Someone quite near to Abrahams said: "They've got hold of Rud…"

Someone was blowing a policeman's whistle outside.

A voice of agony sounded quite near to Mr Abrahams.

"I'm the caretaker of the bloody place. A quiet meeting. They said it was to be a quiet, friendly meeting. Not a *single* policeman. Oh, my God! My God! The *chairs!* Who's going to pay for them chairs?"

Then there was a cracking of timber as part of the platform gave way.

6

Rud was kidnapped before he realised what was happening to him. He was hitting out with his left in order to protect his face from imaginary blows, and he thought at first that it was friendly hands that were thrusting him away from the dangerous corner of the platform. A lot of heavy men were slogging and shouting their way in a line across the platform towards the body of the hall, and it seemed reasonable to duck and push in the opposite direction. His pushing was assisted. He heard Dreed and someone else shouting: "Look out, Rud." Then he fell down some steps, felt his ankle twist rather painfully, and found himself in the open air and being hauled towards Bohun's car. His jacket was pulled over his head and his collar seemed about to strangle him and then tore with a ripping sound. He resisted at the door of the car and was hit under his jawbone in a way that seemed to reduce his face to an uncontrollable jumble of features and obliterate his mind for a time.

He seemed to hear Dreed saying: "Here! Hold on. Wait a bit" – and then groan.

Someone had hit Dreed on the head...

After a lapse Rud found he was being carried like a sack up some steps, the steps of a house.

"What's all this here?" asked a voice.

"All right, constable. One of our men a bit hurt. We'll see to him…"

He was being bumped along the passage of some house. Probably it was the Purple House…

It seemed wiser not to struggle until he got the hang of the affair. He pretended insensibility. He was carried quite a long and complicated way, round a corner, downstairs, and along a passage, and finally he was flung down on a flat surface.

A door slammed and bolts were shot.

An almost complete silence ensured…

Slowly and apparently against great resistances his dislocated face seemed to be reassembling itself. He opened one eye and part of another and listened intently. Very stiffly and painfully he sat up.

He found he was exactly where he had been trying to think he wasn't. He was locked up in one of those cells in number seventeen.

Anyhow, it was a clean one.

In one corner of the cell was a Thermos pitcher. That probably contained water. He felt he would very much like to assuage the flaming ache of his face with some cold water, and he got up painfully and hobbled over to it. But no one had ever put any water into that Thermos pitcher.

He sat down again on the plank bed and contemplated the situation. There was nothing else for him to do…

He went on contemplating the situation…

His thoughts at first were heavy and sluggish and inclined to repeat themselves: then they quickened up and became feverish and incoherent. But they remained uniformly disagreeable.

He had been kidnapped and Lord Horatio had got him.

The Group had been so cocksure about this meeting, all of them. It was to have dispelled Bohun in a storm of ridicule.

It should have done.

But it had failed to do so, and here he was – the Leader! Bashed and in a cell. They had made a mess of things and got beaten…

Rud's realisation of defeat was very rapid. He saw now that it was an altogether inevitable defeat…

The fact of it was Bodisham was a rotten organiser – a lousy organiser. The rottenest of organisers. He ought to have organised an intelligence department. Of course, he ought to have done that. He ought to have known what Bohun was up to. He ought to have been ready for a counter-attack. He ought to have been sure that a counter-attack would come.

This was the Group's first fight and it had been beaten. The Group had been a promise, a dream. This cell was reality. The Group was done for at the first round.

The clearer Rud's mind grew, the clearer grew his convictions of sin, folly, presumption and incompetence. (And now he had to wait for what was coming to him.)

He thought Steenhold's notion of bringing in that masked actor was one of the rottenest ideas he had ever heard of. Absolutely the rottenest idea. But Steenhold always had been a fool – just as Bodisham was a fool. Steenhold had seen some public enquiry about Banking methods at Washington turned to absurdity by introducing a midget and getting the creature to sit on Pierpoint Morgan's knee while he was being questioned. This music-hall turn had been Steenhold's silly imitation of that.

How he had loved the idea! How he had insisted upon it and elaborated it!

Chiffan ought to have warned Rud against it. But there was a malicious streak in Chiffan. There were times when he seemed positively pleased to see everything going wrong. Sometimes you felt you could trust him absolutely and then came that irritating note of derision that filled you with doubt. Why had he fallen in with this fancy of Steenhold's? Because it was effective or simply because it was preposterous? Far better it would have been to have had a straightforward confrontation with Bohun, more political, more statesmanlike. If only he had not given way to Chiffan and trusted instead to his own sounder instinct!

Too late now...

Rogers was just a beefy rough. He was an escape from the National Sporting Club. He had no business in politics. He had been convinced that with these wonderful boxing youngsters of his from Pimlico and Whitechapel he could hold the meeting in order and make it possible to carry the whole scheme through. Well, he had failed. The whole Group had failed. Rogers had wanted a fight and he had had a fight, and he hadn't cared a rap whose career was wrecked in the process. And so Rud had begun his career with his Waterloo. (And here he was landed, with his face in a pulp, waiting for what was coming to him...)

How long would he have to wait...?

And what would happen when Bohun came...?

Discipline? What would Bohun dare to do?

It was remarkable that Bohun had not come already. No doubt that crew of roughs were cleaning up Rogers and his amateurs in the Canton Hall. Maybe Bohun would have to make things right with the police. There had been a blowing of police whistles and apparently a policeman had seen Rud carried into the Purple House. Would they come and take him out of it, and if so, what would happen? But would anyone know he was down here? How would anyone know who it was they had carried in? Dreed knew he had been carried off, but apparently Dreed had been knocked out. None of the others knew. They might not miss him for a long time. They might not be able to get together. No. Here he was and here he was likely to remain – until Bohun saw fit to attend to him. No reason for Bohun to hurry...

He looked at his wristwatch to see how the time was going. But half the glass of the watch had gone and the minute hand was bent up. That was annoying. He seemed to have been here quite a long time, but he could not tell whether he had been lying stunned for five minutes or an hour. How could he manage to reckon? And anyhow, what was the good of reckoning?

Suddenly the light in his cell went out. That took him by surprise and he gave a startled cry.

What did that mean?

Nothing.

Or perhaps a lot.

Unnecessary and undesirable phrases came floating into his mind. "Dead of night," for example. Something very secret and very sinister done at the dead of night. When all the honest, kindly world was fast asleep and beyond call.

He was intolerably thirsty.

That might be part of it. They might keep him here without food and drink, just to weaken him, break him down before Discipline began.

They couldn't very well carry things so far as to kill him.

Not deliberately.

But they might carry Discipline so far as to kill him unintentionally. In England?

"Why not in England?" said his memory of Chiffan.

Oh! Why had he ever launched upon this business? What is the good of meddling with politics unless you are prepared for violence – unless you can stand hard knocks? He had been fool enough to let these others flatter him into the position of a leader. It had been fun for them, but he had been fool enough to be serious about it – drink it all in...

He might have kept clear of all this from the beginning. He might have concentrated on taking an outstanding Camford degree. He could have read law. With this gift of eloquence of his, he would have made a brilliant advocate...

No good thinking of that now...

After all, maybe, his father hadn't been such an utter fool, about the dangers of an aggressive temperament and a nimble tongue...

His thoughts were wandering to unimportant matters. It was difficult to think clearly with this aching face; it seemed as though his brain as well as his jaw was askew. But he had to think clearly and hard and exhaustively before the next thing happened.

Perhaps the enemy was not so clever after all in giving him this endless vigil in the dark to think things out. What was he going to do?

What he had straight in front of him, what he had to deal with first, was Bohun.

Would it be possible to make some sort of compromise with that dangerous fool? Would it be wiser to humbug him or menace him? Suppose, for example, one stood up when he appeared and gave him that damned salute of his? Suppose one said: "I know when I am beaten. This ends politics for me": would he swallow that?

Suppose one said: "I realise now the meaning of Personality, Boss" – or "I realise now the meaning of Personality, Lord Horatio": how would he take that?

"*Gods!*" said Rud, "I don't think I would do that even now."

The beast might just laugh that neighing laugh of his. Vain he was, but also he was cruel.

Perhaps one might say it, less cringingly...

One might offer to make some sort of alliance... As man to man...

And even if one could get by him like that, then what was the outlook for Rud? What chance was there of rallying the old group and explaining oneself to them all?

Rud's attempts to envisage the situation in all its aspects suddenly gave way to a fit of hearty cursing. "Damn you all and damn everything," said Rud, and embroidered that theme.

Which was his way of resigning himself to the conclusion that he had to go through with that Discipline, whatever it was. "Whatever it is," said Rud, clenching his fists until his nails hurt his palms. "I'll get square with him afterwards. I'll get square with him. If I give my life for it."

Then came a phase of lassitude that seemed to last an interminable time, and then his mind was busy again planning where he should go and what he should do after he had got home again, whatever was left of him.

"For whatever happens," he said, "they can't *kill* me. They can't kill me. In England – "

After that a sort of dull period and then a fresh bout of blind cursing.

No earthly way of checking the time at all. For all he could tell it might be morning already. In this infernal darkness one hardly knew whether one was right way up or upside down. They ought to give him a light. Common humanity –

No use shouting.

He wished someone would come.

To judge by his throat and the stiffening of his bruises he must have been here for long hours. Whatever they might do to him, one thing they would certainly have to do to him, and that was to give him a drink.

Perhaps it was morning. Maybe Bohun was sleeping off his exertions before coming down to him.

("Equal with him somehow.")

He passed into a reverie of reprisals.

7

When at last he heard footsteps coming he doubted whether he wanted anyone to come. He forgot what he had meant to say. He wanted time to think that out again.

What was he going to say? "This finishes politics for me. I know when I'm beaten?"

No good to begin like that.

The steps came nearer. A faint light flickered through the inspection wicket and flickered away again. It was like the flicker of an electric torch. His heart was now beating very fast. Someone rattled the door. A voice outside asked: "Anyone here?"

Very like Irwell's voice, but you couldn't be sure. Better keep still. Pretend to be asleep?

Then came another quite familiar voice. "Rud!"

Rud leapt to his feet: "Chiffan! *Chiffan!* Is that you?"

Chiffan's voice, high-pitched and cheerful: "Here he is! Where the hell are those keys?"

And then instantly the light went on again... Somebody was saying something about a fuse.

A key turned in the lock, the door opened and Chiffan stood with a pallid, triumphant face, regarding his leader.

"What is it? Is it still Thursday?"

"Still Thursday, Rud! How long do you think you have been here?"

"Eternity."

"You can't have been in this place much more than three quarters of an hour."

"I was knocked out. I've been insensible. I've been dreaming. What I want first of all is a drink of water. I've got a fever on me. Then a wash."

"What you want is a whisky and soda. Then someone ought to bandage you up."

"But tell me what has happened?"

"Here's Rogers. Rogers, here he is!"

"Are you hurt?" asked Rogers.

"Nothing. Tell me."

"It's gone like clockwork. *What* a scrap! A *lovely* scrap! And right in the heart of the West End. Nothing like it for years. Poor old Horry!"

"What's happened to him?"

"He got a kick in the groin. You should have heard him howl. What a voice he has for the Wilderness! But he's hurt – decidedly hurt… I'm sorry about that. I don't like things happing like that. There's a limit to things. I hope it was accidental. But the rest of the fight was fair and square. I suppose you didn't see one of my Whitechapel kids tackle that all-in man, you know, the Terrible Slew? Dodged his kick and caught his heel and over he went. Just before the platform upset. I thought he'd broken his neck. 'Subsequent proceedings interested *him* no more.'…

"Or maybe he thought he'd earned his pay. A lot of those roughs seemed to get heart failure when they saw what they had to deal with. They thought they were just there to beat up a meeting and get hold of you. There was some dirty work with razor blades, but that was Horry's old lot. Not our chaps, I hope. None of *my* boys certainly. But – this scrap's going to be historical. In the heart of Tyburnia. The police were pretty late. They seemed a bit surprised to find *us* in charge and their old friend Horry doubled up and yelping like a puppy that's been run over.

"Where Horry got all those roughs of his I don't know. He must have a criminal connection somewhere. One or two the Inspector told me were certainly old lags. He got quite friendly with us. Didn't seem to fancy Horry… Half of them didn't know each other, often they were just slogging blind, but my boys knew each other down to the ground. Anyhow, it was the greatest scrap you ever!… It *was* a great scrap."

Rud was still sitting on the plank bed, but his leadership was reconstituting itself very rapidly in his mind. When he spoke again, he spoke as the Chief and everyone listened.

"Here we are," he said. "Except for my temporary obliteration, the whole thing's evidently gone like clockwork. Eh? As we planned it. We've put it over – thanks to Bodisham and Steenhold – and now the thing is to – what's the military phrase? – consolidate the position. What's the right time? My watch is smashed. We must get on to all the press resources available and explain quite clearly what it was all about. 'Thrice is he armed that hath his quarrel just, But he wins out who gets his tale in fust!' We must have photographers. I'll talk to every interviewer that reads and writes"

"But upstairs!" said Irwell. "We've found things. Pictures and things."

"Publish everything."

"But you know – he was a bit of a stinker!"

"Release his stink," said Rud.

Within half an hour Rud was in Bohun's coveted chair, heroically bandaged and heroically talking. The newspaper men stood or walked about. ("If we have chairs up here they'll park themselves," said Rud, taking an entirely new view of the seating question.) Sustained by whisky and soda and an injection of strychnine, he expounded himself lucidly, carefully, and over and over again. It was urgently necessary for the public to understand what had happened. For a long time the Party had been baffled and nonplussed by the increasingly eccentric behaviour of its leader. He had arrested what was essentially a great common-sense movement of the Anglo-American people – the common people –

"Eh? What was that?" said one of the reporters. "Anglo-American?"

Rud repeated his words very seriously. "Anglo-American common people."

They had tried to reason with Bohun; they had meant to have an entirely private discussion; but his Lordship had thought better of it. Or worse of it...

"You can take your cameras all over the Purple House now, and I think you will realise what we were up against. You'll find some queer things. It's yielding up its secrets. But see for yourselves..."

"It's a great story," said one of the newshawks.

"You don't know the half of it yet," said Chiffan.

"And now," said Rud, "the really significant news. The Popular Socialist Party will go ahead. It has rescued itself. It is free. It is rejuvenescent. And it is a natural and necessary Party. It has the vitality of reality. The main points. Listen! What does it stand for? Let me give you our main points exactly over again. How else could it have survived Bohun? No. I'm not a bit fagged. These bandages make talking a bit painful, but that's all. They'll be stiffer tomorrow. I told you how I got this slog on the jaw. Otherwise I should have carried on. But Rogers did that marvellously. Let me talk about the Party and its Future. That's what I want to talk about. The scrap won't make half as good a story unless you put it against its proper background. I'd better get it over now. Not a *bit* fatigued. Go on writing. I'll take on all you newspaper men, one down, another come up. It is the Party of the common man; It's common-sense *insisting* on itself, through me...

"Don't think I am a leader. Don't think I'm setting up to be another Lord Horry. I'm no leader. I'm just the megaphone of common-sense. Get that — the megaphone of common-sense.

But listen to common-sense. What are we going to do next? I'll tell you."

And so forth and so on.

8

It was nearly one in the morning when Mr Abrahams came home.

He opened the conversation as he came into the bedroom. "I'm not a bit drunk," he said, "I haven't touched anything this evening. I've been making history."

"Where have you been, Monty, making your history? You *sound* excited."

"I went to that meeting, darling. The one in Canton Hall. I couldn't keep away. I got a sort of oh *quite* accidental punch in the eye, but I don't think it's going to colour. I was hit by a potato. At one time they were throwing quite a lot of potatoes. That's why I sound excited. But I'm not actually excited."

"I told you – "

"I know. But it was most interesting. I really didn't get a bit excited. I'll tell you all about it tomorrow. A lot of them were *really* hurt. I'll tell you."

She peered close up to his face.

"There's sort of cut on that bruise, Monty. A nasty little cut."

"There was razor blades perhaps in the potato," said Mr Abrahams. "They do that sometimes."

9

It was the news of this explosive emergence of Rud that the old doctor read in his garden. The particulars were not very accurately given, they had been given by Rud, and the triumph of Rud had become much more effective and complete in the telling. And more portentous. In his own admirable phrase he had "clarified the facts." His experiences in number seventeen were entirely omitted from the story, because evidently the reporter had learnt nothing about them. And there was no doubt whatever of the aggressive intentions of the renascent Popular Socialist Party. It meant to "modernise and remake the world," no less, "under the rule of common-sense," as interpreted by Rud. "*Modern* common-sense"; he had apparently said it three times. And first of all he – Rud Whitlow if you please – meant to challenge the country on the American issue...

"And so exit Bohun," reflected old Doctor Carstall. "I guess this ends him...

"If half this stuff about him is true, he's certifiable... Thumbscrews!... Whips!..."

He had been a safety valve. He had put a foolish face in front of all that snobbish, middle-class riff-raff of his. He had wasted money that might have worked mischief. He had been a mask, he had been a gag upon the Fascist drive here. Now it had fairly got loose...

"This young Whitlow will be different. He's ugly as an octopus but he's not ridiculous. There's a tenacity about him. And malice. He reeks, Dick said, of social malice. In these days he may get almost anywhere. He may get a lot of power. What will he do with it?...

"That fellow – I brought him into the world – and he was a trouble even then. Twenty-five hours of it she had with him, and not worth one. (Nowadays I suppose it would be a Caesarian – and over in an hour. Progress goes on – even when it's a case of

213

bringing monsters into the world.) He's a nasty little creature – essentially a nasty creature.

"Intelligent perhaps…

"Some of the stuff he has been telling the interviewers has a kind of plausibility…

"No doubt our government *has* been making a mess of this American business. No doubt this idea of our governing class getting into touch with some imaginary governing class over there is all wrong – and we're getting ourselves up against an angry real democracy…

"Maybe he ha a sort of rightness.

"The last thing one will consent to do is to realise that anyone else is more intelligent than oneself. Maybe I'm wrong. That little beast may be more intelligent than I suppose. Like some of those calculating boys or musical prodigies. A political quick-thinker…"

He picked up the newspaper and began to read over again the account of Rud's coup, as the newshawks had seen it and heard about if from him. Much about the meeting there was, more about Rud, and nothing about that meditation in the cellar. Rud had explained how he himself had thought out that masked caricature as a means of "bringing Bohun up to the scratch."

"It's indecent! Who ever heard of caricaturing a man on a political platform in Gladstone's time? Making up to imitate him! Outrageous. And then the comeback. Fifteen hospital cases. In the good old days the only people who were carried out of political meetings were the ones who fainted. Bohun – kicked in the groin. Whitlow serious contusions. Almost broken his jaw. I wish they *had* broken his jaw. *These* are political leaders up to date! Shade of Mr Gladstone!"

"I'm not going to the *Bell* to night," Mr Whitlow senior announced.

"But, my dear! What will you do at home?"

"There's the radio. And patience. But at the *Bell!*...

"The things I get said to me! Unfriendly things. You'd hardly imagine. It takes way all the pleasure of going out. No *relaxation*, it isn't. No *distraction*. Always harping on Rud, they are. What's Rud going to do next? Where does Rud get his money from? *I* don't know what to tell 'em. He's got into Politics, I say, and that's the truth of it. As for what he's going to do about it – don't ask me. I always said letting him go to Camford was a mistake."

"I expect he's been *led* into it," said Mrs Whitlow.

"Led! I never remember Rud being *led* by anyone," said Mr Whitlow. "It's just his own damned headstrong, ungovernable temper. I spared the rod on that boy – all that stuff about repressions of yours. And here we are!"

"He might have been worse with repressions," said Mrs Whitlow.

"And he might not. Is there such a thing in this house as a couple of packs of cards that Alf hasn't taken two or three out of for his blasted model-making?... Yes, I said *blasted* model-making. B-L-A-R – No! I mean B-L-A-S-I-D model-making. *Now* then... Evening paper? No thank you. I can't take up a newspaper now not without seeing something about Rud. Why! *The Daily Warning* had a photograph of him all tied up like mumps or something."

"He always did set about things in his own fashion," said Mrs Whitlow. "I hope nobody didn't hurt him. He's got a sort of sturdy look about him, but really he's as delicate as a girl."

11

This chapter is trailing as many tailpieces as a kite. The end one shall be a lonely, tall figure, not without a certain sinister dignity, standing at the taffrail of a liner bound for the Argentine, and watching that brilliant theme with endless variations, a moonlit wake. Already as they came into warmer latitudes, dots and thin threads of phosphorescence were becoming frequent in the black-green water.

"Farewell to England," he said. "Farewell to the political life. Farewell to proletariat and bourgeoisie. Farewell to the stink and infinite vulgarity of a mechanised civilisation. And in particular farewell to the Mockery called Law."

He felt magnificently Byronic.

He quoted:

> "Adieu, adieu! My native shore
> Fades o'er the waters blue;
> The Night-winds sigh, the breakers roar,
> And shrieks the wild sea-mew.
> You sun that sets upon the sea
> We follow in his flight;
> Farewell awhile to him and thee,
> My native Land – Good Night!"

He wished he had a better memory for poetry. Then he wouldn't have to go on repeating this verse, night after night.

He was going back to the great freedom of nature – in a general sort of way. Presently Bonina, as weary of that so-called Civilisation as he was, would break away from the tutelage of her trustees and come after him. So she had promised him. They would get some little hundred tonner, they would get together a crew of congenial souls and sail off westward from Valparaiso, to lead lives of untrammelled scorn, defiance and impulse in the South Seas. They would have a great time. They would perhaps buy or acquire some little sunlit island and become Sun Children. They had worn the harness of a decadent social life long enough.

Now they would love like tigers, now they would pursue each other naked about the atoll, slashing at each other wildly and deliciously with riding whips, or rush through the breakers rejoicing, and dive and fight sharks with the long thin knives they would carry between their teeth.

When his leg was better, that is.

And if she didn't change her mind at the last moment...

What were they saying of him in England? (Not that he cared a damn.) But what were they probably saying? Would there be a reaction? Would they want him back?...

There *was* no reaction, no one wanted him back, and so he vanishes from our story to the throb of a steamer screw, into the sweet, deep blue of the sub-tropical night.

BOOK THREE

UPRUSH

CHAPTER ONE

The Enlargement of Rud

Rud's moods in those early days fluctuated widely. There were those narrow and intense moods of fear and hatred, from which he never freed himself. There were simply base phases when he schemed treacherously. There were unruffled moods of lucid understanding, when everything in life seemed cold and clear and plain, but these were comparatively rare. Things he had read, things Bodisham had argued, stray comments of Chiffan's, would flash together then into a transparent realisation. "Of *course!*" he would say to himself. Rare as they were, these clairvoyant interludes supplied the living material for most of his political utterances. He knew their value, he listened to himself then with a detached respect, and he made the fullest use of them.

Beneath all these again, there were moods, more and more exalted moods, of pure reverie. They were no longer the objective reveries of his boyish days, dreams of battle and conquest. Now they were anticipations of a subtler and more intimate ascendancy. They were concerned now with will power and domination over minds. They were pervaded by an intensifying self-appreciation. He kept them secret, as he imagined, from everyone. He would have hesitated to let anyone suspect how highly he could think of himself. He had a power over people. He had something peculiarly great in himself. But not a word about that. He had a feeling that ultimately recognition must come from some outside source, someone must be bound to announce his true quality, but until that realisation came from without, his true quality must remain secret within himself...

In these phases of private exaltation, it seemed to him that his idea of identifying himself with the Common Man was one of the most brilliant inspirations that had ever come to mortal intelligence. It had arisen in his mind with scarcely any premeditation, in the course of speeches and talking. It had seemed at first the merest poetry, just a new bright phrasing of the sympathetic element in the democratic faith. Then he began to realise that it penetrated to the very core of the human situation, as he beheld it. He was something greater than the minds about him. He really was greater. His reveries nowadays were more and more in the fashion of imaginary critical biography. He projected himself outside of himself in order to get a better view of himself.

"The Common Man Emergent," that was one of the phrases he found most acceptable in those opium dreams of his, dreams that he needed no opium to produce. The Common Man gathered together humanity, purified it, rendered it. The Common Man Emergent became his mystical self-divinity.

For the purpose of that imaginary biography he devised a new background of revolutions, a history leading right up to himself. He invented an ancient world before the dawn of history in which the masterful men, the terrifying people, the cruelty dealers, the punishers, the lords and priests, ruled without challenge, and the common man knew his master and obeyed the tradition imposed upon him from the cradle to the grave. To Rud the past had always seemed horrible. There was no golden age for him. It was, he was convinced, a cruel world, that early world of barbarism which first breaks into history. Yet already the Common Man was beginning to wake up, to protest, to assert himself. Plebeians were rising against Patricians, democracies against aristocrats. History opened out for Rud as the Martyrdom of Man, the sacrifice of the Common Man, in face of a gathering protest on the part of the overpowered common people.

Christianity, he theorised, had been an outstanding effort of the common man to find release from repressions, from kings, emperors and priests, Pharisees and the Law, in a frank cosmopolitan brotherhood. It was not only revolt, but in many ways it was the principal and typical revolt. Its insistence on the common fatherhood of God, all men equal in his eyes and so forth, was its fundamental quality. But it had been corrupted early. Instead of a Rud to express it, a lucid, simple Rud, it had fallen beneath the sway of — Saint Paul.

Nobody seemed to love Saint Paul really. Even the theologians. He was the greatest and least ingratiating of all the makers of Christianity, the Founder's whipping boy. But Rud's private blasphemies did not stop at Saint Paul. He dared to think with the most atrocious boldness of matters that even infidels have hitherto treated with respect. His private scorn for the "inefficiency" of the Founder of Christianity for example was fantastic. Here was a Message, he argued; it was a message of the utmost importance to all the world, and he chose twelve disciples to record it and spread it, and *not a stenographer among them!*

Stenographer's a modern idea! Rud would have protested. Not a bit of it. Cicero was using stenography half a century BC. So why wasn't the Sermon on the Mount properly taken down? If it was so important, why wasn't it taken down? Tell me that, asked Rud, in the wicked recesses of his heart. He was incapable of realising the gross incongruity, the indignity, the repulsiveness, of scriptures based on a shorthand draft.

According to Rud, Christianity was done for, within a century of its foundation. For want of trustworthy reporting. By that time it had got itself mixed up with Mithraism, Egyptian Trinitarianism, blood sacrifices and the Hebrew Promise. It had acquired entangling dogmas. What a pitiful story of complication and confusion it had been – all for the want of a man of Rud's lucidity. A good start gone wrong. Corruption had been inevitable. Christianity had found its Marx in Paul and its Stalinites and Trotskyites in the Gnostics and Arians. A swarm of Bishops and Fathers accumulated all over it and they suffocated it. It was dead and done for now, entirely mineralised. Rud tried over phrases in his mind. "Christianity – the best of it – fossilised first-century Communism. And the rest of it, marine-store junk."

What use was it to us? he asked himself. We were way up in the twentieth century. All that work had to be done over again. By less entangled minds...

One might claim to be an early Christian on occasion for controversial purposes, but that was all...

All that work had to be done over again. And again and over again until it was really done. There was no other way for mankind.

For five-and-twenty centuries at least, the Common Man had been making his frustrated upward thrusts against the power grabbers, the bullies, the conspirators and masterful people who enslaved and held him down. All the movements for reformation within Christendom, all the outbreaks of insurrectionary thought beyond its borders, Islam for example; the Renaissance, the Reformation, the great French Revolution; they were all upheavals of human common-sense against the corruptions and perversions that were perpetually developing to restrain it and hold it back. So Rud held. He was, he put it modestly, just one of the billions of common men held down by these conventions and superstitions. He was the commonest of common men. The quintessence. So it was he raged against them. From first to last he was on the side of the rebels. It was in his essential nature. From his swaddling clothes onward, the note of protest had sounded in his voice.

He hated all established things. He hated every established thing, good or bad, and his conception of the Common Man was fast assuming that same attitude of gigantic defiance against all the order and dignity of the world which characterised the cartoons of his Russian avatar, the Marxist Proletarian, hammer and sickle in hand.

In his private reveries the identification of the Common Man with Rud was plainly visible. And in the undisclosed depths of that reverie, his feeling towards every previous exponent of the Common Man idea was one of embittered rivalry. There was no limit to his jealousy.

When someone in the Group suggested that the Common-sense Movement was really Practical Christianity, Rud blew up and revealed something of what he had hidden away in his mind.

"Augh!" he cried, in querulous protest. "Clean all this past stuff off history, and begin again. *If,* after all, we are only going back to primitive Christianity, whatever it was, the 'simple teaching of Jesus' and all that (only I don't believe we are for a moment) then let these Christians find it out. We can't go into all these old disputes of theirs about their blessed Founder, what he was and what he wasn't, what he did and what he didn't do, now. They don't know themselves. *He had his chance and lost it.* Well, didn't he, Dreed? Very fine chap, no doubt, but his inefficiency was awful. And the inefficiency of everyone about him. Think of the march on Jerusalem and compare it with the march on Rome. Think of wandering about in a Garden until they came for him... He's smothered up, they've lost him, and it's for them to find him again. Not us. He's lost under nineteen centuries of theological deposits. Well, *isn't* he? *Any* living leader is worth a dead one, particularly a dead one who wasn't properly reported. What's the good of pretending he was? What's the good of all this smarming over what the Christians have? They haven't got anything clear and sound. Nothing at all.

"If we've got his stuff as you say, then *if it's the reality they care for* and not just a name, let them fall in with *us.* Follow us. Why not? Why should we go after them? Let them sort out their Jesuses until they've got Mr Right. But it isn't *his* stuff they care for. They never cared for his stuff. They care less for his stuff than I do. I'm a better Nazarene than any Christian alive. It's the Name. What's in a name? What *is* there in a name? Will human being never grow out of name magic? Christianity, if it is all they say it is, by any other name would smell as sweet. Modern common-sense, that's what we stand for, and let other people make the identifications...

"Maybe he *was* the first modern Radical. Maybe, I say. But that's only historical speculation. Why go back to that? You've got Christianity plain before you. In the Churches. Look at 'em. Christianity is as Christianity does...

"Christianity! Look at the Archbishop of Canterbury all dressed up to kill, cope and mitre and holy rings and all the ancient spiritual gadgets; look at the Pope in his canonicals. BC all of it, from start to finish. Do you believe any of those fellows are mentally straight? I don't. Who told them they were entitled to speak for that Galilean Radical? If they'd lived in his time they'd have been on the bench with Caiaphas and Pontius Pilate. They think they can put up their bluff upon the masses, and they aren't afraid of God looking at them – for a very good reason. Long ago they said in their hearts 'There is no God.' That's why they won't have these things talked about plainly. That's why they insist on reverence, sacred names and all that. A sacred thing is a protected thing, a thing in retreat. When you want to argue, they say 'Hush! Reverence, please. Lower your voices so that nobody can hear the awful things you are saying. Not so loud, please, and above all, not so plain.'

"They know they dare not have their stuff stripped down to plain words. These Bishops and parsons with their beloved Christianity are like a man who has poisoned his wife and says her body's too sacred for a post-mortem. Nowadays, by the light we have, any ecclesiastic *must* be born blind or an intellectual rascal. Don't tell me. The world's had this apostolic succession of oily old humbugs from early Egypt onwards, trying to come it over people. Antiquity's no excuse. A sham is no better for being six thousand years stale. Christianity's no more use to us now than the Pyramids."

227

So Rud, the Holy Terror, at his most raucous, banging the table, letting himself go about Christianity, in the councils of the Group. They heard him with a sort of horrified admiration.

"You can't say outrageous things like this – *outside*," said Bodisham.

"Not yet," said Rud. "But Mussolini and Hitler said almost as much – and got away with it. Russia again – no longer a Christian country. That thing's not going on for ever. High time it was wound up. We are making a new world, aren't we? – and the old rubbish has to be cleared away. Isn't it absolutely essential that the old rubbish should be cleared away? Or what is common-sense supposed to be doing?

"Why! Think what happened the other day at Forli! Canopy, croziers, censers, banners, little boys in lace and petticoats, and what effect did it have? 'Go home, you old fool,' he said, 'and change those ridiculous clothes. Get into shorts and do some exercises.' And the people cheered!"

"Red belief in Christianity," said Chiffan, "may be at an ebb in the world, Rud, but shockableness is still high. Reverence is something that survives belief. In these northern countries particularly. I knew a little boy once whose head was smacked, smacked soundly by his own mother, for cocking snooks at Stonehenge. I'm not sure I don't agree with her. So you'd better be careful."

"I shall be careful," said Rud. "But Forli, mind you, wasn't shocked…"

"The whole world," he said, "is going Radical again. Fundamentally. In religion. In politics. In law. The Common Man had been trying to get his Radicalism said and done plainly

228

and clearly for a hundred and fifty years. Now *we* take it on. Our movement. The new wave of attack."

"And fill a ditch in our turn," said Irwell.

"Maybe we're over the last ditch," said Rud. "There *must* be a last ditch somewhere…"

"All other revolutionary movements have been experiments so far, Christianity, the French Revolution, the Russian Revolution, are more or less failures. They were experiments in liberation and they did not liberate. The old things wriggled back. But ours may be the experiment that succeeds. *We* may get to the Common-sense World State. Yes – *we* – in this room… Why not? It has to come somehow, somewhen… If it doesn't come pretty soon, there won't be much of humanity left to liberate."

2

It seemed natural to Rud to take the loyal co-operation of his colleagues in the Group as a matter of course. He never felt in the slightest degree beholden to them. He took his leadership over them as confidently as he had taken his bottle from his nurse in the cradle. They served the Common Man and gave themselves without stint to the release of this Common-sense World State from all the foetal wrappings that entangled it. What else could they do? What else was there to do? So why should the embodied Common Man thank and flatter them? He snatched their ideas out of their mouths.

And they chanced to make a team that could co-operate. They kept together throughout twelve crucial years in human history. He did little deliberately to hold them together, but his instinct was for management. His egotistical dominance, his impartial acceptance of the role of the representative Common Man, seemed to check the development of internecine jealousies. During those years remarkably little force was wasted by the Group in internal friction. Day by day it grew, Insensibly and yet rapidly it became a factor, and ultimately a leading factor, in world affairs. Even when it was already attracting public attention, its members still seemed for a time mere incidental outsiders adventuring into politics; commentators rather than combatants. It was by insensible degrees that they became a revolutionary force of the extremest efficiency. They did not appear; they grew.

They differed in one essential from the revolutionary groups from which the earlier dictatorships, the Russian and Italian, for example, sprang. They had no conspiratorial past whatever, less even than the Nazis. They were innocent of the underground methods and free from the tortuous mental habits of the traditional nineteenth-century revolutionists. And after Bohun's collapse no trace was left of any of his Fascist or Hitlerian plagiarisms. Shirts, salutes, symbols, banners, were got rid of. He and his organisation made just their jumping-off board. They had an auction of "unsold stock" in aid of the Movement. "Shirts," they advertised, "can be dyed any colour. Zips not guaranteed." So far they justified their claim to be a new sort of revolutionary drive altogether. They developed the opportunity given them by their picturesque capture of the Purple House and the great fight in the Canton Hall, with skill and vigour. It was their first introduction to political realities. They set about their business with immense seriousness, and they did not only a lot of hard work but a lot of very hard thinking. They tried over definitions and classifications and cleared them up; they listed, they documented, they mapped. They turned the drawing-room floor of number seventeen into a permanent council chamber; they vetted and incorporated newcomers; they were wary of fresh blood but not jealous of it; they were too desperately anxious to succeed to waste any possible co-operation. Bodisham's growing conceptions of organisation, Chiffan's flow of shrewd ideas and Steenhold's ready welcome and support for any entertaining initiative pervaded the place from the outset, and Rud went about masterfully, convinced that he organised everything he learnt and endorsed.

That room still exists for the curious to visit. It is exactly as they left it when three years later they transferred their Headquarters to the Sloten Aerodrome. They kept it on, because at first they thought the Sloten move was a temporary one. The chairs, the tables, and many of the earlier files and charts are still there, but over it all now is that faint, faded quality of thing disused. No morning dusting, no sedulous cleaning can avert that retrocession from reality. All historical showplaces acquire that progressive incredibility. It seems a little room to have sheltered so tremendous an initiative. The custodians of the place had added a collection of photographs of the chief members of the Group before it moved to Holland. As near as possible they are early portraits, and each one stands in its frame at the place where the original was either known or supposed to have sat. (There is no gavel. Rud always banged with his fist on the table.) There they talked out the ultimate revolution and laid the foundations for the Peace of the World.

"Did they think they were playing with their imaginations or did they realise the tremendous reality of what they were doing?" asks Lipping. The answer in "Both". Every war, every revolution and every important invention the world has ever seen, began as a dream. How else can human enterprises begin?

And they end with the voice of the caretaker, reciting his scrap of history, showing round the tourist. "That is where He sat, and generally it seems Chiffan sat to the left of him, rather close to him to whisper things to him, and there, where the chair is pushed back, was Steenhold's place. He was the tallest of them all except Rogers and he used to push his chair back to stretch out his legs...

3

After the capture of the Purple House, Rud insisted on a sort of intensive study of this world they were attacking. His mixture of shrewdness and insight with imaginative vigour was never more apparent than at this time. Chiffan noted his increasing elasticity. Always Rud had had mental bounce, but never so much as this. He would pass at a bound from a private meditation upon his role as the Culminating Common Man, to the most intense practical activity. "I've got to get into relationship with people now," he insisted. "With all kinds of influential people. I ought to do it. We've got to see what they are made of. We've got to get out of our hole-and-corner stage as soon as possible. Marx was hole-and-corner all his life, and Lenin had too much of it for his health. We've got to be different. We've got to escape from narrowness. We're a movement, not a conspiracy. We've got to radiate contacts, and have as many people aware of us as possible. That's living, modern common-sense.

In the various personal encounters in which Rud had made himself known to the worldly powers which might otherwise have impeded the consolidation of his leadership of the renascent Popular Socialist Party, his "living, modern common-sense" became as flexible and slippery as an eel.

He was his loose, large appeal to common humanity spreading and catching on, and he felt not the slightest scruple in talking ambiguously and making vague promises to divert and pacify anyone who might have been disposed to nip him in the bud, restrict his publicity or rob him of police immunity before he was established as a worldwide political fact. Sooner or later a struggle was inevitable, but the later it came, the better for Rud. His instinct was to get all over the picture first.

In the days immediately following the capture of the Purple House he saw as many people of importance as he could, mostly they were people who had hitherto been nothing to him but news and names and portraits. They wanted to see him now, after that bright flare-up of publicity, and he wanted to see them, so it was not very difficult to get together. Opportunities were made for him and he had to ask for very little. Before the nine-days' wonder of the great fight in the West End faded out he knew he had to make sure not only of press but financial support. So he did his utmost to make sure of both.

It was an enormously educational time for him. He grew years older in a few weeks. Chiffan watched him in amazement. Political theorising at Headquarters gave place abroad to practical political canvassing of the most unscrupulous sort. Bodisham and the others schemed, made enquiries, prepared dossiers of important people for him. He went to great pains to make himself "important yet normal" in the eyes of all these key people.

He built up an effigy of himself for their benefit. Deliberately and with great self-restraint, he created an impression that was only effaced in the course of several years. He persuaded or he showed off or he seemed to betray his quality, as occasion required. He wanted them to believe he was the man to capture and sell popular discontent, and they did. After the manner of the British ruling class, they trusted him as a thoroughly untrustworthy man.

He let it be assumed that he was bringing no original ideas whatever into British political life. That, he knew, was fundamentally important. He discussed the internal situation and foreign affairs, discreetly and in established phrases. He read files of *The Times* for some years back to catch the tone, be devoured political memoirs, volumes of collected letters and speeches. He was, he admitted, airing perhaps a few original ideas in what he had to say, but his heart, he implied, was in the right place.

He was to be a national invigorator, he conveyed. He was to profess much, do nothing, and leave everyone the better for it. He was to take on the task at which Bohun had so signally failed. He was to put the fermenting new red wine of popular discontent, popular discomfort and resentment (and popular behaviour in the Midlands and the North was certainly becoming very serious), internationalism, collectivism and all those gathering horrors, back into the brave old bottles of the established order – in his own way. But he must have a free hand. He must not be prevented. Admittedly he was a clever fellow. He conceded that, but all the same, he intimated, they must not embarrass him. They must not attempt to tell him. He began in fact where most Labour politicians leave off.

He let it be tacitly assumed that fundamentally he was a sound, patriotic Englishman and that, in spite of current difficulties, he regarded the staggering Empire, the inert monarchy, the Anglican Church, the Anglican country house, as the lovely and eternal framework of the perfect life. Beyond this frame mankind could progress no further until a thoroughly Anglican Last Day inaugurated an unending Anglican season in Heaven, with the Holy Family playing, very tactfully, the part of super-Royalty. Since they could imagine nothing better, he let it be assumed that he could imagine nothing better.

He had remarkably little difficulty in establishing the fundamental respectability of his intentions. He realised with the profoundest astonishment that a tacit assumption of his Anglicanism was made for him, that it was incredible to most of these influential people that a man could be a born Englishman and still not entertain the completest love and admiration for Anglicanism. He discovered that even the Jews, Atheists and Roman Catholics of Britain are fundamentally Anglican. And there was no question of the entire conformity of the modern Nonconformist. So after all, considering their immense assimilative power, why should they question *him*?

No one in the world of influence asked him what he thought about the established institutions of his native land, and so he told them no lies. They had no suspicion of the fundamental resentments in his nature. They didn't perceive that his scowl was an expression. That he regarded the whole British system as incurably decayed, a crumbling unteachable system of complex and exasperating appropriations and resistances, and that it was the dearest ambition of his black little heart to see it wiped out of existence as soon as possible and replaced by an Anglo-American synthesis with a cosmopolitan trend, remained and undisclosed aspect of his programme. "One thing at a time," said Rud to his council.

"Of course," he said at a lunch party to which he had been invited by Lady Dragnet, "now that we are one day's journey from America, we *must* talk just a little more American than we did." (That was the stuff to give them.) "Frankly, I think we are getting badly out of touch with mass opinion over there…"

"Yes, but suppose you have made a mistake and put your money on the wrong horse. Suppose this recrudescence of aggressive Big Business over there isn't sound. (You know what Americans *are*.) Isn't it well to have a strong popular movement in England in touch with the American Labour side?"

Something in that, they thought.

"I could make just those contacts…"

"It has always been part of the strength of England to have a strong opposition," he explained. "So that when we have got ourselves into a complete mess – as I think, if you'll forgive me, the government is doing now – we've always had an opposition formula to fall back upon. That, we can say, is what we meant all along. That has been our peculiar advantage, a natural, un-premeditated, providential two-facedness. Sometimes foreigners have thought us inconsistent – almost to the point of perfidy. But it is all perfectly simple. England is like a coin with an obverse and reverse. *Has* been, anyhow. A great democratic monarchy is a contradiction in itself; particularly with a House of Lords; it *must* blow hot and cold…

"But nowadays – Our weakness for the last few years has been the ineffectiveness of the Opposition. This Labour Party has never had the quality of a fighting Opposition. It has just sucked the life out of Radicalism. It has never had the definite idealism of the Whigs and Liberals. 'Give us more employment and slightly higher pay and be sure of our contentment,' says Labour. 'We're loyal. We know our place. But we don't like being unemployed.' What good is that as Opposition? It's about as much opposition as a mewing cat. *We* mean more than that. I tell you frankly. Our task, I take it, my task, is to reinstate that practical working Opposition which has always been Old England's alternative line of defence... For the good of all of us..."

He said that.

He had, he intimated, to put the idea crudely in a conversation. He might have to put it still more crudely to the country. But they must understand that he knew what he meant to do. Now and then he might have to use phrases that would make conservative gentlemen sit up a bit. More than sit up – jump. They had to trust him...

"After all, Joseph Chamberlain was a republican Radical who talked of 'ransom'; and look at the Chamberlains now!...

"I don't want support in your papers," he told Lord Thunderclap, the great press peer. "But I want space. Denounce me if you like, but *feature* me. I'd rather be denounced. I don't want to seem to be in with you. I'm being perfectly open with you."

"And I like openness," said the great Lord Thunderclap, and regarded him, as far as he could manage it, with the candid face of a simple, responsible, old-fashioned newspaper proprietor. "I think we understand one another."

"Anything but silence," said Rud, looking if possible even more candid than his lordship.

"Run along," said Thunderclap, like a benign God. "You shall exist."

Thunderclap was particularly impressed by a comparison that Rud, in developing this theory of British disingenuousness, made of Britain to a double-headed eagle, looking both east and west. Thunderclap though this discovery of the essential duplicity of England a very penetrating one. In his past he had been accused, with a certain plausibility, of inconsistency and abrupt changes of front. But Rud's inferential present of a second head seemed to put him all square again. He felt Rud was a clever fellow who ought to be encouraged. He ordered that Rud should be "news" throughout his press.

"I've got the hang of him," he said. "Nothing Red in *him*."

4

Lord Bendigo, another great lord of public opinion in those days, wasn't by any means as easy as Lord Thunderclap. He was one of Rud's more difficult problems. Thunderclap thought in phobias and booms, but Bendigo had ideas of his own. For the most part they were extremely poor ideas. His leading one had been the complete isolation of the British Empire from the rest of the world, which Rud regarded as too obviously silly and impracticable for serious treatment. He thought at first that Bendigo wasn't earnest about this fancy. Then he came to believe that Bendigo was a man of great obstinacy, fighting down a subconscious realisation that he had spent a large part of his life promulgating puerile nonsense.

238

There was something about this man that Rud found curiously congenial. He sensed a malignant wilfulness very like his own. This very resemblance gave Bendigo the quality of an awful warning. "He had pushed himself into a corner and away from power by the very vigour of his egotism," Rud reflected. "He thought he could put over just anything through sheer wilfulness. Things aren't like that. I used to think it, but I've learnt some lessons. He got his luck too soon, and that spoilt him. Primary facts are invincible. You *have* to respect them. Fact is the mountain you have to climb, and the way of it is the way you have to go. It's have only way up. But Bendigo started out to climb a mountain that in fact wasn't there... And he goes on with all the gestures of his Isolationist Crusade long after he has realised its futility...

"I, too, have that disposition... I hate going back on myself. I hate checking up things with other people, but I know enough to know I've got to do it. He must have just *plunged* into that Imperial Isolationism of his. Before he thought over the change of scale or air war, or any of these newer things. Plunged with a million readers. And then held on, like a child in tantrum. *I* did that sort of thing when I was a kid."

Criticism of Bendigo was comparatively easy, but how to get a satisfactory publicity out of him was a riddle. Rud's guess was to go to him for advice about going into Parliament. "Wait, and I will tell you," said Bendigo; "it's no time to start now"; and things were left at that.

Rud tried to convey the effect of a thoroughly dishonest, pushful and able young man ready to sell and be sold, a young man in a state of involuntary admiration and natural envy for a tremendously successful newspaper owner, but even upon these lines he was doubtful if he got Bendigo.

What on earth did Bendigo want? Of Rud or life or anything? There was a wicked scrutiny in his lordship's disillusioned eye. Rud was left with an uneasy memory of that eye. It was an eye that should have twinkled, and it didn't twinkle. It said for a moment, with a touch of the genial fellowship of adventurers, "Well, what are *you* up to?" and then hardened to "You don't get *me,* my boy, whatever you want."

It became the cold, resentful eye of an inordinate man in a disappointing world. Bendigo had thought life was a lark, he had handled it inconsiderately and found it a dead lark in his hands.

Steenhold told Rud there were American parallels. Similar forces produce similar results. Newspaper proprietors were the most paradoxical class in the world. Everybody wanted to use newspaper proprietors, and nobody respected their ambitions. No one expected them to have ambitions. They were vehicles to take people to all sorts of desirable destinations – and wait outside. Never would the public recognise any possibility of direct leadership in them. They became resentful, embittered men. All the world over.

In Britain they wore coronets, often slightly askew, but that made no essential difference. They were once powerful and infuriatingly impotent.

Nowhere in the world, Rud reflected, was journalism anything but a malignant and wanton power. Later on, as the Common-sense Movement grew, he had to think a lot about that. He had to spread a new system of ideas throughout the world, and journalism would neither instruct nor inform nor lend itself consistently to any sustained propaganda.

Both these men, Thunderclap and Bendigo, had an air of really wanting new policies for the country, though they were essentially crazy policies. They were at least kinetic, they wanted to make things happen even it they did not quite know what or how, but the other and really conservative newspaper owners and directors Rud approached seemed simply holding on to the established order.

They displayed not simply a disposition to be unbelievably dull in political matters, they displayed a partisan attitude to dullness; they even carried on dullness propaganda; by way of political education they inundated their readers with the exemplary memoirs of the empty eminent of the Victorian and Edwardian days. They still thought that people would thrill at the pomp and splendour of Lord Grey's mental processes or Lord Oxford's academic dignity. They ignored every social process afoot and everything new, unless it was in some way assimilable to the old order. Nothing, Rud realised, was to be got by a direct association with them. That meant mere submission. It was clear that to win their attention something very emphatic and quasi-successful had to be done.

"Maybe," said Steenhold, "they'd take up our stuff if it came as news from America, much more readily than if it grew under their feet. Or from China. It wouldn't seem so disturbing that way. They still think America and China are oceans away…"

"Couldn't we get a man to write a series of articles warning people against the dangers of the Common-sense Movement?" said Chiffan. "We might launch a controversy. Say it was unspiritual or something of that sort, and drag in the broader-minded bishops to vindicate us…"

"Is there *no* press for ideas, as ideas, in England?" demanded Irwell.

"Only in what they call the silly season," said Chiffan.

Chiffan was inclined to think that the country was in what he called a "phase of discordance" between its press and it public. He sprouted an engaging theory that there have to be "periodic modernisations" in the newspaper world. ("As in everything else," said Rud.) Newspapers succeeded, fell into routines and grew steadily more out of touch with the public mind. They became great estates. They became pompous and aloof. Until at last the gap between them and the latent mental possibilities of a new generation broadened enough to admit a new type of journalism. This, he declared, had happened to Britain with the onset of the new popular halfpenny paper at the beginning of the century, and in America recently with the appearance of the *Time* type of national weekly newspaper. And with each of these phases of modernisation a quickening of the public mind had been made manifest. The times were ripening now for a fresh move in England.

Bodisham picked up this idea and, looking ahead, said that if the movement was to grow it must have an aggressive competitive press of its own. "We must have a press section of the movement – a separate organisation, of course, not a Party organ. We must try out a paper to *pay*. We must try a group of papers… Find men for it. Find men. And keep a Party contact with them. None of these proprietors for us – with their abortive dreams of power – it's editors and managers we want to have with us. We've got to redemocratise the press. Dictatorship is just as bad in a newspaper office as it is in a country. It stiffens. It mechanises. It devitalises."

When the Group turned its attention to the existing leftward papers, Chiffan found still more support for his theory that there were periods of opportunity for publicity, and that now was the time to vary the production and distribution of newspapers. Rud listened to all they had to say, and then went off like a drummer to interest the left press in this new movement he was selling the world.

Any by the time he got talking to them, his bright adaptive mind had developed Chiffan's theory of stale newspaper forms and methods into a general theory of collective fatigue.

He addressed various discreet and dubious Liberals: "What I want to do is to *refresh* Liberalism."

Liberalism, he said, was practically empty. Why not have it done up thoroughly from roof to basement – repainted? "You want to be fresh. How can Liberalism be anything but something fresh?

"The world," he generalised, "is always getting tired of its ruling phrases. Always. Fresh every morning are the old hopes, but the words for them have to be different. People want the same fundamental thing age after age, you say; yes, but they want them in a new dress. We're living in an enslaved and militant world. *You* say that and so do I. And why? We're living in a backward-looking world – black with debts and old histories. 'We?' you ask. We common men. (Think of me, please, as just one of your readers come in to tell you off.) We're perplexed and baffled. We hate the fears and patriotisms that enslave us. Subconsciously if not consciously. We imagined these patriotisms meant local freedom, and now we find they mean

243

universal slavery. Patriotism in a little state is the first resort of a scoundrel. And nowadays all states are too little. Strangulate. We're crushed to death with armies and navies and air forces, and nobody wants them to fight. The common soldiers least of all. We are bored to death of being ordered about – and we don't like the new catering. And the taxes. We're sulking and we want a lead. But where is the chink of light yet in our prison? Where is *your* light? Why don't you go on to something? Everything Liberalism offers the world as an alternative to drill-ground slavery is either really stale or it looks stale.

"Why *is* Liberalism so hopelessly conservative? Worse than any Tories. Everybody is tired of your League of Nations, for example, and yet you are still boring away at it. It's no good arguing whether it's right or wrong or good or bad. It's *stale*. It's – infected. It's infested. It never was anything more than an insincere gesture. No one believes in it now. No one at all. It has missed fire with the common man. Alter it at least, do it up, give it a new name. Wash out the Wilson stuff. Make it world-rationalist instead of internationalist.

"You keep on boring away at that old, old story. Why? Don't you really want world unity? Are you really clinging to national politics subconsciously? Have you asked yourselves that? I misjudge you? Do I? Well, even as a political fraud the old League is pretty well played out. What good will it do you or anyone now? Forget about it.

"That's where your support of the World Common-sense Party would give you a chance... We *have* new formulae...

"We English are profoundly tired of our Empire. Indeed we are. Tired and bored. Don't you realise that? The Empire's become public-schoolmasters' cant and the boys know all the

244

answers. It's being stripped and exposed; it's an empire of kraals and slums, loincloth village and Bombay sweatshops; it has never educated, never released; it has no constructive vitality at all; it's nothing to be proud of. The intelligent boys are ashamed of it. At heart Germany and Italy are just as sick of *their* regimes. But what can they do? They just go on doing the same old exercises and repeating the same old catchwords until something comes along to crystallise their discontent in a positive form. Who can deliver them from the body of this death? They ask that; everyone asks that...

"You didn't know of our movement? You don't know anything of any movement. Your fault, not ours. You just know stale politics... I can understand Liberalism getting stale. All things get stale. But why should it want to keep stale?

"The world, I tell you, is bored – bored now to the explosive pitch. It's bored by all this incessant war preparation. It is bored by aimless violence, now here, now there. It is tired of hatred politics. It's tired of fresh murders every days. It is not indignant, not excited; it is bored. Bored and baffled...

"I don't believe a man begins to know anything of politics until he realises the immense menace of mental fatigue, of worldwide mass boredom. It accumulates. It makes the most frightful convulsions and demoralisation possible. It makes them at last inevitable. Nobody wants fundamental changes in a world where hope and interest prevail. Then people accept their careers, settle down to them, rear children. But throw them out of work, in and out and no sense of security, deprive them of bright expectations, regiment them in masses, underfeed them, bore them with organised mass patriotism, and they begin to seep together into a common morass of discontent and impatience. Almost unconsciously...

"They're like that now.

"If you Liberals really *had* a progressive idea ready for them now, new-phrased and released from old obligations and old associations, you could set the world afire with it. If you had. Eh? Well, *we* have. We Common-sense men are the real New Liberalism. Why be so stuffy about it? You've got to bury old Gladstone sooner or later, just as the Socialists have to bury Karl Marx...

"After all, what we want is to go on with the Radicalism of the first French Revolution. We're just revitalised Radicals. That's what we are. Napoleon was a traitor and the Commune a blunder. Forget about them. *We* want *real* liberty, *real* equality, *real* fraternity... How about 'Back to the Taking of the Bastille' as a slogan? How about 'The Liberators of the Bastille'?"

"But I thought you were all for scrapping old traditions," said the Liberal editor, with an air of making a point.

He had made a point, and Rud had to pull his argument together.

"Scrapping old corruptions," said Rud. "Radicalism – the indignation that stormed the Bastille – is eternally young."

6

Rud returned to the Group in a state of extreme mental excitement.

"I've got it," he said, "about the League of Nations. I understand 1919-20. It's all as clear as daylight."

Chiffan nodded expectantly with a faint smile.

"Yet I never saw it before. These Liberals open one's eyes."

Real affection shone in Chiffan's regard. He was beginning to feel a genuine parental glow at Rud's impassioned discoveries. If Rud neither begat nor conceived nor created, he was, at any rate, a magnificent obstetrician.

"In 1918," said Rud, "the need for such a world unification and socialisation as we are planning was as manifest as it is now. It stared the world in the face. But – "

The Group waited to see its own revelation plain.

"It meant a fundamental change in nearly every system of human activities. That is to say, it meant a reconstructed management. It meant new patterns in politics, world economics, a new world education, a wider way of living for everyone, and nobody among all the worthy people to whom the settlement was entrusted could really stand up to that prospect. Because it meant that they too had to be renewed. They had to adapt or they had to go. An age of extreme experimentation was inevitable. It was in the air in 1918. The rulers and leaders shirked it. Not consciously perhaps but subconsciously the ruling people resisted every rational step forward. It was bound to be a vast, ill-lit step, I admit, and into a strange world. For some of them it was not so much a step as a precipice. So they decided that the mass of people in the world were unprepared for it – while as a matter of fact it was they themselves who were unprepared for it. See?"

Chiffan's face answered that question.

"Lord, what a pleasure it is to get back to you chaps and talk freely! I've been diplomatic all day. Now let me splutter... Where was I? In 1918, I say, the ruling classes everywhere had nightmares of the Last Trump. Everywhere. They woke up again, clear that nothing of that sort must happen. The dear old

247

world, which makes us all we are, must remain. They decided not to resurrect, Last Trump or no. 'What is this about a readjusted world?' they said. 'Let us have no extravagance. Let us go gradually,' they said, 'let us go very, very gradually – in other words, let us do just as little as possible to alter the rules of the game we have played hitherto. It is a played-out game, yes – we admit that *in theory* – but how can any of us learn to play an entirely new one all at once? If we have to drop the control of things, what sort of horrid people will replace us? Let us keep our grip and produce something that will *look* like a World Peace, a Union of Mankind, and at the same time let us see that nothing fundamental is changed about the old Foreign Offices, the old diplomacy, the old sovereignties, the methods we can work, the things we know. Business as usual during the resurrection. We won't attempt to make anything so extravagant as a new world, we will just make a – a nice beginning, an unimplemented promise.'

"In that spirit, I tell you, this great Put-off at Geneva was brought into being. It was a deliberate, almost conscious Put-off. A crash may come later, said their subconsciousnesses; but, anyhow, this patch-up of a League will last our time. Germany must pay and so on, they shall be victims and vanquished according to the best precedents, but the essence of our settlement is that civilisation as we know it will be saved."

Rud repeated: "Civilisation as they knew it! They couldn't think of any other sort of civilisation. Tea when they're called in the morning, and all that."

"That Geneva generation has been tiding over and putting off the new world ever since. Growing old and refusing to see how the real world crisis intensifies with every year of delay.

248

Manifestly to remake the world means a vast obliteration of traditions and class mentalities, but it has to occur. If *they* won't make over, it's got to be made over for them. That's where we come in. That remaking is what *they* call Chaos, and for them it is chaos – the end of everything – obliteration – effacement, anyhow. But for us it is the revolt of common-sense."

"You don't thing there were *any* honest good intentions in that League of Nations experiment?" said Irwell.

"How can one plumb the self-deceptions of the muddy-witted?" said Rud. "There were tons of good intentions. Mountains of good intentions all round the Lake. They were enough to have made Geneva stuffy, even if the mountains didn't. These League of Nations people making believe they were readjusting the world, and elaborately and carefully doing nothing of the sort, *stank* of moral self-satisfaction.

"For all that, the League of Nations was in effect an almost planned and deliberate abortion of the plain commonsense needs of mankind, an elaborate sabotage of the Common Man's hopes. To save trouble. To save face. It was the petition in bankruptcy of the Liberal mind. This, it said, is all I have. And until the whole of this generation of damned disingenuous Liberals is dead, what passes as Liberalism will still be bolstering up this substitute, this sham, this Make Believe of a New World."

And suddenly he became almost lyric. "For three thousand years the Common Man has been fended off from the full and glorious life he might have had, by Make Believe. For three thousand years in one form or another he has been asking for a unrestricted share in the universal welfare. He has been asking for a fair dividend from civilisation. For all that time, and still it goes on, the advantaged people, the satisfied people, the kings

249

and priests, the owners and traders, the gentlefolk and the leaders he trusted, have been cheating him tacitly or deliberately, out of his proper share and contribution in the common life. Sometimes almost consciously, sometimes subconsciously, cheating themselves about it as well. When he called upon God, they said 'We'll take care of your God for you', and they gave him organised religion. When he calls for Justice, they say 'Everything decently and in order', and give him a nice expensive Law Court beyond his means. When he calls for order and safety too loudly they hit him on the head with a policeman's truncheon. When he sought knowledge, they told him what was good for him. And to protect him from the foreigner, so they said, they got him bombed to hell, trained him to disembowel his fellow common men with bayonets and learn what love of King and Country really means.

"All with the best intentions in the world, mind you.

"Most of these people, I tell you, have acted in perfect good faith. They manage to believe that in sustaining this idiot's muddle they are doing tremendous things – stupendous things – for the Common Man. They can live lives of quiet pride and die quite edifyingly in an undernourished, sweated, driven and frustrated world. Useful public servants! Righteous self-applause! Read their bloody biographies!

"This League of Nations of the Liberals is only the last of the endless succession of Make Believes that have baffled the poor, misinformed, miseducated Common Man. I tell you, stupidity, self-protective stupidity, is the fundamental sin. No man alive has a right to contentment. No man alive has a right to mental rest. No man has any right to be as stupid as educated, Liberal men have been about that foolish affair at Geneva. Men who have any leisure, any gifts, any resources, have no right to stifle their consciences with that degree of imposture. The League of Nations has been an exposed imposture almost from the start, an impotent substitute for effort, and it has wasted two decades, twenty crucial years, of human possibility, the first third of the lives of all of us here in effect... We who will never have lives again."

Chiffan put his hands on either side of his chin. He reflected aloud: "This sort of analysis applies, *mutatis mutandis,* to almost every established institution."

"Essentially, yes."

"Established institutions. You hate them all," said Chiffan.

"Because they stand in our way to a rational, happy, splendid world."

Chiffan smiled, faintly sceptical. "You just hate them because they are established institutions."

Rud considered this for a moment and then with a leap of frankness: "Yes, Chiffan — I hate them because they are established institutions. They confine and stifle me. As they do you. But they die, they die. Not fast enough, but they die. And the League of Nations generation is dying, and the dear old scholarly Liberals are dying, the class of the last great Make Believe are dying, man by man, day by day. And as that generation, with all its self-preserving hypocrisies, fades and dies, the stage is cleared — "

"Partially cleared," said Chiffan.

"More or less cleared," said Rud. "Cleared perhaps enough."

Chiffan thought of saying something more. He saw something like an appeal to him in Rud's eye and he said no more.

"For us," said Irwell.

251

"For the Common-sense of the Common Man," said Rud, with a last rhetorical flourish, "to come to its own."

7

Bold and challenging generalisations went rather well at the editorial lunch of the leading Liberal paper. These Liberals felt that so little could ever be done that they were prepared for any suggestions, however extravagant, for doing things. They were as receptive of new ideas as baby-farmers are of babies. They knew they could put away any amount of new ideas and be none the worse for it, politically or socially. But the Labour keymen, in conference upon their newspapers, Rud found rather more difficult to impress.

They were evidently profoundly suspicious of him.

It was his first definite encounter with the wary-eyed, platitudinous, evasive Labour leaders, and he realised at once the formidable barrier of inert leadership they constituted, between the discontented masses and constructive change. They seemed to be almost entirely preoccupied by internecine intrigues and the "discipline of the Party." They were steeped in Party professionalism. They were not in any way traitors to their cause, or wilfully reactionary, but they had no minds for a renascent world. They meant nothing, but they did not know they meant nothing. They regarded Rud just as in their time they had regarded Liberalism, Fabianism, Communism, Science, suspecting them all, learning nothing from them, blankly resistant. They did not want ideas in politics. They just wanted to be the official representatives of organised labour and make what they could by it. Their manner betrayed their invincible resolution, as strong as an animal instinct, to play politics according to the rules, to manoeuvre for positions, to dig themselves into positions – and squat...

"*I'll* get a move on them," said Rud.

"They've got the Trade Unions behind them,"

"I've no use for Trade Unions. They've lasted long enough. They've locked up the workmen in a sort of small-tradesman respectability. We want more than that nowadays. They've hampered the natural political and social emergence of the common man."

"Trade Unions to go!" said Bodisham. "Christianity to go! You're making us take on a lot, Rud. You're a bit of a Terror, Rud."

"You know I'm right. They've gone in Russia, Germany, Italy. They totter in America and France. This country has got to move with the times. We've got to take a lesson from the passion of China, we English and Americans, and wake up before it is too late. I won't be premature about this. Trust me to know when to open fire and how."

"The queer thing is that we *do* trust you," said Bodisham. "In spite of your – extremism."

"You'd better," said Rud with grim conviction. "*I'm right*. What is extremism? The whole truth and nothing but the truth. I ask you."

"It's because of his extremism you trust him," said Chiffan. "It's because in the last resort we believe in his indiscretion, and know he won't fail us even if we fail ourselves. All leadership is extravagance. Extravagance. Going a bit ahead."

Rud did not quite understand that. "It's because you know I'm right," he said.

"It's because," said Chiffan, letting his thoughts run away with him, "to make a new world, the leader must be a fundamentally destructive man, a recklessly destructive man. He breaks his way through the jungle and we follow... We cannot do without you, Rud."

8

Irwell did his best to inform Rud about the City, and get the reactions of his fine inexperience to that complex system of activities. More and more was the Group finding something oracular and decisive in his penetrating detestations. "Of course," they said now to his most startling dogmatisms. "Of course."

Rud and Irwell had lunch with an enquiring group of stock-brokers; and on another occasion, they were privileged to have their views about social credit put right for them by a friendly banking firm which lunched over its offices in a large, graceful room, with such an unpretending splendour of silver and mahogany and cold sideboard, and so protected from outside clamour by double windows and carpeted floors, that it seemed to Rud for a time he must have fallen into some older, wiser and altogether more stable and comfortable world.

But Rud talked none the less effectively on that account. He talked in particular here of his doctrine of the abolition of the Atlantic. America and Britain, with only ten hours to separate them, were becoming one again. There must be some sort of practical coalescence ahead. Must be. But, lunching over a bank, he did not make it as clear as he might have done whether he meant a coalescence of the United States and Britain or a coalescence of the City and Wall Street. "Business," he threw out, "is more plastic than political structure. There will certainly be an Anglo-American newspaper coalescence, for example, in the next ten years."

"It has been tried several times."

"And it will be tried again and again – until it succeeds."

"We're an old firm," said the senior partner.

"But a live one," said Rud.

"If I knew anything of newspaper finance," he added, "I'd try to get ahead with a straddle paper now."

But no one responded to that feeler.

"There's a remarkable feeling of solidarity between the Labour Movement here and those South Carolina strikers – in the rank and file especially. The news gets across, I hardly know how. It's something new. You've never had cotton and steel workers swapping experience and news before – Pittsburg talking to our Black Country. They do now. They know now what the others wear and how they eat and the games they play. If finance doesn't start a Transatlantic coalescence, Labour certainly will. The young men, I mean…"

He shrugged his shoulders and left it at that. He turned to the topic of Social Credit and the increasing interest of the general public in the social effects of finance. "Finance has never been in general politics here yet," he said, "but public attention is growing. The number of small investors increases here. Presently they are going to start asking questions. In America they're ahead of us in that. But we're coming up. The common man over there has been puzzling his brains about currency and credit ever since the days of William Jennings Bryan… It's a tempting field for political adventurers just now."

The junior partner raised his eyebrows slightly and glanced at Rud.

At the time Rud had little more to say.

He had however quite a lot more to say when he reported his talk to his counsellors at the Purple House.

"That City of yours is a morbid excrescence. Wall Street is a morbid excrescence. Plainly it's a thing that has grown out upon the social body rather like – what do you call it? – an embolism, thrombosis, something of that sort. A sort of heart in the wrong place, isn't it? Anyhow – there it is. Everything seems obliged to go through it now; it can hold up things, stimulate things, give the world fever or pain, and yet all the same – is it necessary, Irwell? Is it inevitable? Couldn't we function economically quite as well without it? Has the world got to carry that kind of thing forever?

"What real strength is there in a secondary system of that sort? It's secondary, it's parasitic. It's only a sort of hypertrophied, uncontrolled counting-house which has become dominant by falsifying the entries and intercepting payment. It's a growth that eats us up and rots everything like cancer. Financiers make nothing, they are not a productive department. They control nothing. They might do so, but they don't. They don't even control Westminster and Washington. They just watch things in order to make speculative anticipations. They've got minds that lie in wait like spiders, until the fly flies wrong. Then comes the debt entanglement. *Which you can break*, like the cobweb it is, if only you insist on playing the wasp. I ask you again what real strength has Finance if you tackle Finance? You can tax it, regulate its operations, print money over it without limit, cancel its claims. You can make moratoriums and jubilees. The little chaps will dodge and cheat and run about, but they won't fight. It is an artificial system upheld by the law and those who make the laws. It's an aristocracy of pickpocket area-sneaks. The Money Power isn't a Power. It's respectable as long as you respect it, and not a moment longer. If it struggles you can strangle it if you have the grip... You and I worked that out long ago, Chiffan...

"When we're through with our revolution, there will be no money in the world but *pay*. Obviously. We'll pay the young to learn, the grown-ups to function, everybody for holidays, and the old to make remarks, and we'll have a deuce of a lot to pay them with. We'll own every *real* thing; we, the common men. We'll have the whole of the human output in the market. Earn what you will and buy what you like, we'll say, but don't try to use money to get power over your fellow-creatures. No squeeze. The better the economic machine, the less finance it will need. Profit and interest are nasty ideas, artificial ideas, perversions, all mixed up with betting and playing games for money. We'll clean all that up..."

"It's been going on a long time," said Irwell.

"All the more reason for a change," said Rud.

"I suppose the first gamblers were those caravan Semites who played a sort of chequers in the sand for their camels with dung," reflected Irwell. "They would gamble away everything they possessed. They would gamble with themselves and become slaves."

"Don't you be hard on the Semites," said Rud. "The Cretans traded pots and pans – for profits."

"The Azilians, way back in the Mesolithic, had pebbles marked for some game," said Irwell, unfolding his knowledge.

"It doesn't follow that a nasty habit of mind is any less nasty because it's ancestral. It doesn't follow you can't cure it. Why scratch fleas for ever? Gambling, speculation, is a social disease. It's as natural and desirable as – syphilis...

"Well, we're curing syphilis by telling people about it...

"The City and Wall Street can go back to where these games of property snatching and stealing began. They can play craps for their buttons. It's high time the world stopped being a gaming saloon with the common man's needs and comfort in the kitty. High time... As soon as the common man hears *us* asking for that, *he'll* ask too."

9

Chiffan cleaned up another neglected facet of Rud's education by taking him to the Houses of Parliament, sitting with him in the Strangers' Gallery for a time and introducing him to a friend or two, for whom he had done trifling journalistic services in the past. One or two members who had heard already of the Common-sense Movement in their constituencies were only too willing to be friendly with this ugly, white-faced, erratic talker. Rud was given tea on the terrace and inspected and drawn out.

He surveyed this celebrated Terrace. Narrow, it was, he noted, at the foot of a cliff of sham Gothic stonework, barely a century old and already badly corroded. "Thoroughly Anglican," he thought. Chiffan's friend collected a small group for him, that came and went restlessly.

These politicians impressed him as being the most short-sighted and sceptical men he had ever met. They lived in a little world that was bounded on the one side by "office" and on the

other by the constituencies, and they seemed unable to imagine
that it was not an eternal world. One tall man, he observed, in the
year of grace 1941 was wearing a long frock-coat and a peculiar
half-stiff collar reminiscent of that great parliamentary hand, Mr
Gladstone. They talked with one another about divisions; the
government majority had dropped to twenty; and they talked
about a scene in the House. The PM's manners were becoming
intolerable. Then with an air of relaxation they turned to Rud.
The possibility of altering opinions in the constituencies seemed
a very theoretical one to them. No doubt there were these waves
of opinion in the country, and an intelligent parliamentary
politician observed them and dodged about among them, but it
was quiet outside their technique to consider how the pressures
of opinion could accumulate and be directed.

Rud thought they might be impressed by the breath of his
outlook. He tried to pose as the earnest young enquirer, wanting
to know. He thrust out feelers. Where *is* power in the country?
Where *is* responsibility? In this country? In any country?

But the elusive mystery of political power is no proper subject
for the terrace at teatime. There is nothing to be known about it
and everybody knows all about it. So what is there is discuss?

He tried over a suggestion of Chiffan's that Power is always
being drawn together into a centre, and then escaping again and
diffusing itself. He had not thought much of that at the time, but
now that he heard himself say it, it seemed quite a good idea.
There were, he argued, widespread accumulative phases in
politico-social life, and these were always followed by executive
phases, a sort of diastole and systole, a diastole of accumulation
and a systole of concentrated impulse against diffused systematic
resistances. He tried to impress them with the idea that a phase

259

of diastole was coming to an end, and that the apparent apathy of the day might turn at any moment to the rush of the oncoming systole. But they were manifestly not interested. He might as well have talked to a team of cricketers of possible earthquakes, grass impoverishment and a coming shortage or excess of rain. They returned to the topic of the Prime Minister's lamentable temper.

He came away with an exasperated sense of failure. He denounced parliamentary government root and branch that night. Parliament was doomed. The fact that it had not listened to Rud was only one little conclusive fact in a long indictment. "It has become a series of empty forms," he said. "All over the world, always, the sawdust of reality is running out of the shapes of quasi-public things. Not one British citizen in a thousand watches what is done in Parliament; not one in a thousand Americans follow the discourses of Congress. Interest has gone. Every election in the past thirty years has been fought on gross misunderstandings."

Bodisham ticked off the points of the new Common-sense Movement on his fingers. "The City is rotten and Parliament is rotten."

"But they are!" said Rud.

"Christianity is rotten and Labour politically is rotten."

"But aren't they?"

"The curious thing is that we believe in you, Rud."

"We have much to destroy," said Dreed.

"We have nothing to destroy," said Rud. "All these things are done for already. They are falling in all over the world. They are dead. No need for destructive activities. But if we have nothing to destroy we have much to clear away. That's different. What *is* needed is a brand-new common-sense reorganisation of the

260

world's affairs, and that's what we have to give them. I can't imagine how the government sleeps of nights. *I* should lie awake at night listening all the time for the trickle of plaster that comes before a smash. Ever since they began blundering in the Near East and Spain, they've never done a single wise thing. This American adventure spells disaster. Plainly. Australia has protested already. India now is plainly in collapse. Everyone who has been there lately with open eyes speaks of the vague miasma of hatred in the streets. We don't get half the news from India. Just because there exist no clear idea whatever of a new India, it doesn't mean that the old isn't disintegrating. Things that are tumbling down, tumble down. They don't wait to be shown the plans of the new building. The East crumbles. All over the world it becomes unpleasant to be a foreigner, but an Englishman now can't walk in a bazaar without a policeman behind him..."

The little council hammered out these intuitions and dogmatisms of Rud's eagerly and helpfully. They showed themselves more and more impressed by the soundness of his idea of attracting attention in Britain by specialising conspicuously in a new American liaison and starting from the outset with an Atlantic straddle... The time for it, they agreed, was now.

10

"America," said Steenhold. "Certainly America. Right away. You come with me to America and we'll run round a bit. We can manage a fortnight there. Start Friday, New York Saturday. Partly we'll bus about the country and partly we'll get special planes. I've got it all figured out. There's one or two lads I'd like you to see, and a few bunches I'd like to hear you talk to. There's things brewing there.

"You can talk to the newshawks. We'll give you a press... Tell 'em all how you did in Bohun; he's just the sort of thing Americans detest...

"I shall love to show you America.

"All you lousy Europeans underrate America. It underrates itself. We've been shaping history for a century. Ironclads we invented. We opened up Japan, but you British played us crooked on that. You've always been crooked on Japan and China with us. But never mind that now. We started flying – and we started the popular motor-car. And who invented the machine-gun? Who started big business and mass production? What would have happened to Soviet Russia if it hadn't had American notions? If it hadn't had Americanised Russians to start it? Soviet Russia nearly got away with things, simply thanks to America."

"The British Museum Reading Room had a hand in that," said Rud. "Marx read there, Lenin read there. Litvinov."

"That old gas reservoir! Trotsky was American-trained. And do you know what was the matter with Stalin? He knew nothing real about America... What's the trouble with Russia now? It's lost its American kick. It's ceasing to ventilate. It's going back to Asia. Still I don't want to humiliate you Britishers too much. There's a sort of tenderness – in every American. But there they are, the Russians, de-Americanised and consequently stuck.

"What they want in Moscow," said Steenhold, expanding his theme, "is derision, healthy derision. At first under Lenin. I'm told, there was some."

"Where there is no derision the people perish," said Chiffan.

"Now who said *that?*" asked Steenhold, always anxious to check his quotations. "It sounds familiar."

"I said it," said Chiffan. "Get on with your suggestions."

11

Rud had never been in a plane before. He felt a boyish excitement in seeing the familiar map of south-west England spread out below him in the twilight; he watched the lightships and lighthouse flashing into being, and he soared up, up past a few cloud whiffs, and up and up, into a softly throbbing starlight. He glimpsed the retreating sunset and then lost it again. The sun has gone ahead, he thought, and presently it will be round again and overtaking us, but some day the common man will beat the sun. in which case somehow wouldn't he always be picking up his yesterdays?

That line of thought was too mathematical for Rud's rhetorical mind, and he dropped it. He lay back dreaming and presently a deep blue daybreak came to swallow up the stars.

The plane came down into the lower air. New York, that city of ten thousand bristling towers, facing the sunrise, still with the sleep in its ten million office windows, was a memorable picture. As they droned softly over the Hudson river, the reawakening clangour of that mighty aggregation penetrated the suddenly subdued hum of the engines.

The press had come to the airport for them, eager for a first-hand story of the Purple House. Steenhold had seen to that. They seemed to be more excited than the British press about Bohun. "He's the sort of thing we have to clear away, before

England and America can talk together," said Rud, concluding some pithy comments on his defeated adversary.

"What have *you* come to tell us, Mr Whitlow?"

"Rud – if you please – Rud Whitlow. I've come to learn."

"Anything in particular?"

"I want to know who's responsible for keeping the common man in England and the common man in America out of step."

"Most of us would say it's your government. Especially now."

"I think so too. But there's more in it than that. That's what I want to find out."

"Are you going to talk on the Radio?"

"Ask me. I'll talk."

"Do you talk on the Radio in England?"

"Never. We've got a government-controlled Radio over there now, and they tighten it up and tighten it up, for fear of ideas getting loose. The Anglican Empire has taken to sitting on the safety-valve of free speech; it's been heading back to Dreamland ever since the Abdication. So much the worse when the burst comes. The Bishops and the Court people and the Foreign Office and the Old Gentry and Bath and Cheltenham and Blimpland and all that, are more and more afraid of our common men getting ideas. New ideas. Very afraid. They're done so well by the old set. You know they censor all your American papers? The more they're blacked out, the more we like you. Backwardness is their pride and glory. The Churchmen have stifled our schools and universities for a century. The House of Lords is the sterilisation chamber for newspaper owners and publishers. England's become the great Hush Hush land of the world. Not a land of cruel repression but a land of Hush, Hush. Don't say a word or else you'll wake the babies. Politically the British common folk are the most ignorant and backward people in the world. But maybe now I am over here I'll talk a bit to England on the air."

"The Great Hush Hush Land" made a good headline start for Rud.

The idea of an English common man coming to America to speak his mind to England, was fresh enough in itself to get him a press. "We've never heard of this English common man of yours before," said one reporter.

"You have. What else do you think kept our nobility and gentry from messing up your Civil War?"

"That's true, I suppose," said the news-man.

"And much thanks we common Englishmen get in *your* histories," said Rud.

Some of the Tory press tried to guy Rud. They said he had an Oxford accent and conversely that he rearranged his aspirates. They telephoned to London for facts against him, but they could get hardly any facts for or against him. They tried to find out if he had a "love life". They could not find so much as a blonde hair upon him. They said he was a political monomaniac, but that did not hurt him. They picked the worst photographs of him and issued caricatures. But though they made him grotesque, that did not make him in the least feeble or repulsive. The more liberal papers took him up from a different angle as the New Type Briton. The press fought about him and the Radio people found he had a natural aptitude for "talks", always with something new to say and always in effect reiterating his self-assertion.

"Our common people have been kept apart by politicians and bad history, long enough. We ought to have scrapped old George the Third when you did. That's kept us out of step ever since.

Sorry to be so behind you; but how about getting together now? Our common tongue. Our common freedom. Our common future. While there is still time. Then we'll get these soldiers off our backs, and start fair. That's what I'm here for. That's what I want to learn about."

"Your party *is* the Popular Socialist Party, isn't it, still?"

"We're dropping that name out of respect to his lost lordship. We fired him. We're calling ourselves the Party of the Common Man."

"In England?"

"Throughout the world."

12

The American campaign outran Steenhold's wildest hopes. Rud was intensely excited and met his every occasion with an inspired aptness. He conferred. He addressed meetings. He talked on the air. He dictated interviews. His energy seemed inexhaustible. Always he seemed to be saying something fresh and always he seemed to be saying something obvious. "You *disentangle* things," said Steenhold, trying to give it a name.

In a dozen cities ambitious young men were presently starting nuclei for the Party of the Common Man.

Rud surveyed America from east to west and from north to south from the air. His first impression was an amazing spaciousness. Everywhere there was space. Too much desert there was, too much wilderness; the empty undefended coasts of the west frightened him, the vast unkempt rivers. When later he flew from London to Moscow and thence by way of Constantinople and Rome home, Europe in comparison, with its strips and roads and disciplined waterways, looked like one continuous land of gardens. But everywhere where he descended in America he found communities living in fine great cities, speaking the same language, using the same idiom of thought, and prepared to understand him completely. And he took the utmost care that his great idea was understood.

He kept his end up against Steenhold with difficulty in a long and tedious comparison of these two sections of the English-speaking world. He and Steenhold had absolutely the same ideas and the same vision of things, and yet so subtle is the virus of patriotism that these two professional antipatriots made international comparisons until they argued themselves into a rage. Steelhold was the more aggressive of the two; he was never happy until he had roused Rud to retort. And Rud, in spite of himself, was forced to be partisan and counter-offensive.

"You English," said Steenhold.

"You Americans," said Rud.

"When you aren't as fresh as paint," he said, "You Americans are as stale as old cabbage leaves. I'm amazed at your Labour leaders, at the sort of things you can still take seriously as Presidential Candidates. These leonine reverberators tossing their manes back in order to keep their eyes on the White House – they belong to the Pleistocene. We dropped that sort of head in England after John Bright. When the Revolution is over and I retire, I shall retire as Hitler did, to some remote hunting lodge, and we'll have the heads of Great Labour Leaders and Presidential Hopes stuck all round the Hall. Hippopotami won't be in it."

Rud's picture of the world, under the stimulus of this experience, expanded and became factual with terrific rapidity.

He felt that his Anglo-American idea had been mere talk before, even to himself; that hitherto he had never believed in its feasibility; but now it was becoming immensely credible. "The pivot of our movement has to be in America. The bulk of our Party has to be on this side and" – he paused and looked at Steenhold – "I haven't to come to America more often than *once* a year. For one short week."

"I don't quite see," began Steenhold.

"Public men in America are *too* public. Too accessible. This sitting on the stoop and being 'just folk' was all very well for local politics and the simple farmer days of a hundred years ago, but it's no good for world affairs. Opening flower shows and being genial to babies and all that is out of date. These parish politics methods have to go. The ultimate leader ought to be distant, audible but far off. Show yourself and then vanish into a cloud. Marx would never have counted for one tenth of his weight as 'Charlie Marx' playing chess with the boys, and Woodrow Wilson threw away all his magic as far as Europe was concerned when he crossed the Atlantic. Before he crossed he was a god – *what* a god he was! after he arrived he was just a grinning guest. I've got to be *the* Common Man, yes, but not common like that."

"It's a new thing for America – an invisible Great Man," said Steenhold, considering it, "but I believe you're right."

"I'm right," said Rud, and then with a certain bitterness: "*Look* at me. It would be money in my pocket if I were invisible altogether."

Steenhold considered his leader's visage judicially. "No," he said. "You've got to be careful with it, of course, and you don't want to make it too cheap. I admit a snapshot might make a mess of you. But you've got *force* about you. They never laugh at you on the platform. Not a titter. They gape until you begin, wondering what that scowl's about, and then your voice gets them. But you're dead right about not overdoing it with the cinema and the mike. Aloof's the word. No pomp – but aloof."

13

While Rud was making this American trip Bodisham's conceptions of organisation were being greatly elaborated and defined. For a while his influence made Rud the passionate advocate of thinking things out – even at the price of delay. An obscure instinct for timing may have contributed to that.

Bodisham insisted upon a series of conferences with practically all the Group present and participating. The egg of the world revolution was indeed incubated in meetings very like tutorial classes. Our dramatic and romantic dispositions would have it otherwise, but that was the course reality chose to take. It was begotten of a sentence, it was fostered in talk. In the beginning was the Word. There is no strong, silent man in the history of the world renascence.

"I've got so little to say," said Dreed, and he was the nearest approach to speechlessness in the Group.

"All the more reason for coming to listen," said Rud.

They had to understood each other, Bodisham urged, and to keep on understanding each other. "you have to *talk* a movement into being," he said, "and you have to keep it alert by talk. You have to write and keep on writing memoranda on the different expression of our fundamental ideas, as fact challenges them. It is laborious but absolutely necessary."

So long as Lenin lived, Bodisham argued, he wrote and talked and explained, and when he died progress in Russia turned its face to the wall. The hope went out of the Russian experiment. "You have to play the rôle of Lenin in our movement," said Bodisham. The Common-sense Party had to keep alive mentally even if it risked serious internal conflicts. Rigidity was a sign of death. Fixed creeds were the coffins of belief.

Rud assimilated Bodisham and rendered him with a vigour Bodisham could never shown.

"We've got to bring more men into this, and perhaps a different sort of man, and we've got to scrap any delusion that we're going to make tools of them. Those damned Bolsheviks were always playing obscure games, with each other as pieces, until Stalin swept all the others into the discard. Choked by their own self-conceit. We've got to avoid that sort of thing. This idea of *using* other people and *capturing* other people, is an idiot's dream. We aren't that superior. We've got to find certain necessary supplementary men. What do we know of the air, any of us here? What do we know of transport? What do we know of handling troops? We've got to find men for all that, sympathetic, different men. We've even got to bring them into this council; their new blood, their new ideas, their new point of view; and we've got to assimilate them. And assimilate ourselves. '*Assimilate*', that's the word. But *mutual* assimilation. When we've got a common philosophy and a common objective; then we can advance in open order. We shall be a great team. But we've got to make sure of that common set of ideas. Maybe we shall find our formula difficult for some of these new types. If we keep our minds open, we may find that they are right and that our formulae have to be modified. Probably – it's a thought

270

that shouldn't dishearten us – but probably we don't know everything."

To which Bodisham nodded approval, adjusted his glasses and tried not to look like a teacher hearing a recitation.

14

An idea upon which Rud laid great stress in these pregnant days was what he called *parallel independent co-operation*. It was doubtful whether he himself originated the phrase or Bodisham. Probably neither of them could have answered that question with precision. But even if it was not originally Rud's, he made it his.

A world revolution, he insisted, must advance on a wide front. You could no more standardise the men in a world revolutionary movement than you could make all the parts of a machine alike. Every factor had its own set of functions, and all conscious functions necessitate their own distinctive mentality. The newspaper man had one set of behaviour patterns, and the man in the physical power organisation, soldier or policeman or what not, had another. Research and direction needed a third set; and so on. One big mistake of the Communist movement had been the attempt to stereotype the party member. What was a natural expression for a transport man, say, became mere cant if you forced it on an agricultural worker. The idea of some sort of central omniscience was the fallacy of autocracy. "Don't think of centralisation; think of balance."

"But you must have a centralising body, a nuclear fact, the touchstone, the ultimate reference, the quintessence of the idea," said Rogers.

271

"*I* am the quintessence of the idea," said Rud. "*I* am the uncomplicated, uncovenanted, unrestricted common man. Stalin thought he was, but I *know* I am. I am the sufficient sample."

"For the time being," said Chiffan softly.

"For the time being," said Rud, without extreme conviction and after a moment's pause.

15

Bodisham's organisation charts were destined to become historical museum exhibits of the utmost importance. They have been reproduced in the exactest facsimile a score of times. Nearly every History of the World Revolution displays the "central" one as a frontispiece. He worked at them in that small drawing office, still preserved intact for all the world to visit, in number sixteen. He worked at them with a number of coloured inks and a sublime unconsciousness of the immense possibilities of his scheming. The ink he spilt is still on the faded carpet; the wall is pockmarked by his drawing pins. Occasionally he smudged his work or used an ink-eraser until he nearly perforated the paper. Chiffan came and made suggestions almost daily. He was more than a little jealous of Bodisham, but he had the generosity to respect his quality and admit his own limitations. His own intelligence worked in brilliant flashes, but Bodisham's went on, a steadfastly burning flame, indefatigable. Rud came to survey the developments, making sometimes a pithy comment, and sometimes merely standing in meditation before the great scheme.

The charts showed plainly the developing conception of the world revolution as it grew in the minds of its makers. Bodisham would sit over his big sheets of paper, compasses in hand, breathing audibly, thinking through long pauses, then flinging himself upon some freshly apprehended linkage, scribbling, blotting, tearing the chart from its drawing pins, shouting for his assistant to carry it away and recopy it – for the fortieth or fiftieth time. The whole diagram was enclosed in a huge circle, and in this clustered minor circles, which touched, overlapped, were joined by coloured bands and lines, signalled to each other with arrows, displayed significant tinting. These things meant association of leaders and direction, partial merger of activities, mutual information and so forth.

The all-comprising outer circle represented what Rud called the idea of Common-sense, the idea that a general agreement about life among normal men, based on mutual respect, is possible, and that this common agreement could be made the one supreme criterion of law and collective activity. Sweep away authoritarian ideas, delusions of superiority and inferiority and a general complex of subconscious dishonesties, and that was what you exposed. The was the true Social Contract.

The Party in its more generalised form was little more than a loosely organised propaganda for the intensive reiteration of this one common-sense idea, the idea that the world as a whole belongs to every human being. The only justification for interference with the free domination of the individual was the common good. No claim of authority or of debt was valid beyond that controlling consideration. This was a fundamental concept of the movement, and it meant a continuous attack on everything that set up preferential distinctions and divisions among mankind, that is to say racial, national, religious, sexual claims and assertions, and every sort of artificial advantages and

273

privilege, all hereditary appropriations, inherited wealth or other priorities. It boldly and flatly denied the existence of any broad and essential differences in humanity sufficient to justify privilege, enslavement or control. "No prenatal subjugation," was its leading phrase. "No prenatal debt. Otherwise men cannot be free."

Elaborately Bodisham was working out the implications of this proposition and applying them still more elaborately to the drift of world events.

With this fundamental conception, the new movement faced the world. This "fundamental conception" was the outer ring of Bodisham's diagrams. But so far it hardly went beyond what primitive Christianity, Islam, Anarchism, Rousseauism and all the primary Leftisms, had said before it. Directly one came inside that ample circle, however, the organisers of the new world found themselves against certain practical realities, that so far had frustrated every attempt to reduce human affairs to equalitarian common-sense, and they faced them with an unprecedented frankness.

"They just haven't been worked out," said Bodisham. "They just haven't been worked out."

The chief of these practical difficulties on the way to human unity was the fact that normal human beings are not by nature interested in public affairs. That has always been the little rift in the lute of sentimental democracy. Because man is not instinctively political, as the ant seems to be, all his collective operations have to be directed. Most human beings do not want to be bothered looking after their common interests. They put the real stuff of their individual lives before the common weal as a matter of course. They may be educated or cowed into a practical respect for the common weal, but that is against the natural disposition of their hearts.

It was necessary, therefore, Bodisham argued, to find and select and appoint people of a certain type – Rud called them generally "masterful people" – who would take a special interest in the direction and co-ordination of this or that collective activity, whether it was crop-production or road-making and maintaining, or improving and distributing the statement of fact, or teaching or research or what-not. The whole history of mankind had been and was still and could not be anything else but the struggle of the various types of these masterful men to get collective processes established, either for their own advantage or the collective advantage, against the general contrariety, the resistances, the confused, short-sighted self-seeking and self-production of common individuals. Masterful men come to the top under any condition. But the peculiar sort of masterful men who came to the top depended on the conditions.

"The Common Man can only become conscious of himself and learn his lesson through the exposition of certain peculiar sorts of masterful men," argued Bodisham. "There are people who must 'say it' for the inarticulate and generally inattentive common man. Call them teachers, demagogues, prophets, what you will. Rud is quintessentially that sort. That sort you must have. But also there have to be experts and, furthermore, there have to be men to check back, criticise and justify the expert and protect the Common Man from either tyranny or quackery. All that complexity you must have in human affairs. The essential problem is to use those necessary masterful men and yet restrain them. How to balance them? How to prevent their abusing their masterfulness? They must have authority in their special fields, but you have to put simple power out of reach of everyone.

"That is why the eighteenth century, that most enlightened century, that liberty-seeking century, was so preoccupied by constitution-mongering, and why my great circle here is all cut up by these minor circles and these schemes of mutual checks and co-operations. All through the ages mankind in its communities has relieved its political laziness and cowardice in an irrational abandonment to leaders and rulers. God will provide, the King will settle it, the priesthood will see to it, the aristocracy for the sake of the land, the property owners out of enlightened self-interest, the lawyers, the oligarchy, 'They', the Party, the party leaders, the dictators..."

"The history of mankind," said Dreed, "has been a history of betrayals, the perennial betrayal of the common man by the men he has trusted."

"By the men the lazy, haphazard, childish oaf was too wilfully stupid to mistrust," said Bodisham. "The history of mankind from the very beginning has been a history of over-trusted trustees, corrupted by their unchecked opportunities. And here in these organisation diagrams I am simply trying to assemble in their proper relations, the latest ideas for balancing the interests, restraining the egotisms, and extracting the maximum of good out of masterfulness and the masterful phases of masterful men. It's the eternal problem of politics – once again."

"The problem isn't eternal; it changes"; interrupted Rud. "The conditions have changed. The fundamental conditions have changed. What you don't realise fully enough, Bodisham, you with your out-of-date historical precedents, is that all over the world there is Awareness, such as there never was before. The

276

light penetrates everywhere. Knowledge, I tell you, wins its way. See how ideas spread! See how they run. It's only now that natural science begins to tell what it knows to the common mind. And common people drink it up. For the first time the whole world reads, reads to know. There is a new spirit in the world..."

It was always Bodisham who theorised and planned. Each main function of the new world was presented in his diagram by systems of circles and interesting circles within. Here was the propaganda system, and overlapping it and destined to replace it was organised education. Here were the intimations of a plan for the correlation of research and record and the distribution of knowledge. Here was the organisation of the force balanced against legal power. Here was a quadrilateral of old military organisations, fading out before police, controlled production and the air. Curious green lines intimated the subtle but understandable relationship of "parallel independent co-operation." Here, like an elucidatory veil across this map of the future, was a mighty, new network of universities, of record, discussion and information organisations, of poetry and imaginative creation, that was to furnish the controlling atmosphere of criticism and understanding throughout the world.

To anyone who saw these diagrams in the day before their realisation, they would have seemed like the reveries of a very intelligent but quite impracticable dreamer. Yet they were certainly no more fantastic and far more constructive than was Communism in the days when Marx at Highgate, bothered by tradesmen's bills and earning a precarious living by discreet political journalism, smoked and dreamed.

Plan or reverie, so it was that things shaped themselves in the minds of the central group. The Group grew steadily as it elaborated its conceptions of activity. Never was any revolutionary scheme so little insurrectionary, so boldly and definitely constructive, or so loosely centralised. Naturally the idea of insurrection was fundamental to it, but conceptions of new organisations completely overshadowed it. That idea of parallel independent co-operation proved of the utmost practicability. Rud in those days was not so much the head as the central link of the group's scheme. Nothing so deliberate and detailed and adaptable as Bodisham's net of diagram had ever before been produced by the revolutionary impulse in man. It resembled previous revolutionary organisations as the working drawings for the first modern aeroplane resembled the series of suicidal contrivances from the wings of Dædalus onwards that had anticipated flying. After each disaster people said "Man can never fly". But a few dreamers persisted. After each revolutionary failure men said "Human society can never escape from its traditional limitations. It must live or perish in its self-made cage."

The Group was not of that opinion. It believed in the ultimate victory of design and it was justified.

16

This ramifying group was extending its tentacles to associate itself with types of revolutionary activity that were either novel or had hitherto played a special disconnected rôle in human affairs. One of Bodisham's leading subdivisions within the great circle was the conception of a cosmopolitan pronunciamento.

278

That would not be the Revolution but it would be an important factor in it. There is no revolution while armed forces remain loyal. Both he and Rud were alive to the truth that a few months' drill and a uniform do not make a mechanism of the common man, and now less than ever since warfare had been elaborated and diversified by an incessantly varying equipment. Rulers make wars, but soldiers, sailors, airmen and a complex of technicians carry them on and end in control.

The universal human question: "Why should I do this for that fellow when I might do it for myself?" was more alive than ever in the ranks of the armed and enrolled specialists throughout the world. There was a real psychological difference between the common man and the man in uniform during the eighteenth century, almost as different as the medieval distinctness of the man in armour, but conscription has undermined that antagonism. A small army is the ruler's weapon, but a great army becomes his master.

Bodisham produced voluminous instances of the revolutionary rôle of armies and fleets from the days of the successors of Alexander and the legion-made Caesars down to contemporary Germany; he was particularly erudite about Wallenstein and the condottieri, and about the political side of the Scotch and English armies during the seventeenth century. He invented a plausible history of the Janissaries and he quoted the parts played by the fleets of Turkey, Russia and Germany in reversing governments since 1900. There never had been a fleet, he insisted, without a mutter of mutiny.

Now a new fighting type, the airman, was appearing in the world, men necessarily of a wide geographical range, and all of them living under practically identical conditions. What could

279

prevent their discovering that they had ideas in common, ideas that were totally different from the military traditions of the sovereign states that were so blandly assuming control of them.

"Even the Roman gladiators developed a solidarity of their own," said Bodisham. "The air is not really in the military tradition at all. It is something different and new. It refuses to lend itself to the soldier's tradition. It will develop its own tradition, quite across the old national boundaries." It was one of the less agreeable preoccupations of the military authorities in Britain and America, he pointed out, to keep "seditious" literature away from the "boys" upon the air grounds. "Which they don't," said Norvel, the Group propagandist. "Which they can't. The more you militarise a population, the less purely military the soldier becomes. The more he is amenable to common-sense propaganda."

They found two vividly contrasted organisers for the common-sense propaganda among the military forces of the State, in Reedly, a disgruntled military genius and expert, with a gathering animus against all constituted authority, based on some personal grievance of his own against what he called the "privileged set", and Bellacourt, a brilliant and quite disinterested aeronautical engineer, who had served on the government side in the Spanish Civil War and acquired an intense hatred of any kind of bombing. Both had great energy and organising ability, and neither was in complete harmony with the Rud-Bodisham-Chiffan-Steenhold gospel. But they co-operated on "parallel independent" lines. Bellacourt was a slight, very fair, taciturn, slow-thinking man, but Reedly was a fine big figure of a soldier, built for a uniform and with a big Kitchener moustache. He was conscious of his abilities and impatient of what he thought to be inferior opinions. This disposition, rather than any particular act, had hampered his promotion. He came into the Group now as if he was leading in an army. He came in with the almost naked purpose of showing the authorities what a mistake they had made about him. He meant to use the Group. Rud knew he was taking a risk with him. It was to be remarked afterwards, that Rud rarely interrupted Reedly while he was talking, and that he watched his man even when he was taking no part in the discussion.

Bellacourt, Rud realised early, was a man of one idea. He wanted to take the air right out of national jurisdiction altogether, and to make it a sort of separate world of transport by itself. He was clear that this new mode of locomotion was quite outside the current scheme of human life, but from that point his ideas were in a sort of luminous fog. He wanted to isolate the air just as Bendigo wanted to isolate the British Empire. He had, he said, been studying the problem of the air for years, but his "studying" had meant little more than writing and inducing others to write a stream of pamphlets advocating what he called an "International Air Force". By "international" he meant "cosmopolitan", but in those days "cosmopolitan", for some obscure literary reason, was regarded as a rude word, and "international" was always used instead. He did not discuss how or why any existing government was to be induced to abandon its control of its aviators and machines, and this omission prevented any but a few salaried secretaries, benevolent spinsters and the minor clergy from supporting his amiable proposals.

Bellacourt was a good airman and an inventive mechanician; he had fought and he had tried to carry out a scheme of air photography for the government side in the Spanish War, based on Crawford's work, but conditions had not been favourable to that. Before and after that experience he had played a considerable part, both as an experimentalist and as a financier, in the development of civil air transport. He was a man who did things rather than thought, and his political and social ideas had remained at an almost puerile level for years. "You just have to have an International Air control", and that was as far as he had got. He really believed that existing government might agree to abandon air war.

Then something happened, some sort of afflatus, and his mind took on a new power and energy. Perhaps in some pause in his activities he had read a book or listened to someone, but at any rate he discovered quite abruptly that the problem he had thought a simple one was complicated in a great number of ways he had disregarded, and particularly was it complicated by the fact that nobody with any power to carry out his suggestions showed the slightest disposition to do so. Once his mind was stirred he could be a man of great practical determination. He came round to Headquarters.

"I want a World Control of aviation. Apparently that is impossible without a revolution and a World State. I gather your movement is out for that. Tell me about it." That was his simple introduction of himself to Rud and Bodisham.

Rud sat back observant and let Bodisham explain.

The only way to make the aviation of the world a common world interest, Bodisham explained, was to make every aviator in the air services you could possibly convert, a believer in a Common World Law and an opponent of nationalism. Bellacourt found this a hard saying, and sat with a frown of perplexity on his fair, not unhandsome face, one arm over the arm of his chair, resisting it.

"I thought one might have world peace without this Red stuff – simply through neutralising the air," he said, almost as if he complained of them.

Bodisham elaborated his arguments. He and Rud were not "Reds", he explained, and added his breath, "Whatever Reds may be"...

Rud suggested that Bellacourt should go away for a week and discuss his problem with everybody he met, the more anti-Red the better. "You will find World Peace is only a single problem if you deal with it as a whole," he said. "Then it becomes one and ultimately indivisible. But you cannot deal with any part of it – air union or what-not – as a thing in itself. If other things are not also going on at the same time, you will never get anywhere with that. That is no reason, of course, why you personally should not specialise absolutely upon the question of the air. But in co-operation. We want you with us. We want a man like you badly. We want an organiser of common-sense and Common Humanity in the Air. Just as we want someone to create a parallel organisation in the shipping and in the war material industries. For any service or industry or function, the real necessity is the same. In each case you have to saturate the personnel with identical clear ideas of their individual responsibility. You have to free their minds from blind obedience. We want World-minded Airmen. There is no need for any politics at all for you, and no need for anyone to advocate this air solidarity of yours outside the air forces – and the school and technical schools and factories that lead to the air. But all the same it will be in line with everything else we are doing."

Bellacourt came back at the end of his week.

"I believe you are right," said Bellacourt compactly. "I have thought it out. This air business is not to be done by itself. It has to be done. I will join you for the sake of that."

Rud took a curious interest in Bellacourt's simplicity and directness. It was something he had never met before to quite the same extent. He talked to Chiffan about it. "Do you think machines make men honest?" he said.

"They never take refuge in sentiment or rhetoric," said Chiffan, "and if you try and cheat them they pay you back right away. Whenever a machine goes wrong – it's *you*."

"Bellacourt seems to me a machine-made man."

"I never saw anyone less like a Robot."

"But Robots," said Rud, "were man-made machines. I never felt so sure I could trust anyone in my life – as Bellacourt."

"*This* to your oldest friend!"

"Bellacourt has no sense of humour," said Rud.

17

Another interesting addition to the Group was Thirp, originally a philanthropic prison reformer, a man of some wealth, whose political ideas it seemed were broadening with experience, and who was specially interested in the police side of life. He teemed with ideas about class and type psychology. He was a small man with a thin, fine face and a feminine voice, and his long, lean, restless hands seemed always to be handling details too subtle for words. He had nothing of the conventional revolutionary in his appearance; he was always very carefully. dressed with large, coloured neckties and delicately patterned silk shirts. He liked what he called investigation, and sometimes his investigations about public characters had the quality of personal gossip. Into that, indeed, in a more stable age, he might have relapsed, but for a time at least the movement picked him up and exalted and nourished his mind. It gave his curiosities a purposive quality. He was capable of handling big affairs and at a pinch he would do so, but he preferred the secondary aspects of life.

He too became a separate process in the Party, most closely in contact with Rud. He liked Rud and was curious about him. He was at great pains to please him. He avoided the others, he cut the Group meeting whenever he could, but he talked to Rud alone whenever he had a chance. His brilliant little pamphlet, *The Man inside the Uniform*, had had a circulation of over two million copies in England and America before the British authorities condemned it as a seditious document. On the whole that stimulated its circulation.

Norvel again began as a loosely attached associate of the Group, who gradually assumed a central position only second to the nuclear, indefatigable Bodisham. He was a different kind of tentacle altogether, who specialised in publication and distribution of cheap books on both sides of the Atlantic. He was a born educator and propagandist. His distinctive excitement lay in that. For that he lived. He it was who brought down the price of paper-covered popular books in America to a dime. To most people in those days a change in the price of books seemed trivial commercialism, but he had a better imagination than that. It meant a vast infiltration of rational ideas into previously inert social masses. It meant a heightened social awareness, a step forward in the awakening and release of the common man. Norvel had a considerable genius for business; without any loss of revolutionary zeal, he became one of the controlling magnates in the paper world, and later, when wood pulp ran short, he exploited the manufacture of paper out of light metallic alloys, to the great advantage of the party and the enquiring Common Man.

In his earlier schemes Bodisham had contemplated the development of new daily newspaper as a necessary part of the Common-sense Movement. Then Rud and he had found themselves doubting whether the contemporary newspaper retained any political influence. It had become more and more an ephemeral advertisment-sheet seasoned with news of crimes; catastrophes and gossip. It was slipping away from the centre of collective consciousness. As the big newspaper proprietors realised the futility of their political ambitions, they replaced political matter more and more by distraction. Many daily papers were little more than personal gossip and photographic pornography. Norvel confirmed Rud's ideas of the decadence of the newspaper, and pushed them on to practical realisation. And most of the accepted methods of party propaganda, meetings, processions and so forth, he declared to be also completely out-of-date. Instead of daily papers the Group ultimately found its chief educational medium in small, cheap books of a size to go inconspicuously into a working man's pocket, and before a year was out Norvel had filled at least twenty million pockets where English was spoken, with the stuff of the Common-sense Movement, and incalculable millions more of minds with variations upon the question: "Why do you stand it? Why do you let these out-of-date people play games with your bodies and lives?"

"Out-of-date" is a very deadly phrase for an accepted institution.

286

With the constant reiteration of this question of why people stood what they were enduring, went the plain, clear insistence that in the world it was now possible to have peace and plenty for all – given courage, given tolerance, given plain common-sense. And this Norvel did at a monetary profit to the gathering movement. These little books had much more frontier-passing power than a newspaper that lives and dies in a day. They passed from hand to hand. They played a vital part, a catalytic part, in the brewing of the World Revolution.

CHAPTER TWO

High Tide of World Mutiny

B odisham worked out his diagrams for a World Revolution with infinite care and travail. The talks went on. The Group grew in stature and wisdom. Events were not waiting for the Group, they followed no leadership, they were hurrying the Group along, creating new opportunities, confronting it with new problems, subjecting it to fresh ideas. The state of human affairs in the Brigand Forties was a climax of tension between the traditional life of man and the intimations of a new world. Common-sense and every material reality insisted upon the unification of human life throughout the planet and the socialisation of its elementary needs, and pitted against that was the fact that every authority, every institution, every established way of thinking and living was framed to preserve the advantages of the ruling and possessing minority and the separate sovereignty of the militant states that had been evolved within the vanished circumstances of the past.

The political states of the period, created by the puny necessities of the foot-and-horse phase of human life, were now like grapes in a winepress being squeezed together. They pressed upon, distorted and burst one another. Rud's idea of reconstructing elementary political conceptions and general economic processes on a worldwide scale was so obvious that now it scarcely seems original. Yet the fact remains that to Rud's contemporaries, schooled as they were in an unanalytical history and blind traditionalism, such ideas had seemed extravagantly impossible until his coarse, unqualified assertion of the harsh reality of the human situation swept their inhibitions aside. They may have had some anticipation of the new world order deep down in their minds, but until he and his Group began bawling up the new world, and bawling down the world of accepted practice, they seemed incapable of any practical realisations.

Dr Chanter, in his brilliant *History of Human Thought in the Twentieth Century*, has made the suggestion that only a very small proportion of people are capable of acquiring new ideas of political or social behaviour after they are twenty-five years old. On the other hand, few people become directive in these matters until they are between forty and fifty. Then they prevail for twenty years or more. The conduct of public affairs therefore is necessarily twenty years or more behind the living thought of the times. This is what Dr Chanter calls the "delayed realisation of ideas".

In the less hurried past this had not been of any great importance, but in the violent crises of the Revolutionary Period it became a primary fact. It is evident now that whatever the emergency, however obvious the new problem before our species in the nineteen-twenties, it was necessary for the whole generation that had learned nothing and could learn nothing from the Great War and its sequelae, to die out before any rational handling of world affairs could even begin. The cream of the youth of the war years had been killed; a stratum of men already middle-aged remained in control, whose ideas had already set before the Great War. It was, says Chanter, an inescapable phase. The world of the Frightened Thirties and the Brigand Forties was under the dominion of a generation of unteachable, obstinately obstructive men, blinded men, miseducating, misleading the baffled younger people for completely superseded ends. If they could have had their way, they would have blinded the whole world for ever. But the blinding was inadequate, and by the Fifties all this generation and its teachings and traditions were passing away, like a smoke-screen blown aside.

Before a few years had passed it was already incredible that in the twenties and thirties of the twentieth century the whole political life of the world was still running upon the idea of competitive sovereign empires and states. Men of quite outstanding intelligence were still planning and scheming for the "hegemony" of Britain or France or Germany or Japan; they were still moving their armies and navies and air forces and making their combinations and alliances upon the dissolving chessboard of terrestrial reality. Nothing happened as they had planned it; nothing worked out as they desired; but still with a stupefying inertia they persisted. They launched armies, they starved and massacred populations. They were like a veterinary surgeon who suddenly finds he is operating upon a human being, and with a sort of blind helplessness cuts and slashes more and more desperately, according to the best equestrian rules. The history of European diplomacy between 1914 and 1944 seems now so consistent a record of incredible insincerity that it stuns the modern mind. At the time it seemed rational behaviour. It did not seem insincere. The biographical material of the period

– and these governing-class people kept themselves in countenance very largely by writing and reading each other's biographies – the collected letters, the collected speeches, the sapient observations of the leading figures make tedious reading, but they enable the intelligent student to realise the persistence of small society values in that swiftly expanding scene.

Those values had to die out. There was no other way of escaping from them, and so, slowly and horribly, that phase of the moribund sovereign states concluded.

Beneath the formal surface of their traditional politics the historian of human thought notes the whispering advance of the Common man's party. There can be no question of the value of the phrase "parallel independent co-operation" in preventing it from congealing into a centralised political dogmatism, after the precedent of communism. It was becoming a power, as formless as hydraulic pressure, adapting itself to the particular situations in which it discovered itself. It was everywhere a spirit of critical resistance to authority, resistance not in the name of ease and indolence but in the name of efficiency, this spreading conception of a common aim of efficiency, this spreading conception of a common aim for all human beings. It was the resistance of son to arbitrary father, of pupils to dogmatic and inexplicit teacher.

The essential question was always: "Who are these fellows who give us orders? By what warrant? And how do we benefit and how does the world benefit? But they are doing no good to anyone, no real good even to themselves! This is not government and leadership: this is imposture. Why stand it?…Why stand it?"

The lingering disposition on the part of humanity to personify its general creative drive, that curious diffidence, that persistent infantilism, that made it necessary to ascribe its own

292

urgencies to an outside authority, played its part even from the beginning in Rud's elevation. He became the living symbol of the new world. The same imaginative needs that in the past had evoked the legends of Hercules and Prometheus and Moses, fixed now upon Rud. He had still to have a halo woven for him by great art and music and poetic suggestion, his is indeed still a very uncertain halo, but his essential role in the human imagination was the same. It became his function to say the things men dared not say for themselves. He was the world. Even Rud himself doubted at times whether some masterful pronouncement had not been said first as it were in the world at large and then through him. But the world at large had no such doubts.

The logic of human necessity was bringing the essentials of readjustment into the foreground of the racial mind, simultaneously, round and about the planet. It was sweeping along leaders and adventurers, reactionaries and revolutionaries, masterful men, weaklings and criminals, towards the simplified issues of a renascent world. It was sweeping our Rud along with the rest, but sweeping him now into a foremost place, because of the fact that his vanities and ambitions were sustained by those queer phases of lucidity of his, by his swift intellectual acquisitiveness, and by those outbursts of speech and impulse that predestined him to be, even as he professed to be, the megaphone of the common will and understanding of mankind.

Thus it was fate dealt with him. The mighty, impersonal forces of a world transition, seized upon our scheming little Rud and whirled him higher and higher, until he found himself nominally and physically the head of a new system into which the storm of necessity was forcing the world. It took him and

293

exalted him. His reverie of a new world turned to reality and expanded to exceed his wildest dreams.

2

One might write a very intricate history of the idea of Rud in the world. Always there has been fantasy and falsification in the picture. To begin with, the circulation of his actual portrait was restricted. Instead of a confusing spray of photographs, two friendly studies of him in the pose of a thoughtful Beethoven established a visible personality for him. Later, when snapshots became frequent, these sketches dominated their interpretation. He would never allow himself to be photographed speaking. He had studied the self-exposures of Hitler and Mussolini very carefully, and there survives no portrait of him with his mouth open. Neither was there any legend of his early upbringing in circulation in those early years. "Never mind what *I* am or where *I* come from," was his response to the enquiring journalist. "It's what *you* are, and what you think, and whether what I say is right for you."

Millions of people did not know whether this Rud Whitlow they spoke of was English or American. Millions thought of him as a wise, secluded old gentleman. His white face had been noted and commented upon. In America there was a whispered legend that he was dying slowly of consumption. Another story gave him an unspecified disease in the marrow of his bones that inflicted the most frightful suffering upon him. Sometime, it was said, the surgeons had to saw open the marrow of a bone to relieve him. That gave him the support of many who otherwise might not have suffered his dominance. It was hard to envy a man who moved with pain and harsh to resist one who might be dead tomorrow. There were countless allusions to his tragic loneliness, and a number of religious ministers everywhere believed in and expatiated upon his intense "love of mankind". He hated cruelty, oppression, needless want and war, they said, and he not only hated them but he worked out the way of relief from all these things.

Men liked his radio voice. He had studied the best models. From Tierra del Fuego to Spitzbergen and from China to Peru, there was an expectation that the time for a not very clearly imagined worldwide crisis was drawing near, and that when Rud said "Go", the great day of the Common Man would dawn.

He knew how to arrest this otherwise unstanchable flow of informal warfare, more obviously aimless every year, that still distressed the world. He held the secret of World peace and a common Law. So they believed. The Common-sense of Things; the Common Law, the World in Common; these phrases had an effect of limitless release and enfranchisement from pole to pole.

3

The strike is one of the oldest phases of the warfare between the generality and the overbearing man. The common man comes to a point when his exploitation becomes unendurable, and he puts down his implements and says: "No more". In a rational order this leads to a discussion of the situation and a readjustment of relationships. On ships and in militant armies, however, where the masterful men have elaborated the idea and methods of "discipline", force comes into play forthwith, the strike takes the form of mutiny, and the masterful man, if he is not to be obeyed implicitly, has to be shot or put in irons or overboard. This is the natural consequence of overstressing mastery. The ultimate way of preserving human dignity in the face of arbitrary compulsion is to kill. Here reason and primordial instinct are in complete agreement.

The idea of a mutiny against belligerent governments, against *all* existing governments, seeped infectiously through the world. "Before there can be any world government," said Rud in one of his phases of vivid conviction, "men must realise that *all* their governments are wrong. No existing government can become a world government, and a world government cannot be a large-scale imitation of any existing government. It must be a new thing embodying a universal mutiny."

There had already been a foretaste of this mutinous reaction towards the end of the Great War of 1914-18. All the European fighting forces then were drifting to mutiny. The essential Russian Revolution was a mutiny, and the sit-down strikes of the early twenties in Italy and elsewhere, which immobilised factories and the mechanical plant of civilisation, not by the withdrawal of labour but by its cessation, were plainly experiments of the common man in his revolt against servitude and the exploitation of his necessities. These earlier efforts had failed because they had been local and regional. They had been premature. They had anticipated the necessary approximations and coalescences. They had occurred in a world which was still in a patchwork of dissimilar phases.

It was only now, with the abolition of remoteness, that the entire world was coming into step as one community. Now it was no longer possible to crush revolt in one region before another became aware of the general significance of the struggle. Bodisham and Norvel were particularly energetic and efficient in developing what Rud called this "Simultaneous Awareness" throughout the world. By 1944 there was not a country or region in the world where the "Common Man's Party" was not known, where Rud's beetling forehead had not become the familiar symbol for a vaguely apprehended, vast organisation of release, and where the essential conditions of any conflict against limited, impatient and outworn authority were unknown. All over the world there grew up a solidarity of expectation, a sense of a new order not simply dreamt of, but prepared and approaching.

Those who were most concerned with what still passed for government in those days seem to have been the least aware of the essential connection of a hundred apparently divergent movements that undermined the superficial orderliness of life. Whenever for example there was still definitely an organised military suppression of social adjustment, there was what one may describe compactly and brutally as a "Shoot the officers" movement. This was more apparent in what were then called the authoritarian communities than in those which claimed to be democratic. But it was by no means confined to them. The Nazis for example had never displayed the internal discipline of the old German armies, and there was clear evidence as early as 1939 that the leaders did not dare impose too severe an obedience upon the looting and raping with which the rank and file repaid themselves for the fatigues of warfare. The men put their own interpretation upon their duties, and treated any attempts to moderate their behaviour as disloyalty to their *esprit de corps*. The Japanese staffs and officers again were often too manifestly compelled and terrified men, as the discipline of the hungry and ill-paid hordes of armed Japanese peasants that still swarmed in China relaxed.

By 1939 Japan, for instance, in China, and Italy in Spain, had armies that the government dared not bring home.

There was a constant repetition of the same cycle of phases in the experience of the various demoralised army fragments, great and small, which were now scattered over half the land surface of the globe. First came insubordination, "shoot the officers" and "lead us, Caesar, where we want to go"; a phase of successful lawlessness, a phase of rapine; then a feeling of isolation and fear and a great desire to link up again to some greater order. Bodisham and his staff, watching the world from their headquarters, had great maps flagged to mark down "contrite" troops. Most of these troops had heard vaguely of Rud. As apprehension grew in their minds they would usually claim that they were new revolutionaries, Rud's men. And the countries subjected to lawless brigandage and themselves forced towards counter-brigandage, found their only hope of restoring firm control in the anticipation of a World Common Law. They too claimed to be part of the great reconstruction. Every region too was now infested with denationalised exiles. Their dominant idea was to be legitimated as some new type of citizen. There comes a phase in social dislocation when the desire for order and security, for peaceful living overpowers partisanship, jealousy, possessiveness...

After the great naval losses in the first year of the War of the Ideologies and the development of the military deadlock in Central America and the Old World, the strike method assumed formidable dimensions both in the air forces and among the munition workers. These latter, as they realised their indispensability, began to refuse delivery of particular types of bombs and other weapons whose use they considered inimical to the common interest. The propaganda of Bellacourt had quickened the consciences of the airmen. Everywhere the air forces displayed a disposition to question the decisions of the military authorities. The roar of the planes overhead no longer gave the statesmen and politicians on the ground below a sense of unqualified power. They began to worry about the morale of the air forces, to organise espionage systems among these youngsters.

The propaganda organisations of the disintegrating national governments did an immense amount of work in the spread of the idea of Rud. Each assailed the prestige of its formal antagonists, and found an authority in his phrases, each in undermining the enemy morale sapped its own. Each appealed to Common Justice and the Common-sense of Mankind against its rival. In France and Britain Rud's activities were largely sustained by German money. In Germany his spreading reputation was financed and abetted by Russian, French and British propaganda. Russia paved his way in China and Japan, Germany and Russia in India. The Catholic Church denounced him in one country and claimed him in another, but everywhere it spread his name. There is no better advertisement in the world than to be denounced by an unattractive priest or teacher. With the most definite intentions possible, Rud could still find it the best policy to remain ambiguous. He was vaguely supposed to be revolutionary and "creative", and at the same time he was supposed to be anti-Red. In reality he was ultra-Radical, he left the Reds far behind him. The Common Man emerged at last less by a process of assertion than by a progressive elimination of narrower alternatives.

The Last War on Earth, the Second War to End War, when at last it could be envisaged as a whole, was a huge, ill-managed tangle of conflicts which began informally and did not so much end as peter out. It is difficult to imagine how it could have followed any other course. It was incoherent from start to finish. The name it still carries, "The Ideological War", was first devised for it by that interesting, rhetorical, quasi-intellectual, the Italian Dictator, Benito Mussolini. He too in his time, with his bright phases and his long, heavy interludes, was something of a minor Holy Terror, an opera-tenor Rud.

Already people are beginning to forget Mussolini's role in the restatement of human life. He is following Napoleon into oblivion as a mere energetic personality of no fundamental importance at all. The tendency when he is mentioned is to belittle him. But he was by no means a fool. His fustian was absurd and inconsistent but it was not contemptible. He was a man relatively intelligent among contemporary "strong men"; he had had early experiences of discussion and editorship, and his mind, like that of his Corsican precursor, ran habitually to obvious and often very attractive headlines. He was mentally excitable and as his temperature rose his headlines flushed. He wanted to figure as a Great Man in history, and he was quite unable to foresee the unromantic turn that history was taking.

He realised that for any effective victory in warfare there must be two sides and not more than two sides, but he failed to grasp the further fact that warfare may end without effective victory. He got his antagonisms wrong. The stresses and confusions of the world were more and more manifestly the outcome of the struggle of all the diverse forces making for a common-sense world state, against the obsolescent political, economic, religious and educational institutions, endlessly varied in origin and character, that obstructed them. But he thought the nationalist forms of history were permanent. The primary reality of the age was a worldwide conflict of pressures, parallel all over the world, for which the new order had still to find its definite formulae. To this his own obsessions blinded him completely.

Benito Mussolini, with a surfeit of bad history decaying in his imagination, could not see the plain realities before him. Like most of his generation he dramatised human affairs in incurably geographical patches, and like most of the masterful men of his time his belief in his power to mould the life about him carried him beyond sanity. From the beginning his was an ill-balanced temperament; he would be blatant at one moment, and weeping at another. He beat at the knees of Mother Reality like an unteachable child. He wanted war and conquest, triumph over definable enemies, fierce alliances, and unforgettable antagonisms. He wanted glory. He died, as his last words testify, completely unaware of the fact that the rational treatment of human affairs does not admit of that bilaterality which the traditions of warfare require. "Do we win?" he said.

He persuaded himself and he persuaded great multitudes of people that two great systems of ideas faced each other in the world, "Leftism" and "Rightism", and that he and his associated Dictators embodied the latter. He did contrive finally to impose the illusion of a definitive World War upon great masses of people.

5

In this story of Rud's career we are happily free to ignore the intricate controversies that centre about the riddle of what Right and Left or Red or Fascist or the "authoritarian" and the "democratic" state really signified at any particular time and place.

There is an immense literature on the subject, abundantly unread, but still being patiently added to by the erudite. This material is subjected to microphotography, indexed and so put away out of danger, with so much more of the excessive material of this age of excessive record. It is doubtful if it will ever find any useful application. It goes on and on. It is like Christian theology; it is like the bubbling of salted snails in a pail.

The fact remains that by the fifth decade of the twentieth century there was still a sufficient air of alignment between the two factions of formal diplomacy, alliance and secret treaties to continue. On the one hand, the confused mentalities of the groups, classes and individuals in positions of authority and possession were all sufficiently apprehensive of an advancing rationalisation of human affairs which would call them to account, to be consolidated in a general defensive offensive against something called "Democracy" or "Leftism" or "Reds" or "The Devil"; while on the other a certain number of governments, the so-called "democracies", were less able to make head against the expressive of the renascence of common-sense Radicalism and had to pay at least lip service to the creative forces of the world. The profound and subtle ambiguity of Russia, a fanatical bureaucracy professing the supremacy of the proletariat, sprawled perplexingly, with its internecine feuds and recriminations, across this complex of human interpretations. And still imposed upon the whole fermenting mass were the old boundaries, the old Foreign Offices, the old military and naval traditions, doddering and yet dangerous, that had so astonishingly survived the Great War of 1914-1918.

With a futile sense of complete reassurance the official mind found itself at last definitely at war again. There were actual declarations of war quite like old times. "Who said war was over?" the old order demanded, scared but glad.

"Now we know where we are," they said, when as a matter of fact they knew less than ever where they were. The city crowds cheered, the armies went tanking forward, the expensive navies, according to the best naval traditions, hid from each other in remote inlets behind powerful booms, the bulletins lied even when there was no object in their lying, the planes roared overhead, the bombs crashed, the cities burst, people ran this way and that, clapped on silly gas masks and crowded out inadequate shelters until they were squashed or smashed or suffocated or starved, many millions of living, feeling, human beings were converted into red pulps and messes, and the Great war of the Ideologies moved on for a time, according to the best precedents, to no perceptible objective whatever. For the first six or seven months there was a tornado of battle. Everywhere one was at the front, so to speak, and the entire planet practically under fire. The tale of destruction is as monstrous as it is frightful; it baffled piety, it mocked heroics, philosophy refuses to entertain it, its records remain unread; only very old gentlemen who were in it con that history now for purposes of reminiscence; with a natural human callousness life has gone on and the dead past has buried its dead. Yet even at the time there was a certain amount of cheerfulness, a sense of adventure successfully surmounted, among those who survived. Many of those engaged in these conflicts were too excited to be distressed by their sufferings. Great accumulations of men and war material came into collision and remained in conflict for days and weeks with much slaughter and destruction; and the contemporary historian, trying, at any cost to the truth, to keep up his continuity with the past, called them "battles" and even explained what advantages were gained by them and how, in a technical sense, they decided this or that.

The land war ebbed before the first year was out. In the previous world war there had been a vast accumulation of material wealth to draw upon, and from the beginning to end the supply of men and material increased, to the universal amazement, as though there was no limit to human resources. But the War of the Ideologies followed quite a different course. It began almost at a maximum of equipment, and with populations incapable of much further effort and sacrifice. Armament deteriorated very rapidly at last; instead of the crescendo of 1914-18, there was a more and more perceptible diminuendo. Essential substances were giving out. Makeshift came into its own in the fighting line and famine spread behind it. And then came mutiny. The men of the dwindling air forces, urged to go up in less and less trustworthy machines, and the people in the overstrained munition factories, increasingly dangerous as skilled workers became rarer and material degenerated, passed from reluctance to sabotage and flat refusal.

The European "authoritarian" warships so far overcame the battle-shyness of their crews as to put to sea in order to sweep the Atlantic; and their allies, the Japanese, got across the Pacific to shell and partially destroy San Francisco, cover a futile landing at Panama and another at Valparaiso, round Cape Horn, effect a

304

sort of junction with the authoritarians after the destruction of Gibraltar, and fight that confused series of heroic rearguard engagements known as the battle of the South Atlantic. For nearly a week the battleships of the world, those magnificent pieces of lethal engineering, careered about the seas, greatly afflicted by aeroplanes and submarines, and a bent and battered remnant got back to shelter again. And there it became manifest to the horrified captains that that was where their men intended to remain until the war was over.

Naval strategy became more and more a business of concealing this reality from the opposite side. That last naval war was indeed much more like a panic in a contentious Mothers' Meeting with a wasps' nest upset and mice on the floor, than it was to any of the set naval conflicts of the past. It was monstrous and tragic but also it was intensely ridiculous. After the surviving warships had been tucked away again out of harm's way, the residue of admirals on both sides went ashore, launched into authorship, and after a prolonged campaign, produced the curves of that truncated conflict to fully demonstrated victories. Everybody who had not been drowned or blown out of the water and had escaped to tell the tale, discovered that he and his side had won. The more these gallant survivors wrote, the completer their victories became. There are people who still find an interest in these highly technical discussions.

6

Under the stresses of this War of the Ideologies the quality of the net of Radical organisations the Common-sense Movement had woven about the world was put to the test. And it held.

305

People are only beginning to appreciate the sweeping power of Bodisham's planning, the versatile energy of Norvel and the understanding and unobtrusive competence that appeared almost everywhere ready to co-operate with the Group. Great numbers of capable men had been waiting for some such lead. It was a far broader, more varied and flexible revolutionary system than had ever existed before. It risked no subtleties of strategy; its general direction was definite but broad, and capable of the freest adaptation to special needs and circumstances.

The general decision of common-sense upon the war had no ambiguity. "No," it said, "we fight. We will fight", the Common-sense people agreed, "against the intensive war makers, and for those who propose to liberate. But we have had time to digest the lessons of the Great War, and everywhere we are going to fight conditionally, as free men and women. The governments we support shall justify their professions. They shall not merely pretend to liberate. They shall liberate indeed: This is no war between Make Believes. It is a plain fight to obliterate the very idea of a soldier from men's minds. This is a War to end War..."

Rud talked out the war issue to the Central Group but there was very little discussion. The Group had already shifted its headquarters to Sloten near Amsterdam, close to the new radio centre and the airport. There, in a large room like a departmental boardroom, surrounded with maps and Bodisham's later diagrams, Rud expounded his fundamental plan of campaign.

He banged the table and spluttered with subversive bitterness.

"The war to end war... That is what we are fighting. Over again. Never have sane words been so mocked at, and never were saner words uttered. Someone used that phrase for the last war, and it didn't end war. Ha-ha-ha and He-he-he and also *Yah!* But obviously there has to be a war to end war – and if that fails, another. And if necessary, another and another. How else in the name of the Everlasting White Rabbit, do you think we are going to end war? It isn't really funny that the first War to End War failed to do so. That was a great joke for the Conchies – it seemed to prove them right – but for mankind it was a disaster. It proved nothing that we were cheated by the old gang. Nothing at all. Peace is organised strength. Peace is the discipline of common-sense.

"The last war to end war miscarried. The world wasn't prepared for the idea. The common man didn't realise his opportunity. Very well, since then *we've* been busy. Maybe *this* one won't miscarry. If it does, it will be because *we* in our turn weren't up to the job. This time the common man has got to get and keep control. This time we have to save the world from the old confidence tricks. We English aren't going to fight *this* war, simply and trustfully, under General Timberface and Colonel Blimp with the Army of the Aldershot Tattoo. The crown and the army class and the Anglican padres are not going to jump this war as they jumped our war in 1914. *We've* got to see to that. Nobody is going to stick up proclamations about '*My* army and *my* subjects' in this war, without a protest from us. Let one thing be clear. It is we, the Common Men, who fight, and there are no '*my* subjects'. We don't mean to cheer the cuckoo-clock at Buckingham palace at the end of this war. No. It will be *ours* from first to last.

"The generals and colonels won't jump us this time. Not if we know it. This war has to be won, and won for its definite end, and there's not going to be any other sort of winning about it. These army duffers didn't know how to conduct a war in 1914 when

307

everything was as easy as pie -- Heavens, what a mess they made of it! They had every card in their silly hands in 1916. I've heard decent men talk about it. Now everybody – even they themselves – everybody knows they can't conduct a modern war. If a modern war *can* be conducted. They don't know anything about it. They are just backward boys from backward schools a hundred years out of date. What we are calling a War now is really the opening phase of world amalgamation, it is not a war in the historical sense at all, and the only use we have for our armies now is to destroy the enemy armies and get them out of the way of civilian world controls. This war has to be fought with cards on the table and in the open daylight, with common-sense intervening at every point. Most of that Secret Service of theirs is just a screen to protect the incapables from public criticism. Official Secrets are usually officials' secrets. Never trust a General; let every man under him watch his work. He's no divinity. Why, some of those tin hats in the last war; the men didn't even give them nicknames. Think of that! The men didn't know enough about them. Even for that. Everywhere, all over the earth, we've got to have our organisations saying: 'We mean to help in war. Mean to be told. Mean to know. What do you think you are doing to me? I am a man. What's the idea of clapping me in a uniform and telling me to shut up and do what I am told? That's how you lost the last war for us... Not tell us? Because the enemy might get to know, something! It isn't what the enemy knows, it is what we know that will win the war. And we mean to know it.' "

"That's the spirit of course," said Chiffan a little doubtfully.

"After every big fight," said Rud, "I think the men ought to re-elect their officers."

"That's the spirit," said Reedly, as though an endorsement was expected from him. "That's the spirit, as Chiffan says. I agree. I agree essentially. To the spirit of that. As a modern soldier. Cannon fodder is out of fashion. We want an army alive to its objectives – capable of carrying on if every officer was shot. Give me an army in which every man is fit to step forward and take the place of the man who has dropped out. So far the common soldier must be a responsible man. Yes... Still, there are occasions and necessities... There are times for implicit obedience..."

So Reedly, the "soldier of democracy", sitting square at the middle of the table and already beginning to look a little less like a not too confident deserter, and more like a commander of men.

Then Rud made a speech he had had brewing in his mind for some time. And as he made it, he watched its reception by Reedly.

"Secrecy," he said, and paused.

"Capable commanders will always know when to keep their own counsel – at their own risk," said Rud. "It's all too easy – all too easy – to get blind obedience if the men believe in their leaders. They *like* a leader to do the decisions. But I'm not only thinking of the war; I'm thinking of the end of the war. The vital thing about any rational war is its end. Only sadistic idiots in moments of rhetoric think of war as a thing in itself. You might as well think of a railway accident as a thing in itself. In some fashion or other this war is certainly going to be won by the Radical and Quasi-Radical powers. Not a doubt about it. They've got mass, they've got endurance, they've got adaptability. There will be no separate peace. Make sure of that.

"In some fashion or other this war will be won, I say. There's the rub. That's where the catch comes in. What we do not want is to see the war won in the name of liberty, at the price of liberty. Gently but firmly the common man has to take over from the diplomats and professional soldiers before the war is allowed to end. Even if it takes longer. On the other side as well it's necessary to have not simply defeat but real revolution. In 1918 the Great War was hushed up in a hurry because of the manifest imminence of revolution and communism from the Urals to the Atlantic. The Armistice of 1918 was the *sauve qui peut* of the old order from the dawning understanding of the common man...

"Didn't you realise that? It's not documented, no. Maybe they didn't realise it. But that was the drive in their minds. Our common man now is ten times as clearheaded and made of tougher stuff. He's never recovered *faith* anywhere, since the Great War.

"In 1918 there was no one to say 'A Common Law for the World'. Now everywhere, *we* say it. That's what we are for. That particularly and exactly is what we are for."

He paused. Reedly pulled his moustache. He seemed to be taking counsel with himself, a strong, silent man, but he made no comment on Rud's declaration.

"I could not state our idea more clearly," said Rud. "If I could I would."

7

With intentions thus defined and elaborated, the group faced the formal outbreak of the war of Ideologies. They spread their tentacles as Bodisham had planned them, and the combatant and authoritative forces in the world, seeking to use their propaganda, were gripped by its implications. The Group undertook responsibilities and achieved recognition. Insensibly it became a power in the world. It became an intermediary and then a decisive intermediary. Its informality and apparent flexibility made it more convenient and more non-committal than the official modes of communication between the Allied Democracies.

Few people remarked the rapid gradations by which this party from nowhere and everywhere became a world institution. A year and a half of chaotic warfare and it was quasi-official. The winding up of the war drew near.

So eighteen months to a day after its decision to take part in the war, the Group met in that same room at Sloten. But now they were all wearing the plain grey uniform of New World Police, and the Dutch War Minister and a number of officers of the Consolidated Air Forces were with them. The maps upon the wall had undergone great changes.

The Common-sense Party was in practical and legal control of Holland. The Common-sense Government had an over-whelming majority there. This was true now of ten of the pseudo-democratic powers. And the Group had become the chief consolidating organ of all the allies. The shattered and exhausted militant states had realised its menace for them too late. First they had tried to make use of it under the impression that it was a pacifist influence that would weaken discipline in the Allied Armies. Then discovering that its ideas were permeating backward into their own ranks, they had attempted a futile suppression which had merely strengthened its hold on the Allies. And now the Group was discussing the campaign that would wind up the war, and it had met at the initiative of Reedly who, with an air of subordination that hardly pretended to conceal his growing insolence, had demanded "instructions"

311

from his colleagues. The war, he said, was approaching its final decision.

He had long since abandoned his place at the middle of the table and shifted to the end, so that he faced Rud, and he was speaking now with the air of a reasonable man who exercises self-control in spite of much provocation. "I protest," he said.

He had evidently come charged with that word.

Chiffan's mind went wandering in search of a quotation. "Methinks" – how did it go – who was it – "doth protest too much..."

Reedly was speaking, and Rud was regarding him with brow-knitted attention. Bodisham, at the middle of the table, said very little, but looked occasionally at Rud. Once or twice Rud and he exchanged glances. Dreed and Norvel, the men responsible for education and public information, Thirp for the police liaison everywhere, Steenhold, Irwell, Roots and Holbank, for production, and Bellacourt, the director of air communications, were all, it appeared, treating Reedly unreasonably and unfairly. He wanted the situations cleared up and he wanted to be entrusted with greater powers. There was a demand and a menace in all he had to say.

His position was a peculiar one. The necessity of a unified Allied Command had been forced upon the Democratic powers by a series of military defeats in the European area. But the bitterness of wilful mutual sabotage had made the direct subordination of the acutely nationalist national forces, to the direction of any single commander among them, impossible. The British premier's idea of a Liaison Minister who might develop insensibly into an Allied Commander-in-Chief, was felt to be a brilliant one. It was also the prime Minister's idea to look to the left for this Liaison Minister. The revolutionary strikes of great sections of the munition workers and the refusal of the unified air forces, after the Authoritarians had been virtually driven from the air, to continue to take orders from any source except their representative Bellacourt, had turned the Allied Governments to Reedly as the most hopeful intermediary for a restoration of their internal as well as their international solidarity. Reedly was manifestly far less "Red" and revolutionary in spirit than his associates, essentially he was a good soldier, and nevertheless he was in contact, or he professed to be in contact, with the entire Group, and he became in rapid succession Liaison Minister and then "World Marshal" of the Allied Armies. His commission was vague and he interpreted it as conferring upon him the supreme command over all the forces of the Democratic Powers. There was little resistance to his aggressions. On the whole the allied commanders were not averse to shifting their responsibility to a man who might be set aside at the general settlement. So in a couple of years this disgruntled military expert, this detractor with a grievance, had become an arrogant and aggressive soldier again.

"I come here from the active front and Bellacourt is not here to meet me."

"He is in America," said Rud, "he is dealing with the strike. And Thirp, too, is busy – elsewhere."

"But I need them here. Bellacourt particularly. Believe me, I cannot wind up this war without his effective cooperation. I cannot do it."

He put out his open, hairy hand on the table and clutched, as though he grasped the world.

313

He was now a fine, florid, soldierly figure. He had expanded physically. His elocution had improved. A certain cantankerous note was no longer audible. Thirp, who missed nothing, had pointed out to Rud that he had acquired an artificial wave in his hair. "Vanity," said Thirp, "or ambition? Some vanity, of course. After all, ambition is only vanity with a backbone. That wave photographs better. It makes better personal propaganda…"

Steenhold found Reedly as admirable as an eighteenth-century portrait of a general. He deserved a background of battlesmoke – and a horse. A prancing horse with red nostrils. He was certainly the finest looking captain of men the Group could have produced. He quite outshone the stockish Rogers, who had fallen entirely under his spell.

Reedly opened his big hand again and indicated points upon the chart of the world. "There," he said, "and there and there, you have the last resistances, the last possibilities of a final offensive. This Japanese-Brazilian army here has its back to the Andes. For that region a renewal of air action is absolutely vital. With that we could force a capitulation in a month and then we could concentrate all the air power on this Levantine-Persian-Danube-Elbe complex."

"It's intricate."

"Not so intricate if I had the air."

"And then a general capitulation?" asked Rud.

"Naturally."

"Marches into Berlin and Tokyo and so forth?"

"Something of the sort," said Reedly.

"Nothing of the sort."

"But you want the war to end!"

"Do we?"

"Well?"

"We don't want a capitulation," said Rud. "I think we have that plain. Bodisham can give you chapter and verse for that. You see, Reedly, we don't *want* any excuse for an assembly of the old governments on our side. On our side. The 'democratic' governments and all that. The longer they hide in their dug-outs the better for the New World. From our point of view the war to end war can have no formal end. We've got controlled shipping, amalgamated air forces, pooled finance, consolidated news-services, a common uniform. We want to keep them common for evermore. But the day we proclaim Victory and Peace the diplomatists and nationalists will come creeping out of their funk-holes again with their flags and claims and bills on each other and all that sort of thing. Versailles all over again."

"I agree with that," said Bodisham. "Our revolutionary organisation has become a world war organisation, and now it has to develop into a world peace organisation."

"Even now," said Reedly, "if we fly in the face of national feeling too openly – After all, the war isn't won yet."

"To all intents and purposes it is won," said Rud.

"In order to wind it up," said Reedly, "I want to have complete, unqualified control of the munition supply, and I want to put an end to this ridiculous Air Truce of Bellacourt's. Whoever heard of such a thing? It makes the war – *ridiculous!* Every day now we get a fleet of planes from Sweden going along the lines, inspecting us. Did you know that? I thought you didn't. they just fly over us and go away. Taking snapshots, I suppose. To send home to their friends. It makes a commander-in-chief feel like a fool. I'm like one of those Indian princes under the old British raj who were given armies to play with and weren't allowed big guns. Then there's this strike in America! – going right over the heads of the government… It's fantastic. It's indecent. Here we have the men, the workmen away there, deciding what sort of shell we may have, what sort of guns, if any – and Roots here and Holbank aiding and abetting them. Practically the hold-up of airbombs is complete. Think of that. And not a fighter left. All in cold storage in Sweden. With a war still going on. Fantastic!"

"With an enemy immobilised and not daring to put a plane in the air – even if they had the stuff to do it with," said Bodisham.

"What do we know what surprises they might not spring on us? Or what other surprises may be in store for us?"

"Your business to know that," said Rud.

"Pshaw!" said Reedly.

Never before in his life had Steenhold heard anyone say "Pshaw!" It amused him greatly. It went with that family portrait of a general. Pure eighteenth century. "How do *you* propose to deal with these munition strikers in America?" asked Rud. "If you have a free hand there."

"Clap loyal troops into the factories. British and American regulars. In the past Americans haven't been so particularly gentle with strikers. Didn't they use to have special strike-breakers?"

"They've lost so many of those old freedoms," jeered Chiffan.

"If they try and replace the trained workers in the explosives factories," said Rud, "they'll have most of the factories in fragments somewhere up in the stratosphere. Well, Reedly, you'll be pleased to learn that both Bellacourt and Holbank are in America now, dealing with that situation. There'll be a fleet of bombing planes and reasonable ration of bombs available for Europe or Asia or anywhere quite soon."

"In my hands?"

"In Bellacourt's hands subject to your – intimations."

Reedly was disconcerted.

"I can't work with Bellacourt."

No answer. Rud pulled a grimace.

"I tell you I can't work with Bellacourt."

Still not a word. They all stared at him.

"To be frank I don't trust Bellacourt. What is he after? You don't seem to have thought about Bellacourt. Wings over the World. Air Peace? Dreams and dangerous dreams at that. Or excuses. He's hand and glove with Holbank and Roots. Beware of these men. Yes, Roots, I say it. To your face. Beware of them. If only for the sake of world security – to keep faith with our allies – we have to hold in Bellacourt. After all we are men of honour. We are soldiers first and foremost. The Allied War Office appointed me. Me and Rogers. We can't play tricks on these governments that have trusted us."

Rud sat ostentatiously weighing every word of this.

"I think we understand Bellacourt," he said with deliberation, "Bodisham and I and the rest of us. What we don't understand is what *you* are after. Why do you want control of the air? Bluntly – who is it you want to bomb, Reedly?"

"The situation is complex."

"Obviously. But who is it you want to bomb?"

"I don't want Bellacourt to come sailing over the Pole to Europe on some private expedition of his own."

"He makes you – uncomfortable. I quite see that. But all the same, if you get those bombers, Reedly, whom do you want to

317

bomb? Grossberg is beaten. His army just sticks there waiting for something to happen... Whom do you want to bomb?"

"I don't want other people to be bombed. I want to have things in my own hands."

"You puzzle us all," said Rud. "What, Reedly, do you really want?"

"The end of the war. Peace. The restoration of civilisation."

"Dear old civilisation!" whispered Chiffan. "*Dear* old civilisation."

"And – yourself, Reedly?"

"I shall be content to have done my duty."

"You ought to be. You will be the last World Marshal and the Lord of Peace. You will have done a crowning service to mankind, for which all the world will thank you. Your statues will be everywhere and you'll have more Avenues, Squares, railway stations than you'll know what to do with. Isn't that enough?"

"But," said Reedly, and stopped. He was not nimble in debate.

"Reedly, what *exactly* do you want?" asked Rud, very white and resolute. "Why did you come here? What have you got on your mind? What have you got up your sleeve?"

Reedly sat squarely at the end of the table with that big, hairy hand of his half-clenched. He glanced at his sleeve as though he thought something might be betraying him there. "This is all very well. I'm not a talker. I'm a plain soldier and I want to win this war for the Democratic cause. Mixing the military and civil commands has never been a success, and it will not be now."

"We live in exceptional times," said Rud.

"And that's my answer?" said the World Marshal.

"Yes."

There was a pause. Everyone felt that a long latent issue in the revolution had suddenly become patent.

Rud realised fully that he was at a crisis in his career. It had suddenly come into his head as a bright, clear fact, that in some manner, publicly or privately, in the interest of the newborn World republic, within a year at longest it would be necessary to have Reedly shot...

"Now more than ever," he said, "the supreme duty of everyone in the group is loyal co-ordination. Everyone is answerable for his own department and must keep complete control of his subordinates. Everyone must understand Reedly's plans, in general and in particular, just as we all understand Bodisham's plans. There must be understanding. There must be complete understanding. The Group is one."

"Then I am still to be like one of those Roman Generals With – What did they call those chaps?"

"Questors," said Irwell.

"A Questor at my elbow? – with" – he looked round the room and added three for the absentees – "with *ten* Questors?"

"It works out rather like that," said Rud.

"And away there in America Bellacourt gets his bombs if he wants them and consolidates his position according to his own ideas. Has a free hand."

"You underrate Bellacourt," said Rud.

"And in any emergency I am to be caught short of munitions and helpless in the air!"

"What emergency?"

"How can I tell beforehand?"

"That is your job. To tell beforehand. Military command is perpetual anticipation... But you know that as well as *we* do."

He looked down the table at the sulky face of the great soldier. An impulse from his cruder, earlier days, to have the World Marshal arrested and shot forthwith, had to be controlled. He glanced at the placid face of Bodisham. "No hysteria," he said to himself, "no hysteria. Keep your head, Rud." This situation had been inevitable from the beginning.

"World Marshal," he said, "even if we cannot simplify your task in the way you wish, all the same, you may rely upon all of us being at your service, in the service of our Common world."

He got up, and the group took this as a sign that the session was over. He forced himself to walk down the room to Reedly, lay his hand on his arm and turn him towards the maps.

"Tell us all," he said, "what exactly you think we ought to do."

Reedly seemed disposed to resist for a moment, seemed disposed to throw off Rud's light, nervous grip on his arm; he looked down on Rud like an Alsatian dog being smelt by a mongrel terrier; then he shrugged his broad shoulders and complied.

"I must fly back to Poland," he said, "in an hour or so. Military necessity waits for no man. I cannot give you very long. Let me first explain the position of Grossberg's group of armies..."

CHAPTER THREE

Mastery

Rud woke out of a realistic and frightful dream. He had dreamt he was back in his mean little room in Bloomsbury. He had dreamt that he was lying awake in the knobby little bed, and trying to hold himself perfectly still, because otherwise the man in the next room might come in and beat him up. That dream instant was as clear and vivid as the actual moment. Everything came back to him. He had been shouting because of a terrifying vision of Lord Horatio Bohun and his row of thumbscrews. He had shouted as he awakened. But then the dream, after the manner of dreams, had switched away to other preoccupations. The unseen man had suddenly become Reedly, the World Marshal, loud and vast, bloodstained but indestructible, determined to get at him. "You thought I was dead!" said Reedly. "My sort never dies."

Reedly scorched and torn, unrecognisable except for his uniform and his gaping mouth and thick moustache, and Rogers behind him, with half his face blown away. Without any top to his head and without eyes, with clenched hands and teeth and jawbone exposed, Reedly was, if anything, more frightful than ever.

321

When Rud had seen them they had been lying perfectly still. They had been as dead as rags. Not a kick left in them...

And here they were still in pursuit of him. Still a menace.

Gradually the dream dissolved, but for a time the fear still clung to him.

Then slowly that passed also as he recognised the lovely spaciousness of his bedroom. It was still sufficiently new to be a definite pleasure. He raised himself in the bed, stuck out his feet and rubbed his eyes. "I wish I didn't dream," he said. "There's no sense in such dreams... Reedly has been dead two years."

He considered. "Almost exactly two years. Three days short of two years."

His feet slid down to the smooth, cool, grey-green floor and he stood up and stretched his arms wide.

"Maybe I've worked my brain too hard," he thought. "These are tremendous times. Maybe presently I ought to have some kind of a rest. When did I last have a rest? When have I ever had a rest...?"

He stood still, summing up the situation.

"I've got the upper hand completely now. I've won all along the line. Why should I be troubled? Why should I have these dreams? I have only to go on... But all the same if I could have a rest. Things will not leave me alone. New resistances. New difficulties. Not so great as the old, but still they come.

"Never a rest. I can't leave it. Everything depends on me. Everything depends on me. Everyone turns to me for decision."

He walked down the steps to his balcony and his face expressed a certain grave satisfaction with the martyrdom he had brought upon himself.

He paused under the great arch of the balcony and surveyed the little table on which his breakfast was set out. He had no appetite. He reflected upon the disadvantages of strenuous greatness.

"There was a time," he reflected, "when I *loved* a new-laid egg."

2

But before we can assist at this sunlit breakfast of Rud's, it will be better to relate the main events that had converted Marshal Reedly into a nightmare horror of a frozen, faceless shout, and installed Rud, a nervous wreck, in that palatial sleeping place.

For two years Rud, sustained continually by drugs and the excitement of the struggle, had been living without a pause. He had been suing himself to his utmost stretch. As the end of the War had approached, it had seemed to him that the stresses of his life were drawing to a climax. But thereafter his activities had never fallen below the crisis level. The attainment of world mastery by the Group had not been an end but the beginning of a far more subtle and serious struggle, and only after a two-year crescendo of strenuousness did there seem to be any hope whatever of relaxation in his gigantic revolutionary effort.

Until the very end of the War of the Ideologies it had been in doubt whether the Old World, so far as it was embodied in the Allied Governments, had captured and was making use of the Group and its World Revolution or whether the World Revolution had taken control of them. In the end where would mastery lie? No brain in the world had been more acutely aware of this indecisiveness than Rud's. Day by day, long before the war was over, that ceaseless conflict had gone on, now a point won, now a point lost, now a phase of grip and assurance, now a phase when everything seemed slipping away from him.

Reedly had not been the whole of the trouble; he had not been the heart of the trouble; but he had been its forefront. Reedly and his ambitions and intrigues, his romanticism and his arrogance, his obvious good looks, melodramatically aristocratic, and his obvious contempt for the Common Man, had become the centre and embodiment of the old order of things that Rud was bent upon destroying. He was World Marshal; it was manifest that he hoped to be the first World Caesar. He played off the governments against the Group and the Group against the governments more and more plainly. Until he was destroyed, his destruction seemed to be the final victory for which the Group had to fight. When he was destroyed his destruction seemed only an incident in a far profounder conflict.

In the days before the outbreak of war had brought the Group into official existence, it had carried on its propaganda against astonishingly little resistance. It had slipped in between right and left, with such an air of undogmatic neutrality that few people realised that its fundamental propositions ploughed deeper than either reactionary or "red." It had spread its ideas and phrases about the world with scarcely any counter-attack. To the middle-aged people who constituted the directive stratum in every one of the combatant states, it only became apparent how very definite and uncompromising was the Party of the Common Man and how steadily it was setting itself to create new lines and forms of human activity, when it was already in partial possession of the essential services of the community. The younger officials, the foremen and non-commissioned officer class were already, to a large extent, explicitly or tacitly "Rudite." You never knew, nowadays, among the younger people particlarly, the old stagers began to remark, where those Common-sense ideas might not crop up, and how much these younger men might not insist on disregarding orders in pursuit of some overriding idea. "It is a phase," said the old stagers, uneasily. "It will pass... But we had better do something nevertheless. We don't want this sort of thing to go too far."

As the defeat of militant totalitarianism became more certain the resolve of this active and ascendant Party of the Common Man to keep its grip on the world industries and the transport services it had practically commandeered, and to go on disregarding the national separatisms it had overridden in the name of military necessity, became more definite and outspoken. And with that, resistance to the Group rose.

The hold the Common-sense Movement had secured upon the means of counter-propaganda varied widely in different countries, and Rud realised with a gathering anger that a wide-spread series of movements for national and racial assertion, against "deadly uniformity," against "socialism" and the "bureaucratic control" of financial processes, against "educational tyranny" and "the suppression of local and individual enterprise," were putting up a more and more effective opposition to his rapid drive towards a permanent socialistic world organisation and administration. "After the war," they said, "Restoration." "After the war," said the Common-sense Party, "go on to the new world."

A mind whose operations were becoming of increasing importance in Rud's view of the world at that time was the slow, clear, competent intelligence of Bellacourt. So far Rud had met few engineers or scientific workers, and he found himself dealing with a type of mentality less rhetorical and firmer than any he had encountered before. Bellacourt's general trend was conservative; his disposition was to take it for granted that a vaguely apprehended but highly desirable civilisation was endangered by the failure of something he called vaguely "moral progress" to keep pace with material advance, and that this civilisation had to be saved and reconditioned. After which he was inclined to think no more about it and settle down to what he considered to be his own particular job. He loved the applications of flight to exploration and research, to the taking of food, relief, medical aid to otherwise inaccessible places, to the spraying of crops, the fighting of fires and suchlike humanitarian services. Civil aviation was the very axis of his mind and he could not get away from it.

The whole complex plan of a new world that Bodisham had elaborated had to be correlated with air necessity before Bellacourt could be brought into militant co-operation with the Group. Rud feared he might throw his weight on to the other side, and consent to a premature peace settlement and another hopeless tangle of efforts to put the world back to some imaginary former contentment. His influence in the air forces was enormous. He was, Rud realised, an absolutely indispensable man.

But educational work upon Bellacourt, that Rud and Bodisham found heavy going, was happily for them taken out of their hands by Reedly's eagerness to gain control of the air arm. He found it difficult to regard a man so slight, fair and civil as Bellacourt as in any way formidable. He spoke of him as an "ideologue," a word he used to express the nadir of his contempt. He had picked it up from some *Life* of Napoleon, and by it he meant a man who believed without qualification in his own beliefs, and who was, therefore, a difficult associate. Rud and Bodisham were a little inclined to agree with that opinion, but they let Reedly do the talking. Bellacourt disliked Reedly's moustaches, disliked his overriding, short, sharp manner, his barking judgments that were always wrong when you thought them over. He detested the noises Reedly made coming into a room. Bellacourt was indeed the whole machine-age ahead of Reedly. Mechanisation means lubrication. One can hector men about but not machines, and so they mend our manners.

Reedly's attempts to loosen Bellacourt's hold on the air services of the world forced the latter towards a complete liaison with the Common-sense Party. It was attacking institutions that seemed to him not merely harmless but amiable; he thought its hostility to religion and its educational aggressiveness harsh and unnecessary; but he realised that in contrast with Reedly's dangerous unscrupulousness it was set inflexibly upon the creation of one common air service for the whole world. That was what he wanted.

That was what Bodisham wanted. That was one of the "parallel independent co-operations" that collectively were to make a new world for mankind. It was typically a world service that had to be "put out of politics." And what Rud wanted chiefly was to destroy the old traditional institutions, the old respectabilities and dignities and loyalties he hated, the separating distinctions and time honoured claims, that were now creeping out of their hiding-places and abandoning their protective camouflages again as the defeat of the quasi-modernised Authoritarians became more and more assured.

At first the widespread resistance to World Unification had seemed various in its nature, very human and spontaneous. At first perhaps it was. Rud put it down for a while to the natural perversity of his fellow Common Men. He was disposed to deal with it piecemeal. Then as he heard Thirp's reports upon Reedly's ever-ramifying activities and discussed the accumulating opposition with the organising Bodisham and the shrewd, observant Chiffan, he began to realise the increasing interrelation of these difficulties. They were being drawn together and shaped into a definite, new, reactionary organisation. Very rapidly now.

As usual his mind leapt beyond his instructors.

He summoned his inner cabinet, his most trusted intimates, Bodisham, Steenhold and Chiffan, to his room at the Aerodrome.

"I want to talk to you three about something urgent," he said. "Let me explain…"

They did nothing to prevent him.

"This new movement. It's beginning to crop up, in speeches, books, newspapers, diplomatic conversations. We have all been too busy at our particular jobs to note it. They have a word: 'Federation!' You must have observed it… One hears more and more of it…The way it breaks out here, there and everywhere has puzzled me… Perhaps you don't think it amounts to much. It does. Yesterday I was baffled by a world that looked like a scattered jigsaw puzzle – one thing after another that wouldn't fit in place. Then in the night I woke up."

"You would," said Chiffan.

"And it was all clear. Suddenly I saw it clear. I thought we were just up against Reedly. I thought it would be easy to deal with him when the time came. In fact I thought I had that provided for. But it's something much bigger than that. It's 1918 over again if we don't save it. The world will be cheated again. This Federation movement is becoming a line-up of all the war-battered conservation forces in the world. They blundered into this world war quite on the old lines, and now they want to blunder out of it again quite on the old lines. Instead of *our* Common World Law we are to end in a revised patchwork of what do they call them? – free sovereign countries, a Federal United States of the World. Each of them still with its own little flag and money and religion and finance and peculiar company laws and all that. It's going to be a sort of Reformed Yesterday. An agreement against war – some sort of treaty again – some sort of Geneva again. With a World President (or an Emperor maybe) and a World Senate of dodderers and a Supreme Court to bar any constructive action. Each rotten little state still free to do what it likes with its own common men so long as it doesn't go to war. Sweat 'em – sell 'em. Exile 'em. Like throwing snails over the garden wall. A long time that will last! It sounds so free and liberal – the Federation of the World. Wilson's self-determination over gain. Tennysonian and all that. Broaden down from precedent to precedent, but remain squatting good and tight on your particular allotment of the Common Man... I'll die a thousand deaths before I'll stand it! I'll raise the world against it."

He couldn't sit at the table. He walked about the room, white-faced, gesticulating with clenched fists. "I see it all," he said. "I see it all." They think they've used us and they think they're done with us. And the hand that is drawing all threads together is that hairy fist of the future First World President, the Conqueror of the Last War of All, the ultimate Julius Caesar, *Judas* Caesar – Reedly…

"Who I thought was just on his own…"

And then in an intense voice, and as if he soliloquised, he said something that lifted Chiffan's eyebrows.

"I will not have *my* Revolution assassinated," he said. "No. I will not be tricked now. Now that I have got thus far. I have struggled for this day – for five and twenty centuries. Yes. I and my sort. Five and twenty centuries of it against the bullies and the bouncers and the quiet, sly, plausible people, one down another up. My sort of men have struggled long enough. *My* sort of men. The pre-Ruds and the sub-Ruds, the vulgar, ugly, slighted, cheated, resentful, freespirited Common Men. The Crowd. The Rebels. The Great Unwashed. Me! Do you think I haven't been here before and do you think *all* of you haven't been here before? In the same corner. They can kill us and bury us and burn us up or let us rot away. Back we come again and again. Now, *this* time, we're nearer winning than ever we were. I feel it in my bones…

"Do you think the Son of Man is going to be downed by a chap who neighs like a horse…?"

He stopped short and stared at Chiffan. "Sometimes you think I'm crazy, Chiffan."

"Sometimes I think you're inspired."

"Well, anyhow," said Rud, and stood for a moment like a drugged man. He pulled himself together. "Well, now we have it plain. Come down to hard tacks. How can we grapple him,

Bodisham? How can I set about him? What men can we count upon? Who is with us? What sort of men are with us?

"I knew he had this sort of thing in mind. That talk of his about a United Command! That perpetual effort to get police control away from Thirp and to edge Bellacourt out of the air. Always he was against the embargo on bombing. He's a natural born bomber. Bombing makes him feel like a God throwing thunderbolts. Then his manoeuvres to go behind the Allied Munition Board and have military instead of civil direction in the factories! His pick of officers! His idea of contacting *our* engineers...! Yes, but what we haven't realised up to now were all those forces scattered throughout the world, those multitudes of reasonable able, successful men who've 'got on,' as people say, who dread the Economic World State like the devil, to whom this loose Federation of Mankind they are talking about, without any world investigations, without common financial control, without human unity, will be reprieve, freedom, opportunity...

"We've got these National Dictators licked. They're all sheltering behind their soldiers now – and their soldiers are wondering how to dispose of them. It's like Kaiser Wilhelm in 1918. Grossberg is *their* Reedly. Old Marshal Grossberg is no fool. He knows where he stands. This last war is over. The situation on the European front isn't the deadlock it pretends to be. It's a sham fight waiting for a chosen umpire. Who won't be us. Grossberg means to surrender. His army is sulking. They sit in their dug-outs and their officers keep away from them. They've got to that. On the east and centre, anyhow. *He* may be shot in the back anywhen now. But he means to surrender to Reedly according to all the laws of war, and he doesn't mean to surrender to us. We might hand him back to his own people.

We might do anything to him. He wants to capitulate while he still has an army to surrender. Reedly hasn't reported the state of affairs to us, because he is hesitating. Reedly is still funking Bellacourt. And he has a nasty feeling about Thirp and Thirp's police net, and he feels I mean to shoot him at the first opportunity. As I certainly do. When the shooting begins it will have to be quick work. How are we going to set about it?"

"Whom can we count upon?" asked Bodisham.

"We must bring in Thirp. He's developing amazingly... He's not exactly omniscient – but he's subomniscient."

"There are enormous masses of indeterminate people just now in the world," said Bodisham. "A push will send them in any direction,"

"What are we going to do?" said Rud.

His three familiars knew that he meant to answer that himself.

"I have ideas," said Rud. "I have some ideas."

He dropped into his seat and began to jot down the untidy intimations of notes on a strip of paper. He thought. He rang for his new secretary, Olders, and gave instructions for Thirp to be called to them at once.

"I *had* a sort of intimation," said Rud. "As you know, Bellacourt has been in America twice in the last fortnight. Didn't I tell you? He is there again. He's there with Holbank. After our talk with him – you remember that talk, Bodisham – I had a talk to him myself. It was an afterthought. As a matter of fact, though I didn't bother you others with it, we've done a sort of mobilisation of the air forces. It was Bellacourt's own suggestion – after I talked to him. We've assembled material in Labrador ready to fly it over to Sweden, real war material, and we've been concentrating planes in Sweden. You remember how Reedly the other day objected to the planes flying over his blessed little war. What he didn't realise was that they were photographic planes and that every day for a month we've had a complete photographic record of every movement at the front, and in one or two districts behind. I don't think Reedly knows anything of these highly trained young men in Stockholm with their magnifying glasses, sitting over his little shifts of troops and transport and puzzling out what they signify. Of course, we may have missed one or two little things…

"Frankly, I expect a Reedly Putsch now within six weeks. Bellacourt ought to be coming over Greenland now and his fighting planes ought to be accumulating during the next fortnight. It has to be done quietly. We don't want to frighten the birds too soon. I want this Putsch to happen. I want Reedly to show his hand. That will bring world affairs to one plain issue.

"I didn't perhaps consult you as I ought to have done," he said. He turned to Bodisham with his notes. He was as near to being apologetic as he could be.

"How do you figure this out?" he began.

Steenhold looked at him. He liked this. This was his Rud at his best. It came into his head to say: "Do you remember, Rud, how you came into my flat that Sunday morning – not so many years ago? Just as you are now. 'This is the moment,' you said." And then it occurred to him that this remark might be unnecessary and inopportune, so that he did not make it.

Thirp appeared suddenly. "You're quick," said Rud.

"I have to be," said Thirp.

"Olders had hardly gone out of the room five minutes ago to call you."

333

"He didn't call me. I came of my own accord. I have something very urgent to tell you."

Rud took him aside.

"If it could be just ourselves," said Thirp. "For a moment anyhow. I want to tell you something. It's something so queer – I don't want to argue. Do you mind?"

Chiffan and Steenhold intimated that they did not mind. Bodisham was expressionless. There was something feminine in the way that Thirp would always scheme to get Rud to himself if he could and have little special understandings with him, but it was a pity Rud fell in with this. Bodisham was a philosopher. He had to take Rud as he found him. Rud was essential to the Revolution and that was that. Rud expected to have everything told and explained to him and yet he was always going behind his organiser's back, with Norvel, with Bellacourt, with Thirp – with anyone. It was his way. Bodisham drummed with the fingers of one hand on the table and Steenhold understood how he felt and thought.

Rud led Thirp to an inner room.

3

"It is a very extraordinary thing," began Thirp in his high-pitched voice after he had watched the door close. "But you have such understanding – "

He twisted his long, thin hands together. "It may seem preposterously trivial to you, but what I have to tell you about is the despatch of twelve million coloured postcards from London, to various destinations I have checked. They are all pictures of the same person – "

"Reedly?"

"Exactly. I have known about these postcards for weeks – joining them up to other little things of a similar nature. There are some pamphlets, too – in various languages. Well, I will confess I'm startled. I did not expect these cards to move so soon. No. I counted on three or four weeks yet. I was timing things for that as I explained to you. Then suddenly they have been hustled off…"

"That means something has been precipitated?"

"Exactly. You see – I think. It's very significant."

"The first cat's paw of a storm?"

"Exactly. These postcards are trivial in themselves, but they are part of an elaborate scheme. If they go off, then the whole scheme must be in motion. Nobody would give a particular order, specially about them. Somebody or something has pressed a button. A postcard can show how the wind blows."

"Things are still at a standstill on the front?"

"N-oo. I shouldn't say that. That's exactly it. They can't be. The unexpected must have been busy there. The front has always been difficult to watch. Conditions vary from sector to sector. From their left wing and all up through the Little Carpathians the disposition to fraternise has been very strong for some time. Bellacourt's leaflets, the ones you drafted, have done more there than bombs. Reedly has flatly forbidden them and he has five planes under arrest – "

"Blank mutiny."

"At Constance. I've just got the report of that. You know he has always been opposed to our air propaganda. But he has never dared touch it before. Probably he has some excuse. Things are different on the right there, where the lines bend back above the

335

Jura. What we call the Italian flank. These sectors are more complicated. Old hatreds. There is a considerable artillery activity. The men can't get near each other, and there's Italians against our Spanish. That ugly old feud is as bitter as ever. There's black blood there, and also near the middle where the Czechs are up against the Germans. Now the English and Germans have even stopped sniping... But all that's quite secondary..."

"Let's look at a map."

The map was spread on the table.

"These are details. The right and its little raids and killings is, I say, secondary. What matters is the state of affairs on the centre and their left. There their discipline is in such a state that their Higher Command may come trotting over to Reedly with a white flag at any time. For all I know that may be happening now. I told you that was possible yesterday, but I didn't realise it was imminent. Since then something definite may have happened. Something very definite. Reedly certainly didn't expect a snap to come so soon. Nobody expected it so soon. *I* didn't. He's a great commanding figure is Marshal Reedly, and when he says a thing has to happen, that is the appointed time. Maybe it's got something to do with the food breakdown. Maybe some quite small regimental affair has started an avalanche. Maybe they're shooting their officers like the Russians did in '17... Maybe they're fighting among themselves. But you see, whatever he's been getting ready in the way of a mine under our feet is going to be let off – sooner than was expected – in a day or so... Or earlier. These postcards..."

"You're listening in everywhere?"

"I could a tale unfold. But I spare you. I've got it pretty clear; trust me. I join my slats. The idea always has been to stage an Armistice at the front without consulting you, and to proclaim World Federation and the end of the war straight away. And that's what they seem to be doing now. In a rush."

"Reedly as Jove?"

"Descending upon an exhausted Europa in a cloud of post-cards. Sorry! I'm mixing the ladies."

"And he means to do – what?"

"He will seize the aerodromes and tackle Bellacourt. And that reminds me of another thing about this sudden precipitance. Bellacourt, I find, has been in Canada. Has anything been going on in Canada?"

"You don't know that?"

"No, I don't know that. How could I know it – if you didn't tell me?"

"Well – there *has* been – "

"Preparation?"

"Bellacourt will fight Reedly – yes."

"I wish I had known," said Thirp, and wished silently that sometimes Rud would let his left hand know what his right was doing. "I wish I *had* known," he repeated.

"Reedly must have heard of that," he went on. "Before I did. That may have touched everything off. But anyhow, he is against Bellacourt. He hates Bellacourt if possible more than he hates you. He's a *vain* man. These last months, without any real air fighting and the command of the air in our hands, have made him feel ridiculous. I think I can give a rough guess of what he will do. In one little communication that I happened to hear he said – what was it? – *prig-ridden air.* He'd go straight for the

337

aerodromes and try and recover them from the Allied Air Control, that is to say, Bellacourt. He will seize come of the big power stations. I've been trying to get all that unobtrusively policed – by trustworthy people. He will naturally denounce you for wanting to prolong the war by holding back the air arm. Hey Presto! Civilisation has been saved in the nick of time. We shall figure – as Reds, as World Communists, enemies of religion, enemies of patriotism. All our hard-won respectability gone! Most of us will be arrested."

"He's got all this ready?"

"He's got it *half* ready. In one way or another I've wetted a lot of his powder. Some sort of attack *was* actually brewing here, there's some army die-hards professedly on leave in Amsterdam. Maybe they meant to raid us here. But I've scotched that for the moment, I think, by bringing in about a thousand – nearly a thousand – of my own youngsters. From London... Well, anyhow, they'll be here this afternoon. He's had about three divisions in reserve in Flanders ready to be clapped into trains and rushed here by the end of next week. That I know. Munitions not arrived for them. He's a *bad* organiser. Roots has held that up. We've got all that taped. They're stirring now, but they can't get moving – at least only a few companies might be rushed... With no guns... I'll have the trains held up. I think I can do that. My men will be here in three hours at latest. Nothing much can happen until then."

His confidence had a slightly forced quality.

"Of course," said Thirp, "in a place like Amsterdam... One can't answer for everything – There's always been a strong reactionary movement..."

Rud stood brooding over the map.

"This place might be quite a lively spot in no time," he said.

Olders burst in with a paper in his hand and handed it to Rud. Rud read it silently and then aloud: "Enemy army in open mutiny. Discipline gone. Higher Command and officers ask to surrender to us. They are in great danger. Have ordered Cease Fire and am arranging surrender and armistice. Propose to proclaim World Peace forthwith based on self-determination."

"D'you hear that?" said Rud. "Based on self-determination."

"Only conditions generally acceptable. Trust you and Bellacourt will co-operate…"

"We were prophetic," said Rud.

"And now?"

"Either I shoot Reedly or he shoots me within the next twenty-four hours."

"My lads from London will be here," said Thirp; "it can't take them three hours. I don't see how I can possibly accelerate them… Frankly I would if I could. Tell me about Bellacourt. How does he stand? Can these planes from America be brought here? In time?…"

Rud answered none of Thirp's questions. Instead, he went on extracting particulars of the situation in Amsterdam.

4

Steenhold sat in his place at the council table. He looked sullenly amused. He was reflecting upon the change in his relation to Rud. He had wanted to make a friendly remark to him and he had not made it – out of deference! He was surprised at himself and everything.

There had been a time, not so many years ago, when he had been a sort of patron-philosopher to Rud, when he had disputed with him, quarrelled with him, said anything he liked to him. And paid the bills. Now one waited to be told. This revolutionary business had become real, very real. When he had played at World Revolution in Camborne Square, reality had seemed a hundred worlds away. And yet, had it not been for his helpful money in those early days…

The door of the little room opened and Rud, an exalted Rud appeared. His scowl was at its most masterful and vicious and his mouth was tight drawn in at its left corner, with resolution.

"Listen," he said. "Everything has to be short and quick. The moment is nearer than we thought."

Bodisham turned an attentive face, saying nothing.

"Olders," said Rud, "radio Bellacourt GGG and then wait ten minutes, then repeat and go on until you have the code answer."

"What does that mean?" said Chiffan.

"He'll know."

"H'm," said Chiffan, and his eye met Steenhold's for a moment.

Rud advanced to the table and spoke, standing.

"Reedly's lost his nerve," he said. "He's put his Putsch on – a month perhaps. And here we are. He means to strike. He's got a trainload of French troops coming here from Antwerp, but that may get switched on to the frontier. Evidently he means to grab this place and us. That's for the transport section, Steenhold. What can you do? Thirp doesn't know exactly what he had in the town – but I doubt if it's ready. He's got no guns – anywhere. Neither at Antwerp nor in Amsterdam. Thirp thinks he has some of the groundsmen here… That's the situation. There's no doubt he's moving now. We may have a raid here at any time. But we've got those planes out there? He may have stuff for the four or five he has at Constance. You'd better pack up, Bodisham – in case… We'll keep one plane for you… But that's by the way…

"First of all, the situation here. I want you, Steenhold, to take charge of all this. The police here don't number four hundred, there's only a youngster in command – we don't know anything about him – and Thirp will hand over the command to you. You must have got a section of your transport corps at Rotterdam and some at the port here. They're scattered, I suppose. Can you get them together? We want the aerodrome and the radio station held – and all this. Dreed had better go to the radio station forthwith. You'll assist him to improvise a defence. It's very important to keep the radio going. Steenhold – if you will go with Thirp to the door – your second in command is outside. Thirp and Olders and I are going to vanish. You'll hear from us soon enough."

He went and sat down beside Bodisham and began to talk to him rapidly in undertones. Bodisham nodded quickly and approvingly.

Steenhold felt anxious. Where was Rud going? Oughtn't there to be some sort of council of war?

"I don't understand," he began.

"Steenhold," said Rud, "you've got your orders. Things can't wait for explanations now. You must do something about those French troops from Antwerp. They have to be held up. There's not much time if they are really entrained. Does the line come through Rotterdam? I don't know."

"Gee!" said Steenhold, blew, and then got up and saluted. He had never saluted Rud before.

Rud went on talking to Bodisham.

"That's Rud. That was," said Steenhold as he left the room with Thirp.

They found a bright young officer of police outside, who saluted. Thirp led the way to the ground floor where there was a large-scale map of the aerodrome and its surroundings. "Show the Minister where your men are," he said.

"Is there a siren or anything handy," said Steenhold, taking hold of the situation, "to call the men to quarters?"

The first intimation that Reedly's Federalist friends in Amsterdam had of trouble afoot was the siren at the Aerodrome. Thirp's secret police were already in possession of the Antwerp telephone exchange and were intercepting Reedly's calls to action and taking down the names.

Most of them were caught unawares but not all.

"This is a damned great place to hold with only four hundred people," said Steenhold, standing on the steps of the main building and surveying his area of responsibility. In the afternoon sunshine it looked tranquil almost to drowsiness. "I wonder what one ought to treat as vital points and just where the trouble will come from and what shape it will take."

Steenhold had a lively but receptive mind, he had never been a man of action. He did not feel like a man of action now. He had always looked on at life, egged people on, enjoyed the results of their initiatives. Rud had been his great discovery, his staple entertainment. Now suddenly, an hour after lunch, he found himself with a recalcitrant bunch of disconnected responsibilities thrust into his hands and no one to observe but himself. Hold this place? Hold it how? Hold it against what? Away there by the air station were half a dozen planes lined up and a small one some way off in the corner of the field. These, he supposed, would have to be guarded – the pilots were probably standing by and they would be Bellacourt's men, but there ought to be some police to support them. Rud had said something about disloyal groundsmen. The machines had to be protected from sabotage, a man with a bomb might play havoc there. The half-hidden by the main building was Dreed's radio station. Dreed would be warned and would see to the defence of that, but he ought to be reinforced.

"Three essential points," Steenhold told himself, "headquarters, the planes and the radio. No way of consolidating a central position that I can see. But think – where will the attack come? First there are those French troops from Antwerp. If they come discreetly with pilot engines ahead and a revolver at the ear of every engine driver, it won't be so easy to switch them out of action. But coming discreetly means coming slowly. They'll come along the line and detrain where it is most convenient. Can they afford the time to come discreetly? They'll have to rush. If they rush, they must rush into trouble."

"How near is the railway?" he asked, and then had a bright idea. Even if he couldn't switch those French troops off to some remote destination, as he had imagined at first, he could get a dozen engines or more if necessary from Amsterdam, put them on the line, and simply smash up that troop train as it came up. Before they had time to detrain. He must see to that in a minute, as soon as he was clear about everything else.

Something else? There might be some sort of attack in unknown force from the town. That would come by road in cars. It might come first. It might wait for the arrival of the French. It might not come at all. Nothing might come. He ticked off the items on the fingers of his open hand. Then he asked his second in command how many men he had.

"Seventy-six on duty. The rest are falling in over there by the hutments. About two-hundred-and-ninety-odd."

"Good," said Steenhold. "We join them."

And as they walked across the Aerodrome he arranged for a squad of men under a competent sergeant to go towards the town, hold up any cars and wire the road, while another squad was to reinforce the radio guard, if there was a radio guard, and put itself at the disposal of Dreed. The road party paraded, six men went off to get wire from the stores and the rest marched briskly towards the Amsterdam road in the most businesslike way. Steenhold ordered a dozen men to strengthen the force in the main building and stationed the remainder of a hundred and twenty men in front of the main building as a reserve force that could be turned in any direction to meet whatever trouble might arise. He went through the motions of an inspection of their arms. "We've just got to prevent any disturbance," he told the young officer. Then he went to the planes to assure himself that the pilots and mechanics were on the alert.

He did all this methodically, watchful of his second in command and the two orderlies they had annexed, to see from their behaviour whether he seemed to be doing things right. They seemed to think he was doing things right.

The pilots seemed satisfied with themselves and anxious to learn what was expected to them. He told them to be ready to go up at any moment and they said. "Aye, aye, sir," very reassuringly. Within he felt that faint stirring of derision for the whole business of life which is the salt of the American mentality. Outwardly they are sentimental and enthusiastic and inwardly they are profoundly cynical. All over the world for generations, he reflected, this solemn sort of preparatory business has been going on; commanding officers, with an air of conviction, making their dispositions, sentries being put, passwords fixed, challenges arranged, all the stiffly silly formalities of warfare, everyone being as wooden and regulation-ruled as possible, and the officer never quite sure of himself and carrying it off with an air.

Americans generally have never loved this saluting, uniform-wearing business. They overdid it when they had a chance, because fundamentally they could not believe in it. Probably it was necessary. Probably you could only keep the thing going with all this routine. But what a quantity of fuss, of saluting, heel-clicking, running about, before ever you begin to have anything real happening!

It was just the same with religion. Setting about things, that, in ninety-nine cases out of a hundred, took you nowhere and did nothing that mattered, with the gravest of faces. Being stern, sharp, emphatic – violent if necessary. Before it was necessary. " 'Shun!" "As you were!" "On the knee!" Why did every human concern clog itself up in a tangle of routines, formalities, disciplines, imperatives? Why couldn't one be free? Really free? Guarding one's freedom wasn't freedom at all. Why couldn't one win one's freedom for good and all, and get on with life?

He wished he knew more of the situation. Had Reedly got hold of some planes? If so, would they appear presently? Where was Bellacourt? What had Bellacourt got away there in Sweden? Was Bellacourt playing some game of his own? Why didn't we have our own planes in the air here? When the war began there had been tens of thousands of planes fighting in the air, and then as the enemy had their factories and aerodromes destroyed and their planes beaten out of the sky, there had been this air cessation. Possibly Bellacourt's air strikes had not been altogether unwelcome to the overstrained governments of the Democratic Allies. It had given them an excuse for relaxing their exhausting efforts to produce material and for bringing back the war from three dimensions to two. Yet it was curious we had not made one crowning effort to end the war? Our planes, such as remained, went about looking at things and doing nothing, and the war, which had begun in an uproar of destruction, was dying of inanition. Was there some catch in the business and was it true that the air arm cannot end a war?

Anyhow here we were, it seemed, with war back on the ground again, and Reedly trying to play Napoleon to our revolution, quite in the best tradition…

Steenhold wrenched his mind away from these questions and gave himself up to the railway problem. He spent an active and useful half-hour with a very competent subordinate and then he emerged upon the airfield again.

"And now what is there to be done?" he asked the officer.

"Nothing, sir, that I can see, until something happens." The young officer seemed to think that everything was going according to plan in this best of all possible worlds…

Wouldn't do to ask him what he thought *would* happen… ·

Then suddenly the central part of the main building became active. One of Bellacourt's men with a megaphone appeared on a little balcony high up and began giving orders to the pilots. They became exceedingly active and a truck of petrol appeared out of an archway below. Three of the men went off at a run to

346

the smaller plane. Two more pilots on bicycles shot round the wing of the main buildings and joined them.

It looked all right.

Then Rud and Thirp and Olders appeared upon the steps of the main building, in the company of two airmen. The planes, one after another, began to tune up. Their propellers leapt to activity with a happy shudder.

Something was happening now. The drowsy afternoon woke up. But what *was* happening?

They were going off somewhere and he did not know where they were going. He felt like a little boy who for some inscrutable reason has not been asked to a party. Where were they going? To Reedly? Perhaps Rud had been talking to Reedly and something had been patched up. Or to Sweden where perhaps Bellacourt was in control of things? Or in flight before Reedly struck?

"Why can't I know?" asked Steenhold, with a feeling like tears of vexation in his eyes. "He might have told me. I stood by him in the old days…"

A sound as though someone had snapped a brittle metallic rod and a shiver in the air.

Then a shout from among the planes and revolver shots. Three or four men were moving about very quickly there.

Rud was holding up his hand as if to forbid some action. Sabotage among the planes? Steenhold ran towards the scuffle, pulling out his revolver as he ran, and signalling to the knot of world police who were standing or sitting in front of the main building. There was no further shooting, and two of the pilots seemed to be holding a man, the man, no doubt, who had fired the shot at Rud. A man in pilot's uniform dodged round the head of the nearest machine, and he had something in either hand like

347

a cricket ball. He threw one of these objects under the plane, and seemed to hesitate about the other. Steenhold was running at an angle to the disturbance so that he alone saw this man clearly. He was evidently unobserved by either the spray of police who were running towards the plane or by the men actually about the machines. Steenhold shouted to confuse his attention and fired his revolver. A pilot's face appeared in the cabin of the machine.

The bomb under the machine burst loudly and the machine came tilting over towards Steenhold in a deliberate, drunken fashion as if to meet and welcome him. The pilot behind the glass seemed an inactive, an indifferent spectator of these events. The spinning propeller caught the bomb thrower's head as he turned and stepped back to confront Steenhold, and the bomb he held dropped from his hand and rolled and burst six yards in front of Steenhold's feet.

Steenhold had an extraordinary sense of being struck back and front at once, as though vast aerial hands clapped themselves upon him, and that he had lost his balance as he had never lost his balance before. His feet were off the ground. The plane, with its propeller whirling up the red-brown trophy it had slashed from his scalped antagonist, waved and sank down out of sight and he was staring at the sky...

Everything which had been moving with incredible rapidity now moved with unprecedented deliberation. It was clear to him that Rud had to go somewhere and that he had to prevent any interference with Rud. But nobody was telling him anything. Nobody ever told him anything nowadays. In the past it had been different.

Some sort of mental blank ensued.

He was doing something for Rud.

Had they got Rud? Had he got away? Where was he going?

It was a nuisance to have been hit so that he had to lie flat on his back like this. He dragged a hand across his chest and it was wet. He raised a hand, which had suddenly become very heavy, and it was bright red. He couldn't be badly hurt because there was not the slightest pain. But this blood! There seemed a frightful lot of it. And the taste of blood in his mouth. Where did it all come from? You couldn't possibly go on bleeding like this...

Somebody was saying: "You hurt much?" Somebody with a face upside down looking at him. "You hurt much?"

Bloody fool!

His chest blown in? Some of it anyhow. Mortally wounded? There ought to be a breastbone somewhere if one could raise a hand to feel it. But his hand had gone dead now.

It couldn't be! Presently perhaps, but not now. Not in the very middle of a scrap. Pinned to the ground like this. He'd get up in a minute.

But he knew better. He felt a wave of childish frustration.

He spoke, almost inaudibly.

"Not to see the *end* of it! That's *too* bad..."

They were Steenhold's last words. He felt as though he was being diluted very rapidly. Numbness radiated from his chest in waves. He had a dim idea that he was straining his neck up to look for Rud, but there was no Rud, only blue sky and little white clouds sailing in two columns head, V-wise, across the sky, and then that last faint impression faded.

5

Oblivious of the death of his first substantial supporter, oblivious indeed of everything but the urgency of his conclusive grapple with Reedly, Rud paced the air photography rooms at Stockholm which were Bellacourt's Headquarters.

Bellacourt was already over Norway on his way to them. He couldn't be more than ten minutes away.

Thirp sat crouched and angular with his arms folded, waiting an hour to the minute so to speak; Olders subdued himself to patience by staring out of the windows. They had all come in the smaller, swifter machine from Amsterdam. They had not waited even to learn what had happened to the bombed machine. The others, they knew, were scouting southwards towards Antwerp – except the one that would wait for Bodisham if Bodisham had to bolt.

These Sloten machines carried no bombs or guns, but they were to report any movement of troops to Dreed and Steenhold. Rud had refused to hear any reports from them. He wanted to concentrate upon Reedly. All the rest was detail and it was becoming his habit now to leave detail to others. He paced the long room of the air maps, not looking at them, brooding on what was before him and whistling in his incompetent, small-boy way between his teeth. And presently Bellacourt arrived.

He came straight to Rud, still wearing his wadded coat, and he stripped it off as he greated Rud.

"I got your radio," he said. "What has happened?"

"Everything – suddenly. A full month before our calculation. I was right about the facts as I told you them when last we talked. Where are the bombs and the bombers?"

"Twenty close now. Following me. Not half an hour behind. Twenty more from Reykjavik. Fifty in reserve, starting from Battle Harbour in an hour. In all this I'm guided by you."

"Then we can be in Poland with that load – your twenty – when?"

"Well before sundown."

"You have plenty of other planes here but no bombs for them?"

"Several hundred without bombs."

"We could take men in those?"

Thirp intervened. "I've got a detachment of my men here who've been trained for that. They can drop. Mostly they're Russians. Lovely youngsters. I just took them over. They've always been good at the parachute game."

"Good," said Rud. "Now the next thing is to locate Mr Reedly exactly."

"We've got all the positions in Poland photographed from a thousand feet," said Bellacourt. "I haven't worked with Crawford for nothing. We've been doing that for weeks now. I doubt if Reedly understands that. If you'll come into the Long Gallery, where the boys are working, I can show you – his GHQ and everything. Fresh and nearly up to date."

"Bellacourt, you hate bombing, I know," said Rud, "but this time you will bomb in a good cause. Just let me tell exactly why we have to blow the World Marshal to bits, now."

And as they went towards the Long Gallery, where Bellacourt's photograph readers were working at their daily examination of Reedly's movements, Rud, with elucidatory remarks from Thirp, explained the urgency of the situation to Bellacourt.

Bellacourt led the way to the long table devoted to the photographic examinations. There, arranged for comparison, were the long strips for yesterday and the day before and the day before that. An assistant stood by with lenses while Bellacourt explained the reading of the photographs. "There's his dug-out. Pretty big and deep. That heap of earth came out of it. It casts quite a shadow, you see. That's the shadow, that black mark. That gives us the height of the heap. There's the Officer's Mess. There are the kitchens. You see the tracks made by the orderlies going to and fro? Those pale streaks. Pretty work reading these photographs! You see that shadow there; that's cast by the photographer's own plane. Its size and its distortion gives its height and the angular measure for all the other shadows."

"You could bomb all that – this afternoon?"

"I can blow it to rags – all this area – before sundown tonight. We've got quite enough stuff for that. But how can we be sure he will be there – and not somewhere else, or down in that dug-out? Impossible to get him if he's in the dug-out."

"He'll be there all right," said Rud. "I'll arrange that with him."

Olders was called away for a moment to take a radio message.

"You'll *arrange* it – with *him!*" said Bellacourt, puzzled.

"With him – by telephone. Why not?"

"You mean he'll *tell* you – himself! Where to bomb him?"

"He'll tell me all right and then we shoot. This is a very simultaneous world. You can't shoot a man unless you know where he is, can you? But if you know exactly where he is you can shoot him halfway round the world."

"But – !"

"Perfectly simple," said Rud. "I've been talking to him already – from Sloten. And when we are clear about these maps... You might bring a strip of that with you while I telephone again."

Olders came with a message. "I think you might know we've just got this: 'Troop train from Antwerp derailed near Dordrecht. No further trouble here. Wilson.' "

"Who's *Wilson?*" asked Rud. "I wonder why Steenhold didn't sign that. He ought to have signed it."

He wondered only momentarily. Then he turned his mind to the business in hand again.

They went to the room with the radio apparatus and Thirp sat down to get the World Marshal. When he did he handed the instrument to Rud. Bellacourt sat beside him with the air photograph of Reedly's Headquarters on the table.

"That you, World Marshal?" said Rud...

"Quite all right...

"No, nothing has happened. What did you expect to happen? I have been thinking over our last talk. I still think you may be too precipitate... Of course if Grossberg has surrendered, you must treat him decently. But what about his army? What state are they in?..."

Lengthy reply. Thirp listened to anything he could catch and Rud winked at him suddenly.

"But don't you think that before you communicate with the Allied Governments, you ought to come to Sloten again and consult us? After all, you *are* a member of the Group. Or aren't you?...

"You have a double responsibility you say. Even then you ought to keep in touch with us. You could be in Sloten before sundown...

"You have Grossberg and his staff on your hands... Naturally – every courtesy... Yes, yes, as one soldier to another and all that.

Naturally you'll dine with him. We civilians are apt to forget that professional brotherliness. Would you like me to join you?...

"Tomorrow more convenient. And you will be entertaining the defeated this evening. I should be in the way. Yes? Seven, I suppose. About then?"

Rud gestured noiselessly and triumphantly to Bellacourt and Bellacourt stuck a pin in the Officers' Mess. "Can I ring you up later? You'll be at the Officers' Mess, if I want to get you... After seven for certain. Wait a moment...

"You don't think there's much more to .say? Maybe you are right. But I warn you the Group may feel a little out of it if you insist on carrying on negotiations without them...

"Bellacourt? I *told* you he was in America. Getting munitions specially for you...

"Oh, we'll settle something, trust me. Maybe the Group *has* overrated itself... You think so. I've always been a bit afraid of you, Reedly. I've always felt you had that idea of us... Still, things are in your hands. You have said it. Bon appétit."

He put down the instrument. "That's that," he said.

"Wonderful," said Thirp. "He's fixed. I can't help feeling – "

"Feel it later," said Rud. "Now what exactly do we mean to do?"

Bellacourt began: "I get my planes refuelled and inspected."

"What we do," said Rud, "is this. You, Bellacourt, I take it, go high with those twenty bombers of yours, high, high, high – out of sight in the blue – until you are just out of hearing of him. About here say."

Bellacourt made a rapid calculation and indicated a spot with his pencil. "Twenty thousand feet," he said.

"You will be leading. Your men will have copies of these air maps. Well, as many as there are copies. Possibly not if you think it unnecessary. The light will be good for two hours yet. Then you stop your engines and down you come. Without a sound. Down, down, and then flatten out and let out the engines. They'll hardly hear your engine before you are on them. Then – all this area – "

"Goes to smithereens," said Bellacourt. "You can count on it. It's disgusting work. We shall be beautifully accurate – as we shall do it – trust me – but none the less it's disgusting. This makes ordinary assassination a gallant enterprise. You know I admire the way you've fixed him but by God I don't like it... Ah well, perhaps I'm a bit finicky. I'll try and think I'm getting square with those damned Germans at Guernica. You know, I saw all that... I did."

"Meanwhile," said Rud, "Thirp and I go over the enemy lines in that modest little plane we came in and drop down in these flats here."

"Olders and you," said Thirp. "I had better stay here for a bit and then go back to Sloten."

"You think?" said Rud.

"Sure," said Thirp.

Rud turned to Bellacourt. "You're sure we can make a good landing there?"

"It's been used as an airfiled," said Bellacourt. "You can see the tracks. Look. With the lens."

"We land there then," said Rud. "While your Russian boys, Thirp, in their parachutes, are already drifting and falling like thistledown over all this bit, each with his little gun and his ribbon of ammunition."

"I wish I could come," said Thirp.

"You expect to find mutineers there?" asked Bellacourt.

"I expect you'll find a Soldiers' and Workers' Committee," said Thirp. "Talking mostly."

"Is that what they call it?" said Rud. "Soldiers' and Workers' Committee! Delightful! It's 1917 over again. But this time the sequel will be different. We are the Revolution from the West and all fast-colour Revolutions come out of the West."

"Suppose they shot you as you come down?"

"No guarantee they won't. Then it will be all up with our Common World and nothing else will matter to us. I wish I talked better German. But they will have heard of me."

"Suppose they take pot shots at our parachutists?"

"Most of them will be gaping at Reedly's Headquarters, over the way. They won't shoot unless they're shot at. They won't know who we are."

"And the Allied Army?"

"Stunned. And then fraternisation…"

6

The World Marshal spoke in Anglo-German out of compliment to his distinguished guests and prisoners.

He hated talk when he encountered the loose, unaccountable minds of the intelligentsia; you never knew what they meant by it all; that brought out all the strong and silent stuff in him; but when it came to talking to soldiers and gentlemen, who used exactly the same phrases and metaphors, had identically amorphous ideas and could understand him perfectly, he could be fairly eloquent.

He was now in a state of sombre exaltation. At last it was his Day. He had told himself quite a number of times that afternoon that he had crossed the Rubicon. Except for a faint uneasiness about the possible recalcitrance of that crazy pacifist Bellacourt, there was not a shadow that he could see upon the road to world dominion that opened wide before him. He was grasping control of a disordered world on the very verge of social dissolution. He felt like General Monk, who had been one of his boyhood's heroes. He felt still more like Bonaparte after that whiff of grapeshot had put an end to the revolutionary vagaries of Paris. He, too, in his turn was saving civilisation – and civilisation – he would see to it – was going to be jolly grateful to him.

Just before he rose to speak he talked about Rud and the Group to the officers about him.

"Every sign of the completest collapse of the Common Man Movement. Every sign. They feel Destiny closing in on them. They realise they are outwitted and outmanoeuvred... Yes, I've good evidence of that – the best of evidence. Listen to something I have to tell you. I never believed in this man Rud Whitlow, though for a time it has served our purpose to have dealings with him. Anyhow, now I can wash my hands of him. Queer fish! Born double-crosser. Now he wants to go back on his associates. They'll all try that. They'll all be coming in now, ears down and tails wagging. It's in the breed. Twice he has been talking to me today on the air, trying to get to some sort of terms with me. Would you believe it?... Oh, I humour him. What is the use of his talking now? He's a doomed man. What use can they be in the world now? Short and sharp – against the wall. Eh?"

He nodded. His hearers nodded appreciatively. Then after a brief interval he stood up to make his speech, a manly man-to-man speech, but in its way, brilliant.

He said he did not want to make a speech, he never wanted to make speeches, he was not the talking sort, but he felt he could not let this occasion go by without a word of cheer, of fraternal greeting, as one soldier to another, for the great Christian gentleman, that clean, honest fighter, their enemy and brother-in-arms, Marshal Grossberg.

"We know only too well, to our cost, some of us, what a stout and sturdy warrior he can be, and on our side too we understand what it must mean to be stabbed in the back by those who owed, for every reason, high or low, loyal co-operation. None of our backs here have been perfectly safe. From the soldier's point of view, and as far as soldiers, real soldiers, go, this has been an honest, straightforward war. Modern weapons, but the old spirit. Alas! It can never be fought to a finish now, because never at any time has it been possible to keep out the enterprises – the interferences of shall we call them outsiders? Shall I speak more plainly?"

He paused and warmed up – "The filthy activities of cosmopolitan rogues, the incessant interference of ambiguous civilians, men who boast of their treason, men without faith or flag." (Sounds of agreement.)

"We soldiers, Marshal Grossberg, have had neither hand nor part in ths foul propaganda that has undermined your discipline and turned every other man in your ranks into – what shall I say? – the perplexed tool of the forces of malarial – of malignant disorder." (Applause at the phrasing.) "Even our espionage system has been honest, Marshal, here at the front, a soldierly espionage of fact, not a burrowing under the very roots of human life. This has been a great war and a fine war, but now we realise that there are issues profounder than any immediate war aims. The whole social order, Christianity, chivalry – Christianity here and chivalry in the Far East – honour, obedience, property, the purity of women, the discharge of obligations, plain honesty, love of country, the breed of horse, clean sport, everything that makes the orderly succession of seed-time and harvest, peace and war, is at stake. The sword, that clean white symbol of disciplined force, has been ousted by the ink squirt, by the creeping activities of mental germs viler than any physical corruption – viler than any disease germ, any poisoning of the wells." (Hear, hear.) "While we fight here at the front, humanity behind us crumbles down to a diseased dementia." (Sounds of approval.) "The first duty of a soldier is and always has been *not* to make war – no – but to keep the peace and to keep it with a strong hand. War is the soldier's exercise, his natural purification, but it is not his primary function. His primary function is discipline. And now we soldiers under all our flags have to stand shoulder to shoulder in the name of discipline – of disciplined democracy, strong and silent. I give you The Soldiers' Peace, the mastery of the sword, obedience and preparedness. An end, gentlemen, an end to this cosmopolitan folly…"

Something seemed to happen to his voice. It was as if he no longer had a voice. Something had engulfed it.

"What's *that*?" cried Grossberg inaudibly, staring with sudden apprehension out of the window.

The World Marshal's voice had been drowned by a great roar of aeroplanes, an eruption of huge, ugly, undulating, hungry sound, and he, too, turned to see the black bulk of the leading bomber sweeping over the Mess. It did not seem to be coming out of the sky, it had skimmed so low as it opened out that it seemed now to be rising out of the ground. It rushed up out from beneath the edge of the glowing sunset, a swift, expanding blackness. It was like a gigantic black skate in an aquarium swimming towards him very swiftly. It just cleared the nearer barracks and it had already risen sharply up out of the field of his vision, when the two bombs it had delivered, burst.

Hard upon it roared its fellows, rising right and left behind it and blotting out the sky in their turn. Beyond came others... Everything seemed to burst as the bombs burst. The corner of the window flew in towards the World Marshal. It flew at him, attacking him; a great knife of glass... It was coming straight for his moustache.

That was his last impression of life. He felt nothing more. The glass cut through his face like a knife thrown at a meringue.

He was extinguished.

7

The airfield behind the front lines of the Authoritarian Army was already deserted, and the shell-torn area beyond seemed equally abandoned, except for the World Police who were dropping down out of the air, making their more or less dexterous landings, and coming together into little groups. Farther to the north west and slanting away westward lay the broken country of the trenches and a couple of ruined villages, and still remoter, flame-shot masses of smoke rose from the Allied Headquarters against a clear golden sunset.

The bombing planes had zoomed up overhead and vanished in the eastward sky. They swept round in a great curve and went straight back to Stockholm, leaving everything to Rud. Bellacourt knew he could not stomach the sight of his handiwork. The thought of Guernica proved to be no consolation to him. But from Stockholm he sent on his planes from America as they came to hand, and put them at the service of the World Police. They spiralled down out of the twilight and dropped more and more parachutists.

Rud and Olders advanced across that wartorn landscape, and as they did so, the descending men of the World Police converged upon them and fell in as a sort of guard. A rabble of soldiers joined them. A huge cat bolted out of a shell-hole, and then another. "The cats eat the rats and the rats eat us," sang one of the Totalitarian soldiers. Men's heads an shoulders came up out of the ground, watchfully. They decided to clamber out. An increasing number of men emerged from the trenches and dug-outs ahead. The desolation became populous.

"What's German for Fraternisation?" demanded Rud.

"Try Verbrüderung," said Olders.

It seemed right.

Then the men began to realise that this determined looking little gnome who had come to them out of the air was Rud, the World Director, the Voice of the Common Man. The Soldiers' and Workers' Committee came to him as a matter of course.

Fraternisation, they discovered, had already gone far since the order to Cease Fire had released the pent up goodwill of the common soldiers. There had been a confused struggle on the Democratic side, which were mostly English in this sector, to maintain discipline and keep up the attitude of a victorious army. Protesting officers had ordered the men back to their trenches and flourished revolvers. But where the men persisted they had usually decided not to shoot. This was the state of affairs along most of the front. There were very few American or British officers murdered. There were more on the opposite side, especially among the Bavarians and Prussians. If Rud had ever had any doubts of the effective permeation of the Common-sense propaganda, his reception on either side of that deliquescent war front would have dispelled them.

No one seemed to question his authority and the droning of Bellacourt's planes overhead endorsed it. The bombing of the central group of buildings had left the entire army in a state of dismayed interrogation. It was, as Rud had foreseen, stunned. An army is a vast organisation trained to take orders; for an hour of agonising paralysis there was no one at all to give it orders, and then Rud and Olders appeared, with an escort of World Police, confident and assured, under the aegis of the planes. The decapitated host crystallised about its new head, fell naturally into postures of obedience. Here was order anyhow. And Orders. Life seemed to have become rational again. Officials came to Rud, saluted, reported their functions and were given directions.

Rud had the word passed. "Maintain discipline. All is as it should be. Reedly wanted to make himself Dictator of the World. He had prepared a coup d'etat and he has been killed. Every man to his quarters..."

The prostrate routines of life stood up again...

"Tomorrow," he said to Olders, "we shall have them playing football."

8

Rud had never been to a shoot, but he must have seen a picture of one in some illustrated paper, and the scene amidst the smoking ruins of the General Headquarters reminded him grotesquely of the game spread out at the end of the day's sport. The twilight was depending into night, and a miscellany of lights, electric lights of all sorts, oil lamps and the bursts of flame from the wreckage, added strange shadows to the orderly accumulation of bodies outside the ruins. Reedly had been found, Rogers, Grossberg and a score of others.

Rud looked at the scorched and tattered bodies before him.

"I hate to see them. But − It was necessary I should see them... I shall see them in my dreams."

He turned green.

"I don't like this sort of thing," he said to Olders. "I've always been oversensitive to horrors. Couldn't stand them. It's just because I hate cruelty and bullying − "

He turned aside and vomited.

A stranger appeared before him presently and saluted. "Radio, sir," he said. "Headquarters' control."

"Well?"

"What is to be done, sir, to those officers who tried to seize the radio station of the thirteenth army − they seem to have been acting under Marshal Reedly's orders?"

"Shot," said Rud.

"All of them?"

"Every one of them. Now. Once you start shooting... You have to go on. The fewer stories we have about this, the better."

Olders marvelled at him. He had been physically sick after he had seen the body of Reedly and now he had recovered as if nothing had happened. Now he was going to the radio to talk to Dreed at Sloten and launch his view of the facts, a highly clarified version, upon the world.

"Is that Dreed?" he said. "It is all over. You can tell the world there has been a Dangerous Reactionary Conspiracy. Got that? Nipped in the bud by the Master Director. It was an attempt to surrender to the Nazi Commander and set up a military dictatorship with Reedly as a sort of Napoleon. Make that clear. The Group has taken control and the situation is well in hand. There was a brief struggle in which World Marshal Reedly and most of the General Staff of both armies were killed, and also a certain number of officers of lower rank, orderlies and other attendants. Full lists of casualties, which amount in all only to about three hundred, will be published later. You need not give particulars of the fighting. The air force has behaved with unswerving loyalty to the Common World Cause and the armies have fraternised and acclaim the World Directorate. D-I-R-E-C – you have it?"

Rud had decided to call himself Master World Director, and nobody disputed the tittle.

Dawn found him still working. He had had repeated injections of strychnine and he seemed indefatigably active. Bodisham had come to him from Sloten and was enormously resourceful.

A little after sunrise Rud broke off to eat. He and Bodisham and Olders swallowed eggs beaten up in rum and milk by way of breakfast.

Thirp came from Stockholm about ten o'clock to report on Bellacourt's state of mind. Bellacourt was all right. "You have been working," said Thirp.

"And you?"

"I've been getting reports from all over the world. It's been like firing an unexpected pistol in a drawing-room. They're stunned. But they are going to accept it. Generally."

"There'll be trouble."

"The work's only beginning," said Thirp. "But they will take it – they will take it."

"Well, it's here we begin the real World Revolution," said Rud, rubbing his jaded face to refresh himself. "Here and now. All the rest has been just preparation, just getting a grip. Now, right away, we have to set to work stamping out this poison they call Federation. It is separatism trying to get back disguised as union. This is only the first outbreak. Reedlys are a prolific family. He's got brothers, cousins, all sorts of them. Every nation. Black Reedlys there are; red and yellow. All over the world there will be every sort of resistance to a World Common Law. All over the world fellows saying: 'Now is my chance.' Directly the fear of war is lifted, everywhere the old things will flame up again. Trust my prophetic soul. All the old-world people who were scared into silence for a time will be coming back, leaping, crawling, flying in a gale of hope – like sparks, like burning twigs and branches. It will be like beating out heath fires in sultry weather. But we've got to beat and stamp now until the world is one for ever...

"Because, you see," he said, with a sudden swoop from rhetoric to reality, "nothing else is possible for us now. This is the way we have to go, the only way. If we falter – "

"We are shot," said Thirp.

He reflected. "Reedly would have shot you, anyhow," he said.

"And you," said Rud.

He went on working without sleep until nightfall. Then Chiffan, who had arrived in the afternoon, affectionately masterful almost in the old fashion, carried him off to a chateau some miles behind the lines and put him to bed. He slept for twenty hours.

He was not told of the death of Steenhold for some days. He heard the bad news manfully at last.

"Rotten luck," said Rud. "Poor old Steenhold!" and never spoke of him again.

9

That had been close upon two crowded years ago, and for all the intervening time Rud, with Bodisham perpetually at his elbow and Thirp going to and fro on the earth, had been struggling to make that day's victory real and to secure the absolute dominance of the Common World State against a vast complex of antagonisms, insubordinations, inertias, apathies, unanticipated administrative difficulties, physical difficulties imperfectly foreseen and sheer exhausting intricacies.

For the bare idea of a Common World State there was now a vast majority of mankind, but directly it was defined as a positive reorganisation of human affairs, as the establishment of a common economic system. A common education, a common transport system, free movement about the world, involving the rupture of a thousand boundaries and a readjustment of the daily routines of the great majority of lives, resistances began and grew. Mankind was quite ready to accept peace but not to seek peace and ensure it.

A great and intricate warfare in the human imagination had followed the obliteration of Reedly, attempts to explain, attempts to compel, misrepresentations, denigrations, glorifications, false simplifications, tactical and strategic lying, detractions, stupefactions, hysterical reactions, blind insurgence.

Gradually things began to fall into place as the idea that the Common World State had come to stay prevailed over the belief that it was merely a provisional arrangement, pending a satisfactory restoration and adjustment of old claims. Everywhere a larger proportion of people, especially in the younger generation, set itself to learn new ways of living and abandoned the thought of returning to the old routines. What had been Utopianism a few years before became normal common-sense, and romantic traditionalism retreated into that world of imaginative reality from which Utopianism had come.

The Group, with vastly increased resources and now everywhere in control, resumed its pre-war propaganda of world unity on an enormously enlarged scale. It was undercutting rival conceptions of life by withdrawing endowments and subsidies, taking over schools, taking possession of religious buildings in the name of art and history. It had deprived reactionary newspaper propaganda of the incentive of gross profits by its rigorous censorship of newspaper advertisement and by its separation of newspaper finance from general speculative activities. The complex public controls of economic life that had come into existence under war conditions were retained and amplified to carry on the peace. Profit-seeking production and distribution had already been squeezed into a mere corner of

367

life; the main staple industries and housing and transport were already in the hands of the munition controls of the victors, and this time there was no storm of financial racketeering. Without a break the world war passed into world adjustment. This time there was no Peace Conference and no Peace Treaty.

The Group had found and unexpected amount of support from the world of scientific men. After a deliberate survey of contemporary fact the World Association for the Advancement of Science had produced a lucid and unemotional exposition of the attitude of the ever-multiplying class of scientific workers to the World Directorate. In less than two years after the coup d'etat that had made Rud World Director, the World Association produced its official declaration that the Common World State was also the Scientific State, and that the whole body of organised knowledge was definitely in support of the Directorate. In effect the scientific body was deliberately taking upon itself the role of the Church in the theory of Medieval Christendom, it was becoming the repository of knowledge, the directive power in education, and the criterion of all social organisation and readjustment. It was not so much proposing itself as tacitly becoming a new sort of Church, a progressive Church, a monistic congregationalism with ministers indeed, but without priest or pope.

Its declaration surveyed the biological situation with an unemotional explicitness. The human species had to adapt its life to the new conditions material inventions had created for it or perish. It embodied and applied ideas that were already apprehended by such liberal intelligences as old Doctor Carstall while Rud was still a rebellious undergraduate. They were now the universal ideas of the scientific world. Without world unification the species would destroy itself by the enlarged powers that had come to it. This, said the men of science, is no theory, no political alternative; it is a statement of fact. Men had to pool their political, economic and educational lives. There was no other way for them but a series of degenerative phases leading very plainly to extinction. They could not revert now. They had to got on – up or down. They had gone too far with civilisation and in societies, to sink back into a merely "animal" life again. The hold of the primates on life had always been a precarious one. Except where they were under human protection all the other great apes were extinct. Now plainly man had to go on to a larger life, a planetary existence, or perish in his turn. The survival of a degenerate man, a sort of "poor white" in the kingdom of nature, was for many reasons unthinkable. These many reasons were given succinctly in the declaration. One that struck Rud with a sense of novelty was that the rats could do that sort of thing so much better.

Thus the men of science. That declaration had come to hand a few days ago, and Rud had read it with a certain feeling of self-applause. He had been doing what he had done in the name of the Common Man, but apparently he had been doing the right thing all the time. If he found anything to object to in this declaration it was that there was a certain failure in it to recognise his own guiding role in the release of the Scientific State.

There was an impressive array of signatures. He ran his eye down the list. Several were the names of men he knew to be in administrative positions. Then he saw "Richard Carstall."

He stopped short at that.

"Richard Carstall," he whispered. "Richard? Dick? Dick Carstall. That's the man! And I went to school with him at

Hooplady House! And afterwards he was doing research at Camford. They gave him a fellowship the year before I came down. Old Carstall's son. Old Carstall the atheist, who made a job for Alf and Alf thought it was an answer to prayer!"

Afterwards he recalled that. He thought of Carstall in the night. He saw him tall and self-assured, telling him just what was "done" and just what one didn't do. Now as Rud contemplated the vast view from his balcony, that sustaining declaration came into his head again.

"They might have said all that two years ago," he remarked to the mountains and the sky. "But these scientific people always like to be quite sure of things before they do anything. I've been doing the heavy work while you've been theorising – and don't you forget that, Doctor, Professor, my good Lord Carstall. It's all natural forces and inevitable and all that – so you say *now*. But your theories are excellent, and I don't see why they shouldn't be made the basis of our new political education...

"I bear you no malice about it. None."

He went down the steps to the balcony on which he would have his breakfast.

10

The house he occupied had been built not so much to his designs as to his suggestions. For after the nature of his type, he had strong architectural impulses. It was built into a cliff that jutted out upon a wide bend of the River Durance.

All the world was busy then rebuilding or building anew or irrigating or planting or restoring soil. For centuries men had developed the art of resurfacing their cities and roads, but now they were blending and manufacturing soils as they needed them and distributing them where they could be cultivated most conveniently and agreeably. None too soon had world afforestation been taken in hand. The old competitive order of little nations and private finance had already stripped the world of half its forests and a third of its soil and exterminated seals, whales and a thousand once abundant resources. But now with the establishment of a real Common Ownership, a tremendous recuperation had begun. It was already in hand by that time.

But it had not seemed unreasonable to Rud, or indeed to anyone in the Group, that a large number of artists, architects, experts and skilled workers of all sorts should be diverted from the general reconditioning of the world to the special task of making a great cluster of residences and halls, laboratories, work-rooms and offices for the occupation of the chief members of the Group, upon a site that Rud had chosen. It had its aerodrome; it had great roads leading to it; it was in immediate nervous contact with all the world. It was a lovely piece of country he had hit upon, and this towering assemblage of structural loveliness challenged every palace and splendour of the past. Rud's own quarters had taken precedence of the rest and had been completed for his occupation with an incredible swiftness. It was, so to speak, a first intimation of all that lay before the new world.

It was Rud's own fancy that he should sleep in a bed upon a dais in a great arched loggia, into which his dressing rooms and so forth opened from behind, and from which he could descend to the open-air life of his grand balcony. His early upbringing in stuffy little rooms had given him a sort of architectural claustrophobia.

A considerable staff of secretaries, assistants, messengers and domestic workers had already been assembled about these first completed portions of the new World Centre. Bodisham was accommodated and Thirp was coming soon. The place undoubtedly had a magnificence surpassing that of any of the kingly and presidential residences and places in which he might have taken up his quarters. But it was free from old world associations and suggestions of inequality and pretension. There was no regal state about all this, there was no pose of aristocracy, no court. There was an insistence upon simplicity in its splendour. There were no bows nor salaams nor prostrations, and nothing in the nature of ceremonial.

For Rud after all was no exploiter, no tyrant; no sweater of his fellow creatures. He was very clear in his mind about that – clearer than many other people. He was the Director of an equalitarian world, a natural leader. He was just the Common Man – triumphant at last and enthroned.

Book Four
Zenith Transit

CHAPTER ONE

World Trustee

In a few short years the multitudinous common man throughout the earth had to make what he could of a stupendous fact, of which he had no previous warning, namely Rud, the World Trustee. And Rud being himself, as indeed he always alleged, no more than a common man, had also, with scarcely more preparation, to make what he could of himself. The mystical personification of himself as the universal common man was the most congenial interpretation that had occurred to him, and for a time he clung to it.

He would like to have said to mankind that he was just themselves in a concentrated form, and that what seemed good to him was necessarily good for them all, yet more and more did Thirp make it clear to him that the pervading infantilism of his fellow creatures demanded no such mystical and incomprehensible identification with him but objective leadership and paternalism. They refused to live *in* him, they kept themselves to themselves, but they were quite ready to live under him. So with a rapidly diminishing reluctance Rud allowed a sympathetic yet heroic version of himself to be built up in the public mind. And as this objective version was established throughout the world, it brought conviction to himself. Except in rare moments of private exaltation, he ceased to be that universal man of his profounder speculations and instead he became merely the greatest and most greatly advertised of men.

At first Norvel was manifestly much less convinced than Thirp of the necessity of presenting Rud to the world as the Hero of the Revolution. Norvel disliked Thirp and suspected his motives. But gradually as he studied the strange novel thing upon which he himself had to work, this newborn world-mind in the cradle of its education, his distrust of Thirp relaxed. There was understanding in Thirp's idea, whatever desire sustained it. Immature humanity has indeed, Norvel was forced to admit, an insatiable craving for exaggerated personalities, for vast effigies publicised about a core of fact. Humanity still insists upon them; it has always had its gods, as it has had its saints when its gods became metaphysical, it craves for powers and princes, for celebrities, champions, stars. It would take more than two eventful decades to alter that. Norvel, always reasonable, allowed himself to be persuaded by Thirp that unless Rud could be magnified, projected on the screen of the heavens, made dominant in the world imagination, it was inevitable that this urge to deify, round and about the world, would create for itself local dissentient and disintegrating figures, Robin Hoods and William Tells perhaps, Wallaces and Bruces, Gandhis and Garibaldis, to the great injury and confusion of the nascent common unification of mankind. Better let Thirp have his way...

Norvel, like so many of the Group and their associates, was growing rapidly to the scale of his occasions. He was getting a firmer and more comprehensive grasp upon his particular aspect of the world problem, and he was gathering round him a school of colleagues who shared ideas and purposes with him. It was a parallel process to Bellacourt's consolidation of the world services of transport and distribution, to Irwell's successful invention of a monetary and financial network practically free from speculative corruption, and to the scientific reorganisation of production by Roots and Holbank, who were now, among other innovations, manufacturing soil from crude rock and resettling agricultural workers at the rate of a hundred square miles a week.

Norvel had observed the decadence of the newspaper, in the days before the War of Ideologies, until it had become a mere daily entertainment and bazaar display, he had developed and dominated the worldwide distribution of cheap books, and he had acquired a very extensive mass of experience with all the new multiplying appliance for mental stimulation and exchange by cinema, radio, microphotography and the like. He had organised an effective world survey of schools and colleges, and he was now in a position to remodel, multiply and expand them as he chose and so far as the available material would let him. That was a tremendous task. The Revolution had indeed crippled the power of business interests and the old religions to hinder the liberation of the human mind, but it had done little to equip the minds it had emancipated. For the purposes of a world community, he found the world even in its most progressive regions, *thinly* educated, thinly to a dismaying degree. Quite as much as Roots and Holbank, who had realised the limits set to vegetable growth by soil insufficiency, he found he had to begin the new crop of humanity from the ground upward.

Education still for a large majority of human beings meant little more than teaching them in a primitive fashion to read and count a little. It was only in the most advanced communities that the need of continuous education throughout the whole life was recognised. For the multitude, such world pictures as they had, had been supplied in a haphazard fashion by the talk of the people about them, by the unscrupulous statements of the advertisement newspapers, concerned chiefly with the sale of worthless drugs, adulterated foodstuffs and plausible commodities, by political propagandists and the appeals of religious organisations. A few hundred so-called universities, of unequal merit, a flimsy network of impecunious scientific societies, a loosely organised trade of book publishing and distribution, were all that there was to guide the general mental operations of the entire world community. The common man at large had reminded mainly ignorant even of what was known, and had floundered through life in a muddle of prejudices, misconceptions and downright delusions. That was the educational level of the middle twentieth century, and upon this insufficient and decaying detritus of the petty cultures of the past it fell to the new educational administration to translate Bodisham's hopeful network of circles and liaisons into reality, and build the stout mental organisation needed by the new world.

Norvel found himself involved in a gigantic extension of the old structures of thought, research and instruction, in the evocation and training of vast armies of teachers, in the application of film and aerial to school use and the establishment throughout the world of millions of those community centres that manifestly had to replace the schools and home instruction of the past. He had assembled a magnificent group of associates and an ever-increasing multitude of mentally quickened helpers; he was sustained by an increasing realisation that most human beings want to learn and are ready to meet capable teaching half-way; but for all that it had become plainer and plainer to him that to establish even the broad framework for the mental reconditioning of mankind would be a task that would demand the sustained devotion of hundreds of thousands of workers through some scores of years.

And in the interim, what was to be done for the passing generations? For the present and for the rest of his lifetime, it was plain to him that he would have to endure the spectacle of vast masses of the population, white, yellow, brown and black, undereducated through no fault of their own, and for sheer lack of equipment, staffing and organisation, still largely uneducatable. With a job too big for him before him, it was manifest he had to economise all his resources. He had to concentrate first upon the bare scaffold of the new intellectual order and work for progressive increments in enlightenment, and beyond that the multitude would have to be left to much the same methods of information and suggestion as had served before the Revolution.

"We may stop some of the quack medicines at the source," he said, "but until we have put doctors, teachers and then more and more of the public through the mill of the real education, they will still prefer to be given quackery. We have got our Revolution, but we still have to establish it and make it real. Revolution or no Revolution, we have for the present to let the public from China to Peru have what the public wants. Putting more and more of our own proper stuff into the mixture as time goes on…"

"Precisely," said Thirp.

"So since a Revolution seems to be impossible without an incarnation," said Norvel, turning to Rud, "we have to hand you over to a press agent and the Revolution has to organise a publicity department for you. You have to be Trustee for Humanity, no less – until Humanity comes of age."

Rud tried to suppress a faint gleam of excitement. "So be it," he said.

"You have never, I suppose, read Frazer's *Golden Bough?*"

"Never had time," said Rud.

"About those sacrificial kings," said Novel. "You'd be interested."

2

At the bottom of Rud's nature, covered over and suppressed there had always been an acute sense of his physical inferiority. He had even an exaggerated sense of his own ugliness and his bodily feebleness. He had a passionate impulse to exercise power, but his primary method of exercising power was to destroy, and he consented only to the vast constructiveness his movement was developing, because that alone guaranteed the complete disappearance of the institutions, restraints and compulsions he hated. It was at first with a definitely reluctant scepticism that he found Thirp, with Norvel's connivance, building up a detailed legend of a pseudo-personality for him. Modesty with him at any rate was fear of failure. Maybe that is always the essense of modesty. So that when at length he realised that Thirp's propaganda might indeed attain its ends, his confidence in his essential self blossomed.

It would need vast volumes after the manner of Tom Harrisson's Mass Observers to convey the hundreds of millions of individual reactions to the intricate advertisement process by which the vaguely apprehended World Director of the Common-sense Revolution became a concrete living personality in the human imagination. It followed upon the best precedents. He was "displayed" by word and picture, put upon postage stamps and on public buildings, written up, systematically alluded to; a thousand anecdotes were invented about him. Skilful photographers arranged lighting about him and contrived novel angles of approach, and for every picture of him that went into circulation, scores were destroyed. His scowl upon his ample brow became an expression of concentration upon human destiny; his eyes caught an abstracted benevolence. He looked less and less into his mirror and more and more at those approved photographs. He became more and more interested in the press cuttings expounding himself, that his secretaries selected.

He talked upon the air at chosen intervals, and millions of simple homes to which the Revolution had brought security listened to his indignation at the disorders of the past and to his promises for the future. Never more would a bomb descend upon a house nor a son be taken off to war. He made a practice of explaining in simple language the developing merits of the new order, using the modest yet regal "we" and unobtrusively annexing all the credit for the bold constructive work of his multiplying associates. These men and women were building now like bees, but he figured as the beekeeper. To the simple mind everywhere in the world, he became the Promethean figure that brought the light and heat of the Power Administration into the social circle; he also was production and his name was Plenty; he was distribution and his name was Service; he it was who now fed the world variously, employed it interestingly, instructed it, released it for holidays and travel about the world. He had slain soldiering, slain it in the person of Reedly. He had guided the world through the terrific opening crises of the Age of Adaptation to their present universal hope and freedom. Now one was free; now one could learn and live.

Norvel in his private thoughts decided that was as good a working embodiment of the scientific ordering of the world as mankind could have for the time being, and as good a use as any for Rud. Personal Leadership the multitude would still insist upon until his schools made a new generation. Until the human crowd could respect itself it might just as well concentrate its respect upon Rud. Meanwhile a new world-brain organisation would grow and spread, the proportion of critical and enlightened intelligence would increase in geometrical progression, irony would creep into loyal gestures. In due time Rud would die in glory, revered as the father of a new civilisation, the last and greatest of the culture gods; and the human mind would be ready to adjust itself to the realities of the great transition, and ultimately get him back into his due place in the universe.

While common men were still amenable to the idea of power, still anxious to say "Yes, sir" to someone they felt would be protective, the only ways of abstracting the commanding quality from ownership, money, class, rank and elected authority, was by concentrating it for them in this way upon a single individual – who would at any rate be mortal. Norvel assumed that gradually they would acquire the habit of doing their jobs without any other inducement than the intrinsic interest of the job. So, under Rud, acquiescing in Rud and sustaining Rud, he set himself to his essential work. Irwell, Bellacourt, Roots, Darwin and all the able new chiefs who were coming into the comprehensive network of Bodisham's scientific replanning of human life on its new scale, worked in much the same spirit, content that Rud had cleared the way for them, and Thirp was allowed to fence off a special department for the organisation, according to the best precedents, of Rud's publicity, his establishment in the human imagination as the sole, unchallengeable Trustee of power.

Thirp did not do this work himself, but he made all the arrangements for its being done. His essential quality was a feline curiosity in the less obvious motives of his fellow creatures. It was this that had first attracted him to criminology and prison reform. He was interested in human errors and misconceptions, his life as a watcher and shepherd of rebellious sprits, was primarily one of vicarious anti-social activities. He had Rud's fear and hatred of stark power, but in a subtler, more penetrating form. He had worked with energy, he had become a party man, because he realised the trend of the old order towards a mosaic of military and spasmodically moral tyrannies, but he had no desire whatever to establish a new order with possibly even austerer disciplines of its own.

He was tied up now to the Revolution, he did not dare turn against it, but in the place of the new strenuousness of Norvel and Bodisham, all his instincts would have preferred a gently rotten society in which the essential queerness of humanity could have been stimulated and released in the fullest abundance. He did not believe in anything that looked simple. He had a fear of simple things. To his intelligence they were rigid things without escapes. He had a mind for orchids, queerly shaped fungi, peculiar insects, drugs, wicked little carvings in jade and ivory, occult phenomena and Rosicrucian mysteries. He was the strangest, most alien of all the adherents of the last Revolutionary Group.

But Rud had a use for him. He felt in him a kindred fear of restraint, to which the others were oblivious. He perceived Thirp's animal alertness to any antagonistic movement in the world about them. It was, he remembered, Thirp's sharpness and his own natural distrust which had saved him and the Revolution from Reedly. The others in the Group would have been caught. They could take care of everything but themselves. Bodisham would have been killed like Archimedes over his diagrams.

The old world had left over a very considerable class of advertisers, personal journalists, agents, impresarios and the like, many of whom were odd characters and so very attractive to Thirp, and with the return of confidence now that the revolutionary blood bath and blasting operations were over, gossip, organised entertainment, social life and a disingenuous patina upon behaviour, were reappearing in the world. Caricature looked up, and little non-political local talk papers, living on their merits, broke out in every language. The leading figures of the pre-Revolutionary world, from kings to cinema stars, had had their publicity cultivated and protected by experts of outstanding brilliance, many of whom were still alive and available for Thirp. Dimly apprehended behind the arras of history is Quinlan, Rud's publicity manager, building up his official picture and arranging interesting and characteristic events for him. He made all Rud's publicity comings and goings important; he made his birthday a great public event from pole to pole.

All over the earth on that auspicious day flags were flying. Rud, in one of his rhetorical moments, had designed a world flag. He had seen a man handling a pile of cases for some public use. On each was a little national flag of the country of origin, and this man had a piece of white chalk in his hand and just crossed off the flag on each packet. Some national clash had to be considered. "Of course!" said Rud. "Cross off all the flags." He made the world flag a white saltire on azure. And for all regional or local purposes he had a white saltire, imposed upon the national or provincial colours. All over the world now the birthday bunting fluttered, bearing over every racial or cultural symbol that white clamp of peace.

A practice of personal relationship was fostered by Quinlan. It was physically impossible for Rud to meet the entire human brotherhood and shake hands with it, nevertheless people were emboldened to write and even telephone to him. His fan mail attained astronomical dimensions. To meet that Quinlan was creating a huge staff of Director's Correspondents, many of whom could produce a fair imitation of Rud's handwriting or speak almost with his voice. They were most of them polyglots, and there were very few languages in which Rud's composite personality could not reply. So that Rud, at one and the same moment, could take an interest in a little girl's white rabbits in Pekin, parley with a young Norwegian who was disappointed in his preliminary trials for the air service because of a poisoned hand, and promise an enquiry into the troubles of an old lady tied in knots by arthritis who didn't like her doctor in Perth.

"Who wants Providence when they have me?" said Rud, and "Isn't it amazing that neither the Vatican nor British Royalty ever thought of this!"

Thirp collected half a dozen convicted but now reformed forgers who could do the most brilliant variations of Rud's signatures.

Operations of this sort stimulated the worldwide desire for closer contacts and nearer relationships still further. Strange imaginations appeared.

"Seventeen women today," said Quinlan, "want to bear him a child. That is mild. It was thirty-seven last Saturday."

"The old morality never sat very well on the ladies," said Thirp. "No... But they endured it as women will... All races, I suppose?"

"Practically," said Quinlan, "but mainly Americans and Europeans."

"You haven't let Him know?"

"Not a word."

"Good," said Thirp, with his head on one side, putting his long hands together as if in prayer. "In a way, it's an attractive idea. I don't know...if anything of the sort did occur... Something might be done. But it would have to be kept a profound secret. Just a trifle *too* modern... I suppose that sort of thing will come. If there are Dictators a hundred years hence it will seem quite sensible to make them the Fathers of the People. I'm surprised they didn't try that in Russia."

Quinlan consulted the eugenists. He thought, too, that something might be done about it, and that something of the sort might come, but it was clear that for the present the business bristled with difficulties. He did not put the matter before Rud until his own ideas about Rud's possible reactions were more definite.

3

After all Rud ate an egg that morning. That beautiful house of his was a reassuring setting. The mountains were benevolent. And it was, he suddenly remembered, his birthday.

The mists of his nightmare evaporated in the warm sunshine of the great terrace. He forgot that sense of a vindictive pursuit that marred so much of his nocturnal existence. The sense of being the overworked servant of mankind passed into a glow of righteous self-applause. "I am forty-four," he thought, standing at the parapet and surveying his particular lovely piece of world. And when I was twenty I was messing about Camford in a dog's-eared mortar-board and a patched gown and I hadn't the dimmest idea of what was to become of me! At least – yes; I *had* even then, a dim idea...

"There was all the world to take and I took it. Luck? I suppose so. Vision? Inspiration? My twenty-first birthday: where was I? I remember. Took Chiffan on the river. Twenty-second? Poor old Steenhold made what he called a 'porty' for it. Still at Camford that was. Twenty-two years ago...

"I took some risks. Nobody knows how I funked Bohun. Lord! How I dreaded him! It was a close thing, too, with Reedly. I timed that well. I knew my man. I chose my moment. H'm. and now I have to put this silly little old world in order for good and all – and make sure the old rottenness doesn't creep back – before I go. Giant's Task. Who would have thought it – twenty years ago? Great Accomplishment. And still gigantic things to do. Four and forty – I wonder how long I shall last.

"It's all thrust into my hands now, almost in spite of myself. I'm still not sure. Never sure. Unless I see to things myself. If I could only trust those others to carry out their jobs without me. Bodisham – Bodisham is good – no doubt he is good – but he has to be urged. Circumspection. He sees difficulties. Over-elaborates. He is an old spider with those round shoulders of his and those glasses – How round his shoulders are getting! but all his plans and diagrams would change back to spiders' webs again if I did not insist upon their being translated into steel and living substance. I am his life giver – his reality giver. Says I am rough-handed – impatient. But things have to be done. He's practically a man of science – and God knows that men of science are Devils for not hurrying. I found him dreaming. I made him what he is, my constructive truffle-hound. Bellacourt, too, is good – in his way. Most people would have been afraid of him – that fool Reedly was – but I knew better. I wish they were all like Bellacourt. Sticks to his job. I've done some good picking in my time. Roots was my find, and I certainly saw the quality of Holbank as soon as anyone. Irwell – in a sense he has always been in the movement, but – anyhow – I never got rid of him. Norvel? – just a little loose-minded, loose but abundant. And conceited. Sometimes irritatingly conceited. No good telling him things. At the most he pretends to listen. He's be speeded up too much. Never relax, but never hurry. One could imagine he expected to live five hundred years. Do we want all these school of his? Don't people for all practical purposes know enough already? And he goes behind me and doesn't do the things I say – unless I say them very definitely. He's all for letting – what is it? – individual initiative run loose. But I suppose he has all this academic, scholastic business at his fingers' ends. There is nobody else like him. It would be amusing to go back to Camford one day and see what he has done down there. He does a lot, but he hasn't Thirp's flair for what is happening. Things grow up behind his back.

"If I'd the educational machine in my own hands I'd have nipped this new Catholic movement in the bud... I may have to see to that yet...

"Olders? Olders is coming on. The typical Civil Servant, able to carry out anything and start nothing. A sense of duty to anyone who will give him orders. The world would fall to pieces if there weren't such men.

"Dreed, of course, might easily be brighter than he is...

"And Chiffan is Chifffan – good old Happy Thoughts. With a trick of saying things just before I do, or anyone else, damn him...

"I couldn't do without Thirp. At first I didn't like him because of his queer voice and his flat hair and his face like an earnest spinster – and those hands. Like a praying Mantis. But how penetratingly he works! He looks under things and through things – that cynical touch – a cruel sense of reality. And he tells me things. He finds out things I don't know. The others are beginning to keep things from me. Fear my critical glance. After all, where would the world be now, where should we all be now, if Thirp hadn't known about those postcards of Reedly's? He's sharp as a terrier in spite of that drawling eunuch's voice...

"Thirp is my extra eye...

"I suppose altogether it's as good as team as I could have assembled. That's where my Revolution beats its precursors. I am building up a World Civil Service. I am making my Code. *My* Revolution has come to stay. *My* Revolution!

"All the same, essentially, the world's still on my shoulders. On my shoulders. Prometheus-Atlas. I didn't ask for it..."

So, if not quite so definitely as we have worded it here, thought Rud on his four-and-fortieth birthday.

He thrust the little breakfast table away from him.

He touched a button and a young man appeared.

He and Rud were living now in an equalitraian world. Nevertheless there was a certain deference in his manner, for as yet equalisation was incomplete.

"I'll go into conference," said Rud. "Will you tell the Group I am coming to join them? I have to keep in touch."

4

The conference received him without undue excitement. Only Bodisham, Norvel, Dreed, Roots and Chiffan were present. He sat down in the place reserved for him at the head of the table, and regardless of what point they might be discussing at the moment said: "Well, tell me all about it…"

For some time they had been drawing up a document which Bodisham had originally suggested and which Rud had embarked upon with much enthusiasm. His conception of it had been rather different from Bodisham's; but in the long run Bodisham's tenacious mind became dominant in its production.

The title at any rate was Rud's. It was to be called The Fundamental Law, and its general purpose was to present all the structural ideas of the new world society in such a form that they could be used in schools and colleges everywhere and made the criterion, the standard pattern, for administrative and subsidiary legislative action. But Bodisham had conceived something of the systematic detail of the Code Napoleon. It acquired the bulk of a handbook, the tone of a textbook. It cited authorities; it not only made statements but proved them. Chiffan made some bright interpolations, but Bodisham's tendency towards a serious practicality prevailed over him. The rest of the Group contributed little to this "Bible of the New World". (One of

Rud's rejected phrases.) Thirp, Bellacourt, Holbank, Darwin, and the indefinite fringe of new and occasional members who came and went to the administrative centre at the instance of Bodisham and Rud, rarely put in an appearance at these deliberations.

Rud was greatly excited by the composition of the exordium. He drafted that, rewrote it again after a long and fruitful discussion with Bodisham, argued a number of minor points, lost his temper, recovered his balance, rephrased the final version. But after the exordium his interest waned. He was becoming more and more impatient with detail; it irritated him; it irritated him to realise how much more ably almost any practical question could be handled by his colleagues; once or twice, in order not to contradict himself, he had walked out upon some unexpected issue on which he had given way to impulse and taken the wrong line. No one ever reminded him of these occasions, but they went on with the planning under Bodisham's direction as though he had not intervened. He began to come late, and on one or two occasions he had absented himself altogether.

The exordium is by itself a fairly comprehensive document. It recites ably and clearly all the primary ideas that had grown out of the crude popular Leftism from which he and Chiffan had started. But they had been tried out now, scrutinised, polished. It incorporated Bodisham's analysis of the meaning of power, and the essence of Rud's mysticism.

"The whole planet earth," it commences, "is inalienable heritage and possession of the Common Man. The World Revolution bases its methods of rule, law, production, distribution, its education and its finance, upon that conception of a common ownership." Then with a sweeping thoroughness it disposes of the pretensions of sovereign states, of non-functional proprietorship, of sex, race, caste or class, of usurers or any type of creditors or successful gamblers, to qualify that principle of the indivisible sovereignty of the whole race. Food, shelter, freedom, the healthiest possible life and universally accessible knowledge constituted the birthright of every mentally and physically sound child born into the world.

In accordance with this initial statement the exordium goes on to define the main branches of human interest and activity as they have henceforth to be administered. All Rud's fundamental maxims and all that he had picked up and assimilated from the more penetrating dicta of Chiffan and the more scientific and comprehensive approach of Bodisham are woven into this general statement. And it repudiates the idea that it has any unnatural and arbitrary quality. It insists on the logical necessity of the Revolution. Now and again an unmistakable biblical echo, due to the early education of Chiffan, appears in the phrasing. "The Revolution," it says explicitly, "came not to destroy but fulfil."

"The whole earth belongs to everyone. That is not a doctrine, that is a fact – long overlooked. We restore what individuals and groups and gangs and nations have appropriated in the past. But restoration is not a reversal of human conditions. It is only a clarification. There is no real distinction between political, social and economic control, that is an error that has crept into social life as it has developed. They are inseparable in rational order. Individual wages, money, properly shrink in importance as competent directorates are established. That is no Communist dogma; it is common-sense..."

And further, the exordium of the Fundamental Law explains: "The essence of the Revolution is to abolish the attainment of unqualified power of man over man either by vote-getting, money-pressure or crude terror. The Revolution repudiates profit or terror altogether as methods of human intercourse. It turns the attention of men and women back from a frantic and futile struggle for the means of power, a struggle against our primary social instincts, to an innate urgency to make and to a beneficial competition for pre-eminence in social service. It recalls man to clean and creative life from the entanglements and perversion of secondary issues into which he has fallen. It replaces property and official authority by the compelling prestige of sound achievement. Eminent service remains the only source of influence left in the world..."

That last idea is pure Bodisham, but the voice is the voice of Rud.

5

When Rud read over his final version of the introduction to the Group, they endorsed it very cordially. "You could not have put our common faith better," said Chiffan. The others murmured approval in the same key.

A wave of conscious nobility swept through Rud. "This – to be blunt about it – is the time when we might usurp, and I won't," he said, in a mood of real magnificence, and proceeded at once to a completeness of usurpation that dwarfed all precedent.

"It is clear," he said, "that the effective reorganisation of the machinery of administration is an immensely intricate job, and that any attempt to establish a democratic control by these shattered, inexperienced and mentally confused populations must wait upon the creation and working of Norvel's educational machinery. They would not know at present what was needed nor what to ask for. A crude return to electoral politics would give every mischievous rascal in the world an opportunity, and it would revitalise all the national, religious, racial organisations that are down and out indeed but still in a sort of attenuated existence. I think we are right in assuming a general acquiescence. Here we are, and there is no effective revolt against us. What I propose we do is to go right ahead, establish our world system first and then as an educated generation comes along – "

"When?" asked Norvel.

"In two or three decades it will be becoming effective."

"I hope," said Norvel, and continued to regard Rud thoughtfully.

"And until then we do things by decree. We will assume we have been elected and we will decree. Afterwards we will ask them what they think of it. The game for power is over – yes – and we have won. We cannot risk having everything upset by a new squabble for power. We'll have no power politics and no politicians again, until the new world is in working order, and then we will ask whether the world wants them back. We will establish everything firmly on the basis of this Fundamental Law, and face them with actuality. How else can we do it? Finally, I assume we will establish some sort of conference for the endorsement of the world order and, if necessary, for its revision – we shall crown the work with a representative legislature – a more or less representative legislature, representative I suppose by callings and services rather than localities. For we have de-localised the world. There are still local populations, but there is no more local community. The abolition of distance means the end of political geography. Isn't that the way, Bodisham?"

"I agree entirely," said Bodisham, recognising phrase after phrase as his own, and nodding quietly as they passed him, while the others acquiesced. "That is our way," said Bodisham.

"Then and then only," said Rud, "my task will be completed and I shall give way to – whatever we find is the best way of co-ordinating our various World Administrations, and I will resign and end my days simply as the common man I am."

There was a pause. Rud sat at the end of the table looking modest but firm.

"You couldn't say fairer," said Chiffan.

6

One of the minor difficulties of these conferences to produce the Fundamental Law was the instruction of a number of suggestions for minor changes in the natural texture of life, in numeration, time reckoning, symbols, language and the like. Some of them were manifestly overdue reforms, and most of these were carried through automatically by the ministries concerned. Revolutions are always hurried and hustled processes; they never make novel reconstructions except by accident; but on the other hand if there is any cut-and-dried rationalisation waiting to be accepted, they carry it through almost automatically.

The reform of the calendar is a case in point. A variety of rearrangements had been exhaustively discussed, and a rough outline of what was needed had been established. Norvel was very uncompromising in that matter. He accepted the World Calendar Association scheme which has given us our twelve months of thirty days and the necessary intercalary one, but he would have no further changes. He wouldn't have the months renamed or the count of the years broken. He wouldn't hear of a ten-day week. He overrode Thirp on these points.

Thirp had hinted at a renaming of the days – or at least of three extra days – and even thrown out the suggestion of the Rud-day. Possibly even a Lenin-day and a Darwin-day.

Chiffan had glanced at Rud when this suggestion was made.

"Nonsense," said Norvel hastily, before Rud had time to express an opinion. "We *must* keep on the old calendar days, weeks and months, just as much as we can. They have character. No substitute for the Semitic week," he said, "has ever yet been thought out. Maybe it doesn't suit every sort of industry, but working spells and rest intervals ought to vary with the nature of the job. Ten days would be just as much a misfit as seven. We're not going to do the sun and the moon and Thor and Freyja and all the rest of 'em out of their days of the week, and personally I'd hate to call the ninth and tenth months anything but September and October. These are interesting fossils of the mind, and they do no harm that I can see. They remind us of our intellectual origins. You'll want to shut our earholes next because they come from primitive gill-slits. I'm all for continuity in unimportant things. So don't let's start a new era.

"I don't know how it seems to you," Norvel went on, before anyone else could cut in, "but that Year One of the Republic business and all that, has always struck me as more than a little vulgar. It's like calling Petersburg Leningrad. Let the Christians keep the tale of years and Greenwich the first meridian. After all, nothing really happened in AD one. Even our Dominus wasn't until AD four."

"No," said Rud, with an eye on Thirp. "No. Of course he wasn't. We have to recognise that arbitrary unmeaning points like the Greenwich meridian and AD one, *are* the best for reckoning. We don't want to prejudice history. The old world tried to put its propaganda in everything, from eras to postage stamps. The new world – I agree with Norvel and Chiffan – can't do that."

"I never said anything," said Chiffan.

"I read your thoughts, Chiffan," said Rud.

"It was a mere passing idea," said Thirp, taking his cue.

"And, after all," thought Chiffan, "he *is* on the money and the postage stamps."...

In the same spirit the Fundamental Law conference would have nothing to do with a duodecimal system of numbering. "Leave all that sort of thing alone," said Norvel. "Who knows how science will be dealing with sequences and dimensions in the next hundred years? Our sufficient business is world unity – with such material as we possess. Man counts by tens because he has ten fingers. That trouble began with our amphibious ancestors, I believe, somewhen in the Palaeozoic. It's too far to go back. It's too far to go back."

7

Nor would Rud listen to any projects for a World Language. There he not only followed Norvel and Bodisham, but his own natural indisposition to tamper with the rhetorical instrument he had mastered.

They were all three inclined towards a simplified and phonetically spelt English as the common speech of the world, because they were English-speakers and because the English speaking communities had been the backbone of the revolutionary

397

movement. But they realised the element of bias in this disposition. They knew that language was bound to change with all the other changes in progress, that it needed not merely new words but new idioms, that the vocabulary of every tongue that remained in use must inevitably be enormously enlarged and refined, and that the speech of the future, whatever its basis, would necessarily by syncretic and greatly polished by attrition. They favoured English so far as to institute phonetic spelling, make it compulsory to print books in this reformed orthography and optional to print them also in the classical alphabet, and establish basic English the official lingua franca. But they suppressed no other language teaching. When there was a non-English-speaking population the local language was the primary one. They felt that in this way a mutable English speech might be imposed upon the patchwork of Babel, much as the white saltire unified the world's flags. Useful and expressive novelties could be incorporated from any other language and made worldwide by the cinema, the radio and the ever-multiplying schools. English has always been the Autolycus of languages, taking its own where it found it. Against this leisurely advance towards a naturally developing, synthetic, world language, the Idoists, the Esperantists and their like raged in vain.

"It is remarkable how patriotism still lingers in the blood," said Dreed. "I like to think that the coming world language will be English."

"It will be almost as much English," said Norvel, "as Middle Saxon is the English in use today. Less like. It will have dropped a thousand ambiguous and deflated terms. It will have received from every language under the sun. It will probably have new pronouns and new prepositions. We can no more foresee that than we can foresee the fashions of five hundred years from now.

"All we can do is to prepare for a universal language that will go on changing for ever. We don't know everything. We aren't final. I wish we could make that statement a part of the Fundamental Law."

"We could work something about that into the exordium," said Rud. "I think we could make it sound rather fine."

8

On the morning of his forty-fourth birthday Rud sat down at the head of the table in the place reserved for him, and regardless of what the Group might be discussing at the moment, said: "Well, tell me all about it…"

They had come to the position of women in the new world.

"We were saying," said Chiffan, "that women have played a curiously small part in the Revolution."

"So far as I know," said Rud with conviction, "they haven't played any part at all. What are you working upon now here?"

"They constitute fifty-seven per cent of the species," said Chiffan.

"Well, the Fundamental Law provides that there shall be no discrimination of race, religion, class, sex?"

"Wait a moment," said Bodisham. "Sex?

"We provide," said Bodisham, "that there shall be no legal disqualification or handicap on account of sex, but that does not end the matter. First we have to consider that vast mass of human beings, which is already expanding proportionately again, Norvel's particular field, the young below the age of citizenship, and next and linked to that we have certain occasions between man and woman. How far does the law interfere?"

"As little as possible," said Chiffan.

"In every affair the law must interfere as little as possible. The Fundamental Law makes that clear."

Norvel spoke. "We have to consider first of all the supply of children in the world. Sooner or later we may have to forbid marriage – no, not marriage, but bearing and begetting – to certain definable types. Biological science isn't so sure yet – but it will get sure. That is as much a part of the World Health Service as the compulsory notification of infectious diseases and the establishment of cordons."

"It will be liable to abuses," said Dreed.

Bodisham raised his eyebrows by way of reply. Every law is liable to abuses.

"All that sort of thing is pretty straight sailing," said Chiffan. "There is no dispute about the principles involved. The real problem is just how far the modern world can regulate – embraces."

Rud scowled at him. "That," he said, "is part of the individual life. There is no need even to talk about it here."

"You think that apart from licensing parenthood and subsidising motherhood," said Roots, "the state should leave sex alone."

"*Embraces*," corrected Chiffan, heedless of Rud's objection. "Embraces! You can't ignore the social aspects of sex, you can leave the actual embraces alone, but you can't avoid the social recognition of the groupings that ensue."

"There have always been marital rights," said Dreed, unheeded. "but were they ever – enforced?"

"It affects our housing projects, for example," said Chiffan. "Whom do we embrace and where and when? Are we to build for monogamy, polygamy, polyandry, promiscuity?…"

"There is no such thing as promiscuity," said Norvel.

"Well – an obliging looseness, let us say. An amiable laxity. Is this new world ahead to be a world of tight little, right little homes, or a patriarchal kraal or a sprawl of lovers against a background of maternity homes and foundling hospitals? I admit every day and in every way, parentage becomes less involuntary. It seems to me that this also releases human affectionateness at a less austere level. Cupid with his bandage off and armed with a revolver. Still – "

"That would be a problem for the constructive ministries to meet, according to the varying local requirements," said Roots.

"It is remarkable," said Dreed, "that we should be sitting here discussing the future of all womankind on earth, without a single woman present. Ought we not – ?"

"We don't want any women here," said Rud. "They would take sides where we differed, but they would contribute nothing."

"They would demand complete control of the whole business," said Norvel. "with a certain air of reasonableness they would say it was their particular business."

"And they would do nothing whatever about it," said Rud. "We don't want women here. We don't want them."

"Not even to give evidence?" said Norvel.

"*What* an inquisition!" chuckled Chiffan, manifestly amused. "I can imagine – "

He stopped short at the sight of Rud's scowl.

"I suggest that the Fundamental Law deal with the young and with any eugenic aspects of the matter, and leave all the rest to the natural development of social life," said Rud.

"Nevertheless," Norvel persisted, "I think we ought to have some representative women here. We ought either to make a special committee of them to report and suggest, or bring them into consultation."

"What *are* representative women?" demanded Rud, with a gust of impatience. "What *makes* them?" And then, as if the whole question was too trivial for his attention, he pushed back his chair, rose slowly and departed.

Chiffan watched him go.

"And now?" began Norvel...

"Being a woman so far has been the major profession of the species," said Roots. "In a few specialised forms it is grossly overpaid; in nine hundred and ninety-nine cases in the thousand it has been abominably underpaid. It is not so much a sweated industry as a bluffed and racketeered one. Being a wife is still the main profession of women in the world, and yet the financial and well-disciplinary conditions of two people, married or not, who are living together, amount generally to a fight for the upper hand. It is a fight very much out of the cognizance of the law. Most of the events occur without witnesses, both sides have an age-long tradition of lying abominably about the other, and at the same time standing up for each other, and interference between husband and wife is consequently very difficult.

"But it is only in the intimate life that interference is difficult. Economically the problem is much simpler. An increasing number of women are taking up professions now; at architecture, catering, various industries, normal teaching, secretarial work, hospital work, for example, they are practically as good as men or better, and there we need only carry out the principle of absolute equality. And it seems economically and socially convenient to make motherhood a paid social service. If that is done and if the allowances go to the mother, with a reasonable right of the father and the local authority to intervene in cases of cruelty or negligence, we shall have put womankind for the first time in history on a fair and equal footing with men, so far as economic freedom goes. Nothing need prevent a woman being a man's salaried housekeeper or his nurse or what-not with or without marriage. If she enters into a form of marriage involving a contract, that contract will be subject to the laws we shall certainly impose for the limitation, periodic revision and annulment of unreasonable and undesirable clauses in all contracts. There the Fundamental Law stops short. Sexual amour-propre, jealousy, what are called marital rights and so forth are no concern of the state's. If they lead to crimes the law deals with the crime. All that seems very simple."

"The World State, I take it," said Bodisham, "will protect individual freedom, from conception to cremation. It will protect individual freedom from menace and monopolisation. It will protect the young from any premature decisions they will be unable to reverse. It may also presently set about protecting the young from diseased or defective parentage. As our knowledge of dysgenic processes advances. Beyond what is implied by that much protection, it will leave men and women absolutely free to conduct themselves as they choose. There lies the scope for a free literature, novels, dramas, poetry, spectacle, suggestion, inspiration, exaltation of every sort turning upon conduct and interpretation. There may be cults. We have to prepare for life in unprecedented profusion and variety… But the state has to stand aside from all that."

9

"It's curious," began Chiffan, and stopped short.

"Yes?" said Bodisham, who had a marked tolerance for Chiffan's excursions.

"I suppose," said Chiffan, "that with man just as much as with any other social animal, sex was the original binding force of the community, and I suppose our religion, our morality arose mainly out of sexual subordination and sexual tabus. So the anthropologists tell us. If perhaps I temper my Freud with Adler, still all the same I think the main strand of emotional life is sexual. Maybe fear, hunger and the power-craving are more elementary than sex, but sex is bound up with most of the power-craving…"

Norvel nodded his head.

"Well, here we are organising a world first to defeat, distribute and disperse the power-craving and so end war, and secondly to secure and distribute abundance to everyone. Good. We shall do it. What of sex? We are going to release something which hitherto has been kept under the severest restraint, which hitherto has been the chief force harnessed by morality, which has been in fact for most people the significance of morality, the sexual urge and the sexual imagination. That is, I have to point out, a complete change of function for the social organisation. Our Fundamental Law is just bundling the original social force out of the court room to do what it likes unchallenged…"

"What have you to suggest?" said Bodisham. "Are you suggesting a control?"

"I am suggesting nothing," said Chiffan. "I am reflecting."

Bodisham began to fiddle with his pencil. He had expected a project of some sort.

"Sex," Chiffan went on, "is something absolutely primary in this queer beast, Man. Perhaps I see things with a certain bias, but it appears to me that when the animal man is neither afraid, nor hungry, nor exhausted, then it is that the energies within him, the endocrines, the chemical conspirators that drive him, are turned in the direction of self-assertion through sex. Concentrated on that end. Security and abundance release sex. Wherever there *is* sex to be released. I think the intimate history of what one might call emancipated classes in the past – courts, aristocracies, plutocracies for example, points in that direction. Sex is released, exposed and elaborated. Life ceases to be serious. Gallantry and art break out. Sex lies in wait for every sort of success. It follows success about. That has always been so, and I think it is likely to be so always. No Revolution can change that."

"Yes, yes," said Bodisham. "But how does it affect the Fundamental Law?"

"I am considering the problem of surplus energy," said Chiffan, "as an explosive force. I am speculating about what is to happen when the Common Man begins to realise that the scramble for life is over for good and all. Our Fundamental Law is ensuring his permanent immunity from violent termination by explosives, machinery and insane hatreds and intolerance. But also it is creating a curious *gap* in living – unknown to the adult life of any other animal – leisure, active leisure, leisure with surplus energy... And now, says the animal, what am I do?...

"While we were all within a reasonable distance of being shot, life was eventful and we had no sense of any emptiness in things. A man with someone in hot pursuit of him was never really bored. But now, now it is going to be different."

Norvel, with his hands relaxed on the table, considered Chiffan. Bodisham began to draw little diagrams on his blotting-pad as he listened. Dreed seemed lost in thoughts of his own, and Roots, who had to fly back to the Sahara irrigation works before night, turned to stare out of the great window at the afternoon sky.

"When the pursuit relaxes," Chiffan went on, "then our problem changes. Two things, I imagine, may happen to a hunted man when the hunt is over. He may doubt if it *is* over. He may think that the hunter is still about, but hiding and creeping – and he won't know what to do about that. And that will make him uneasy. And also the mere fact of having made his escape and won his flight will also leave him rather at loose ends."

"You mean man in general?" said Norvel.

"Man in particular," said Chiffan. "Perhaps I am talking of Everyman when in fact I am really thinking of the Common Man who has come through the Revolution. He is going to feel 'something is still coming for me and I am doing nothing about it, something is escaping me and I am doing nothing about that either.' That may led to complicated trouble. The World Peace we have won was well worth living for and dying for. Now we have it, it is nothing. It is just a danger abolished. We have to go on living."

"Creation and constructive work," said Bodisham. "There is no end to that."

"Knowledge," said Norvel. "Men are scarcely beginning to explore life and their own possibilities."

"Common men don't realise that," said Chiffan. "At present, Norvel. Until you and your colleagues educate them up to that realisation, it's just as though it wasn't so... Common men, I tell you, are going to be most damnably bored – in the years ahead of us. Men much more than women. Maybe sex is the actual line of relief. An efflorescence of sex – and sublimated sex, art, decoration and music may be the natural and necessary relief... I don't know."

He stopped short and shrugged his shoulders.

"I suppose you will draft this section, Bodisham?" said Norvel.

Bodisham nodded and pushed his scribbled blotting-pad away from him. Dreed sat up and Roots returned from his contemplation of the clouds. The session was over...

Norvel spoke to Chiffan as they left the room.

"I have been thinking, very much as you have been thinking," he said. "I too think – the Common Man – in particular – in one particular instance – may be getting bored – and I don't know what to do about it."

10

Rud returned along the painted corridor to his own apartments.

He felt irritated by his Fundamental Law conference and he realised that his irritation was unreasonable. Evidently they had to discuss women even if they discussed them only to thrust sex out of the main propositions of the Fundamental Law. But why should they have chosen that topic on this particular morning? And why had they not kept it high and austere? It was Chiffan's touch. Why should Chiffan drag in a word like "embraces", a discomfiting word, a warm, enervating word.

Hitherto in his strenuous life he had kept these suggestions out of his imagination, except in those vague phases that come between sleeping and waking – and then they were soon disposed of. But here they were invading the day. Here they were producing something like a self-betrayal to his colleagues. Here they were a plain intimation that he might forget himself...

He fretted about his apartment for a time. His mind seemed to have lost all its discipline. What had he to do with embraces? Damn that word! He decided that he needed to refresh his sense of the mighty role that he was playing in the world, to get things back into proportion. In fact he went to look for himself. He made his way over an arcaded bridge that spanned a gorge to the series of offices in which the development of his personality was in progress, and there he found Quinlan ready to refresh his memory.

"And how am I getting on with humanity today?" asked Rud.

Quinlan showed him a vast pile of photographs, papers, trial records and beflagged world maps of the birthday celebrations.

"It is amusing to think that no religion has ever had this universality. Never has Christmas for example ever been celebrated as *your* birthday is being celebrated."

A gleam of satisfaction appeared upon Rud's pale face. "I suppose not," he said. "I suppose not."

Then came a twinge of modesty. "Of course it is all this new apparatus. It is just the new scale of things that makes it more universal."

"But so it is," said Quinlan. "None the less."

Rud looked at the methodical assemblage of Quinlan's publicity machinery. He felt as if he was standing on stilts a mile high. It was perfectly right, reasonable, fantastic and mad. Alexander, Caesar, Napoleon, Hitler, had anticipated this sort of thing, but never had the significance of their elevation been brought home to them to quite this extent. The stilts seemed steady enough, but the perspective was terrific.

"We have some new schoolroom cartoons," said Quinlan. "They hit reaction hard."

Conspicuous in this display was a cartoon of a mighty winged figure with the face of Rud, idealised and yet recognisable, and in his hands was a drawn sword. He defended the world against a squirming mass of necks and heads, bearing crosses, mitres, crowns, red caps, Federalist shakos; all the symbols of the principalities and powers of the pre-Revolutionary world.

"Of course, this is an immense exaggeration," said Rud. "I suppose that in a way it is necessary."

"It is no exaggeration. Maybe it symbolises. It is a symbolical statement. It is the only way in which we can get the Revolution over to ninety-nine per cent of them. This – for the run of mankind – is what you are."

"After all," said Rud, searching in his mind for ideas that were fading away from him. "It is their own collective self..."

Quinlan was too busy with his display to discuss meta-politics.

"There will be much to tell you tomorrow," he said, "as the reports and pictures of all that come in and are analysed...

"Of course, if you would like to see something of what is actually happening now, for example – " He considered the buttons before him and decided: "*Here.*"

He motioned Rud's eyes to the screen. It lit up and an elfin clamour of cheering voices became audible. "This is Pekin," he said. "they are celebrating you. Look at them."

The crowd was just a waving stipple of faces, an undulating close-spotted snake's skin. It bustled with banners bearing inscriptions, in the new Chinese alphabet. Save for faint floating iridescences it was as real as direct vision. Everyone was singing some sort of shrill song to pseudo-oriental music.

"Here you can see them quite closely," said Quinlan.

And suddenly almost within touching distance were flushed faces and bright eyes, and mouths that shouted his name. Mostly they were quite young girls and their excitement poured out upon him.

"That's enough," said the World Trustee abruptly, and turned away.

The apparatus clicked and was still.

"All over the world," said Quinlan.

"Thank you," said Rud, dismissing him, and went out through a further arch that opened upon a rock garden. He strolled slowly up a winding path with occasional steps, and came to pavilion in which he seated himself. "All over the world," he repeated. "And here I am – solitary."

"All over the world."

He had never thought of his home for years – he had indeed deliberately not thought of it. Now he imagined that forgotten family of his joining in the world chorus. Would they realise that this great Rud was indeed their – Rudie? And then, thrusting all the rest of them out of the way, came his vehement little cousin Rachel. He had pulled her soft abundant hair and they had scuffled. It all came back to him intensified. He saw and felt her face very vividly close to his. She was gripping his wrists, she was putting out her sharp red tongue at him and saying "Yaaaa" at him. Was she still somewhere in this conquered world, marvelling at him? He hoped she was still in the world. He would like to feel he had got square with her.

What had become of her? What would she be like now?

Queer, but she must be, she was, the only girl he had ever come to grips with. He had never seen her since. Her mother took her abroad, to South Africa was it? Or Australia. And after that slowly he had become aware of his Destiny. Slowly his Destiny had enveloped him, absorbed him.

He imagined Cousin Rachel was sitting beside him and that he was talking to her about the intervening years.

"In a way I have done my task too well. I stand over the world like that mighty archangel you may have seen out there, the Guardian of the Revolution. I am frozen in the same attitude. On guard against any reaction. But I am not really frozen through. I am not really a mighty archangel. Not altogether. I am something more. I am living man – most terribly alone…"

(What was that book Norvel spoke about? *The Golden Bough* and sacrificial kings? I must read it.)

"You are wonderful," said Cousin Rachel, sitting beside him in his imagination and speaking very softly.

"Sacrificial king of the world. For whom no sacrifice could be too great, my Master."

Rud started at the extravagance of his own thought and looked round guiltily for fear that someone might have observed what he was thinking. Cousin Rachel had evaporated. His haunting fear of self-betrayal occupied his mind again. This sense of an ever-watching eye in the open spaces cancelled, as it so often did, the ease of his Atheism. He sat up and then let himself droop into a pensive pose as who should think thoughts for all the world.

11

Chiffan was the least administrative of all the Group out of which the first World Administration grew. He remained what used to be called a Minister without Portfolio. He joined in the irregular councils that Rud assembled and on increasingly infrequent occasions he talked to Rud and Rud annexed his ideas. But the great World Ministers were developing their own methods of dealing with one another, and the new conjoint sessions of the Law, Education and Biological (Health) Boards were acting as an organ for arbitration and taking more and more responsibility off the shoulders of the council. Rud maintained his closest relations with the World Police under Thirp and the rather ill-defined Ministry for the Protection of the World State, and Chiffan, with his generous salary as consultant-general, was as near an approach to the old-fashioned "independent gentleman" as the new world could show. He spent his days in appreciative living and leisurely writing. With the rapid increase of the world's wealth, a new leisure class of released and superannuated workers was appearing. There were more gentlefolk than ever, and more and more. The normal life labour contribution was now twenty-five thousand hours; there was already great freedom in the way this could be distributed over the lifetime, and it ensured a comfortable minimum existence throughout life. Above that level, there was a great variety of rewards and fortunes to be earned by competent contributions to what was called the surplus of life.

Chiffan lived in a pleasant villa in the Rhone Valley, ten minutes' flying from the Centre, and there he lived with the most intelligent and congenial of all the women he had ever met, his wife, Phoebe Chiffan, who was indeed the twenty-ninth "real mistress" of his philandering career. Their mutual affection was as manifest as their mutual tolerance, and though she was, as people say, "faithful" to him, she viewed his active and imaginative interest in the whole spectacle of womankind with an amused sympathy. The only person in the world about whom she felt a twinge of jealousy was Rud. She felt Rud was a monster, she thought his leadership of the Group uncanny. When she saw that Chiffan was troubled in his mind and asked him point-blank what he was worrying about, and when he said, "I'm bothered a bit over Rud," she said "I thought as much."

"You are stupid about Rud," he said.

"No – you are."

"He's getting into a – a state of lonely misery."

"Isn't that his own affair?"

"You're inhuman."

"I'm feminine."

"I owe everything to him."

"And he to you. It's fifty-fifty."

"I've got a sort of maternal feeling about him. I've known him – "

"Four times as long as you have known me. What right has a man to be maternal?"

"Men are – and even some women."

413

She leant out of the hammock and pulled his hair. "All right, Chiff-Chaff," she said. "Tell me about your Rud."

"What I – What we have always liked about him," said Chiffan, "is a sort of diabolical energy. His drive. There is something outrageous in his make-up that won us all. And something that still intrigues me. There are times when I want to follow that man about like a child following a circus show. *Why* does he do things? He's an abject coward – these are things not to be repeated, my dear – and also he is a desperate fighter. Do you know I think at times that he is the master of the world today simply because he has a frantic fear of power – in the hands of anyone else."

She ruffled Chiffan's hair by way of showing she was listening.

"So he has got it all into his own hands," she said.

"And he doesn't know what to do with it, and now he doesn't know what to do with himself."

"But isn't he putting the world in order at a tremendous rate? Everybody says so."

"No. *We* are. At least, the others are. All that he does is to watch – and make that keyhole Minister of his, Thirp, watch – that nobody anywhere turns any official authority conceded him, into power. And Thirp – well, Thirp bothers him with suspicions. Things are going well with the world, but unless they go a little wrong, what is the use of Thirp? Thirp sees to that. Thirp keeps him irritated and uneasy and he has no distractions. I'm sorry, darling Phoebe – you know I love you, you know how I love you – but I don't want my ugly little Thunder-god to culminate in misery. He has made the whole spectacle of life rich and ridiculous for me. And now he is – he has a sort of greyness.

He bored or angry or afraid – afraid of things coming back – all day, and at night they give him drugs – and the best of drugs lower one and give one dreams. I know he has dreams. I didn't think things would take this turn with him and it distresses me. It distresses *me*, my dear. Love me, love my Rud, Phoebe. I did a lot to make him what he is. You help me with Rud."

"How can I help?"

"Advice. The wisdom of your sex. Give me ideas what to do for him. You are all born with a natural interest in us. You are twenty years younger than I, and all the ages wiser."

"It is good for men to have such beliefs," said Phoebe. "But you must tell me first what you think, and then I will tell you just how right you are."

"That may be the way of it," said Chiffan.

"Well?"

"I said Rud had been driven by fear. He has been driven by an extreme dread of domination. He cannot endure the thought of anyone having domination over him. Until he became World Director he never felt safe about that. He needs constant reassurance still. That is plain enough even for *you* to see, my dear."

"Did you say just now that I was all the ages wiser than you?"

"Yes. When things are put before you. But what I have only glimpsed by fits and starts about him – until quite recently – is something else. Rud, I realise, has a profound, maybe innate dread of the closest of all forms of domination – love."

"Go on."

"His capacity for love – if he ever had much capacity for love – has atrophied. Or you can put it, if you like, in quite another way. It has vanished and then returned in a vague, cloudy desire

415

to be appreciated, admired, obeyed – loved by all the world. Without any return. All this accumulating desire for public adoration, all this increasing exhibitionism – "

He thought profoundly.

"You see, Phoebe, you and I *assuage* each other's egotisms. To a very considerable extent. Unless they get-wasted, or crippled or perverted in some way, men and women get together as you and I have got together at last... We get a domination over one another. And so long as things seem fair and equal we don't resent that. We begin with liking and love-making – yes, we keep on with love-making – but the chemistry of body and mind works so as to give us a control over each other's self-respect... That's ·the sane way of life. For anyone with a rational imagination. When a man is happy with his woman and a woman is happy with her man and they are happy in their friends, neither of them *aches* – as he does – to possess the world and the sun and the moon. Am I right?"

"Sweetheart, you are right. Though it took you some years of sedulous research – "

Chiffan waved aside what threatened to be a troublesome digression. "You kept out of my way," he said. "The point about Rud, Phoebe, is just what you have said to me. There is nobody in the world to say to him 'Sweetheart, you are right.' "

"And that aches?"

"Damnably. It is the fundamental ache. The better you are fed and clothed and gratified, the more that ache for reassuring appreciation takes hold of you. The core of happiness is to have someone with whom you are essentially right and important – however wrong and ineffective you are. Rud hasn't loved, doesn't love and doesn't know how to love."

"Now *why?*" said Phoebe, with her chin between her two fists.

"Missed it."

"You don't mean he's homosexual?"

"No. Not a bit of it. And besides, I'm told, *they* can be quite affectionate."

"Asexual?"

"Nobody is."

"Then, what?"

"I said that his ruling motive is dread. Something happened. Something humiliating. Quite early perhaps. But something that turned him back upon himself."

"Narcissism."

"If you like to call it that. A trifle too floral for my taste. We want a third word; there's homosexual and heterosexual – why not autosexual? He is afraid of women. He dare not risk an approach to them. He is afraid of humiliation, he is darkened by a dread of them. And, my dear, dimly, he wants what you give us. He missed the coarse enterprise of adolescence, which lays the foundations of confidence. He feels now that that triumph – it *is* a triumph, Phoebe – is not for him, and so he has trained himself not to attempt, not to betray a flicker of desire."

"Queer creatures we humans are!"

"Am I right? Can you imagine him as a lover?"

"Ugh!"

"For any woman?"

"Women are queer things. Not all alike. More variable perhaps than men in these things. I can't put myself – can't imagine myself – in any woman's skin but my own. There is a brutal fastidiousness in *my* physical make-up anyhow. Let alone that I love you, so that I'm specialised now for you. But before ever I met you I am certain he would have seemed not simply indifferent, but repulsive – disgusting."

"I wonder," said Chiffan, "how far you speak for even a majority of women?"

"Any woman who answers for the behaviour of any woman but herself is a fool," said Phoebe.

"But even as what they used to call a Platonic lover?"

"Some women seem capable of monstrous toleration. You and I are imaginative, sensuous people. We can't stand people who are not good-looking. We are a normal easygoing couple. There are women without sensory imaginations, without physical price, gross women, acquisitive women, prestige lovers, women with a sort of blunt, savage brutality of ownership... But go on."

"Well, you will see now what I mean when I say that Rud is living in an unbroken egotism, all inside himself. A sort of moral potbound plant. Love is the natural force that breaks down egotism, takes you out to living, to personal self-forgetfulness, but he has never had even a sentimental relationship. He had no intimate life, no life of the affections, at all; and so his egotism now has become inflamed and dreadful."

"But what am *I* to do about it?"

"Help me to do something to break down his loneliness."

"But how?"

"Make some sort of social life for him. Get him into contract with human beings, easy, delightful, everyday human beings."

"But how? And where?"

"I don't know how. That is why I come to you. Social life is woman's work. He distresses me, I tell you. in a way, Phoebe, I love him. He's been a great fact in my life. And I can't think what to do about it. There he is away there, either working or alone. I've been watching him. Things are getting urgent."

Phoebe swung down out of the hammock and confronted Chiffan.

"You darling," she said. "*You* broke out of *your* egotism quite early in life. You tore it to rags. I suppose you've always been breaking out of your egotism in all directions – when did you begin, dear? I never thought being a rake was a synonym for altruism. Bless you – I don't mind – as long as you don't dwell on it. I'm glad you've loved so many people. I will think of something – somehow. You've made me do some difficult things. But this – what shall I call it? – rehumanising of the Master Director!"

12

"Rehumanising the Master Director" seemed a good phrase to Chiffan. Phoebe was learning the trick of phrase-making from him, as women will acquire even the most recondite tricks from their men, and he had that impulse to quote her cleverness which is part of the pride of love. The change in Rud's moods and manners was attracting the attention not only of Chiffan, but of most of those who were in any sort of personal contract with him, and he was being observed and discussed as he never had been before – intimately. The thing was leaking out towards the public mind. And Thirp was not one of the least active of those who speculated about was not one of the least active of those who speculated about the Master's disposition. He caught up Mrs Chiffan's phrase with approval.

419

"Of course!" he said, in his high-pitched voice. "How clever of that young woman! No human being can keep going as he has kept going for the last ten years without *some* relaxation. Worse than a term imprisonment. He needs distraction sorely.

"Everyone says he needs rest," said Thirp, "but rest isn't a negative thing. It is no sort of rest to do nothing. Prisoners have told me that. The best mental rest is a change of preoccupation. For – I don't know how long – he has had no – what shall I call it? – no personal life. All that side of his life has been inhibited. Queer I didn't realise this before!"

Thirp's mind went off at a tangent from that.

Thirp was certainly the most incongruous of all the Central Group, the least constructive in spirit and perhaps the most active. There was something about the motions of his hands and about the passing raptures on his face that made Norvel, who disliked him thoroughly, think that he ought to have been an old-world dealer in scents or sweets or precious stones. He was always astonishing Norvel by the extraordinary penetration of his occasional comments and by his barely concealed indifference to the vast conception of social reconstruction throughout the whole world which dominated the rest of the Group. He lifted his eyebrows, he lifted his voice in a slightly derisive appreciation of the reconditioned world about him. He intimated that he felt it was too good and much too rapid to be true. There was none of the hive-builder, nothing of the beaver about Thirp; his constructions were webs.

He went to and fro in the world, always a little secretly and unexpectedly, and his friends were mostly the younger men of his organisation, agents he used and somehow had to protect, and a certain sprinkling of accidental womenfolk. His taste in atmosphere was for variety, contrast, richness and the recondite. He had an instinct for the out-of-the-way. He would spend a few days in some Chinese household that had miraculously survived the social convulsions of the age, or he would stay for a week in some remote monastery or lamasery that the tides of destruction had left untouched, or he would go to his own villa among a group of artistic friends, near Montserrat in Catalonia, and return with renewed zest to the control of his immense organisation of information bureaus and the obscure activities of his Ministry for the Preservation of the Revolution.

This last was the most ill-defined of all the World Administrations. It was in effect a political police which had grown up about Thirp as a centre. It had its prisons and its oubliettes – often prisons taken over from the old order and very incompletely modernised. It watched for an anticipated militant reaction, and particularly for any systematic attempts to revive a nationalist feeling or race antagonism, it was as underhand as the evils it attacked, it was suspicious in spirit and its methods secret and arbitrary. It was all in his hands, and Rud was an insistent to keep it entirely in his hands as he had been to maintain Bellacourt's independence of Reedly.

"You honest men don't know anything about treason," he said to Bodisham. "You must set an intriguer to deal with intrigue."

Bodisham said something about universal fairplay nowadays.

"Sedition," said Rud, "knows nothing of fairplay."

Rud surprised Norvel one day by telling him of a rather acid comment upon Quinlan's St Michael poster he had made at a private dinner party.

"Good God!" said Norvel indignantly. "Do we still live in a world of political espionage?"

"*You* do," said Rud.

Chiffan's phrase about "rehumanisation" set not simply one train of ideas but two separate systems going in Thirp's busy brain. One was the rehumanisation of world affairs through what he called "the reappearance of women", and the second was the imperative necessity for him that any personal "rehumanisation" of Rud must be in his own hands, if his present influence in world affairs was to be maintained. Whatever happened, Chiffan was not to rehumanise Rud.

"The reappearance of women", he expounded to two or three of his leading agents in the Arab dining-room of his chambers at the police headquarters.

"In war and during the turnover of revolutions, women have a way of disappearing from the centre of the human stage. They are just blacked out. They are shapes in the background. They nurse, they supply the rough material for outrages, they do a lot of love-making, but in a hurry, unimportantly, as the inferior partner. There is espionage – but the popular mind exaggerates about the beautiful spy – and they work in munitions factories and act as substitute men, clerking, driving cars and inspecting tickets. It's all minor roles they have. But now as things are getting into shape again, as the tension of conflict relaxes, you see them coming back not merely to equality; but to a special sort of power and predominance. They are less and less wanted for jobs; they are more and more wanted for their pretty selves. Beauty becomes significant again, important in itself; they dress, they make-up. 'Society' life is resumed. Men compete again for their approval and their favour... I have never set much store upon the achievement of women myself," said Thirp, "but

I admit they are becoming now as interesting as they have ever been...

"Even though the World War left more of them alive than men...

"All over the world, I observe, social occasions are arising and women are becoming self-conscious again. The way the pretty creatures begin to dress – and undress! Oh! I suppose we shall never see the kind of entertainment there used to be in the great private houses of the past, huge gatherings coloured by the personality of a monarch or a merchant prince, but with the increase of wealth that is going on there is sure to be a tremendous development of large public assemblies where everyone can see and be seen. On any sort of excuse. Dancing is spreading and parades and pageants.

"Dress, I remark, is already extravagant, but some of it, I admit, is lovely. It's funny how men too are beginning to dress up again. These new community centres that are replacing the old schools everywhere are becoming social centres and adding assembly rooms – oh! palaces we should have thought them – everywhere. As fast as they can run them up. It makes all that one remembers of the old world seems grey and cheap and shabby already. I thought we were going to have a plague of unemployed artists and decorators, but it seems there aren't enough to go round. The world is swarming with wandering painters and jewellers and singers. And – I don't know what to call them – these itinerant lovers. Queer people, they are – very.

"Mere boys and girls now work like devils for a year or so and then go off round the world to spend the money and leisure they have earned. Not a frontier, not so much as a toll-gate to hinder them. We've had the world peace established for hardly three years yet and already we are keeping holiday and holding a fair. It's a peace carnival. People who were dodging bombs and hiding in shelters only three years ago. No end of these handsome young fellows we see at play everywhere have worn uniforms and clicked their heels and been in the trenches. Everywhere you go now you see the Trustee's picture; he's on the money, he's on the notices in the streets, and he looks well and hearty everywhere – except when you see him himself. And he's – he's bored. He's bored and uneasy. I've been told that he dreams. He cries out in his sleep. I have it on good authority. It's my business to know things…

"What I am saying I wouldn't say to everyone, my dear Horatio, but the World Revolution which has been such a blessed reality for hundreds of millions of people, has been a sort of joke played upon him. For him it isn't real. He's hoisted up – right out of it. He's become – " He took a quarter out of his pocket and showed the ennobled visage on it – "*this*… He may end by hating the sight of himself.

"The strain of the Revolution went on so long that it has left him with a dread of a return. He *will* look back. He seems incapable of sharing the general gladness. If only I knew how – if only we could contrive…"

13

Thirp and Chiffan competed in the rehumanisation of Rud, and Thirp won easily. Mr and Mrs Chiffan entertained Rud once and he would not come again. He appeared a little distrustfully among the "easy, delightful, everyday human beings" she had assembled for his entertainment. He brightened for a moment when she took his hand and smiled at him, and then darkened when he saw her exchange a glance with her husband. He was definitely clumsy with the other women. They were a little at a loss for something to say to him, and he gave them no help.

He became less and less responsive as the evening wore on. His mute demand, Why the devil had they got him there? Became insistent. He made a premature retreat and left the little gathering in a state of unwonted dismay at its own unattractiveness. It occurred to Chiffan then, that never in his life had he ever known Rud to indulge in general conversation. Even at the Steenhold flat he had either sulked in his corner under his caricature or broken out into monologue. But there had been no luring him into monologue that evening. In the old days his one topic had been the coming Revolution, and now the Revolution had come he was tongue-tied.

One young woman tried to interest him in her bracelets and necklaces of fire-opal set in silver. They seemed to be old, but she could not find out where they had been made. Opals were supposed to be unlucky. Rud looked at them with an effect of not looking at the neck and arms that wore them. "Thirp," was his sole comment, "could tell you all about them. *He's* interested in that sort of thing."

Rud indisputably was not.

He went early and yet it seemed to Phoebe that he went reluctantly. She felt, as she told Chiffan afterwards, that if things had been different and there had been different people and he had been different, he would have liked to stay for quite a long time.

"He went away slowly," said Phoebe, "with an air of going off to something worse."

425

Thirp took a different line with him altogether. He set about entertaining the World Trustee with inferiors and performers. He did not invite him formally, but one evening when they had some minor matter to discuss, he asked Rud to come him because, he said, he was treating himself to a show. Rud was difficult to entertain because of his habitual abstemiousness, but Thirp induced him to eat a cheese dish he had had prepared for him specially and drink some fine Burgundy, and then he produced his show. He had discovered a little round-faced, round-eyed, yellow and black, exceedingly impudent, Siamese girl conjurer. She had a great sense of humour and some excellent tricks, and very soon she had Rud at his ease and laughing. Then came a dance of masked Siamese girls to a lilting Westernised tune which also took Rud's fancy, so that presently he was beating time.

"He likes them funny and he likes them little and he likes them young," Thirp noted. "The smaller and the younger and the more weakly impudent they are, the less he is afraid."

That was enough for the present, thought Thirp, but at the end of the evening he told Rud he often had little shows of this sort. He felt it well to keep in touch with the amusements of the people. If Rud would care to come again – ?

Rud was not unwilling to come again. "Relaxation," said Thirp.

"I liked that little conjuring thing," said Rud. "She made me laugh – and somehow I seem to have got out of the habit of laughing."

Thirp repeated this entertainment, but without undue alacrity. This time two wriggling Japanese maidens served the dishes for Rud's austerely excellent meal.

Four or five time was Rud Thirp's appreciative guest, and then it seemed time for Thirp to – to use his own phrase – "arrange a little tête-à-tête"? That demanded thought and preparation. He talked to Rud of health and fatigue, amusement and rest, and of the extraordinary sleep-provoking power of massage. At first Rud seemed as likely to expose his bare skin to the mauling and pinching of massage as to dance naked in a market place. His accumulated modesty barred the way. Then by a well arranged accident he was given a glimpse of the infantile but appetising charm of Miss Chubby Fielder, and a little later, when he was in a phase of neurasthenic discomfort, Thirp persuaded him to give her an opportunity...

14

"It isn't my fault," said Chubby Fielder. "It isn't my fault. I tried everything.

"I wish there were nunneries. I must go way from this. I must hide. He got so *angry*...

"If ever I take a lover the Master will kill me."

"But He didn't say that!"

"No. He didn't *say* it. But he was so *upset!* He was *so* upset. At having forgotten himself. *That's* what upset him. All crying and then furious. Overbearing and then kind of ashamed of himself and them ashamed of me. 'I'd like to wipe you out of existence,' he said. He said that. Suppose he meant that! And then he kissed me and kind of threw me away from him. I'm *terrified*. How can I get out of this? Where can I go, Mr Thirp?'

"Don't you worry, Chubby, my dear," said Thirp, and made a sort of dabbing pat at her bare shoulder as if to reassure her. "If necessary you shall vanish. I'll just smuggle you away. Though I doubt if I'll have to do that. But, mind you, never talk about this. Never say a word and you will be safe. But if ever he thinks you have told on him, even as little as you have told me, I can't answer for it."

"But what have I told you? It isn't anything – it's what I feel. I haven't said a thing. Not actually. *Have* I said anything?"

"No."

"I've said nothing. Practically it *was* nothing."

"It's just how much it was nothing – that you mustn't tell anyone," said Thirp. "If you talk – "

"Is it likely?" said Chubby.

"If you don't talk, Chubby. If he believes you haven't talked. If you keep everything there was between you, between you – even from me. Maybe – I can't promise, mind you – but maybe he will see you again…"

"Bert – " began Chubby, which was her way of saying "But."

"Yees, Chubby," said Thirp. "Quite possibly. If you are silent and discreet. Very discreet.

"And if ever you find yourself with him again, Chubby," said Thirp. "Say this to him; say – 'You are God.' "

Chubby repeated that in a whisper.

"But why?"

"He'll like it."

"I shan't see ever be with him again," she said, "so what's the good?…"

Rud did see her again, but all that happened between them was wrapped in mystery even from Thirp. Quite possibly little or nothing happened between them. *Honi soit qui mal y pense.* And Chiffan to the end of his life never even knew that there was such a person as Chubby, much less how much more pleasant the company of a being like Chubby could be to the unlimited, fear-haunted egotism of Rud than that of any fully grown, level-spirited woman.

15

So much of Rud's intimate life has to be told and discussed to make the picture of him complete, but beyond that there is hardly anything significant to tell. For the rest we can emulate Chubby's discretion. The significance of what has been told is its insignificance. One or two other feminine figures flicker on to the record, but they were mere passing incidents. There was the lady who professed to be able to induce dreamless sleep by mesmeric passes. She appeared, dark, handsome and impressive, betraying a beautiful blue veined marble throat, waving large white hands. From the outset Thirp distrusted her, he felt she might have the makings of a female Rasputin in the world autocracy; nevertheless, since it was in Thirp's scheme of things that Rud should continue to be concerned about his insomnia, she was given access to him. Something happened. She emerged from Rud's private apartments with a scared expression on her handsome face and nothing portentous left about her.

"Not a success," she said to Thirp, pushing past him. "Not at all a success."

Then Rud: "That disgusing woman! Never let me see her again."

Lady Susannah Shakespeare, that splendid golden blonde, the perfect woman, Flaming Susannah, Susannah the Terror of her Elders, as she was known among her intimates, was outstanding among those who would have conferred fatherhood upon the Master of the World. Her pursuit of Rud was open and shameless, and she fought her way at least to the presence of Thirp.

But Thirp was stangely discouraging.

She had met Thirp for the first time, and she found him antipathetic. He was so much more feminine in an elderly sort of way than herself. "You know," he said, "if you go on as you are doing, it might be felt you were making him a little ridiculous. None of us would like that, Lady Susannah. The Secret Police, I'm credibly informed, might not like it. *Indeed,* they might not. If you go on as you are doing.

"I think," said Thirp, in a tone of profound meditation, "I think you'd better not. I really think you'd better not. I think you'd better not even talk any more about your idea."

And it suddenly entered into the mind of the perfect woman that she had better not.

16

About this time a woman interviewer made a great scoop by discovering the Master Director's Aunt Julia and getting access through her to Mrs Whitlow. "A great man," said the woman interviewer, "owes everything to his mother."

"Never did I know anyone so simple, so *direct-minded*, as Rudolf," said old Aunt Julia. "I was always *very, very* fond of him. There was something enchanting about him. A naturalness. A straightforwardness. I should say he is the one single human being I have ever known entirely free from any complex. He went straight to his point, whatever it was, like an arrow."

"He was a strange, thoughtful boy," said Mrs Whitlow, when at last the woman interviewer had got past Aunt Julia. "I would wonder – I would ask myself – what is he brooding about? He was aloof among his playmates, communing with himself. His soul was like a star and dwelt apart. Sometimes he would ask questions that it puzzled even me to answer. When he was still only a little fellow of five or six."

The woman interviewer's thoughts flitted for a moment, and in all reverence, towards another mother in ancient Nazareth. She wondered if in this case there had been any sort of Annuciation. But that was difficult to ask. "You felt he was a child of Destiny?" she asked.

"He had that *something*," said Mrs Whitlow...

"He puzzled his poor father," said Mrs Whitlow. "His father never understood him."

"Mother fixation," said the woman interviewer. "They say he has never cared for any woman but you."

"He's had so much to think about," said Mrs Whitlow, modestly.

It occurred to Rud, when he read this, that it would be a natural and popular thing for her to visit him. He had hardly given her a thought for years. A mother fixation might not be a bad thing to have. And it might be still more gracious to entertain Alf and Sam... They'd open their eyes. He would conspicuously do nothing for them. So that there would be no talk of nepotism. Would Alf turn out to be as religious as ever? Sam would be frankly envious and spiteful, but Alf's behaviour was more uncertain. He got Thirp to make enquiries.

431

"He has got rather fat, he is a minor distributive official, and he thinks you are anti-Christ... You know that Neo-Catholic idea?"

Rud decided not to rediscover Alf.

But he made a large public visit to his mother and talked to her of what the world owed to her for what she had done to him, and she said he hadn't changed in the least, he reminded her of how he used to come home and tell her he was top of the class at school; he had just the same eager, boyish expression. How happy it used to make her!

She talked of some new mind cure for her nervous dyspepsia, and he told her that every specialist in the world was absolutely at her disposal.

She spoke of various neighbours of their early days. She did not know what had become of his cousin, Rachel. She had lost sight of her after her husband's sister died in Australia.

"Do you still have those sick headaches, Rudie?" she asked. "Always so suffering and so patient you were..."

CHAPTER TWO

The God Caesar

Because of the effective control of the press exercised by the World Directorate during the period of world readaptation, people at large heard practically nothing about this physio-psychological eddy in which the Master Director was spinning. Only some years later did vague rumours of it become current. They did not know that he gave way now to long spells of indolence with occasional interludes of relaxation under the complaisant management of Thirp. The world as a whole believed him to be the active administrator, as sexless as a modern God, who was, with a certain peremptoriness, but unquestionable rightness and ability, putting the world's affairs into a more rational and happier frame than they had ever been in before. They understood that he lived a simple, strenuous and very secluded life, in the performance of his great task. For them it was Rud's Peace that ruled in the world.

And for a span of fruitful years the rational reconstruction of human organisations, boldly scrapping traditional entanglements and boldly tackling difficulties that hitherto had seemed insurmountable, went on swiftly and without any conspicuous disturbance. The diffused liberal thought of nearly a century of ineffective years was being given a scientific form and a scientific application. It was a process parallel to that discursive multiplication of ideas about electricity that went on before the eighties of the nineteenth century and the swift onset of the electrical age that followed. The new social advance was so vast and rapid and universally interesting that for time it was received with a worldwide, uncritical satisfaction. It was indeed whispered here and there that the pursuit of counter-revolutionary tendencies was becoming closer and keener. It was whispered that the secret police was responsible for the disappearance of this or that too outspoken antagonist of the new order of things and even for one or two disappearances that had nothing to do with politics. Freedom of publication was certainly declining, but there was very little visible tightening up of restriction. People were too actively intent upon their individual shares in the new order of thing to note this diminution of dissentient expression, much less to look for reasons for the decline. These were matters affecting intellectuals, reactionary spirits and the religious, and they scarcely qualified the plain reality that mankind as a whole was living far more abundantly and happily than ever before.

Then came an event which sent a very perceptible quiver through the quickening conscience of the reborn world community. This was the sudden death of Bodisham at the age of fifty-two. He was taking a summer holiday with his wife, a married son and daughter-in-law and four grandchildren in the Aland Isles. He was taken ill in the night after a boating picnic and, in spite of an immediate concentration of medical skill from all parts of the world, he died in six days. His seizure threw Rud into the greatest perturbation. His first words when he heard the news were "They've poisoned him." He leapt to that idea. He flew straight to his older colleague and became a great nuisance to everyone in attendance upon the sick man, demanding long interviews with the doctors and insisting upon repeated visits to the sickroom.

Thirp, with one or two discreet looking investigators, followed hot upon his master's heels and immediately began checking up on the procedure of the experts in attendance. The situation became irritating for everybody and unfortunately certain disagreements about diagnosis and treatment broke out among the physicians. They quarrelled among themselves, and in their desire to discredit each other upon minor points of procedure they did something to discredit themselves in public opinion.

For the first time Rud admitted to himself and those about him how much he had been dependent for his decisions upon Bodisham's shrewd advice and how helpless he would feel without him. He wanted to have stimulants administered so that he could "discuss matters of primary importance that could not wait"; he insisted on talking to the sinking man.

"He must be left in peace," said the doctors.

"But what shall I *do*?" he demanded. "He is my right hand. Right hand, do I say? He is the half of my brain."

He commanded the doctors to save Bodisham at any cost; he was imperative, he would hear of no alternative to recovery, and menace began to mingle with his urgency. With a gathering dismay they realised that they were going to be held responsible if the patient did not recover. They decided that nothing should be neglected. They disputed, therefore, about the minor details of his treatment, and amidst their indecision he died.

Their public trial followed, and it amazed the new world. The hand of the World Director became only too perceptible in the proceedings. The dominance of Thirp, he shone in organising the evidence, and the remarkable way in which minor differences and trivialities were woven into a charge of malignant conspiracy, ran entirely contrary to the spirit of balance and candour which Norvel's vast system of adult education was disseminating through the new community colleges and the swelling literature of information and discussion. The prosecution was reactionary in temper, albeit it was undertaken by the Ministry for the Protection of the Revolution, and the constitution and procedure of the Court aimed at conviction from the outset. That secret distrust and hatred of doctors common to all mankind had evidently existed in Rud in an exaggerated form, and now flared out plainly and conspicuously. These unfortunate men, gathered from the most varied sources and having little in common but their scientific prestige, were sentenced, four of them to death and the rest to indefinite terms of imprisonment. And being so sentenced they vanished abruptly from the public eye.

That sudden black, silent shutter was even more disconcerting than the trial and the sentences.

Intelligent men and women all over the world found themselves asking: "When were they killed?" "How were they killed?" "Were they shot?" "And where?" "And what had become of the others?" There was no answer to any of these questions. The condemned men had disappeared. And with a curious discomfort people began to realise that in this exhilarating, renascent world of theirs there existed somewhere the organisation, the machinery for an invisible, voiceless incarceration and for the hidden execution of suspected men.

Bodisham's wife appeared transitorily in the background of the case. "A very kindly woman," the official reporters had it then, "a Jewess – the mother of five admirable children." Her intervention availed nothing. She seemed to play an ambiguous part in the drama because of her evident pity for the incriminated doctors and her indignation at the methods of the court.

2

The death of Bodisham marked a definite change of phase in the history of the World Revolution. Up to the date of that event it had seemed to be one whole process, complex in detail but homogeneous in form. Now it began to be plain that the World Revolution, like all its less universal precursors, like every Revolution, was woven of two essentially distinct strands. There was, for one strand, the innate insubordination of the human animal which lies in wait for all decaying, hesitating or needlessly oppressive systems of social control, an insubordination compounded of fear, resentment and vindictiveness, and embodied in its final dramatic phase by Rud and Thirp. And contrasting and interwoven with that was the creative urge for order and achievement in the human mind, an impulse more deliberate and sustained, finding its expression in a progressive organisation of science, a progressive extension of the scientific method to human affairs and the systematic establishment of a new education, a new order and a new regime of law. The two strands co-operated at first in their attack upon their common objective, the old order of things. It was not at first evident that while one aimed to destroy, the other sought to replace. It was not necessary at first that it should become evident. Together these two allied contraries produced the World Revolution, which had not to so much been evoked by the Group as found its centre of expression therein.

Long after the formal defeat of the decadent old order was manifest, long after the obsolete boundaries, the antiquated Foreign Offices, the armies and navies, monetary manipulation, and the unconscionable appropriations of private ownership in collective businesses had been swept away. Rud's intense fear of reaction and revenge enabled Bodisham to maintain his argument that the only sane barrier against counter-revolution was the establishment of a satisfactorily working new order in the place of the old. To Rud the new institution were essentially fortification against the old. He did not see them as collective organisations imposing fresh codes of behaviours and necessitating an education of their own. So, Paradoxically enough, Rud, this power snatching, essential rebel, this instinctive lawless grabber, this antisocial egotist, sustained the forces of constructive control on earth through their early years of growth, while Bodisham implemented and co-ordinated them and protected them from any serious release of the destructive instinct in Rud. Concurrently and, as it came to seem in the retrospect, naturally and necessarily, there grew up an untrammelled and arbitrary Caesarism in which political power became increasingly concentrated, while system of production, distribution, transport, education and biological control, the living body of that planetary civilisation which the new material conditions demanded. To many it seemed like the complete confirmation of Hobbes' *Leviathan,* the ultimate realisation of autocratic efficiency on a scale altogether more gigantic than Hobbes could have foreseen. To others it seemed a necessary phase that had to come to an end through the casting-off of autocracy, as an eagle breaks out of its egg. The idea that absolutism might be the necessary way to the world republic had been floating in men's minds long before the last War to end War and the rise of the Group to power. Young Dick Carstall had foreshadowed it long ago when he talked with his father about his own outlook on life.

The full quality of Bodisham's genius only became apparent after his death. Released from his subtle interventions, the two revolutionary strands began to part company forthwith. Then, as young Carstall had foreseen, it began to dawn upon intelligent observers throughout the world that the spirit of insubordination and irresponsibility which leads through ascending phases of lawlessness and violence to lawless personal rule is, by its very nature, doomed to an ultimate grapple with a growing system of law, order and economic justice and sanity. For years Bodisham had been staving off that conflict. His untimely death left Rud, a little heavier, less active and quick-witted, soaked now in preposterous flattery and very much under the sway of Thirp, as the sole actual controller and intermediary of a still very loosely knitted network of world ministries. That young Heir of the Ages, the New World State, suddenly found itself under the guardianship of quite a different uncle. It was confronted with the problem of the liberator become tyrant.

Norvel, who was probably, after Bodisham, the most powerful and energetic intelligence in the Group, contemplated the new situation with undisguised dismay. He was already in conflict

439

with Quinlan and Thirp upon the question of the extensive use of his educational and publicity services for the propaganda of Rud-worship. Bodisham's interposition had damped down the tension; but now he would have to deal with these self-appointed slaves and masters of Caesar directly, and come sooner or later into open conflict with the Master himself. He hated and dreaded the issue to which he was being drawn, the issue of the balanced and deliberate man face to face with lop-sided energy. He reproached himself for his acquiescence in the development of this cant of the Master Director, beside which the cants of personal devotion to Hitler, Mussolini, Stalin and God-save-the-King-whoever-he-is of his boyhood seemed tolerable affectations. The ennobled portraits of Rud now decorated every community centre from pole to pole, the children of a new generation were being trained to a servile salute of the supreme figure, they were being assured of his love and wisdom, there were endless songs, hymns rather, sung in his honour. Usually the schools began work in the morning with something very like an opening prayer to Rud and the Revolution. The children took to it with a disgusting readiness; the mediocre teachers liked it sincerely, mainly because they found it so easy to impart. Everywhere Caesar, the Czar, the Shah, the Mikado, the dear King and Queen, the Leader, our Stalin, the Duce, Providence and God Almighty had been or were being ousted form the facile childish imagination of mankind, as the reassuring symbol that justified submission to the restraints and routines of life, in favour of this half-deified newcomer, this aggressive, querulous individuality with indefinite powers of interference. Who did not now seem to Norvel so harmlessly and satisfying mortal as once he had done. The rapidity of this mental infection under modern conditions astounded even Norvel, who was in as good a position as anyone to have anticipated it. He had known how quickly now new things could be spread about the world, but he had not realised how rapidly old things could be dropped and forgotten.

Rud might live for another quarter century. By that time Norvel's slowly growing educational machine might be shattered again, and a universal, clumsy worship of Caesar, a habit of acquiescence in the dogmatic state, be clamped upon mankind. That imprisonment of the human mind might continue indefinitely, and when at last it found a release, what sort of etiolated and distorted thing might it not have become?

"They'd better go back to God," Norvel said to his wife. "Far better go back to God for a bit – Providence the Unready – whom anyhow one can trust to keep his fingers out of things...

"Though I suppose we should soon get some Thirps in canonicals, inventing a 'Will' for him and starting out to defend him against the doubters...

"Some counter-balance there must be. There can be no right, there can be no truth, there can be no healthy life – without some dissent, without some opposition. A Society without criticism is like a hand without a thumb...

"Sooner or later this must come to a fight," he told her... "It may be – uncomfortable for us."

"I'd hate to be comfortable," she said, "If it means your standing anything we didn't think absolutely right. You go on and I'll come with you."

"And if, in my disingenuous way, I falter – ?"

"You'd better not," she said.

"Ugly things can happen in a prison – things worse than mere clean shooting. A man's behaviour can be lied about. His wife may be lied to."

"Giving in," she said, "is the worst sort of death. I'll stand by you to the end. Maybe I'll stand by you if you do give in, but then I shall feel like mad Queen Johanna who carried her dead husband about with her in a coffin of lead... Trust me, my dear. I'm sure of you. Don't I know you through and through? Whatever they say, whatever you do, I shall believe in you."

3

Rud's fundamental idea that he had in effect become Everyman, had given him a far less tolerant attitude towards anything that he regarded as a reactionary force in human affairs than this primitive Radicalism would have enforced. His particular grievance against Norvel was the increasing patience the latter was displaying towards the old faiths, the old customs and usages, even the old patriotisms that still stirred and protested beneath the brave new surface of the world state. These idea systems were not only alive and active in the minds and habits of the surviving pre-revolutionary generations, they were still more vividly alive in the bulk of literature, in the accumulations of art, in customary metaphors and a thousand turns of language and social attitudes. Through these media they infected the young far more than through the immediate teaching of their elders. Rud, like the early Christian fathers, like the Emperor Shi-Hwang-ti, like the early Moslem who destroyed the library at Alexandria, like the German Nazis, was a natural born bookkeeper. Norvel, although he was perhaps in his ultimate texture a far profounder modernist than Rud, had a much more patient, comprehensive, tolerant and respectful view of human tradition. He realised that inheritance is possible without parricide.

Rud considered Norvel's methods vacillating and tinged with insincerity. Several times he had urged Norvel to a more stringent suppression of any literature or teaching that ignored or ran counter to his new-world Caesarism, even if it did not specifically attack it. Then, finding Norvel negligent of his protests, he began to ignore him and to turn to Thirp and the Secret Police for the defence of the Revolution. There is more than one way of restraining education. Norvel discovered that teachers, professors, students and writers were being warned and arrested for "counter-revolutionary activities." The lessons he incited them to give in the schoolroom were being used as evidence against them.

This exasperated him, but he found himself powerless to prevent it. Fundamentally he had as little use for the organised religions of the pre-revolutionary period as Rud, so far as their dogmas and sacred symbols went, but his conception of their role and destiny was entirely different. He realised that whatever else these organisations had imposed upon mankind, however much they had hampered enlightenment, they had also provided a shelter for a vast amount of devotion, a conception of self-control, valuable moral suggestions and a justification for much gentle living. It seemed to him just as silly to believe in nothing as to believe in Mumbo Jumbo. It was possible, he thought, for hard-minded men of mature years to frame their lives in social co-operation, but his vast enterprise of training the whole world for one community of life and behaviour was bringing him to a conviction that for the young and the vulgar at least, the idea of an interested heavenly father was a practical necessity. He did not like the little child atheists who were brought up before Thirp's investigators to witness to the secret vice of prayer or hymn-singing in their parents.

Rud's instinctive hatred of religion was becoming more and more marked. He had learnt at his mother's knee to resent the existence of another being more important than himself. At first he assailed only the endowments of the churches, and that only as a part of the general socialisation of rents and monopolist profits. But his confiscatory methods included religious buildings and monuments of all sorts. It has to be recognised that the traditional religious bodies stood up very ineffectively to his persecution, if one can call it a persecution. It is the heretics and innovators of all sorts who have been persecuted in the past, and the authorised religious organisations that have persecuted. When in their turn they have suffered effective persecution, their collapse has been prompt. Rud saw to it that their finances were austerely treated and the ensuring decadence was swift and irreparable.

But out of the crushed ruins of the churches there came presently oozing a mental juice, a seeping and penetrating recrudescence of religiosity. This was going on not merely in the former Christian countries. It was easy to rout Allah out of a mosque, but Allah hidden somewhere in a human heart was an altogether different problem in eradication.

Rud was particularly exercised by the New Catholic movement, which broke out a year or so after he had had the satisfaction of converting the entire Vatican quarter into a public monument under the control of the Roman Archaeological Department. Christianity was now as homeless again as its founder. These New Christians claimed to be the original Catholic Church, they were mainly Catholics, but they had associated with themselves very considerable bodies of adherents from the other shattered Christian churches. The reunion of the churches, so long dreamt of by Liberal priests of every denomination, had been greatly facilitated by the disappearance of highly salaried posts for the heads of the various communions. A general loyalty to the Pope, who was now in hiding, was asserted by these Neo-Christians, the mass was celebrated, at first publicly and then – when that was prohibited because of nationalist demonstrations that followed its celebrations in various old Catholic countries – in secret. Rud's rough hand was provoking reprisals.

The Pope hesitated for some time about the form Christian resistance should take, but a number of more or less representative religious leaders already spoke out boldly against the World Director as Anti-Christ. The Pope in various messages to the faithful distinguished meticulously between the autocracy of Rud and secular education on the one hand, and the new financial, economic and political unification of the world on the other. The former he condemned unreservedly, the latter he commended. In one respect the Holy Father was inconsistent. Although on the one hand he denounced usury, on the other he complained bitterly of the confiscation of the ecclesiastical investments.

In imitation of the early Christians who refused to burn incense before the effigy of Caesar, these Neo-Christians were refusing stoutly to stand up and salute at the mention of Rud. This idea spread to Islam, and huge crowds would shout defiantly whenever the saltire was displayed. Rud came raging to Norvel with the discovery that a considerable proportion of the teachers in the elementary schools were Neo-Christians, Jews, Moslems, Hindus and the like, some secretly so, some outspokenly.

"But I *must* staff my schools with these people," said Norvel. "If there are to be schools, if there are to be any teachers at all. There is no one else available. Before we can completely modernise the school centres we must have twenty million highly educated teacher – twenty million – and how are we to get them until we have built up something better than these poor little old scattered universities of ours? It's a marvel people know as much as they do. It's a marvel they are not ten times more ignorant and credulous than they are. I'm driving on with it. But, as you know, the birth rate is going up again. I'm building my intellectual dams and sluice gates against a fast rising flood of babies..."

"You go on printing the Bible," said Rud. "It's time that rag-bag, that collection of fever rags, was suppressed."

"You do not need to suppress it. So far as it is historically misleading, and so far as it sustains that horrible doctrine of a Chosen People, it is already lapsing into complete incredibility. It's a curious book and some of the stories about those artful old patriarchs are told with a bald simplicity that is very effective. I don't mind its being superseded but I object to its suppression. I mean to print every book that people ask for, until the paper supply gives out. There it shall be for them to read if they want to read it, and for them to ask other people to read too, if they value it as much as that. There it is, evidence for or against them."

"And so it all goes on!"

"I'm not so sure that for human beings under twenty-five to thirty the idea of the Fatherhood of God isn't a very good idea.

Suppose it *is* artificial. Aren't clothes artificial? You have to wrap up a child's body in chilly weather. Why not its mind?"

Rud was not listening. He was prowling about the room.

"They've still got a Pope dodging about somewhere," he said suddenly, coming to a stop. "They conspire to hide him. It's becoming a sort of sport to frustrate me. But I'll get him. I will not let life remain worthwhile for anyone who sets up to be Pope against me..."

Norvel laughed abruptly. "To think of it! A Pope-hunt! Just as *they* used to hunt the Albigenses. It's funny. These Pope-hunters of yours ought to wear the old Nazi swastikas; your white cross is improper. You can't have Crusaders hunting a Pope. No... But you're all wrong about this. You're going to enlist on the side of the old religions just the very force that made you a fanatical atheist!"

"*What!*" shouted Rud.

"Resentment at authority. You will make men believers and martyrs who never gave a thought to God as a ruler, before your pressure began. As an alternative, purely as an alternative to you – they will fall back upon him..."

"I never thought of this," said Rud.

"It's elementary social psychology. Gods have been man's refuge from human power since the very beginning of history."

"I never thought of that. I never saw it like that," said Rud, and looked at Norvel as though he had seen him suddenly in a new light. "That accounts for a lot of things. Gods the alternatives to rulers –. God become Leader of the Opposition..."

"But why should people dislike the new order as I give it them?" asked Rud. "Why cannot they be rational? Am I anything but the embodiment of the Common Interest and the Common

447

Will? What have they to complain of? Think of what the world was like fifteen years ago?... See what I have done for them!... I suppose it is the older people... It isn't the common people; it can't be. It's something organised. Some subtle undermining. Where is the leakage? Why do these ideas survive? Are you *sure*, Norvel, these schools of yours – ?"

4

Thirp put it into Rud's head that Norvel, instead of using the cinema in the schools to display the rapid development of the new life of mankind, the public festivals, the sunlit crops, the triumphs of engineering that were in progress, all with a montage in which the Beethovenised head of Rud, the ruler and guide, was displayed in such manner as to evoke and sustain a world-wide enthusiasm, was diverting the young with old romantic and trivial stories and propagating a cult of disintegrating laughter, even resorting to the pre-revolutionary period for his material.

Accordingly Rud asked Norvel to show him a selection of the still popular classics. Norvel, who knew nothing of what Rud had in his mind, was pleased by this sudden interest in his work. "I've been reviving a lot of old stuff that I remember as a boy," he said. "Perhaps you would like to see that. The comic stuff for example. The taste for romance and heroism seems to have changed. That sort of thing is too remote from our world today even to seem funny. Our children nowadays can make nothing of Cinderella or the Fairy Prince. But when it comes to sheer absurdity, it's a different story. Certain sorts of fun seem to be universal and perennial. Look at this, for example."

He motioned to the operator to run first one and then another of those old-fashioned quaintnesses, very early films, old cartoons, *Felix the Cat* and so forth. "We use this sort of thing to illustrate the history of the films."

At first Rud was amused. He forgot Thirp's suggestions for a while. Then suspicion crept back into his mind.

"That," said Norvel, "is Charlie Chaplin. He has a curious human absurdity no one has ever excelled. All these films of him were suppressed in Germany during the Hitler regime. You notice the moustache?…"

"I did not realise they have a political significance," said Rud, and became more intent.

Norvel came to the post-war period and traced the development of Walt Disney's art. Gradually as the plain Micky Mouse gave way to his coloured version and Donald Duck appeared, silence came upon Rud. And then to the infinite astonishment of Norvel he broke out suddenly.

"Who *is* this Walt Disney? He seems to me to be a *very* dangerous revolutionary. This − all of this − is underhand sedition. I'm not such a fool −. I see his point. This Donald Duck! It's subtle but I get him. I *get* him. The busybody who interferes and tangles up everything. That's the suggestion. That's how I'm lied about. That's what they want to say of me − if they dared. He's even got the sailor's cap I wear at times. The way the forehead is shaped! Exactly the same! The grave look he gives people before he does something decisive. It is insidious. It is abominable. It is deliberate. This Disney ought to be shot. Where does he work? Where is he to be found?"

"These films were made before the Group existed," said Norvel, recovering slowly from his amazement. "I don't know where Disney is. Probably he is quite old by now. He was doing his work before the Last War. I don't know if he is still alive. Maybe he is still making films, happily unconscious…"

Autocracy was making Norvel a facile liar. He had as a matter of fact been talking to Disney three days before, and discussing a scheme for a great series of operas with him. But he saw no reason why Rud should intervene in these matters.

"I don't believe it!" said Rud, suddenly pathetic. "If these films were made long ago, why didn't I see them? They're new. Or they've been altered… It's so cruel, Norvel, so unjust to me… Why do you show them? Don't you realise the drift of them? Or do you?"

He paused interrogative, his head a little on one side, his skew mouth like a beak slightly open. In the back of Norvel's mind was a realisation that this incarnation of the Common Energy of Mankind *was* after all just a wee bit like Donald Duck.

5

One day Chiffan said something very disturbing to his Phoebe. He had been unusually moody, silent and distraught for some time, and excessively gentle with her, never saying an absurd thing. Then late one afternoon, as they sat together in their loggia that looked out upon the tennis courts where they had been entertaining half a dozen friends, he broached his trouble.

"This can't go on," he said.

"We're happy!" she answered, astonished.

"Rud," he said.

"You are still troubled about him!"

"I am troubled about the whole world. On his account. We have made a sort of God of him…"

"Isn't that enough?" she asked as he paused.

"It's too much. To all intents and purposes, Phoebe, he is mad. Characteristics in him that used to be amusing are becoming monstrous and evil. He discovers danger everywhere. This infernal secret police of his is arresting people, making them vanish, killing them… Because he is afraid…"

"But what can you do?" asked Phoebe.

"I ought to do something. I don't know what, but I ought to do something. In a way I am responsible for him. I was his impressario. In those old days I launched him on the world."

"But nowadays you hardly ever see him. He avoids you."

"I ought to see him. I ought to know more about him. Now I get all these queer things about him at second hand. I don't know what is happening to him. I don't know whether he is going mad or simply getting loose. Sometimes I think he's just an imaginative egotist, who has escaped from all restraint. Maybe he is what many men might prove to be with the escapement off. I – in a sort of way – was his escapement… I ought to have stuck closer to him…

"He used to listen to me. If I went to him now and spoke plainly…He might be sulky but he would take it in.

"Maybe I am the only person alive able to recall him to his former self."

6

Chiffan found it more difficult even than he had expected to get an audience with Rud. He had to apply, he had to wait, he was kept waiting in an antechamber for three-quarters of an hour. When at last he was admitted to the Presence, he found himself in a long room with a polished floor that slanted upward to the dais that carried Rud's desk. Halfway there was a flight of seven shallow steps, too wide to be taken two at a time and only about five inches high. They would have reduced the most confident stride to a totter. He thought how much Rud had improved upon the crude methods of Bohun's reception room, and the reminiscence served to sharpen the blade of hard derision in his make-up, already whetted by his unnecessary wait outside. He was no longer the affectionate and persuasive Chiffan he might have been.

Rud sat at the desk pretending to be occupied by some papers and peering under his shaded desk lamp at the approach of his old friend. Chiffan, entering, and seeing this pose of preoccupation, advanced at a leisurely stroll, hands in pockets, and realising the difficulty of the shallow steps, halted there, turned his profile to the Dictator and professed to consult some memoranda, humming and – as Rud seemed still occupied – producing a pocket pencil and making corrections. Rud decided to conclude his sham work with a sigh and turned his face towards his visitor.

Chiffan packed up his memoranda, clicked his pencil together, pocketed it and strolled up to the desk. "Hope I don't interrupt your – annotations," he said.

Rud stood up, came to the corner of his bureau, and stared at Chiffan in silence.

Chiffan's first impression was that the lop-sided scowl had become intenser and then that Rud looked overstrained and ill. His face was a deader white than ever and his eyes burnt with an unwonted fever. It was going to be harder to bring this Rudlike creature back to the Rud of the summer school and Camborne Square than Chiffan had anticipated. But there was no time now to alter what he had in his mind to say.

"Hello, Rud," he said. "How goes it with the representative Common Man?"

"You wanted to talk to me?" said Rud.

"As one common man to another."

The malignity of the scowl increased. "About what?"

"About that idea of your being the supreme embodiment of the common man and the effect that it is having upon the world."

"Well, w*hat* effect?" asked Rud.

Chiffan had meant his talk to develop gradually, but this compact answer spoilt his approach. He felt himself blundering directly into the gist of what he had to say. "There is a feeling abroad," he said, "that your role of being a sort of incarnation of humanity is being – to put it bluntly, Rud – overplayed. It was, you know, one of the greatest of your inspirations to make our Revolution the Revolution of the Common Man, not to set up yourself or the gang or anybody as the Heaven-sent leader of mankind. It was a great phrase to call you the World Trustee and make you, so to speak, the Commonest of the Common, in the common interest... You *were* the common man, yes. *The* common man. On those terms we won the World Revolution. But now the job's done and finished, and I take it you have to be *a* common man again. Because if you don't, you will come to be in a sort of way a new Caesar, a new Imperator, Boss of the World, a tyrant, traitor to the Revolution."

"Well," said Rud. "that is plain enough, anyhow."

"I didn't mean to begin as bluntly as this with what I have to say."

"But you mean to say it?"

"Yes."

"A sort of Message, eh?" said Rud. "Telling me my times are at an end and that I have to go. Mene, mene, tekel, upharsin, Eh?"

"Don't make me feel like a Prophet of the Lord rebuking a wicked King of Israel," said Chiffan.

"And what in the name of the Lord," said Rud, "is this message you bring me if it is not that?"

"Well," said Chiffan, "if that is the tone we are to adopt, then let us speak plainly; the time *has* come for you yourself, as the last crowning service you can render to mankind, to prepare for the liquidation of your trust."

"The liquidation of my trust?"

"The restoration of the world to the heir."

"Who is?"

"The common man – the common-sense of mankind."

"Go on," said Rud darkly. "Go on. Tell me more of what you have in mind."

"I came to tell you – plainly – as no one else will dare to do – that you are hanging on to power too long. You know how to overthrow, Rud, you know how to guide and you don't know how to let go."

"And you – on behalf of yourself and friends – I suppose you have come to tell me to let go."

"I came of my own accord."

Rud tried to look penetrating, but he merely looked cunningly sceptical. "Assuming that is true," he said, "go on. I am to let go. Well? I want to hear all you have to say against me."

It appeared to Chiffan that Rud had become endowed with a new defensive obduracy.

"It's not against you," he said.

"Go on," said the Dictator. "Now you are here."

"Well, Rud, in the old days you used to face up to facts. I ask you not to think of me as an antagonist. Why should you? You never did that in the old days. Hear me out. You have played a great part in this changeover of the world. You have been the star in the limelight, but – "

"Yes – but? Go on. Go on."

"You are not the whole play. Damn it, Rud, you *must* face up to that? This new world didn't begin, and it won't end, with you. You have wiped out finance, which had grown like a cancer in the interstices of business, and you have wiped out every sort of sovereignty, public or private. There is no sovereign state and no sovereign owner any more. You exorcised them both. And the world now is full of able people setting about the complex – the very complex – readjustment of social life to its new physical conditions."

"You are telling me this? You are coming into my remote, secluded life to tell me this?"

"This new world isn't your making, Rud. That is what I am telling you. All you have done is to release it. It was struggling into existence before we were born. It was dawning on men's imaginations already in the eighteenth century – if not before."

"You make me feel as though I was in the history schools again," said Rud.

"But look at the facts!"

"And to whom am I to give way? Tell me that. Who is to make the new directorate? You and these friends you speak for?"

"Rud, again I tell you, I have no friends behind me in this. There is no conspiracy or movement or revolt against you. None at all. But I want to warn you. It will come, Rud. Unless you relax this grip you have taken upon the world movement. Men will not stand it. Rud, I implore you, listen to me. I have always done my best to stand at your elbow, warn you and supplement you."

Rud was nodding his head in silence. He regarded Chiffan with a faint, derisive, grin, and there was hatred in his eyes.

"Who is to make the new directorate? When you have got rid of me?"

"There is no need of a directorate. We did need a destroyer, we did need someone to break up the old system, and that is done. There are no States now; there are Services. There is a new sort of man taking charge of things. The mentality of men of science, of technicians, of responsible critics and functionaries, is spreading through the whole race. The old struggle for power is over."

"Men of science!" said Rud with bitter scorn. "Technicians! I can make 'em and break 'em."

"You can break them," said Chiffan.

"But not make them?"

"No. And you can't do without them."

"You are just a theorist, A constitution-monger, an ideologist."

"Gollys! Why! Who *was* it? Why! – *Reedly* used to abuse ideologists. You're not going the way of Reedly, Rud?"

A spasm of anger betrayed itself in Rud. He controlled himself.

"So I am to give way. I am to retire. I suppose I had better go off fishing, eh? And some sort of Royal Society and World Civil Service and new Universities and so on, what your friend Norvel – Oh yes, he's your friend, I know – calls the Knowledge Organisation, My God! are going to take over the world that I – yes, *I* – have liberated and unified. Am I permitted to be sceptical? I tell you, Chiffan, I have had time for thought and experience since you and I talked nonsense together in those old days. And there is nothing whatever to override Will in human affairs. And like it or not – and *you*, – you know hardly anything of the burthen I carry – I am the Will."

Chiffan swung half round with a gesture of despair, took a step away from Rud and then turned upon him.

"Rud," he cried. "Don't be an idiot! What has come over you? Will is all about us, the collective will, guided by the free wisdom of thousand of brains. Will can never be concentrated in one individual. Power you can grab but will escapes you. You of all people understood that so well – once. Parallel co-operation! Your own phrase, man! And now, here you are, lonely, secretly wretched, implacable, trying to clutch everything. *Why?* Can you trust nothing free outside yourself? Come off it, Rud. Come off it."

He stopped short and began again on a less strident note.

"Why should I lecture you like this? Remember yourself, man. Remember your humanity. Remember how shabby we were when we met. Remember our long tramp together and how hungry we used to get in the afternoon. Remember that punt – the rabbit and onions – that visit to Jim Flab's headquarters at Balting – that stinking little major! What has happened to you to forget such things?"

"Yes, I remember all that. Yes."

Rud's pallor seemed to increase. He had something very urgent to say and he did not know how to begin. It looked almost as though he was going to be sick. He brought his face closer to Chiffan's. When at last he spoke, he spoke in a close undertone and a new bitterness had come into his voice.

"And I remember you bragging about that Lancashire girl's neck. I remember that too. You talked about having her and how easy she would have been. In the punt you talked. I remember every word of it. I remember you fleering and jeering at me about my having to give up all thought of sex. Afterwards on the road. After Balting. All through our lives you have relieved yourself about that. Always. *Do* I remember? Is there a thing I forget? Your ill-concealed envy of my – my genius, and your attempts to compensate your inferiority by all those petty triumphs over women – and me. Envy, incarnate envy: that is you, Chiffan. You, the cheerful friend with a sneer! And still you are unsatisfied. Now you would like to see all that I have done, undone. You want to see me and my Revolution – yes, *my* Revolution – prostrate and shattered. You would welcome back a thousand things I have dismissed, just to spite me, just for the satisfaction of seeing my name and my pictures taken out of the schools, just to stifle the love the people bear me all over the world. That's what you can't endure, Chiffan. That's why you come here spitting malice and venom at me. Taking the risk. What a long story it makes from first to last! Flaunting your mistresses under my nose! Always you have done that. Winding up with that painted wife of yours! *You* are virile, aren't you? *You!* I've had to be continent while you've had the fun. Chiffan the free-and-easy; Chiffan who say what he like and does what he likes; Chiffan the gay smiler; Chiffan the debonair! The playboy of the revolution! While old friend Rud is the Power Grub. Poor old Rud. Shrunken old Rud. But now – and now – we come to a reckoning. *Now* the Power Grub *has* you."

Chiffan stood stunned in front of this fantastic outbreak of long-hidden resentment.

"Well," said Rud, "you chose to come to me and ask for it. It was only an anticipation – It wouldn't have been long before Thirp came for you. I know about you. You have been watched. You have been overheard."

He stopped short, resolute but unable to say clearly the purpose in his mind. The two old associates stared at one another.

"So it's like *that*," said Chiffan at last.

"How else can it be?"

Chiffan shrugged his shoulders.

"I have known – I have felt it coming. And yet – it's incredible."

"Inevitable. Incredible to you perhaps. While you have been dreaming, Chiffan, about this dear, dear old friendship of ours and how you could always win me over whenever you wanted to do so, I have kept wide awake. Wide awake. You come here to tell me all sorts of things, but now *you* have been told something, fair and square. Is there any need to say more?"

Chiffan stood still and silent for a long second or so. But Rud had finished. The audience was at an end. Then slowly and meditatively Chiffan spoke.

"I'm not sorry, Rud, for what I've done for you in the past. Whatever I *have* done for you. We've had a great time together with this little world."

"*We!*" said Rud.

"Yes – we. I taught you many things. At the start… And – like all pilots who're dropped, I don't like to think of you without me. Silly, isn't it?…"

Rud made no answer. He stood sullenly mulish.

"Goodbye," said Chiffan.

And then: "Goodbye, Rud."

There was no answer.

He walked down the long slant slowly, resisting its urgency to quicken his steps – never once looking back.

Rud remained silent and motionless until the door had closed on Chiffan.

"He jeered at me," he whispered. "always he jeered at me. Always. Him and his *Bitches*… All those women… He was jeering at me right to the last. The pilot. *Him!* The *pilot!*"

He went to the great desk. There for a little space he was immobile. At last he pressed the telephone button and gave Thirp formal orders for Chiffan's arrest.

"Tell Rothberg to deal with him," he asked.

"Do you *mean* this?" asked Thirp, and for once he sounded overawed.

"Yes," said Rud, "I mean it."

He held his telephone and there come no sound of replacement from the other end.

Perhaps Thirp would say something that would alter the situation. Nothing came. He must have put down his instrument noiselessly.

Something caught at Rud's throat. His indignation evaporated. He felt that Chiffan had dealt very badly with him and forced this tragic situation upon him. He had *made* Chiffan. Yes, Chiffan was his making. He had discovered him a tramp on

460

the roadside. He had like his freakish humour. And – it was true
– they had had good times together. They had been young
together, and that in itself is to have a good time. Before the
terrible responsibilities of power forced them apart. There had
been a sort of friendship. Even if it was a mistaken friendship...

He stood telephone in hand. He raised it to recall Thirp, but
Thirp was still waiting there in silence.

"Yes?" said Thirp at once, receptive and colourless.

Rud hesitated.

"Let everything be done – with the utmost consideration," he
said, and then slowly replaced the instrument.

He addressed the empty room. "*No*," he said. "No man shall
undermine me. My Empire before all other conditions. Even my
dearest friend..."

A wave of self-pity submerged him. In his emotion he
relapsed into temporary Deism.

"My God up there – you! I am as lonely as you are. Yes. As
lonely as you, the everlasting God. Was there ever anyone human
– as alone as I? Deserted by my last friend! And now – nobody
knows it, but I am getting ill... I feel ill...

"I must have strength. I must keep fit. My task is not yet done."

Then as if some contrary consideration was attempting to
assert itself: "My task is not yet done. While I live I must guard
this new life I have given mankind. It is *my* Revolution. *My*
duty..."

7

One moonlit summer night a few weeks later Thirp was
murdered by a young man to whom for some reason he had held

461

out dazzling prospects and then disappointed. The particulars of his death are no part of this history, only its suddenness and its effect upon Rud concern us here.

Once more for a brief final phase of lucidity he realised his own personal inefficiency. One more he felt matters beyond his management were being forced into his hands. It was a greater loss even than Bodisham, because while Bodisham left him diagrams and projects, plain, open and completely understandable, Thirp had been deliberately secretive. He had always kept his methods to himself. Rud did not know very much even about his agent's immediate underlings, and now for a time at least, until he could gain a controlling knowledge of them, he must be his own watchdog. Rothberg came to him at once obviously intent to play the same confidential role that Thirp had filled so satisfactorily. But Rud did not like Rothberg. The evil in his nature had none of the redeeming dilettantism of Thirp; he made Rud feel unsafe with him; he was of the hard, dark police type who hated his quarry, took every advantage in the hunt and exulted self-righteously in a kill. Now Thirp had always behaved as though a political murder was a sadly regrettable necessity. For him it was a curious aspect of this strange, unaccountable game of life. He made Rud feel that though he could inflict death, he would never inflict wanton humiliation. He would do everything as it were under protest – though quite effectively. But Rothberg flushed with zealous animosity when he heard the mere name of a marked man.

Rothberg's impulse for self-assertion through destruction was far cruder in its expression than Thirp's, cruder even than Rud's. He was not merely a killer; he liked to stamp them down.

Norvel's theory that the Dictator was a necessary evil and that the forces of progressive adaptation could live through and live down any dictatorship, was losing its validity with every fresh aggression of Rud's. And Norvel was losing his temper. As one intrusion of the political police into his new universities and school organisations followed another, as he found even his best school teachers were being terrorised, his clearest thinkers silenced and his carefully planned instruction in biology, history and social science more or less systematically and ignorantly confused, revised or suppressed, he began, reluctantly enough at first and then without reluctance, to scheme for the restraint and elimination of Rud.

He was not a good conspirator. He had begun as a publisher and propagandist and he had grown into an educator; these are outspoken activities, and he did not know how to set about any secret plotting. He sounded several of his colleagues. Neither Bellacourt nor Holbank nor Roots seemed to be greatly stirred by the suppression of thought and discussion. They were entirely preoccupied by their own immense jobs, they were interfered with very little, as yet. It seemed a matter of secondary importance to them who was fed, clothed, carried about by their always more competent material organisations. They disliked the idea of any disturbance of this vast rationalisation of the general world economy. They wanted things to go on as they were going. But Heming, who was in control of the world's health, and Lacoste, who was a sort of Minister for a miscellany of biological services wilderness conservation, deep sea conservation, genetic reorganisation, a service leading possibly to human eugenics, population regulation and the like, were in closer contact with the mental organisation of the world. Their work overlapped Norvel's at a number of contacts, and their general outlook was very similar to his. They disliked the systematic falsification as much as Norvel.

So that when they found themselves in conference upon a project of Lacoste's for eliminating various infections, disease carriers and insect pests once and for all from human experience, it was natural and easy to fall into a discussion of the ever-intensifying World dictatorship.

They had dismissed the assistants, secretaries and stenographers; they sat together at the end of the long table in the main conference chamber of the Education Office and their voices dropped to undertones. Now and then one or other of them would glance over his shoulder to be sure that they were still alone.

"Well?" said Lacoste, watching the departure of the last secretary.

"We did not mention all sort so things," said Heming; "for various good reasons. we seem to go about our business in blinkers. I have been feeling all along that the gist of our discussion was unspoken."

Norvel sat with his arms folded on the table. "Can things go on much longer?" he asked, "as they are going?"

"Things are so secret," said Lacoste. "I only heard about Chiffan six days ago. I can get no particulars. "Chiffan?" asked Heming. "What is this about Chiffan?"

"Shot," said Norvel.

Heming shut his mouth tight, saying not a word. His astonishment was more eloquent than any outcry.

Norvel looked at him. "something has to be done," said Norvel.

"And what do you think has to be done?" said Lacoste.

"That is the riddle," said Heming.

"This new world of ours is merely a scaffolding – so far," said Norvel. "A struggle for the leadership might bring it all down. Can we bear to see this World Revolution lose its headway, as the Russian Revolution did when Stalin and Trotsky fell out? I would rather be boiled in oil than destroy the work that has been done already, that he as leader has done – the ending of war, peace throughout the world.

"But he himself is beginning to destroy it," said Heming.

"They are increasing the secret police," said Lacoste. "They have been interfering lately with the collection of our vital statistics. They want to inspect the confidential answers to our questionnaires in one or two places where they are after people. People who have been denounced."

"That infernal little weasel Rothberg wants to found a special college for detectives," said Norvel, "a spy and sneak factory."

"What will you do about those confidential answers?" asked Heming of Lacoste.

"Hold them as long as possible and then burn them if we're pressed."

"But then *your* people will get arrested."

Lacoste shrugged his shoulders.

"There is no prospect of an insurrection – anywhere?" speculated Heming.

"Do we want an insurrection?" said Norvel. "I don't think so. Partial insurrections are quite possible. They are probable. There's plenty of inflammatory stuff in Islam for example. But that sort of thing means disorder, disintegration. And as a matter of fact, and it's more a matter of fact every year, the young, the masses of young people, white, black, brown or yellow everywhere, believe in Rud, swear by him. They identify him completely with the new world... We must let them down gently. No one of us ever foresaw the tremendous power of modern mind-moulding. The old Nazi and Soviet methods have been developed now to a tremendous efficiency. From the infants' school on. The young don't understand how it is with us. They would not understand any move to limit or restrain him. The mischief's done. I do not see how we can disentangle ourselves from this – this Tyranny without a social disaster."

"How long may he live?" asked Lacoste. "he looks pretty ill at times. He keeps changing his doctors."

"He's a nervous wreck," said Heming. "But still he may live for years. It's mental strain with him far more than bodily. Quite possibly he'll go mad."

"That won't help us," said Norvel grimly.

"If he went quite obviously mad," said Lacoste. "so plainly mad that we could hustle him into a mental hospital – ?"

Norvel turned to Heming with a new idea. "Even if he *wasn't* mad," he said, and left the suggestion at that.

"He chooses his own attendants. It would be impossible," said Heming, thinking it over.

"Some accident," said Lacoste.

"You mean, in one word, assassination?" said Norvel.

"Open assassination – unless it was done by an actual certifiable lunatic – on some personal score... No." Lacoste shook his head. "It would be a tremendous social shock.

Rothberg might jump the situation. No, I mean an accident – an aeroplane, a car."

"I don't care a rap for Rud. I never did care for him," said Norvel. "and since this Chiffan affair I hate him. Simply and plainly I hate him. I think the original Group laid the foundation of all this trouble by letting him acquire this preposterous personal power. There was no need for it. He grabbed under their noses, – and with their consent. None of us three were in the original Group, and we know nothing of the magic of early associations. No. He has to go. I don't care how he goes, so far as he and I are concerned. Nevertheless I will consider no way of disposing of him that would subject this New World Order to stress and danger. That's the difficulty. That's the real problem."

"But how can men of our sort conspire?" said Lacoste.

"It has been trained out of us. Which of us three would be the most incapable, if it came to dealing with the First Murderer, the Second Murderer, and so on? Which of us could deal with a Rothberg? We are not that sort of stuff. We could as soon go down on all fours to fight dogs. We are different animals."

"And so there is nothing to be done?" said Heming.

"Chiffan dies and nothing can be done," said Lacoste.

"My schools are shattered," said Norvel. "My universities are debased and nothing can be done... I won't stand that. And yet – how the devil – ?"

He was pallid with impotent hatred. And with his hatred went a strong infusion of self-contempt.

"Oh! It is intolerable," he cried, "that the lives of hundreds of millions of people should be dishonoured beneath the vanity and folly of one single man. It is intolerable that Chiffan should be murdered and we do nothing. I more than anyone, am to blame.

467

The worst sort of treason is the treason of the teacher. And I gave him the crowd. I. I let his propaganda go. I helped it. I, as much as anyone, am responsible for this servitude. Prospero slave to Caliban! Horrible!"

"But what can we do?" asked Heming. "what can men of our type do?"

(It might have been a echo, a third of a century later, of Father Whitlow's: "What can you *do* with a boy like that?")

"Protest, resist, disobey, suffer, carry on to the last moment," said Norvel. "we could at least do that. I intend to become more and more insubordinate – to take his pictures out of the schools, to drop his salutes, to teach history faithfully. Half my teachers are with me in that."

"And if he strikes you down?"

"I shall be struck down. Such things have to happen. Some of my teachers will certainly carry on."

Every characteristic of Norvel conspired to make him despise as well as hate Rud. He was a man of immense practical ability, as great or greater than Bodisham's though he lacked the world co-ordinator's imagination; but he had nothing of the one commanding quality in Rud's composition, his rare flashes of social and political insight. So that he missed the one quality in Rud which had first attracted and bound the Group together. He despised his incapacity for detail and he would not recognise his occasional inspirations. Rud, Norvel thought, was just a needless accessory to the Revolution; he had not been necessary to its development; he would not even concede him the honour due to a foetal membrane. He jabbed his pen-nib into the table. "To hell with leaders," he said. "Why do we endure them? To hell with dictators and every form of monarchy. Why cannot we agree to kill this little beast and have done with him, and get on with our work?"

"*How?*" reiterated Heming. "How?"

9

Deep down in Rud's heart, suppressed and denied, stirred a profound conviction in complete agreement with Norvel's question. Why did no one kill him? He had had this feeling ever since the death of Chiffan, and sometimes it forced itself up almost to definite realisation. He perceived an increasing quality of menace in his bearing towards the people about him, though he tried to soften it with a spasmodic geniality and familiarity, he sensed that he was becoming too much for them and surely therefore, he decided, they must be whispering and scheming his death – as in similar circumstances he would have whispered and schemed. Of course, they were trying to kill him. They would try to do it unobtrusively, but they would do it.

He surrounded himself with precautions. He was amazed already at the recklessness with which he had exposed himself to Chiffan – if Chiffan had decided to stab or shoot. He had not thought of that. In his natural, generous way he had let the threatened man come to him. That must not happen again. Henceforth guards must hover invisibly about him and behind them other trusty guards must watch to see they attempted no treason upon him. But precautions were not enough for Rud. He had never been able to wait for an attack. The tension of his long wait for Reedly had been a torture to him. His instinct was to strike first and unexpectedly. So now he spent a considerable amount of nervous energy, peering so to speak into the world

469

about him, to detect any possible gathering of conspirators against his Revolution and himself. He wanted to destroy every stratum of recalcitrance in the world, before it could assemble a definite attack upon him.

Christianity he had always detested, and his persecution of its assemblies and formal worship was now intensified. Quite a number of young rather stupid men who might otherwise have gone from the cradle to the grave unlit by any touch of nobility, died like saints and heroes under the secret interrogations of Rothberg. Then Rud chanced upon a book about the Jesuits and realised that they constituted a special and efficient branch of the Christian campaign against modern enlightenment. The spirit of Loyola had been revived by the Church's disasters, and to their energy and efficiency he attributed the exasperating phenomenon of a vanishing Pope. He had wanted to offer rewards for the Pope, "properly authenticated, dead or alive," but Thirp had dissuaded him. From the Jesuits his imagination passed to Freemasonry. That mysterious body also has been suitable material always for the politically suspicious, and it required quite a lot of research before he unearthed its secret, which was that is· had no secret at all, and was one thing here and another there and nothing in particular, a mere excuse for assemblies.

Then the searchlight of his suspicions swung round upon the Jews. It swung round upon them and centred and settled upon them. In his earlier years he had adopted a very liberal attitude towards the Jews, if only on account of the indisputable "race" of his maternal grandmother. But now the chosen people drew his attention again. It flickered away from them and returned; for indeed they are a peculiar people. Focussed, the Jew became a burning centre of mental inflammation. When all the rest of the world was becoming one community, why did they still cling to their peculiarities of food and observance? It was odd, he said in the troubled hours of a sleepless night, and at once the old witch of dreamland set about supplying nightmare explanations of this oddity. From which dreamland he came trailing clouds of vague distrust about him, into the common light of day.

Once he was started on that slippery slope he could not get the Jewish question out of his head. It became an obsession. It became the nucleus of a tangle of fear-born impulses to extravagant violence. Assuredly there was something wrong about the persistent separateness of these people. He discussed them with Gentiles who were interested in them, and most of the Gentiles who were interested in them disliked them because it is not reasonable for a modern intelligence to be interested in Jewish particularism without a resentful irritation. Gradually the conviction grew upon him that all Jewry constituted a conspiracy, though it was never quite clear in his mind what the conspiracy was about. Nobody could tell him what the conspiracy was about, or whether it was as non-existent as the secret of the Freemasons. They were just a peculiar people, to their own and the universal discomfort. That made that unknown, hidden objective all the more sinister. It was impossible to believe that they were still genuinely worried about the Exodus from Egypt or the Captivity or the destruction of Jerusalem. Yet still they seemed to brood and wail over these things and bear a grudge against the Gentiles on account of them. There was surely something more immediate behind this affectation of remote sorrows. But what was it? They impressed him as a savage is impressed by an inexplicable incantation. They made him feel uncomfortable and apprehensive...

471

So in the brain of the World Trustee the potentiality of an ultimate pogrom accumulated. And Jews themselves supplied all the food that was necessary for his conspiracy mania to grow. As ever, there were Jews demanding differential treatment and preparing themselves for that perennial surprise which has pursued them through the ages of finding that this differential treatment, when it comes, is not preferential. The more intelligent Jews were assimilating rapidly to common mankind, but an obstinate remnant persisted, and the more it felt it fulfilled its destiny.

"It's that damned Bible, with its Chosen People poison. Isaiah was the first and the worst of all the Nazis!" said Rud. "Until that book is stamped out and forgotten, the Jews and Christians will coagulate and recoagulate about it... You don't understand, Norvel."

Norvel declared that the new generation of Jews were as much ashamed of Isaiah as the new generation of Germans were ashamed of the Hitler period and the Nordic legend. "Educate," said Norvel.

Rud would not have it. He appealed to sayings and doings of the remnant. "Why do they go on being Jews at all *now*?" he said. "Why do they keep it up? All through history the Jew has been hunted like a dog with the Bible tied like an old tin can to his tail. Why can't they cut away from that old tin can, now that they have a chance? I want to free them. Just as much as I want to free the rest of the world. What is good of pretending that Judaism isn't a conspiracy against human unity? Read their Holy Books, man! Read Isaiah."

It was only too evident he had been reading Isaiah.

He closed synagogues, he prohibited the printing of Bible or Talmud in spite of Norvel's remonstrances, he began to provoke the younger Jews to defiance and heroism just as he had provoked the Neo-Christians to heroic martyrdoms. Everywhere his attacks were reviving these moribund religions as convenient centres of resistance to his deification. They dared to do as members of a sect what they did not dare to do as individuals. History, in its loose, inaccurate way, was repeating itself. They would not burn incense to Divus Caesar.

"Don't heed them," said Norvel. "they will assimilate. They are assimilating. It is just a dwindling cult now of old ladies, old rabbis, sentimentalists, eccentrics, Zangwills, men with caricature profiles which they cannot escape, professional champions, who keep the old Promise alive. They're like those Druids who meet at Stonehenge on Midsummer morning. Leave them in peace. They will pass. Judaism will pass as all things pass. Leave it to *them* to come over."

"Jews never assimilate," said Rud, regardless of his maternal grandmother. "Once a Jew always a Jew."

And then when Norvel was about to speak, Rud went on.

"Maybe there are fewer Jews," he said. "But these Christianised Jews become Neo-Christians. All of them. You haven't observed that. I have. *They're* not a dying breed. They go on. Christianity always has been a Jewish sect."

"But," protested Norvel, "the Christian idea is the exact opposite of Judaism. Christianity is the broadest universalism; Judaism the narrowest nationalism. Everything you and I need and care for can be put in terms of this Neo-Christianity."

"You ask me to believe that!" shouted Rud, pacing up and down the room, and stopping with outstretched fingers to make his points. "You ask me to believe that! Then *why* the Bible still? Yes – you'll talk about the Old Dispensation and the New

473

Dispensation. You know that's a quibble as well as I do. You say they are as opposite as the poles. You pretend Christianity is a Gentile religion. Why! Even after the crucifixion, after it was all over, after the Resurrection and everything, still for a time none of them breathed a word about letting in the Gentiles. Not a word. That came later, with Paul and all those animals Peter saw in a sheet – what was that vision? Not a word from the Founder… I ask you! He comes to earth to make religion universal – and he forgets to mention it! Eh! Not much of a story, that!"

"There was the story of the Good Samaritan," said Norvel, but Rud's voice overrode him.

"New Dispensation, they say! The more the Jews and the Christians differ, the more they remain the same thing. Why do the Christians trail that old Bible about with them, if they have outgrown it? Why don't they denounce it plainly? Why do they still read the Psalms and the Prophets in church? Answer me that! You can't. Every Christian, I tell you, is a Jew or a Jew proselyte."

The gleam of mania appeared in Rud's eyes – but his voice became gentle and persuasive. He appealed to Norvel as a man might appeal to a child with incredible delusions. "Are you blind, Norvel?" he said. "Do you really and truly think that Christianity changes Jews? Not a bit of it. It disguises them. It makes them more than ever the same thing. Why are there so few Jews? Because there are so many Christians. The Jews breed and breed and never increase. Isn't it plain? They're in the other Warren. All that is left of the Christian Churches today is three parts crypto-Jew. Three parts, I tell you. You will see. You will see – one fine day something will happen to me, Norvel,

474

something will happen to me... Something will happen to my Revolution... *They'll* manage it. Unless we strike first."

He walked away to a window and came back. He brought his hot face close to Norvel's and Norvel hoped that his own expression would not betray his eager wish that something should happen to Rud.

"And then, then at last, at last, when they think the time is ripe, they will push one of the real race into my place, and you will have a Jew World dictator, a Jew Emperor – a Son of David, Lord of the World! Solomon, with wives and concubines, all complete. So that the Promise shall be fulfilled, and the Jews inherit the Earth! That is the eternal dream of the Jews and they will go on dreaming it. What else can they be dreaming about?... Unless we deal with them, Norvel – now..."

So far Rud was following in the footsteps of his German precursor, Hitler, in his attack on the Jewish riddle, but it is to be remarked that, quite unlike Hitler, he never betrayed any traces of that physical race mania which is so frequent an aspect of the pogrom complex. He regarded the Jews as a conspiracy. Hitler felt them as a biological pressure, multiplying around him and his kind. He bore a personal sexual hate for them. But Rud had no sense of race. It was not the Jewish race he hated, it was the Jewish idea.

"Stamp it out, stamp it all out now," he would mutter between sleeping and waking. He would lie in bed pursuing a reverie that passed into a nightmare of triumphant violence. Should he make them renounce the God of Abraham, Isaac and Jacob? In so many words? Would an enforced renunciation be enough? He planned a worldwide Sicilian Vespers – Jews and Christians butchered together. No ghetto seclusion, no exile, would satisfy his imagination. It would have to be a worldwide terror this time, a cumulative massacre...

Whom should he use? Whom could he trust? How could he prepare for this last and final world purge, get thousands of people straining at the leash, and yet take these doomed Bible cultures by surprise? The Pogrom would have to burst simultaneously throughout the earth. It must be like the fall of some tremendous meteorite. Out of a blue sky. Abruptly in every cinema he would appear, full of menace, advancing, filling the picture, until there was nothing to be seen but his eyes and nothing to be heard but his voice roaring in their ears, drowning every other sound. Or should he appear in great effigies thrown across the smokescreened heavens? Everywhere all over the world the loudspeakers would shout together with one terrible voice: "The Day of Wrath, the Day of the Wrath of Rud, has come." They would hear what was coming to them in the cinemas, in the marketplaces, in their homes. That voice, that face of hatred, would pursue them everywhere.

Everywhere too Rothberg's police, reinforced a thousand-fold, would be picking out the special victims. This time there would be no place to shelter them, anywhere on earth. Earth and air would howl against them. *Conspuez* – what a good word that was! His reveries became more and more gigantically apocalyptic. Mountains were thrown about like ninepins. The seas were tinged with blood. No more Jews. No more Jehovah.

More and more did he brood on this crowning surprise for mankind. It began with him as a dream; then it became a willful imagination which he would conjure up at will. "Rud," he whispered. "Thud. Thunder." They thought he had done what he had to do, did they? They thought he was played out. He'd show them. Why! He was only beginning. Wait just a little...

He would wander about his carefully guarded apartments and gardens. He would come to a standstill, a small dark figure in some vertically tremendous archway. Far off stood Rothberg's unobtrusive, trustworthy men shielding him from danger. He would sit alone on his terrace, elaborating it all. He whistled thinly through his teeth just as he had done when as a boy he had wandered over the countryside fighting imaginary battles...

10

It was not merely the planning of the last and greatest of all pogroms that fevered the now almost unsleeping brain of Rud. It was indeed the dominant theme of his disordered mind, but at times it receded to give place to narrower, intenser moods of uncontrollable distrust. Perpetual vigilance is the seed of madness. It trails a perpetual wakefulness. His mind was festering now with suspicion whenever two or three were gathered together in any sort of co-operation.

Every sort of association made him uneasy, every professional solidarity made him uneasy. He had never subdued his fear of medical men after that vindictive trial and execution of Bodisham's doctors. He felt all the doctors were now his enemies. Then there were men of science. The physicists, the mathematicians, seemed tame cats for the most part; the biologists, the psychologists were more outspoken; but they all hung together. They, too, he felt, had their shibboleths, their hidden understandings. They, too, looked at him now with incommunicable thoughts in their eyes.

He suspected even the teachers of mathematics and physics, Olders found him one day crouched together, sitting on his feet in a big armchair in his bureau, puzzling over a textbook of mathematical crystallography, trying to detect the treason behind the pinacoids.

His doctors he subjected to the most searching questioning. He was always consulting fresh ones secretly and then confronting them with any apparent contradiction from the diagnoses he had extracted from their fellow experts. His general malaise increased. He was ceasing to eat as well as ceasing to sleep.

At this stage, with a profound distrust of all other doctors, suddenly he bethought himself of Carstall and turned to him.

In spite of his flatterers and worshippers, in spite of his growing sense of divinity, Rud had still a curious feeling about Carstall left over from the days of Hooplady House, a faint, exalted, snobbishness. It came to him now as a thing supremely desirable that Carstall should be willing to stand over him and fend off these impalpable treacheries that menaced him. He had always wanted Carstall to care for him – from their earliest meeting. Now he decided that Carstall should indeed care for him – that Carstall should leave whatever else he happened to be doing at the time and become Rud's personal attendant.

11

Carstall regarded the Master of the World, and behold he was still the Stink and the sickly-faced orator in the Camford Union, exalted but the same. That little tadpole of a boy with the large head had simply grown to cosmic proportions, and all that remained now of the bold oratorical quality that had swept undergraduate Camford off its feet was something wordily shabby. He affected a stern dignity and it did not suit his fragile smallness. His looks hadn't improved, his eyes were bright with mania and bloodshot, they seemed to have sunken deeper into their sockets, and his voice was harsher. Master of the world!

Carstall received his instructions with an expressionless face. He nodded gravely to a recital of symptoms and asked a few questions. Rud urged him to come into personal attendance forthwith.

"No," said Carstall. "You must come into my clinic. It is not thirty miles from here – you know – near my house opposite that great cliff on the bend of the Gorge of the Loup. You need continuous supervision. You've been overdoing the strychnine."

"How did you know?"

"Everyone nowadays under such stresses as yours takes strychnine in some form. But I think I know what to do with you. I want you under close observation and control. And to be frank, I can trust my own staff, but I'm not so sure *here*."

"You haven't *seen* anything definite?" asked the Director with a flash of wild suspicion in his eyes, that vanished almost as soon as it came. "If you think there is anyone."

"No. But this is, what shall I call it? – an office palace. Where there is a concentration of power in the hands of any single man, there is intrigue. Politics blow in like draughts here whenever a window opens. For a time at least I want to forget what you are and treat you as a case."

"I shall be glad of a rest," said Rud, consenting.

"That you shall have," said Carstall.

12

"He came to me too late," said Carstall. "He had gone too far. He had to die."

"Who knows of it?" asked Olders with white lips.

"I do. Krause, the analyst, and his staff. We have only men nurses here. Do you want to hush it up for a day or so? It can be done, you know."

"It is a catastrophe. Nothing is ready. Anyone may seize power."

"I will issue a bulletin that he is emerging from a crisis and must remain insensible for fifty-eight – or say, sixty hours, And then we can have a phase of coma before the end. Meanwhile suppose you as secretary stop all these pending executions."

"You think?"

"I am sure. And you add as a note to my report – not stressed but as a matter of course – that otherwise everyone, everywhere, carries on – as usual. If there is no sudden shock things will go by inertia. For a time anyhow."

"You think?" said Olders.

"Sure of it. I'm in control here. I can answer for this end. And by the by, there are certain medical formalities – There must be no suspicion about his death, you know."

He insisted upon a searching post-mortem and this was carried out by the great analyst Krause with his assistants. Carstall had suggested that either strychnine or arsenic would appear, but the autopsy reveled nothing. "Sheer overwork then," said Carstall, and the faithful Olders bowed his head and murmured, "He died for us all."

"He died for us all," Carstall agreed...

"We are still keeping back the fact of his death," said Olders next day. "I – have given a hint here and there."

"Who knows?" asked Carstall.

Olders looked reluctant but not treacherous.

"One or two possible successors have to be watched," he said.

"I am going to bring in three fresh experts and have the body embalmed. They, too, are absolutely trustworthy. No one will know they have come here. And then, why not wait a little? A pickled dictator is better than a living dog fight."

Plainly Olders was shocked.

"Sorry," said Carstall, 'But there was no one like him. Was there? The succession was never settled. He kept us guessing. No rational man wants a world civil war. In this sprawling newborn world now – it would be unending. There would be Caesars here and Caesars there. Nationalism isn't dead yet; its scorched in the grass. We might be carried back to that old world again... If once it starts. But it needn't start... And nowadays does anyone considerable, really want Power? As power. *You* don't want to be his successor. You want to go on as a sort of world secretary. As you can. And you don't want any particular one of the possible successors very badly. Do you?... *No.* I thought so. Neither do I. Suppose we take his embalmed body back home in an ambulance and put him to bed in his own room at the executive centre. Suppose you go on being his secretary."

"I shouldn't dare."

"If I stand by you. If presently you find others standing by you. All the strings are in your hands. Nobody else had your executive knowledge. The castle there is like the centre of a spider's web. You were loyal to him. You believed in him. Believe in him still and keep this new world united and at peace. We will help you."

"We?"

"There are competent men in the world still. None of these would-be successors dare move in the dark. They're a poor lot.

481

Not like those fresh, raw Dictators of the twenties and thirties. I know their quality. The conditions have changed. Tell everyone to carry on. And get Norvel here. Norvel particularly."

"But who are *we*?"

"The men in the various World Controls – Bellacourt, Roots Heming, Holbank, Sen, Lacoste, Rurik, Norvel, men like that. In love with their jobs. They'll all carry on if they can. It's in their make. Not one of them is a power politician. It's amazing how financiers and politicians have died out in the last few years. You'd have thought the breed was eternal. I did as a young man. But the desire for mere power – either in the form of money or as direct control – seems to have evaporated. Reedly had it, and Thirp, in is own peculiar twisted way."

He checked himself on the verge of adding "Rud."

"It's the natural desire of a not very social animal forced into a society too large for it and frightening it. But now we are getting a sort security, and the impulse to hoard up power is assuaged. The Dictators eliminated the power of finance, and now here, if you will, is the end of political power. Concentrated into an individual, then into a spot, now into a mathematical point, nothingness."

He closed and clenched his hand. Was he saying too much for Olders? He stared at him and felt reassured.

"A dictator, Olders," he said, "seems to be necessary whenever there is broad readjustment of human relationships. Apparently a major power system is necessary to destroy any minor power system that preceded the readjustment or arose out of it. Hence there must be a dictatorship. But no dictatorship can go on indefinitely. This isn't a new discovery – at least not a very new one. They're teaching it, *sub rosa,* now, in the new universities.

But Lenin, who was head and shoulders above his generation, saw far beyond anyone else at that time, into these inevitable phases that have to follow a revolutions. His language was clumsy, he spoke with a strong Marxist accent, but he had the heart of the Power question clear. This now is what Lenin was trying to foretell when he talked of the disappearance of the state. Here it was." He held out the fist he had clenched and opened it wide and wiped the palm with his other hand. "Presto, it has gone!"

Olders assented silently.

"Stalin reversed all that," said Carstall. "Stalin went back on Lenin because he did not understand this."

"Yes," said Olders.

"The man to take hold of this situation now is Norvel. And between ourselves, thank God Thirp is dead."

Olders nodded agreement.

"Who is there to make trouble if you and Norvel and all of us say simply 'Carry on'? There's not the shadow of a Reedly in sight, and all that nationalist Federation stuff is just fading out of men's minds. Rothberg? That bloodstained little ferret! No... You think he'll just hide? So do I. He'd better.

"If there *was* another possible leader, would he have a following now? All the conditions have changed. The world is busy. There's few idle hands or people and the ones there are, are scattered. Common people don't want trouble now. They're full of hope. In the day before the Revolution they were full of resentment. They relieved it, and the time for Revolution is over. There is no early reason whatever for another Dictator in the world – none. Not for centuries. Now that common-sense has got itself organised and unified it is mere common-sense to abolish an individual head even as a symbol...

"So. Let the Master Director sleep and sleep, and then let him pass into a coma – and need that coma ever end? He had done his work. He was deadly tired. It is amazing but true; he has destroyed so much, so many irritating boundaries, so many poisonous traditions, that he has united the world unawares. Why should we not go on now – with an embalmed dictator?... I mean it, Olders.

"Perhaps they had something of that sort in their minds in Russia when they embalmed Lenin. Years ago I saw him once. Lying there in the little mausoleum outside the Kremlin wall, like a man, a rather tired little chap, asleep. But Trotsky and Zinoviev and Stalin and Co. had not the loyalty to carry on together. That Russian gang seems to have been a poor band of egotists – tortuous self-justifying egotists – not good enough for anything of that sort. And the Russian community was anaemic and overstrained. Now comes a chance of trying it again with all the sane men in the world to draw upon – and people busy. People, Olders, are busy. Busy. Hang on to that. He was beginning to scare them but *now* they will forget these last bad years."

"Do I dare?" said Olders.

"What else can you do, Olders? There's no possible successor who wouldn't shoot you within a year."

"Of course *I* have thought that the world now was, so to speak; a going concern again," said Olders. "*He* cleared away so much... You put it all with such confidence....Almost" – he paused for the smallest fraction of a second – "almost as if you have thought it out beforehand."

Norvel became at once a central figure of the reconstituted Group of administrators who now took charge of the world's affairs, and he showed the liveliest curiosity about the last hours of Rud. He insisted upon having the fullest particulars of his last illness from Carstall and his assistant Krause, and while he did so he looked hard at Carstall. But Carstall met his enquiring eye imperturbably and agreed that the cause of death was quite obscure. "Krause here," he said, "did the post-mortem. He *ransacked* the body."

"I want to see the body," said Norvel. "I want to see the body for my own good."

"We are going to treat him very much as they treated Lenin," said Carstall. "He has been embalmed, and presently all the world will be able to come here, like pilgrims, and see him for themselves."

Until the Mausoleum could be prepared Rud lay upon a slab in the clinic, and thither went Norvel and Carstall. The chief embalmer met and accompanied them and gave a few unnecessary explanations; then, having no reason to remain, he departed. Norvel regarded the yellow and waxy visage of the departed autocrat with tranquil distaste. Carstall was absolutely expressionless. "He's nothing much to see," said Norvel.

"They will want to see him," said Carstall.

Norvel had made his hostility to Rud no secret from Carstall. And Carstall had neither agreed nor dissented.

"To think of it!" said Norvel. Carstall turned silently attentive to hear what Norvel had to say.

"To think that such a creature should have terrified the world and made millions of normal men quibble and lie! Completest surrender of their dignity! And scores of millions, hundreds of millions, made a sort of God of him! To think of it!"

He grunted and shook his head.

"Do you know, Carstall, the other day I routed out his eldest brother Sam – and I got some realistic reminiscences of our God-Caesar out of him. Sam hated him. Always had hated him. Told me how he used to sit on his little pot in the nursery and threaten his brother about what he would do to them directly he'd done. They used to make faces at him. And there was a story of a mess in the corner, the pot tilted over or something broke in some sort of scuffle, and that is why they called him the Stink. I forget the exact particular already. I didn't think them as funny as brother Sam did. I thought they were nasty and pitiful. But evidently he was like that.

"I don't blame him very much for becoming Dictator of the World, Carstall, but, by God! I feel sick at the crawling of the millions before him. Was it really the snake that God condemned to go on its belly all the days of its life? Or the other party? I'm not sure. Perhaps both parties were in default...

"It takes the heart out of life to think of all that subservence. I do what I can to respect myself. I make a brave story about myself. I tell myself I am doing my share in the making of a new mankind. I keep it up that we educators and biologists are setting out now to breed and educate a race of gods – statesmen, teachers, thinkers (as we used to call them), poets. And then I think of the recent history of mankind! I think how a thing like that thing lying dead there can lead them to war or worship or massacre! Mankind! Mud! Shall we ever do more than make mud pies out of them? What else can you do with mud? Educated mud is still mud. Adam was mud and all his seed are mud…"

"And that is how you feel about it?" said Carstall. "You have the makings of a fine late-Georgian poet in you, Norvel. Did you ever contribute to their paper? – *The Criterion,* wasn't it? No? There ought to be a refrain to this little song of yours, '*Let us get drunk.*' Does this mean you give up your mud-modelling work? Resign the directorate of education?"

"Not a bit of it," said Norvel. "what else is there for me to do?"

"Exactly," said Carstall.

"Conceiving what you say as a mere passing mood about mankind, I am inclined to agree with you," said Carstall. "But mud is mixed stuff and even in *that*" – he nodded to the embalmed Dictator – "there were some bright gleams."

CHAPTER THREE

Post-mortem

Krause had refused one or two invitations to visit Carstall in the new home the latter had made for himself near Gourdon in eastern Provence. At a fourth intimation he went. He had seen very little of his former teacher since the death of the Master Director, ten years before. He had gone to preside over the big Research Station at Chicken Itza in Maya land, and his work on the latent infections in these jungle sites had been subtle and fruitful.

Carstall was installed in a modernised castle that was built into the cliff of Gourdon, looking down on the gorge of the Loup. He had given up active practice for some years and had reverted to certain problems of physiological chemistry from which he had been diverted during the economic collapse that had preceded the War of the Ideologies. So far he had published no results of very commanding originality. He had a very lovely wife, dark-eyed and still, she was fully a dozen years younger than himself, and she had given him three boys and a daughter.

Husband and wife were evidently upon the most affectionate terms, they could not meet without some trifling caress, but it seemed to Krause that they talked very little. Once or twice he saw her looking at her husband with a gentle scrutiny, as though she felt unsure of him and of what he might do next. It seemed odd to Krause that he should be aware of this and Carstall apparently unaware, or else so used to it as to be indifferent to it. It was as if beneath the general candour of his bearing he had kept something essential, some belief or disbelief, some habit of thought or action, out of that relationship, and that she felt that incompleteness.

Krause sympathised with Mrs Carstall and thought Carstall ought to have lived or behaved or done something different to avoid this faint but perceptible aloofness. Perhaps the disparity in their years had been too wide a gap to bridge, or perhaps the very love they had for one another was a barrier between them. Krause had seen that happen before. Passionate love, which can bring two humans closer than breathing, can at the same time keep them worlds apart. Krause was one of those quiet, observant, unaggressive men who go about sympathising mutely with pretty women, and particularly with the wives of their friends, but who never think of themselves in the role of lover. He thought all men were unworthy of women and he made no exception of himself. Which left his sympathies unhampered.

He thought all men unworthy of women and generally his estimates of his friends were qualified. He never allowed this to appear in his demeanour, but it was a private consolation for his own sense of inadequacy.

Krause had begun as Carstall's pupil and the tone of their old relationship of mentor and enquirer still flavoured their intercourse. Krause was a subtle and original worker, but his make-up had an ineradicable junior quality, and by nature Carstall was a sixth-form boy. So Carstall usually had the conversational lead. And it presently became clear to Krause that Carstall had a bias for talking about the Master Director.

By imperceptible degrees Krause apprehended what was coming.

They were sitting together after lunch one afternoon on the terrace, indolently aware of the mountainous loveliness spread out before their eyes. Nice could be seen through a thin veil like a burst sack of microscopic crystals poured down a slope, and far beneath in the gorge the Loup was a thin, bright-blue line winding its way down through a nearer wilderness of crests, cliffs and wooded slopes towards the Mediterranean.

Carstall reverted again to Rud. What was Rud's significance in the world? What had he achieved? Had his work been done when he died? At last he blurted out what he wanted to say, speaking with an affectation of casualness: "Did you know it, Krause? – I killed him."

2

So he had said it at last.

All the muscles of Krause seemed to tighten. For a space he was silent. Then he said: "*I* thought you killed him – until I made the autopsy."

"I saw you did at the time. That is why I insisted on the autopsy."

"But how did you manage it? How could you have killed him?"

"You suspected me?'

"Then – yes. Arsenic. There was that curious depression of his spirits before the end – and the fluttering heart. But my autopsy yielded nothing. There wasn't a trace. Of anything."

491

Carstall studied Krause's pensive profile.

"There were tons of arsenic in him. His body had to be soaked in it. After all that strychnine he'd had… Primitive, I admit, but it happened to be convenient."

"Then how?"

"Can you remember now after ten years, how, where and when you made your tests?"

"I've been over it time and again in my mind."

"That does not always improve a memory. But let me refresh the facts for you. We took our material from the body together. You had every facility in the hospital laboratory. Yes…But in the hospital patients die every day."

Krause turned his face to Carstall, in surprised interrogation.

"Yes. While you and your assistant were busy with your reagents," said Carstall, "I handed you fresh material. From another subject. I had it ready. Yes. You did all a man could do under the circumstances. And your assistants checked your results. I have always felt, Krause, you could not be trusted with a secret − with that secret anyhow. At that time your scientific habit of telling the truth might have caused a lot of trouble. Everything might have gone to pieces. Some adventurer would have got people excited. I might have been shot. And I did not want to be shot."

Krause made a weak sound of protest.

"I'm afraid I should have been shot. But now as this new regime settles down it does not matter. At last, thank the stars, I can talk. Even if you ran out now and denounced me nobody would believe you after all this time. It had to be done. He was hopelessly mad at last. He was frantic with vanity and fear. There was no other way with him… No way that I could imagine… I did right in killing him... He might have gone on disintegrating for years... And murdering and degrading other people... Putting everything wrong again. Spoiling his job. I killed him to save what he had done...

"Did you know, he was my schoolfellow? No? He was. I was head boy in the same school and I tried to prevent the other fellows calling him The Stink. It was a sort of link between us...

"I don't think I ever liked him very much, Krause, but he had, I know, a sort of unsatisfied desire to – to come it over me. I *mattered* to him. I felt that – and I confess it made – what I did to him– a little more difficult...and then there were the traditions of the profession. Good traditions. He was a patient...

"But I had seen his pencil list for the next massacre. He scribbled it in bed in the clinic... And there was that Chiffan story. That hardened my heart. Chiffan had been his closest friend. No one was safe from him at last. There was nothing for it but to finish him... I think about him a good deal. What did *you* think of him, Krause?"

"He impressed me as a very Great Man. I don't think anything can change that impression."

"I suppose... So far as there are great men...You admit he was mad?"

"At the last. But consider the immense things he did! The magnificent sweep of his imagination. His inflexible will!"

"I suppose he was a necessary evil."

"He was the supreme superman. If you could look at him, not with the eyes of an old schoolfellow but with the eyes of the world. Hundreds of millions worshipped him."

"You will never really grow up, Krause. Numbers mean nothing."

"Even now, forgive me, Carstall, I feel a sort of horror – " ·

"At what I had to do to him... Even *you*...

"But then you are fifteen years younger than I am, Krause, and when you grew up he was already a great light in the sky...

"You would have told...

"I realise more than ever how right I was to keep my own counsel. And anyhow, you know, I had no right to drag you in. Or anyone else. Before or after. It was no slight to you. Krause. I had to do it on my own, absolutely on my own."

3

"Sometimes," said Krause, "I am afraid of you."

Carstall sat silent with the corners of his mouth tucked in. He knew that Krause was not in the least afraid of him. Why should he be?

Carstall dismissed the topic of Krause and his fear. The vision of a dirty-faced little boy miserably and viciously jabbing a penholder at his schoolmate occupied his mind. He had not thought of Rud in that way for years.

"The Stink," he said at last, and then weighing the one word against the other: "Superman? Divus Cæser? The truth I suppose lies in between...

"The fact is, Krause, I am right about his quality and you are right about his scale. Poor little devil he was, just a poor little murderous devil at heart – and he was blown out by the chances of life, as little urchins used to blow out frogs. Just a nasty, frightened kid, greedy but frightened, horribly afraid of violence, always in a panic, living in a age of panic and expanded a million, a billion times. Until in a world of utter cowardice, he filled the sky. He killed a multitude of people, he destroyed institutions, traditions, boundaries, in his terror – and praise the stars! they were institutions that had to be destroyed. Or at least he was the instrument –

"Those dear old institutions, social classes, private property, religious cant, patriotism!…They had become shelters for every slinking meanness in the human make-up.

"I have watched these Dictators from their beginning when I was a schoolboy, to now when they are all over and done with. I've lived through it all. And these fellows had the same quality of being driven to do something, feeling that they were creatures of destiny, they all began like that, and then, not being able to understand, not being able to give themselves simply to the thing that gripped them, they went mad. History, Krause, is a case-book for the alienist. Thus far. All began as demagogues, all of them began like men aware of and feeling for and being used by some drive – Rud was driven highest and furthest. He was the ultimate dictator. I compared him just now to a frog blown out by an urchin…Yes… But what was it really, Krause, that inflated him?…What was it, Krause?"

"Call it the Spirit of Mankind," said Krause.

"Spirit of Mankind? Not a bit of it! Not even the Spirit of Life…I don't care for that word, spirit… Forces of which we still haven't the faintest understanding made him and used him. As they made and use us. He had to live, it seems, and certainly he had to be killed… His kind *asks* for killing and our sort has to kill them…The pattern of life requires it. And as for the pattern of life – ! How can we know? What can a man know of reality beyond the life that is *in* him while he lives?

"Here after two brief generations of conflict and destruction we are in a renascent world. No doubt now of the renascence. New standards and a new scale. The Blood Dance of the Dictators quite over and done. Dead already, all of them now, as dead as last year's mutton. Think of their last days!...

"But they had to dance, of course. They had to dance in their turn...

"We are going on to a new way of living altogether. Who can doubt it? People may make another legend of our Rud, a greater Caesar, a mightier Alexander? A Moses? Maybe they will. Yet I question that. He had a pathetic greed for fame, had Rud. I hope he isn't away somewhere in space, waiting for his press-cuttings... Or eavesdropping on us...

"Queer lot these twentieth-century dictators. They broke out like wasps in a dry summer. Conditions favoured them. A peculiar species they were. A crescendo of scavengers because the unadapted world was rotten with shabby evasions and make-believes. It asked for blowflies and wasps. Not a loyalty, not a religion left that was not dead and stinking. These dictators were master stinks, stinks like burning rubber and creosote, in a world of cowardly skunks. Superficially like gangster chiefs, they were, or like the pronunciamento bosses of those little old republics there used to be in South America, or Greek tyrants. But only superficially. More like Caesars, but not really like *them*. Spreading further and less intense... In the human community, a difference in scale means a difference in kind. As in most other things. They weren't simply blown-out frogs, they were burst frogs, inflated to nothing and burst; they were just the skins and faces of men.

"When these scientific historians who are coming along with their biology and their psychology, when they have done with your God-Caesar-Rud, Krause, he will be left with about as much greatness and divinity and as little power over men's imaginations as the wired-up skeleton of a dinosaur in a museum. Just a memorial of reptilian energy, vestiges of a slobber in the mud. Remarkable, but no precedent for us...

"Very anthropocentric our values are still...We still don't stand up to the truth, Krause. Measured against infinity, is a dinosaur any greater than an ant? The ratio is the same. Ants are in the pattern of life just as much as dinosaurs – and our noble selves. We're too snobbish. We do our brother under God, the ant, an injustice. We blackball him for the Ethical Club. *We* are spiritual, we say, and all that, while he's just a little bit of clockwork instinct. The only *real* gentry, the Lords of Creation, God's chosen animals are we! More particularly we of the upper classes. *We* who crawled at the feet of the Dictators and were too currish to make an end of war. Pink rats, Krause! Diseased pink rats! If *we* had to be, then surely those great handsome deinosauria and deinotheria had to be – they had to play *their* part. The ants too are playing their part. Every little ant. *Has* to. And the little Stink I knew at school, playing *his* part, became the Marvel of Mankind.

"He ended war forever. He did. He rationalised property and money. He inaugurated the Age of Plenty. He reconstructed world education. None of that was his original work. It had all been thought of before. It was already there as the common-sense of mankind. Much of it had not been simply thought of; it had been thought out and planned. Bodisham digested it all for him. Only we hadn't the courage and honesty. *He* was needed somehow to make it real. He – *eventuated* it. After all he had – a certain desperation. There was honesty in him, honesty in the frantic fear that drove him on, honesty in his hate of subjugation. He liberated and he was frightened by the freedoms he had released. He did what he had to do, and doing it, lost touch with his fellow creatures. And at last he became a public danger and we did not know what do with him. Until the arsenic I gave him made his poor little heart beat very fast and then stopped it altogether. The Stink. Master of the World."

4

Carstall tilted his chair back and with his hand behind his head gazed serenely at the sky.

"Yes. You frighten me," said Krause, after a pause.

"You don't agree with my point of view, you mean?"

"I agree with you, Carstall. That's why I am afraid. I am afraid of this clear, unsentimental life in you. And in so many of our young people. A life consciously as small as an ant's maybe, but as proud and self-reliant as God's. Where will it take us?"

"Beyond my particular limits, I don't know and I don't care... *Now*... I did once... That, Krause, is what I mean by that excellent phrase, Living by Faith. Live by faith in the unknown pattern. What else can a reasonable man do? There is a pattern. That is all I know...That is all you know, Krause...

"I have to be myself to the utmost, and none of my questions will ever be answered. That is my creed. *Why* do we go on living, Krause? *You don't know.* Neither do I. But we *have* to go on living. *Could* we know? I doubt it. Mysticism and Stoicism. We live in the dawn of a mystical and stoical age. *Hard* perhaps by the old standards. Free of lots of the old scruples but with new scruples, very exacting scruples some of them, of its own. I like this new life around us and I wish my old father could have lived to see it. I like what is happening. It's a clear, fresh morning with the promise this time of a really bright day...

"It's a great relief to talk to you like this, Krause. I've had to keep this Rud business to myself for ten full years. Absolutely to myself... I've continually been thinking of him...You'd be surprised... He had to be killed, you know. He *had* to be killed..."

Carstall paused, but Krause said nothing.

"I didn't like doing it. Why should I?"

Silence from Krause.

"I killed him because I knew that no one else among you had the guts to do it. There was something – a prestige – about him. But he had to be killed...

"After I killed him he became more important. That I have always found rather queer, Krause. I began to ask myself what exactly it was I had killed. Was he exceptional or was he a perfect sample of what we all are? Stink and insight? Rats with unexploited brains? Toads with jewels in their heads?

"That peculiar intelligence that he showed at times! In the early days particularly. It seemed to be something almost entirely independent of his personal self. As though his brain lit up. Everyone who knew him says that. I suppose it's something of the sort you get in real poets – or in cardinal men of science. Like something hidden in the dark suddenly lit by a searchlight. As though a higher mind is imprisoned somewhere behind the human brain. Getting free now and then – partially.

"Presently, now that so much has been cleared up in the world, it may get free more and more frequently. What do you think,

Krause? Suppose man is only just beginning to realise what he can do with his brain? Or suppose our brains are only beginning to realise what they can do with us? Or that some sort of brain behind all brains...

"The world state in which we live isn't a magnified militant sovereign state of the old type; it's something essentially different, something new and better. Maybe this Man in Common is something different too – not a man magnified, but men aggregated, a superman with larger thoughts and aims, something not so much collective as quintessential. The real Leviathan – not the State, as Hobbes had kit, but man's entire achievement."

The mind of Krause moved in a narrower orbit than Carstall's "It was a pity you *had* to do away with Rud. I see your case. But it was a pity. It seems so – so ungracious. After he had done so much."

"It was a pity the world couldn't do its business without a Rud – from the beginning," said Carstall. "I suppose Rud was necessary, but I cannot see why he was necessary. I suppose these new biological philosophers now can tell a sort of story about individuality being a necessary step for realisation and all that sort of jargon..."

"*Individual as Tentative*," said Krause, quoting the title of a current popular book.

"The way he used to call himself *The* Common Man," said Carstall..." What did he mean by that really? What was he getting at? I've never quite got to the bottom of that. A sort of return from individualism at large, wild individualism, to – one might call it – co-operative identification... *Individual as Tentative,* I haven't read that book. But that's the idea. Perhaps we are all drifting to that. In his own peculiar self-centred fashion, I suppose he was doing just what you and I are doing in our work, what religion and morality have always been doing. That's the line of thought. He was certainly conscious of being impelled to develop – not himself exactly, but how can I say it? – his particular aspect of that common man who is hidden in all of us, that unknown common man, that undying, unhurrying incessant man in common who says this through one man and that through another, and who comprehends and transcends us all?"

Carstall enunciated his phrases slowly and carefully, with his hands behind his head and his eyes among the clouds.

"*He talks like a book,*" thought Krause. "*He might be dictating to his stenographer. That last bit might be in capitals... And he poisoned the Master Dictator like a rat!...*

"*And where,*" reflected Krause, "*would he and I and all this free and lovely life of ours be today if it hadn't been for the vehemence and vindictiveness of the Holy Terror?*

"*Or – to be just – that dose of arsenic? I suppose that too was necessary... As he said, the rest of us hadn't the guts...*

"*Hard and cold. Think of it! Living with that lovely wife of his and never breathing a word even to her... Ten years of silence for fear she wouldn't understand. Or so as not to make her an accessory after the fact... As though she'd have told on him!... Or not to put a strain on her gentle mind... That too I couldn't have done. It's too much self-control altogether for me...*"

Carstall said no more, pursuing his private meditations over his cigar, and Krause went on thinking.

"*Lusts of reptiles, stallion pride, dog hunger, anger of apes, obstinacy of urgency and obstinate resistances, cunning and double-crossing – so it is we got here. It is too much for my poor under-standing,*" thought Krause. "*It is too much for any understanding.*

He talks like a book, and quite apart from that poisoning, quite apart from that, he and this free and handsome new world of his make me afraid. Perhaps I should have been a little afraid in any world. He talks like a book and yet I have to admit that what he says is harshly true. Mystical Stoicism is as much as we can make of it...

"*As much maybe as any of us individually ever will make of it,*" thought Krause. "*But could there be this greater sort of mind, this* co-operative *mind? How would it work? Couldn't we somehow know of it? It would be such a mitigation. Isn't it after all a sort of God...*"

"Carstall," he said aloud. "That transcendental mind..."

The idea escaped him.

Carstall glanced sideways at him and seemed to understand what he was unable to say. "So far as we go now," he said, "Thinking of these things is like shouting to catch the ear of a star. When we are young we think the stars are looking down on us – entirely sympathetic. And when we have lived through our personal lives we come out on the other side – and find this. The stars in their courses going away from us. Inexplicably. Like people leaving a theatre...

"*We have been played...*"

5

A few days afterwards Carstall came upon his youngest son curled up on a grassy slope beneath a bank of purple iris, reading Memoir of the Master Director.

He was absorbed in the book. "Gosh!" he exclaimed.

Carstall stood over his son unnoticed.

"What do you think of him, Bunny?"

The boy sat up with a start. He answered after due consideration.

"Think of him? I think he was a Holy Terror," he said. "Worse than Napo or Musso or any of them. I suppose you knew him quite well, Father? Talked to him and all that?"

"Your grandfather brought him into the world and I – I was his schoolfellow. We knew a lot about him. Yes. I was called in. I assisted at his last illness. I suppose it tells you that."

"And it was you made up their minds for them that the Dictator had done his task and that we did not need another. Good old Daddy! They say it was his desire. He turned to you at the last."

"It says that? It says he turned to me at the last?…"

"You knew his work was done?"

"Yes…"

"He must have been a Holy Terror to get on with, though, if half of this is true," said Bunny, after a pause for reflection… "All the same…"

"Yes?"

"He got a move on things…"

Carstall considered that for some moments. Then he expressed the other side of his own unsolved perplexity. "Maybe," he said, "the move was there anyhow; maybe it just took him."

But Bunny was five-and-twenty years at least too young for predestination, Mystical Stoicism and that style of thought. His father's doubts flew over his head unheeded. "It was marvellous the way he seemed to get hold of people. I suppose Bodisham had a very powerful mind; the great world organiser, they call him. And Bellacourt the Air Master. And Norvel. Re-educating the whole world! And those others. But they all worked for *him*.

He was horrid at times; he had people shot and he killed his best friends. But always they stood by him. Didn't they? It says here 'he cleared things out of their way'. It says here 'he seemed to make it possible for them to work unencumbered'. And they seemed in a way to like him, even when he treated them badly. There must have been something about him... And he did, it says, he did 'clean up the suffocating tangle the world was in'. What a world it was! So *mean*. Everybody doing everybody in. Profits, usury, appropriating things, taxes upon taxes, patenting, monopolising, sweating, stealing, frauds, gambling... He cleaned it up. I wish I could have seen him once. I missed him by just two years – two years and a month. At least I wasn't born, I mean... I suppose you did all you could for him?"

"Yes," said Carstall slowly. "Yes. I did all I could for him. According to my lights. I did my best for him – and his work. Quite at the last, you know. When he turned to me."

He took the book, flicked over a few pages, mused over it, and handed it back to his son.

"This book exaggerates here and there – and it simplifies things. It simplifies a lot. What else can a book do? I suppose that makes it easier to read. It brings life within our compass... Broadly anyhow it is the truth. The condensed truth about the World Revolution. It is as real as most other historical stuff..."

H G WELLS

THE HISTORY OF MR POLLY

Mr Polly is one of literature's most enduring and universal creations. An ordinary man, trapped in an ordinary life, Mr Polly makes a series of ill-advised choices that bring him to the very brink of financial ruin. Determined not to become the latest victim of the economic retrenchment of the Edwardian age, he rebels in magnificent style and takes control of his life once and for all.

ISBN 0-7551-0404-8

H G Wells

In the Days of the Comet

Revenge was all Leadford could think of as he set out to find the unfaithful Nettie and her adulterous lover. But this was all to change when a new comet entered the earth's orbit and totally reversed the natural order of things. The Great Change had occurred and any previous emotions, thoughts, ambitions, hopes and fears had all been removed. Free love, pacifism and equality were now the name of the game. But how would Leadford fare in this most utopian of societies?

ISBN 0-7551-0406-4

H G WELLS

THE INVISIBLE MAN

On a cold wintry day in the depths of February a stranger appeared in The Coach and Horses requesting a room. So strange was this man's appearance, dressed from head to foot with layer upon layer of clothing, bandages and the most enormous glasses, that the owner, Mrs Hall, quite wondered what accident could have befallen him. She didn't know then that he was invisible – but the rumours soon began to spread…

H G Wells' masterpiece *The Invisible Man* is a classic science-fiction thriller showing the perils of scientific advancement.

ISBN 0-7551-0407-2

H G WELLS

THE ISLAND OF DR MOREAU

A shipwreck in the South Seas brings a doctor to an island paradise. Far from seeing this as the end of his life, Dr Moreau seizes the opportunity to play God and infiltrate a reign of terror in this new kingdom. Endless cruel and perverse experiments ensue and see a series of new creations – the 'Beast People' – all of which must bow before the deified doctor.

Originally a Swiftian satire on the dangers of authority and submission, Wells' *The Island of Dr Moreau* can now just as well be read as a prophetic tale of genetic modification and mutability.

ISBN 0-7551-0408-0

H G Wells

Men Like Gods

Mr Barnstaple was ever such a careful driver, careful to indicate before every manoeuvre and very much in favour of slowing down at the slightest hint of difficulty. So however could he have got the car into a skid on a bend on the Maidenhead road?

When he recovered himself he was more than a little relieved to see the two cars that he had been following still merrily motoring along in front of him. It seemed that all was well – except that the scenery had changed, rather a lot. It was then that the awful truth dawned: Mr Barnstaple had been hurled into another world altogether.

How would he ever survive in this supposed Utopia, and more importantly, how would he ever get back?

ISBN 0-7551-0413-7

H G WELLS

THE WAR OF THE WORLDS

'No one would have believed in the last years of the nineteenth century that this world was being watched keenly and closely by intelligences greater than man's…'

A series of strange atmospheric disturbances on the planet Mars may raise concern on Earth but it does little to prepare the inhabitants for imminent invasion. At first the odd-looking Martians seem to pose no threat for the intellectual powers of Victorian London, but it seems man's superior confidence is disastrously misplaced. For the Martians are heading towards victory with terrifying velocity.

The War of the Worlds is an expertly crafted invasion story that can be read as a frenzied satire on the dangers of imperialism and occupation.

ISBN 0-7551-0426-9

OTHER TITLES BY H G WELLS AVAILABLE DIRECT
FROM HOUSE OF STRATUS

Quantity	£	$(US)	$(CAN)	€
FICTION				
ANN VERONICA	9.99	14.95	22.95	16.50
APROPOS OF DOLORES	9.99	14.95	22.95	16.50
THE AUTOCRACY OF MR PARHAM	9.99	14.95	22.95	16.50
BABES IN THE DARKLING WOOD	9.99	14.95	22.95	16.50
BEALBY	9.99	14.95	22.95	16.50
THE BROTHERS AND				
THE CROQUET PLAYER	7.99	12.95	19.95	14.50
BRYNHILD	9.99	14.95	22.95	16.50
THE BULPINGTON OF BLUP	9.99	14.95	22.95	16.50
THE DREAM	9.99	14.95	22.95	16.50
THE FIRST MEN IN THE MOON	9.99	14.95	22.95	16.50
THE FOOD OF THE GODS	9.99	14.95	22.95	16.50
THE HISTORY OF MR POLLY	9.99	14.95	22.95	16.50
IN THE DAYS OF THE COMET	9.99	14.95	22.95	16.50
THE INVISIBLE MAN	7.99	12.95	19.95	14.50
THE ISLAND OF DR MOREAU	7.99	12.95	19.95	14.50
KIPPS: THE STORY OF A SIMPLE SOUL	9.99	14.95	22.95	16.50
LOVE AND MR LEWISHAM	9.99	14.95	22.95	16.50
MARRIAGE	9.99	14.95	22.95	16.50
MEANWHILE	9.99	14.95	22.95	16.50
MEN LIKE GODS	9.99	14.95	22.95	16.50
A MODERN UTOPIA	9.99	14.95	22.95	16.50
MR BRITLING SEES IT THROUGH	9.99	14.95	22.95	16.50

ALL HOUSE OF STRATUS BOOKS ARE AVAILABLE FROM GOOD BOOKSHOPS
OR DIRECT FROM THE PUBLISHER:

Internet: **www.houseofstratus.com** including synopses and features.

Email: **sales@houseofstratus.com**
info@houseofstratus.com
(please quote author, title and credit card details.)

OTHER TITLES BY H G WELLS AVAILABLE DIRECT
FROM HOUSE OF STRATUS

Quantity	£	$(US)	$(CAN)	€
FICTION				
THE NEW MACHIAVELLI	9.99	14.95	22.95	16.50
THE PASSIONATE FRIENDS	9.99	14.95	22.95	16.50
THE SEA LADY	7.99	12.95	19.95	14.50
THE SHAPE OF THINGS TO COME	9.99	14.95	22.95	16.50
THE TIME MACHINE	7.99	12.95	19.95	14.50
TONO-BUNGAY	9.99	14.95	22.95	16.50
THE UNDYING FIRE	7.99	12.95	19.95	14.50
THE WAR IN THE AIR	9.99	14.95	22.95	16.50
THE WAR OF THE WORLDS	7.99	12.95	19.95	14.50
THE WHEELS OF CHANCE	7.99	12.95	19.95	14.50
WHEN THE SLEEPER WAKES	9.99	14.95	22.95	16.50
THE WIFE OF SIR ISAAC HARMAN	9.99	14.95	22.95	16.50
THE WONDERFUL VISIT	7.99	12.95	19.95	14.50
THE WORLD OF WILLIAM CLISSOLD VOLUMES 1,2,3	12.99	19.95	29.95	22.00
NON-FICTION				
THE CONQUEST OF TIME AND THE HAPPY TURNING	7.99	12.95	19.95	14.50
EXPERIMENT IN AUTOBIOGRAPHY VOLUMES 1,2	12.99	19.95	29.95	22.00
H G WELLS IN LOVE	9.99	14.95	22.95	16.50
THE OPEN CONSPIRACY AND OTHER WRITINGS	9.99	14.95	22.95	16.50

Tel:	Order Line	International
	0800 169 1780 (UK)	+44 (0) 1845 527700 (UK)
	800 724 1100 (USA)	+01 845 463 1100 (USA)

Fax: +44 (0) 1845 527711 (UK)
         +01   845 463 0018 (USA)
         (please quote author, title and credit card details.)

Send to: House of Stratus Sales Department   House of Stratus Inc.
          Thirsk Industrial Park   2 Neptune Road
          York Road, Thirsk   Poughkeepsie
          North Yorkshire, YO7 3BX   NY 12601
          UK   USA

PAYMENT (Please tick currency you wish to use):

☐ £ (Sterling)   ☐ $ (US)   ☐ $ (CAN)   ☐ € (Euros)

Allow for shipping costs charged per order plus an amount per book as set out in the tables below:

CURRENCY/DESTINATION

	£(Sterling)	$(US)	$(CAN)	€(Euros)
Cost per order				
UK	1.50	2.25	3.50	2.50
Europe	3.00	4.50	6.75	5.00
North America	3.00	3.50	5.25	5.00
Rest of World	3.00	4.50	6.75	5.00
Additional cost per book				
UK	0.50	0.75	1.15	0.85
Europe	1.00	1.50	2.25	1.70
North America	1.00	1.00	1.50	1.70
Rest of World	1.50	2.25	3.50	3.00

PLEASE SEND CHEQUE OR INTERNATIONAL MONEY ORDER
payable to: HOUSE OF STRATUS LTD or HOUSE OF STRATUS INC. or card payment as indicated

STERLING EXAMPLE

Cost of book(s):..................... Example: 3 x books at £6.99 each: £20.97

Cost of order: .... Example: £1.50 (Delivery to UK address)

Additional cost per book:.............. Example: 3 x £0.50: £1.50

Order total including shipping:.......... Example: £23.97

VISA, MASTERCARD, SWITCH, AMEX:

☐ ☐

Issue number
(Switch only):   **Start Date:**   **Expiry Date:**

☐☐☐   ☐☐/☐☐   ☐☐/☐☐

Signature: _____

NAME: _____

ADDRESS: _____

COUNTRY: _____

ZIP/POSTCODE: _____

Please allow 28 days for delivery. Despatch normally within 48 hours.
Prices subject to change without notice.
Please tick box if you do not wish to receive any additional information. ☐

House of Stratus publishes many other titles in this genre; please check our
website (**www.houseofstratus.com**) for more details.